THE
WISDOM
OF THE
FLOCK

FRANKLIN AND
MESMER IN PARIS

STEVE M. GNATZ

The Wisdom of the Flock
Published by Leather Apron Press
Wheaton, IL

Publisher's Cataloging-in-Publication data
Names: Gnatz, Steve, author.
Title: The wisdom of the flock / by Steve Gnatz.
Description: First trade paperback original edition. | Wheaton [Illinois] : Leather Apron Press, 2021. | Bibliography included. | Also published as an ebook.
Identifiers: ISBN 978-1-7353480-0-1
Subjects: LCSH: Historical fiction, American. | United States—History—Revolution, 1775-1783—Fiction. | Franklin, Benjamin, 1706-1790—Fiction. | Mesmer, Franz Anton, 1734-1815—Fiction.
BISAC: FICTION / Historical / Colonial America & Revolution.
Classification: LCC PS374.H5 | DDC 813 GNATZ–dc22

Cover and Interior design by Victoria Wolf, Wolf Design and Marketing

For information, contact info@stevegnatz.com

For Gloria, and all who now fly with the flock.

ACKNOWLEDGMENTS

MY SINCERE THANKS GO TO everyone who made this book possible. I would especially like to thank Dr. Stanley Finger for initially introducing me to the interaction between Franklin and Mesmer. Also, Claude-Anne Lopez for her marvelous books on Franklin in France. The Bakken Museum, and particularly Elizabeth Ihrig, librarian, for access to original source materials. Dr. Susan Walsh for enlightening me about hypnosis and the unconscious mind. Steven Bauer of Hollow Tree Literary Services, for his insightful advice and early editing. Also, a heartfelt thanks to the very helpful folks at MyWord! Publishing, Kirsten Jensen, my editor Jennifer Bisbing, and designer Victoria Wolf.

And of course, my wife Aileen, and daughters Dana and Kiera, who have encouraged me immensely.

The writings wherein attributed to Benjamin Franklin, Pierre Beaumarchais, and others, reside now in the public domain but they are theirs. I have used a unique font in the text to alert the reader that these are their words, not mine. I thank these authors for their thoughts and expressions.

This novel is a work of historical fiction.

It is based on real events and people who lived a long time ago.

While I have endeavored to be as historically accurate as possible,
I have filled in many of the blanks in the historical
record with the fruits of my own imagination.

Still, it might have happened this way...

Benjamin Franklin

"IT IS NOT ENOUGH TO SAY that Franklin is handsome. One must say that he has been one of the world's most handsomest men and that one knows no man of his age who could equal him. All his proportions reveal the strength of Hercules and at seventy-five years he is still supple and light-footed. His large forehead suggests strength of mind, and his robust neck the firmness of his character. Evenness of temper is in his eyes, and on his lips the smile of an unshakable serenity. Work seems never to fray his nerves. His wrinkles are gay; they are tender and proud, not one of them careworn. One can see that he has imagined more than he has studied, that he has played with the sciences, with men and affairs. And it is still almost a game that in his declining years he labours to bring into being the greatest republic. They have put under his portrait that laconic inscription: Vir. There is not one trait in him nor in his life to belie it."

—*Pierre-Samuel Du Pont de Nemours, upon viewing the 1779 portrait of Franklin by Joseph-Siffred Duplessis*

FRANZ ANTON MESMER

"ANTIQUITY GAVE MUCH PRAISE to the system of the Stoics, who considered man merely a portion of the universe; but this system, which died out in the human heart because it had an improper basis, will now, if Mesmer tells the truth, have all of nature as its support. This union of man with the universe seemed only a beautiful dream, but according to Mesmer it is the physical theory of the universe. The physical and mental phenomena which I admire in myself every day without understanding them are caused by the same agent which develops around me the phenomena of vegetation, which I do not admire less because I do not understand them. This universal fluid penetrates this great tree in every part and filters through the canals of the sap which animates it. It is this fluid that produces the leaves, the flowers, the fruits, just as it produces when it is filtered in the nerves of my brain, thought, movement, and life. My son and this young elm under which he sits are two beings of the same age, developing in the bosom of nature by the power of the same agent! They receive and transmit in turn this fluid which circulates from one to the other for the common good of both. All beings are therefore my brothers and nature is the common mother."

— *J. M. A. Servan in defense of Mesmer and his theory, 1784.*

FOREWORD

"**PERHAPS THE HISTORY** of the errors of mankind, all things considered, is more valuable and interesting than that of their discoveries. Truth is uniform and narrow; it constantly exists, and does not seem to require so much an active energy, as a passive aptitude of soul in order to encounter it. But error is endlessly diversified; it has no reality, but is the pure and simple creation of the mind that invents it. In this field the soul has room enough to expand herself, to display all her boundless faculties, and all her beautiful and interesting extravagancies and absurdities."

—*Historical introduction to the Report of Dr. Benjamin Franklin, and other commissioners, charged by the King of France, with the examination of the Magnétisme Animale, as now practiced at Paris (1785)*

PART
I

October 28th, 1776

BENJAMIN FRANKLIN AWOKE, disoriented and alone. His tall, muscular frame fit the built-in bed poorly. It creaked as he shifted. A gray circle of light hovered in the air above his feet, weakly illuminating the room with a ghostly pallor. He ached all over. His stomach churned. The walls seemed to undulate, adding to his discomfort. Ben groaned as he rubbed his forehead in an attempt to soothe the throbbing. Perhaps he had drunk too much wine last night. Yet he didn't recall overindulging.

"I'm getting too old," he muttered.

Ben hauled himself up on the side of the bed. His feet hit the wooden floor. It was cold—devoid of the carpet they would have touched at home. There was a distant rumble of thunder. Ben shivered. Where was he?

The cobwebs cleared quickly from his mind. He had set sail from Philadelphia only yesterday, his final destination Paris. Ben had accepted a formidable responsibility. He had been named the unofficial American ambassador to the French royal court. He carried a copy of the Declaration of Independence, recently signed. Back in America, skirmishes between insurgents and the British had already occurred. An all-out war could erupt at any time. Assuring French support would be key to winning any larger conflict against the British.

There was not much to hold him in Philadelphia now. After the passing of his wife Deborah, Ben had returned from England briefly to put his domestic affairs in order. But he had found his daughter Sally had his house on Market Street well in hand. Ben welcomed the new assignment to travel to France—until this morning, that is.

The sky of the prior evening, with high clouds streaked bright crimson and gold, had been stunning. "So much for 'Red sky at night, sailor's delight,'" Ben grumbled.

Ben had coined more than a few of his own witty sayings over the years, but not this one. And he realized that predicting the weather was hardly an exact science. Yet, he had hoped for at least a few days of calm sailing based on the ancient adage. But the weather had definitely taken a turn for the worse, with wind gusts and hard sheets of rain buffeting the ship. She tilted severely from swell to swell.

Cautiously, Ben fumbled toward the gray circle of light. Through the porthole, he could glean nothing except the gray sea and sky, indistinguishable even at the horizon. As he watched, the sky lit up with a flash, and a crack of thunder immediately followed. The ship trembled. The lightning strike was very close by, possibly even a direct hit.

Ben sent up a prayer that the lightning rod was in working order. He certainly wouldn't want to find himself attempting to swim back to shore in these seas. Still, the ship seemed solidly built and up for the stress of a rough ocean crossing. Her timbers creaked, but they appeared to be holding firm as Ben dressed in foul weather gear. He burst out the door of his cramped stateroom, in search of fresher air.

October 28th, 1776

FLORENCE, ITALY

MARIANNE DAVIES PUT DOWN HER PEN. Her letter to Ben was written, yet she felt unsatisfied, restless, uncomfortable. The late autumn sun was waning; her room began to fill with gloom. She felt a wave of fatigue wash over her. Marianne recognized the feeling only too well. She looked over at the cut flowers on her bedside table. They should be brightly colored, she knew, yet they appeared gray instead. There was not a wisp of breeze. No sound from the street, no smell. She was being enveloped by "the darkness."

Almost in slow motion, she picked up the scissors that lay on her writing desk. She sniped a lock of her hair, kissed it, and placed it gently in her letter to Ben. She knew that she should miss him terribly. Yet she felt completely empty, devoid of any emotion at all. Automatically she dabbed the paper with her perfume—although it held no fragrance for her. She cut and then tied a gray ribbon, which she could only hope was pink, around the envelope.

The scissor blade was sharp Austrian steel. She held it like a knife in her hand. Marianne put the tip against her chest and pushed ever so slightly toward her heart. She felt nothing. It wouldn't even hurt going all the way in, she thought. Her hand released the scissors, and they dropped to the floor.

Marianne lit a candle. The feeble light barely escaped past the edges of the flame. She melted her sealing wax and applied it to her letter. She snuffed the candle flame out between her thumb and finger. No pain, no feeling at all. She climbed into her bed. The darkness engulfed her.

October 28th, 1776

AT SEA

THE CREW WOULD BE STARTING their breakfast soon, yet food was the last thing Ben wanted. He made his way to the cloth-covered part of the deck. The thick oaken planks were wet with rain and sea spray. The area he sought was sheltered from the howling wind. Ben found the air on deck to be electrically charged and more invigorating than usual, exactly what he needed to settle his stomach and pounding head.

Ben sat down on a deck chair and spread a heavy wool blanket over his legs to shelter himself from the cold ocean spray.

"Do you believe in God, Doctor Franklin?" a deep voice asked.

Ben jumped, flailing his arms out of his lap. He hadn't realized he was not alone. He squinted through his bifocals to make out a gaunt man, completely dressed in black, occupying a nearby chair. He was as emaciated as a saint but with the haughty countenance of a bishop. It was the Reverend William Smith.

"Reverend, I fervently hope that not only does He exist on such a foul day as this ... but that He has a benevolent nature," Ben replied.

The Reverend sat back and pulled a blanket up around his neck. "Well spoken," he said with a chill in his voice.

Ben had learned long ago that there was no gain to be had in debating religious faith with devotees such as the Reverend. It wasn't that Ben didn't believe in God; it was simply that he didn't have proof. And Ben needed proof of things. He could think of only a few aspects of his life that he was willing to take on faith. The love of his late wife came to mind. But then, that belief hadn't been based entirely on faith either, for she had had ways of proving her love to him. God was a different matter altogether. A painful memory flashed of Ben praying to God to spare his son Francis from the pox, but the four-year-old succumbed. While this certainly wasn't proof that God didn't exist, though, it had shaken his faith. However, Ben knew that, like any true believer worth his salt, the Reverend would have an explanation for God's lapse. Ben decided to change the subject.

"That bolt of lightning was close just now," Ben said. He gazed out at the clouds that flashed in the distance.

"Aye, a bit too close for comfort," the Reverend said. "But we can thank the Almighty for the effectiveness of your lightning rod. Lord knows how many ships were destroyed by fire before you were inspired by Him to invent it."

Ben had not been certain that the clergyman would even know about his invention. Smith's reply encouraged him to go on.

"Thank you, Reverend," he said. "The Lord works in mysterious ways, even through men such as me. Though I am sure He's familiar with how the rod works, I wonder if you are?"

The Reverend sat up a bit. "I know only that the lightning bolt was somehow prevented from striking the ship," he replied.

"Oh no, the lightning almost certainly struck our ship just now," Ben explained. "Our mast is the tallest point for miles at sea. When I began studying the behavior of lightning, I noted that it always seeks the highest point in the landscape. Not only that, but also that lightning always seeks its way to the ground. My lightning rod simply creates a safe channel for the lightning to pass through the ship, so as not to endanger the vessel or its cargo. If the lightning were to strike a mast, there would be damage or fire. And if the damage were severe enough, it might even sink the ship.

"My rod is placed at the highest point on the ship and attracts the lightning. But that alone isn't enough to prevent catastrophe, for I also found that I needed to channel it through the ship to the water. A thick metal cable runs from the lightning rod to below the water line to accomplish this."

"A truly marvelous invention," the Reverend replied. "Thanks be to God. But I thought you said that lightning always seeks the ground. Wouldn't you have to run your metal cable back to the Colonies for the rod to be effective?"

"Excellent, excellent," Ben exclaimed, "that is just the sort of question a man of science carries within him like a man of the cloth seeks to understand the mysteries of his faith ... but I do beg to remind you that our country is now called the United States of America."

"Oh, yes! Force of habit," the Reverend exclaimed.

"Perhaps not a bad habit to maintain until your mission is accomplished," Ben said. "Your Anglican Church does not support independence for the people of the United States."

"That doth vex me," the Reverend replied. He sunk back in his chair.

Ben resumed his explanation animatedly. "You will observe Reverend, as I did early on, that lightning is an electrical fluid that has no trouble traveling quickly through the air. Through careful experiments, I also found that this electrical fluid travels through water, albeit more slowly. Hence, there's no need to run a cable back to shore so long as we are connected to the earth by water. Scientists around the world have taken to calling this electrical fluid 'electricity.'"

"But what do you believe to be the source of this 'electricity', as you call it?" the Reverend asked. "The Bible tells us that lightning is sent down from Heaven by God."

A slight shiver traveled Ben's spine. Was it the cold sea spray or a sense that the Reverend was once again testing his religious beliefs?

It had not been so many years since scientists had been treated as heretics and persecuted for their belief that natural forces might be studied for the benefit of mankind. Now, in modern-day 1776, in this age of enlightenment, a fragile truce existed between religion and science. Ben believed the truce had occurred in part because of advances in natural philosophy—the science of the natural world and medicine.

The revelation that tiny creatures seen through the microscope by Van Leeuwenhoek and others in the last century might be the cause of human diseases was gaining wider acceptance. With increasing frequency, descriptions of these microbes and their associated diseases were being published in the proceedings of the Royal Society in London.

Ben had a personal stake in understanding the spread of disease and in making others aware. Smallpox had claimed the life of his beloved son Francis over forty years ago, and still claimed the lives of thousands each year.

It was disheartening that despite the advent of effective inoculation against smallpox, the Church continued to consider the medical technique to be inconsistent with the established canon. Ben had stormed out of more than one sermon when the clergyman had condemned vaccination as unholy.

"Reverend, you may if you wish, believe that lightning represents the wrath of God ... sent down to avenge the sins of mankind," Ben said. "But I believe that this electrical fluid is simply another natural force—no more mystical than the powerful flow of water through a stream that the miller uses to turn a wheel and grind the grain from the field. Mankind has learned to harness many natural forces. While it is wild and dangerous today, I believe that electricity may someday yield tangible benefits to mankind ... if we can learn how to channel it appropriately."

The Reverend appeared to be deep in thought. He raised his eyebrows and shrugged. "What do workers gain from their toil? I have seen the burden God has laid on the human race. He has made everything beautiful in its time. He has also set ignorance in the human heart; so that no one can fathom what God has done from beginning to end," he said.

"Ecclesiastes," Ben replied. "But what do you mean by it?"

"Ben, don't you see that there might be mysteries that are not intended to be known to man? That God has intended for some things to be taken on faith? That your natural philosophy both cannot, and I dare say should not, attempt to provide a proof for everything under the Sun? That by attempting to do so, by requiring proof for everything, you denigrate God and His power?"

"No, I don't see it that way at all, Reverend," Ben said. "I believe that God would want mankind to discover the intricate workings of the universe that He has created for us to live in. I believe that He has designed us to be probing, intelligent beings; designed us to yearn to discover and elucidate the hidden workings of the universe—not designed us as sheep, blindly following established doctrine."

The Reverend looked as if he might object but said nothing.

Ben went on. "Take your own situation as an example. You do not believe that the Anglican Church is right in backing the British in this conflict over our freedom, correct?"

The Reverend squirmed in his seat. "Aye."

"And the Church would say that you should accept their decision blindly, that it is God's will, correct?"

"Aye."

"But you do not see it that way. You have seen the injustices inflicted by the British on our people. You have thought independently and asked yourself why God would want things this way. The answer we agree upon is that God would want our people to be free. It is the Church that has a different goal, the Church that has a need to maintain the status quo. Your Anglican Church claims to know the will of God in this matter ... but do they? Once you start asking questions, as you have, once you start demanding proof of things, as I do—then you will ultimately find the correct answer: that the will of God and the will of the Church may not be one and the same."

"Yes, I see your point," the Reverend replied, "but what of God's true will? Would it not be one of the mysteries that cannot be proven? Isn't God's will ultimately something that must be taken on faith?"

Ben didn't have an answer to his question, but during the time they had talked, the storm had abated enough that his appetite returned.

"Reverend, what say we see what the cook has prepared for breakfast?"

"Nay, I'm not yet ready to eat, sir. I'll sit out here a bit longer, contemplating what the Lord may have in store for me."

Ben bid the Reverend good day and headed for the galley.

Along the way below deck, he stopped to peek in on his two grandsons, Temple and Benny, in their quarters next to his own. Ben opened their stateroom door quietly and observed they slept soundly. He went on.

As he entered the cook's galley, he observed several large pots boiling on the stove, sending up thick clouds of steam. His glasses immediately clouded over, rendering him momentarily blind. The smell of creamy bubbling porridge and the heavenly odor of frying bacon quickly supplanted his loss of vision.

"Top of the morning to you, Tom," Ben called out.

Other than the captain himself, Ben was the only one on board allowed in Tom's galley. Most sailors would not dare to enter, and those who did would surely regret it. Ship's lore had it that Tom had once hurled a butcher knife into an especially persistent sailor. Ben didn't know if the story was true or simply promoted by the normally amiable cook to discourage interlopers. However, one icy stare from Tom caused even the most cock-sure sailor to think twice about attempting to snatch a tasty morsel from the kitchen. Tom was both a good cook and a respectable fighter, so everyone stayed out of his galley.

The prior evening, their first night out at sea, Tom had impressed Ben with the meal he'd cooked for the captain's table. Ben had decided to take a moment after dinner to stop by the galley and extend his compliments. And not knowing any better, he'd entered the galley boldly, walked up, and warmly shook Tom's hand.

Though Tom had been visibly taken aback by the intrusion, he gathered himself and rose to the occasion. "It's an honor to cook for you, Mr. Franklin," Tom had said. "You're welcome here any time."

Captain Wickes, who had quickly followed Ben into the galley and was intending to pull his distinguished guest out of harm's way, was left speechless.

Later that night, over a snifter of Madeira, Wickes had said, "Ben, I guess your fame has earned you a very special privilege on the Reprisal."

As the evening wore on, Wickes had regaled Ben with story after story of the Reprisal's adventures in the West Indies, right up to their current assignment. Ben was grateful to have such men fighting for his cause—an independent United States of America. However, he was also aware that many of the sailors in his navy were mercenaries and would go to the highest bidder.

His glasses finally cleared of the fog, Ben saw that Tom was tending to a huge rasher of bacon in a vast cast-iron frying pan.

"Tom, your dinner last night was superb, but this morning I find that once again, I'm famished," Ben said.

"Sit yourself down right there, Mr. Franklin," the cook said. He motioned to a table in the corner of the kitchen.

"No formalities, please, Tom," Franklin said. "Call me Ben." He sat down.

"All right then, and thank you, Mr. Ben. What will you be wanting for breakfast? I've got porridge and bacon cooking for the men, but today the ship's stores are full. I could cook you anything you fancy. In four weeks' time, there'll be nothing left but salt pork and weak beer."

"Porridge and bacon sound just fine. Have you any tea?"

"We just come up this way from the West Indies where we took over every British vessel we encountered. The best tea is secured in the captain's locker, but I'll fix you some of my favorite Indian black tea. We even have cane sugar to go in it."

Tom deftly placed a few slices of orange on a plate. He handed it to Ben. "I don't want you getting the scurvy, Mr. Ben."

Ben bit into the juicy orange.

Tom went on, "Mr. Ben, I know about you because I've heard every volume of your Poor Richard's Almanac."

Ben looked up, surprised, "Heard?"

"I have a lady friend, name of Margaret, a widow, back in Norfolk who saved your papers up for many years, and she reads them to me when I'm not at sea."

Tom set down the tea. "I never learned to read myself, but Margaret is teaching me, using your Almanac. Now I know all my letters. And I enjoy your sayings; I memorized my favorites. 'Little strokes fell great oaks' and 'He who lives on hope will die fasting.' You certainly do have a way with words."

Ben swallowed a bite of orange. "I published those little pamphlets over twenty years ago, Tom. I'm glad to hear that they are still useful ... May I ask how you became a ship's cook?"

"I always liked to cook," Tom replied. "Not that we had much food growing up, but my father made the most of what we had. My mother died in childbirth a few years after I was born. I don't remember her at all. Dad raised us, kids, alone. We hardly had clothes and never had shoes, but we always managed to eat well enough because he taught us to hunt and to cook what we had.

"Dad worked on a tobacco plantation whenever there was work. I tried that too, but it didn't suit me. I learned to swim because it helped ease my aching back from working in the fields. I can still recall picking all them leeches off my feet after swimming across our lake. I knew I had to get out of there. As soon as I was old enough to sign up onboard a ship, I did. When they asked me what position I wanted, I told them I could cook. My first job was as an assistant to the cook, peeling vegetables and the like, but in time I got a chance to show what I could do. Eventually, I got my own galley. I've always fancied myself more a lover than a fighter, but I reckoned that if I was ever captured, even the most blood-thirsty pirate might spare me if he learned that I could cook."

Bemusedly, Ben sized Tom up as a potential ladies' man. The thought that women would find this grizzled, badly weathered old sailor attractive, with his several missing teeth and more than a few ugly tattoos, almost caused Ben to laugh out loud.

Captain Wickes poked his head into the galley. He scanned the room with the eye of a man who watched every detail. It occurred to Ben that this quality was a part of what made him such a good captain.

Tom must have sensed the small inspection also. "Everything's in order here, sir," he said. "Breakfast can be served in five minutes if you will send the men to fetch it."

On a navy ship, the cook had no dedicated staff. The sailors had drawn lots to determine who would be assisting Tom these first few days. Later, the captain would assign kitchen chores to any sailor who needed a reprimand. This early in the journey, the original rotation schedule held.

"That will be Cartwright and Harrison this morning," Wickes said.

Clearly, the captain had come prepared, having checked the duty roster prior to visiting the galley.

"Ben, will you join me for breakfast at my table this morning?" the captain continued.

"Of course," Ben said. "But first I must check on Benny and Temple. By now, I hope they've been rousted by the noise of the crew."

"Very good," Wickes said and headed off to continue his rounds.

The boys were indeed up and dressed as Ben entered their small cabin. While the same size as Ben's, it had been fitted with bunks on one wall. This arrangement had delighted seven-year-old Benny, who, upon their arrival, had quickly claimed the upper berth. Temple, at sixteen, was more nonchalant. He acquiesced to his cousin and settled in the lower berth. This morning, those bunks held a jumble of blankets and sheets. The boys greeted their grandfather happily.

"That was quite a storm we sailed through last night, wasn't it, boys?" Ben said. He gave each a pat on the shoulder. "Did it wake you up?"

Benny looked a bit sleepy, and his hair was a squashed mess. "What storm?" he replied.

A crewman entered the room with a small bucket of water. Fresh water for bathing was a luxury reserved for the captain, officers, and special guests such as the Franklins. In fact, Wickes had told them that they themselves might have to dispense with bathing later in the trip, if they did not get much rain on the voyage. But after the deluge last night, the cisterns would be full, Ben surmised.

"Wash up, make your beds, and come to the dining hall," Ben said. "I'll be having breakfast with Captain Wickes."

Ben instructed the boys to go to a separate table. Given the sensitivity of their mission to France, Ben didn't want the boys to know too much. Not that he mistrusted them; he simply felt that it would be safer for them if they were not able to inadvertently divulge any details. Temple was entrusted with a bit more information than Benny, as he was older. Temple had also been assigned the role of secretary for the American delegation in Paris. He'd read and collected the letters Ben had received from the Continental Congress's Committee on Secret Correspondence (referred to simply as "The Secret Committee"), which provided Ben with his instructions. Naturally, the knowledge obtained from keeping those letters had given Temple more insight into the activities they would pursue in Paris. Nonetheless, Ben had specifically kept other information from him, such as the Reprisal's mission beyond delivering their party to France. Ben thought this might be the topic Wickes wished to discuss over breakfast.

Ben descended below deck to the large room that served as the mess hall, general recreation area, and meeting room for the sailors. He sat down at the captain's table and was served porridge and bacon along with more hot water for his tea. He was just wondering if it was proper etiquette to wait for the captain before starting to eat, when Wickes walked briskly up to the table and sat down.

"No reason to let your food get cold on a navy ship," Wickes said.

Ben took a big spoonful of porridge. Wickes was served steaming scrambled eggs with his bacon. One whiff and Ben instantly regretted not having taken Tom up on his offer to fix something special.

Wickes looked around to see who was within earshot. "Do you reckon our Reverend Smith is a spy?"

"I can't think of any other reason he'd be on board," Ben said.

"So you don't believe his cock and bull story? He told me he was traveling to England by way of France to pick up some clerical document," Wickes said.

Ben laughed. "Is that what he told you?"

"Perhaps we should toss him overboard to feed the sharks," Wickes replied.

Ben eyed Lambert Wickes, whom he had only known since yesterday. The captain, being a military man, would be accustomed to meting out swift justice to traitors and spies. He was, at the most, only half joking. Ben quickly calculated just how much Wickes needed to know about the Reverend's true mission in France.

"No, that won't be necessary," Ben said.

Wickes chuckled. "So, what would you do with him?"

"I'd treat him the way I treat any spy," Ben replied. "I'd provide him plausible but false information that I wanted him to pass along to the enemy. For example, I assume you've familiarized yourself with the orders for the Reprisal after you discharge us at Nantes?"

"Of course. I read the orders as soon as we reached open water."

"Well then," Ben said. He paused and looked around to assure himself that no one else could hear. "Suppose that it were to become known that the ship was headed back to the West Indies after our party disembarked?" Ben asked.

"That would be plausible but false," Wickes said.

"But the information must not come from you or me," Ben said. "It will be much more effective if this information happened to slip out when our good Reverend overheard a few sailors talking. Perhaps towards the end of our passage, the men could begin grousing about having to sail all the way to France just to turn around and go back. What say you?"

"I'll make sure that it happens just as you suggest," the captain replied. He flashed Ben a broad smile. He seemed pleased at the opportunity to serve his country with a bit of cloak and dagger directed at the suspicious cleric. "Then, as we are working our way up the English Channel and around Scotland, the British navy will be searching for us in the Caribbean," he said.

"Quiet now," Ben said softly. "Only you and I know the true future mission of the Reprisal. I'm hopeful that, when you do return to American shores, you will do so with your ship's hold full of confiscated black powder and weapons for our soldiers."

"Yes, and maybe a few other choice prizes."

Ben smiled. "I thought that there might still be a bit of the old pirate in you."

"Only in the name of God and Country now, my dear sir."

Ben studied the face of the young captain. Wickes was ruggedly handsome, tanned, and with a cleft in his chin that ladies would undoubtedly find irresistible. He had a full head of curly hair tied back in a ponytail. His naval uniform was impeccable, well tailored to his tall frame. Ben already knew that the captain ran a tight ship and had a keen eye for detail.

"Do you have a family back home?" Ben asked.

"No," the captain replied. His expression became pensive. "I always reckoned there would come a time when I wouldn't return from the sea ... so why leave a widow with young ones to raise alone?"

"What makes you say that?"

"Both in my prior career as a privateer and now as a captain in our new navy, I judge my chances of dying outweigh those of living almost every day. I guess the fact that I've made it this long—attacking and commandeering larger and more fortified vessels than my own—must say something. Yet, the odds don't favor my survival."

"I do hope you are wrong in your assessment," Ben said. "But I recall I once wrote: 'Fear not death; for the sooner we die, the longer shall we be immortal.' Of course, I haven't taken my own advice, having lived seven decades this year."

Wickes laughed. "Begging your pardon, sir, but my understanding is that you have failed to take your own advice many times."

"Whatever do you mean?"

"Well, for instance, I recall you once wrote: 'Be temperate in wine, in eating, girls, and cloth; or the gout will seize you and plague you both.' While I can't attest to any other vices you might have, I witnessed the huge allotment of wine you stowed on board. Not that I'm complaining, mind you, having thoroughly enjoyed your fine Bordeaux at dinner last night. I'm simply making my point."

"Well, in that case, you see, I do know something of which I speak, for the painful gout does attack me from time to time." Ben hoisted his left foot up on his knee and rubbed his big toe as if to soothe it. Thankfully it was not hot, red, swollen, or painful just now.

Ben went on. "Alright, we all must have our weaknesses. Regardless, I do make it a habit to rise early in the morning and exercise daily."

"I am sure that has been just the recipe to keep you 'healthy, wealthy, and wise.'"

Both men then took up their spoons in earnest.

Done with his breakfast, Ben walked over to the table where the boys were seated and drew up a chair.

"Temple, I'd like to get into a routine of working on our correspondence after breakfast, if that suits you."

Ben caught the look of disappointment on his grandson's face. Temple must have assumed that since no mail could be picked up or delivered while they were at sea, there might be a reprieve from such duty while they were on board. Ben had other plans. Temple would soon find that his grandfather could generate a prodigious amount of correspondence that he would be expected to copy, index, and file away for posting later. Not having to read any incoming mail left Ben even more time to generate lengthy letters to his business associates and friends.

Nonetheless, Temple's secretarial duties were his passage to Paris, and Ben observed that Temple never complained, even if he might have inwardly questioned the need for the level of detail and the sheer volume of written correspondence that his grandfather produced.

On the other hand, Ben found the absence of a daily incoming stream of mail almost unbearable when at sea. He felt cut off from his friends and associates, who kept him informed about matters in which he had important interests, both business and personal. On his prior transatlantic crossings, he had kept himself busy with scientific experiments and measurements of the ocean currents. But this time, circumstances were different. He and the others on the Reprisal were insurgents, enemy combatants ... and would be treated as such by any British warship they faced.

There is much more uncertainty in the world today. It occurred to Ben that, even assuming he survived the voyage, he might arrive in Paris to find that the American colonists had reconciled with England, and he had been recalled. He might go all this way just to turn around and go home again. But where was home now? Ben had grown up mostly in America but spent half his adult life in England. If home was where the heart is, perhaps it would be with Marianne. Something about that thought caused Ben to pause.

November 1st, 1776

FLORENCE

MARIANNE SLOWLY BECAME AWARE of her sister's presence. The room was light, possibly morning. She couldn't recall how long she had been in bed.

"Marianne," Cecelia said softly. "Marianne, please wake up."

"Go away," Marianne replied.

"Oh, so at least you are not dead."

"Not entirely, I suppose." Marianne could smell the rich Florentine coffee Cecelia carried on a tray. Her stomach growled. She realized that she was hungry. The return of these senses meant that the darkness was lifting. "How long have I been in bed?"

"Three full days."

"Did I miss a performance?"

"No, but we are scheduled this evening. Will you be able to play?"

Marianne observed that the flowers on her bedside table were brightly colored once again. She could hear the birds singing outside her window. "Yes, I believe so," she said.

Cecelia looked relieved. "Mother will be glad," she said.

"Yes, I am sure she will," Marianne said sarcastically.

"I will be glad too," Cecelia said. She smiled warmly at her sister and squeezed her hand.

Her touch felt warm to Marianne. She sat up in her bed. The mass of strawberry-blonde hair cascaded down over her shoulders. It tickled.

Cecelia giggled. "I will have to brush your hair for hours to get out all those tangles," she said.

Marianne reached for the coffee cup. Her arm felt unnaturally heavy, stiff, and wooden—but at least she could feel it. She took a sip. The warm, pungent liquid flowed down her throat with ease. It tasted divine.

"The only good thing about the darkness is returning from it," Marianne said.

Cecelia looked apprehensive. "It scares me when you are like that," she said.

Marianne paused for a moment. "Me as well," she replied.

"I fear that you will not awaken."

"I know." Marianne squeezed her sister's hand and smiled as best she could.

They spent the remainder of the day preparing for their performance. Marianne tried to put the darkness aside. She scrubbed in a leisurely bath while Cecelia attended her hair. She dressed in a velvet gown that her mother had borrowed for the evening. It was fashioned for a woman twice her size, billowing and huge when she first donned it, but Cecelia was able to pin and quickly baste it so that it fit just right.

The two sisters decided to practice the songs they planned to perform. Not that they needed much in the way of rehearsal—they had been performing together since they were children. But Marianne was concerned about her strength on the harpsichord. At first, her fingers were sluggish, her rhythm off tempo. After a particularly weak attempt at a sonata, she slammed her fingers on the keys and screamed. At least it hurt. Cecelia was patient, though, and massaged her hands until the pain was gone.

"It will get better," she said.

"Not fast enough," Marianne replied.

"What about playing the flute instead?" Cecelia offered.

"No, let me try at this a bit longer. My strength is returning—and you are not nearly so happy with the songs I can play on the flute."

Marianne stretched out her fingers. She stood up and straightened the soft velvet dress. She took in a deep breath and exhaled even more deeply. She closed her eyes and pictured Ben's sweet face. She told herself that she would play for him—like she had so many times back in London. When she next struck the keys, it was as if a different woman had returned to the instrument. She played a soaring Scottish air. Cecelia joined in singing after the first few notes. Their harmony was perfect; the tone sublime; the timing just right. At the end, the two sisters hugged, and Cecelia sobbed softly.

"I'm so glad you are back," she said.

Marianne just smiled and wiped the tear from Cecelia's cheek.

November 25th, 1776

AT SEA

As they neared the French coastline, the Reprisal encountered an opportunity. Wickes first spotted the ship near the horizon. "Fat pigeon at two o'clock," he bellowed from his position on the captain's deck. Ben and the boys rushed to the starboard side to observe the activity as the sailors manned their positions and readied the ship for combat. They checked and loaded the cannons. The master-at-arms unlocked the armament lockers and distributed muskets and pistols to the men.

Though Ben hoped that he and the boys would remain observers in this process, he accepted a pistol for himself and Temple as these were passed out. "Better to be prepared," he told the older boy. Benny scowled, disappointed that he would get no gun.

Ben marveled at the captain's precision. First, Wickes maneuvered the Reprisal into attack position in relation to the other vessel, making sure he had the advantage of the wind. As they drew closer, it became clear to all that their prey was a merchant ship.

The sailors relaxed a bit as it seemed unlikely that there would be much of a fight, but Ben still felt apprehensive. When the crew could see that the two-masted brigantine flew the British flag, their spirits rose again.

Wickes drew the Reprisal expertly up to the side of the brig, which tried in vain to elude capture. Not a shot was fired as the boarding party leapt from one ship to the other.

"These merchant seamen have been through this exercise before," Ben said to Temple. "Their cargo is insured and not worth risking their lives over."

Half a dozen merchant sailors were held at gunpoint on the deck of the smaller ship and watched as the men from the Reprisal set up a series of ramps and rolled barrel after barrel out of her hold. Wickes talked briefly with the merchant captain and then sent him off, his ship now empty.

"He wanted to discuss a ransom for his goods," Wickes told Ben. "They will contact us in Nantes, if we are so inclined."

"It depends on what's in those barrels." Ben smiled.

"Nothing but tar, turpentine, and some low-quality claret," Wickes said. He appeared clearly disappointed.

"That may not seem much of a prize you took today, Captain, but you surely have an efficient system," Ben said.

"Ben, today was easy, but that is not always so."

The following day, Ben found out what Wickes meant as they went through the exercise again. The captain spotted and pursued a merchant ship that proved more of a challenge to the Reprisal's prowess, either through the talent of her crew or the prevailing sea and wind. Where the day before they had overtaken their prey effortlessly, this brigantine slipped out of their reach several times. For over two hours, the Reprisal chased its prey, and Ben was not sure that Wickes would be able to attain her.

Each time the ships came close, the two crews yelled obscenities across the water. Given the passivity of the prior day's adventure, Ben was surprised when a shot rang out from the other ship.

He looked around and saw that a young sailor had slumped down directly in front of him and the boys. Ben instinctively shoved Benny and Temple toward the stairs that led below deck. The boys ducked their heads, locked hands, and ran for cover. After he saw them reach safety, Ben rushed to the side of the young sailor, but Tom was already there. He was applying pressure to the man's shoulder. At the same moment, it seemed that all of the other 120 sailors on the Reprisal's deck started shooting at the brig, causing a tremendous thunder.

In the face of that barrage, the crew of the other ship, including their captain, dove below deck. This gave Wickes just the chance he needed to swing the Reprisal alongside in position to board. As soon as the two ships were close enough, sailors from the Reprisal swung on ropes over to the captured vessel. From below, they quickly brought up the merchant sailors with their hands on their heads. Ben feared a bloody retribution might follow. However, Wickes bellowed, "Hold your fire."

All of the sailors quickly lowered their weapons except for those directly guarding the prisoners. Wickes then came over to attend to the wounded sailor. Tom was kneeling by his side, applying pressure to the wound.

"It's a shallow wound and should heal quickly," Tom said reassuringly.

"Take him downstairs, clean his wound, and give him some brandy," Wickes barked.

"Ay, Captain," Tom replied. Two nearby sailors came over to help the man up, and they headed below deck. Other sailors had meanwhile set up the ramps between the two ships as they had the day before, in preparation for moving the cargo out of their hold. This time they also had set up a gangplank joining the decks; it angled steeply down to the smaller ship.

Wickes walked past Ben. He said, "Well, I'll just go see what they could be carrying that is worth dying for." He bounded gracefully across the gangplank onto the deck of the merchant vessel, despite a rolling sea. Ben watched as Wickes marched up and greeted the other captain cordially. They sat down on deck, and both men seemed relaxed, although a sailor stood nearby with his gun drawn.

The other merchant sailors had been bound at their hands and feet and tied with ropes to the two masts. Ben could not hear what was being said between the two captains, but from their gestures, Ben could tell that the other captain was apologizing profusely. Ben watched as the Reprisal's men emptied the hold. When they had completed their task, they pulled back all of the ramps, and Wickes left the deck of the other vessel and climbed the gangplank. The merchant vessel was set adrift. As the ships floated apart, Ben could see their captain was untying his men from the masts and preparing to head back to port empty.

Wickes set a course for Nantes and then handed the wheel to his second-in-command. He walked down on deck, where Ben remained standing.

"No need to take prisoners in this game," Wickes said.

"I was concerned that our men might seek revenge for the shooting, but you controlled them well," Ben said. He felt the color slowly returning to his face.

"Thank you, Ben. My men are all seasoned ... although I admit—some are more hotheaded than others. But you look a bit shaken. Come with me."

The captain put his arm around Ben's shoulder and directed him below deck. When they got down to the hold, Ben saw the newly acquired barrels already stowed neatly on racks and the sailors lashing them with ropes to keep them in place.

"What was their cargo?" Ben asked.

"Flaxseed oil and cognac," Wickes replied. "I doubt the former is what they were trying so valiantly to protect." As if by magic, he produced a pair of snifters from behind his back and offered one to Ben.

"Let's give it a try," he said. He tapped an oak keg inscribed Rémy Martin 1751 and drew an ample amount of golden elixir into each glass.

Ben lifted the snifter, inhaling the heavenly aroma deeply.

"Ah, this is truly a wonderful *eau de vie*...aged in oak for twenty-five years," Ben said. He sipped the cognac and whistled in admiration.

"Oh, dah, what?" Wickes asked.

"I apologize," Ben said. "The French have such a high regard for this liqueur that they call it *eau de vie*—the water of life. We only know it as cognac because it is produced in that region of France. I think *eau de vie* is a much more appropriate name, don't you?"

Wickes took a deep sip. "Most certainly," he said. He swirled the drink in his glass. "I will always refer to this drink as 'Oh dah vee' in the future."

Ben laughed. "We will have to work on your pronunciation, my friend ... if you are ever going to talk on the streets of Paris."

November 26th, 1776

QUIBERON BAY, FRANCE

ONE NIGHT AT SEA, Ben had a dream. He found himself standing on a deserted city street—definitely not Philadelphia—in the early morning. The atmosphere seemed vaguely European, but Ben couldn't quite place it. The cobblestone street was too clean to be London or Paris. It was lined with tidy shops and cafés, above which the shopkeepers lived. Vienna or Hamburg, perhaps.

Ben heard the unmistakable lilting, plaintive sounds of a glass armonica playing softly in the distance. As he marveled at the sunlight breaking through the early morning fog, a female figure appeared, walking toward him down the middle of the street. He recognized Marianne instantly. Her long, plush strawberry-blonde hair caught the morning sunlight. She wore nothing but a sheer nightgown.

He appreciated every curve of her luscious figure as the sun illuminated the fabric from behind her. His eyes feasted on her beautiful face, her soft, freckled shoulders. Her full breasts slightly swung as she walked. Her hips undulated slowly, as rhythmic and enticing as ever. Her delicate feet seemed to glide across the cobblestones. She did not appear to be aware of Ben when she passed but rather continued looking directly forward as if in a trance. In front of her, she carried a shiny metal object in the shape of a semi-erect phallus.

Ben tried to call out her name, but no words came out. Nor could he move, he found. He was only to be an observer in this dream. Ben would have to content himself by taking in another lusty look at her from behind as she passed.

She turned away and headed for the opposite side of the street. It was only then that he noticed that a door on the far side of the street was ajar. It was completely dark inside the vestibule, but a streak of sunlight lit one lower corner by the door. There Ben's eye was drawn immediately to a lavender satin fabric with elaborate, colorful swirls of embroidery done in golden and silver threads. It looked like the edge of a wizard's or alchemist's robe. However, it quickly vanished, pulled back by its wearer into the darkness of the doorway. He strained to make out any other features of the person lurking there but could not. Marianne approached the dark doorway and entered. The music that until then had been hauntingly pleasant became notably louder, more discordant, and screeching. The door closed behind her. She was gone.

The screeching became unbearable.

"Marianne!" Ben yelled.

He awoke with a jolt to realize that the screeching was the frenzied calls of seagulls right outside his porthole. The cacophony had become incorporated into his dream.

"No time to contemplate the meaning of that dream now," he said out loud to no one. "We've reached France."

December 1st, 1776

NEAR AURAY, FRANCE

AFTER LANGUISHING IN QUIBERON BAY at the mouth of the Loire River for four days waiting for a favorable wind to take the Reprisal south to Nantes, Ben decided to disembark. He went ashore at the French town of Auray. Upon inquiring at the livery, he was told that it was possible to arrange transportation over land by coach to Nantes. But the road was rough, and there were not many services along the way. It would take several days. While not an easy decision, Ben ultimately agreed. The boys were anxious to get off the ship, completely bored playing deck quoits, and even tired of watching the sailors tie knots or clean their guns. The colorful stories the sailors told as they sat around idle seemed to be getting more grandiose each day. They had little else to do with their time. Ben thought these tales would probably not overly influence Temple, but he wasn't so sure about Benny, who was still talking about the shootout they had witnessed. Captain Wickes, Ben surmised, would be glad to discharge his civilian passengers and get on with his mission up the English Channel and beyond.

After a month at sea, the lack of written correspondence had become even more distressing to Ben as well. He longed to know what letters would be waiting for him in Nantes. He anticipated word from Silas Deane, updating him on the complex political environment that he would soon encounter in Paris. But even more, he found that he was desperately longing to see a letter from Marianne. Since leaving England almost two years ago now, Ben had written to her at least monthly. She had written back with details of her performance schedule around Europe. As Ben thought of her, he could almost smell her perfume on the envelope. He was hopeful that she would write of the rendezvous they had planned. Overall, Ben felt that it would do all of them good to be making progress toward Paris.

To celebrate the Franklins last night on board the Reprisal, a few of the more rambunctious sailors put on an impromptu play. The plot involved some British soldiers trying to fleece two American rustics in a tavern. The Americans, of course, outwitted the soldiers, playing cat and mouse with them, ultimately enticing them into an awaiting ambush by Revolutionary troops. The British soldiers, initially portrayed as full of bravado, surrendered immediately and started crying, whimpering like cowards. The Americans finally gave them a good thrashing and sent them on their way. Though the play was mostly improvised and completely amateurish, the sailors provided a witty satire that had everyone, including Ben, howling with laughter.

As Ben tried to fall asleep that night, he wondered what America would be like without British rule. He believed that the people of America were strong, but he feared what was ahead for them. Would they ever be free to pursue happiness? Ben had helped write those words of hope on the Declaration of Independence. He resolved to do all that he could to achieve his dream of a country free of British tyranny.

The next day, the Franklins and the Reverend boarded a coach in Auray. They required a second large wagon to transport their belongings. As promised, the road to Nantes was indeed rough, muddy, and poorly maintained. It was rumored that outlaws lurked in the woods. Ben would have felt more comfortable if he'd been able to take a few well-armed sailors with him, but he took consolation in the fact that their coachmen were three strapping young men who looked as though they could provide some protection.

It was impossible to read in the coach. No sooner had Ben fastened his eyes on a word, than the coach jolted and threw him off balance. He watched the boys play games or sleep. The Reverend seemed particularly uncomfortable. Ben didn't want to ask in front of the boys, but he suspected that the clergyman might be wrestling with his conscience regarding his decision to take a stand against his Church.

Late in the day, Ben dozed off briefly. It was around dusk. The sun sank lower in the west, and the sky took on a warm, late afternoon hue that contrasted with the gray of the early winter landscape. Sunlight raked the plowed fields, producing a magical mixture of light and shadow. When he awoke, figures on horseback seemed to appear in the distance out of nowhere. The road took a sweeping curve so that Ben could see from his window that the riders were ahead on the same road.

The horseback riders loitered near a grove of trees on the edge of a small town. The scene would have been pleasant if Ben had not been worried about bandits. He put on his glasses and squinted to get a better look. The figures ahead seemed to be wearing mostly dull-colored clothes, but Ben perceived a flash of brightly colored fabric on a few of them. Odd for bandits. The coachmen noticed the riders too and said something in French that Ben didn't catch. However, it didn't sound as if they were overly concerned; in fact, it sounded as if one of the men said, "*Ooh lá lá.*"

The figures were riding at the side of the road in a leisurely fashion, clearly not headed for anywhere in particular. As they drew closer, Ben had a hard time keeping them in sight. For early December, the weather was not cold by American standards, but with the sun waning, and the speed of the coach, it would have been very chilly to stick his head out the window. Besides, he didn't want to appear overly concerned. As the coach drew closer,

Ben was able to pick out more details. His apprehension dissipated as he was finally able to see that the would-be bandits were instead a group of local women out for a horseback ride in the country.

Ben frequently advocated horseback riding for exercise. It was his favorite physical activity after swimming, he thought. Then he realized his error and smiled. Since his wife Deborah had passed, and he had been separated from Marianne by the Atlantic Ocean, it seemed that he'd actually had to settle for his second and third favorite forms of physical activity more often than not. "Hopefully, that will change in Paris," he thought.

At that moment, the coach slowed down. Out his window, Ben got a better look at the eight countrywomen, varying in age from their teens to middle age. The group was made up of mothers and daughters, perhaps aunts and nieces, with a couple of single women who didn't resemble one another. The warm light of the setting sun highlighted their hair and caressed their cheeks, already rosy from the cool temperature and the exertion of riding. Ben would later describe one of the women in a letter as "One of the fairest women that I have ever seen." But his perception of her heightened beauty, Ben recognized, sprung out of the juxtaposition to his imaginary bandits. What power the imagination has ... to inject emotion into a scene, either menacing or sublime.

The women approached and spoke with the coachmen in French. There was an exchange of what sounded to Ben like the asking and giving of directions.

"We must be getting near our stopping point for the night," Ben told the others in the coach.

As evening fell, the Franklin party retired to a spartan, but comfortable, roadside inn. After the boys were tucked in, Ben sat down by the fireplace with a delightful bottle of Grand Cru Bordeaux he discovered the innkeeper had reserved for a special guest such as himself. As he recalled the women he'd seen out riding that afternoon, his thoughts drifted to Marianne Davies.

The first time he'd ever seen her—now nearly fifteen years ago in London, she'd been performing, of course. Marianne was *always* performing. On this occasion, it was a concert using crystal bowls. Over the years, Ben had heard other musicians use the popular crystal bowls, or even wine glasses, to produce music. The practice of filling different sized glasses or bowls with water and then rubbing a moistened finger over the rim had probably been around nearly as long as the glass itself.

Though when Marianne played the crystal bowls, she didn't just make pleasing tones; she produced sweet music that touched Ben's soul. When Ben first heard her play, it was as if they shared a direct emotional bond— even though they'd not yet met. Ben felt she played for him alone, despite being in a room full of people. But Ben also noticed that her method of playing the bowls seemed to cause her pain. She could not play more than a single song before she was forced to stop and wring her hands.

As Ben walked home from her concert, he conceived an invention. He would eventually come to name it a glass armonica. Ben sketched out a series of nested crystal bowls that lay on their side in a tub of water. The bowls would be drilled exactly in the center and fastened in ascending order of size to a rotating spindle driven by a foot pedal. This unique design would keep the bowls properly wet and spinning so that the player could simply touch the rim of whichever bowl she wanted, in whatever order, to produce music. Ben had the first glass armonica made for Marianne. When he presented his gift to her and showed her how to play it, she kissed him.

There had been a spark between them, even at that early point. Ben came to understand that Marianne cared passionately for him, yet there was always something reserved about her. She seemed melancholy. There were times when she hid away in her room for days or even weeks when she suffered from more severe melancholia.

Marianne's mother, Mrs. Davies, was a shrewd, practical woman who strictly controlled her daughter's every move. She acted as manager, promoter, handler, and chaperone. She gave instructions that Marianne's younger sister Cecelia, who Ben judged as possessing a decent singing voice, always be given top billing when the two performed together. Ben thought that Marianne deserved more of the credit. He judged Marianne's singing voice to be at least as good as her sister's and far more pleasant to his ear. Besides that, she could play the harpsichord and flute in addition to his glass armonica.

But never able to live independently and constantly controlled by her mother's regimented schedule, Marianne lacked self-confidence, Ben decided. Sometimes she locked herself in her room, claiming a headache or fatigue, refusing to come out even for meals. Ben imagined that this allowed her a modicum of control over her life in the only way that was available to her. This behavior did come to benefit Ben more directly later, he recalled. As they started to see more of each other, Marianne would excuse herself from her mother's supper table with a "headache," retire to her room, but then slip out to rendezvous with him.

Mrs. Stevenson, Ben's landlady during that time in London, had an uncanny way of knowing when Ben desired privacy. Most days, Ben was like any other member of the Stevenson family. He took many of his meals at the family table and had free run of the house. But when Marianne came to call, Mrs. Stevenson would disappear into the kitchen with her daughter Polly. Early on, Ben had offered to meet Marianne at a cafe, but she had felt this too risky. Someone who knew her mother might spot them. And, in fact, Ben didn't like her walking the streets of central London after dark.

When she and Ben first met, Marianne and her family lived in the Soho district, a good two-thirds of a mile from his lodgings with Mrs. Stevenson on Craven Street. It would not have been appropriate for Marianne to be walking down Haymarket Street alone after the King's Theater closed. Ben insisted on meeting her at the end of Haymarket so that they could walk arm in arm past the few inebriated revelers still out at that hour.

But then, after a few years, her family moved closer to the theater. Ben never discovered if Marianne had somehow orchestrated the move or if it was simply a stroke of luck. Nonetheless, the shorter distance was much appreciated by his feet, prone as they were to the gout.

When she entered the privacy of Ben's room, Marianne always started with music, their first common passion. Music was a universal language they both understood and deeply appreciated. There was no need to talk when they had music.

Often Marianne would play something new that she had just composed or heard. Her music always seemed tinged with sadness, even when the song was a happy one. Ben never objected to this aspect of her playing though, as the depth of her passion and emotion caused him to truly experience what she felt as she played. Occasionally they played duets. They had fallen into each other's arms for the first time at the completion of one of these duets. The emotion and passion of their music flowed naturally into their coupling. Ben recalled that when he had first touched her, her reaction was so passionate, so rhythmically synchronized, so completely immersed in him that it was hard for him to tell where the music stopped and the physical world had begun. He learned to play her body like a musical instrument, and she his, until they were both completely satiated—and exhausted. Later they would walk back to her lodgings through the empty streets in the chilly London fog, warmed by their lovemaking.

Ben closed his eyes and sensed that warmth now. He sighed as he realized that it was only the heat of the crackling fire. He wished that he knew where Marianne was right at that moment. "All the more reason to get to Paris," he thought. He drained his glass and went off to bed.

December 1776

THE ROAD TO NANTES

THE NEXT THREE DAYS proved altogether uncomfortable and downright boring on the road to Nantes. However, as they got closer, it became clear out the window that their party was drawing attention. Benjamin Franklin was already well known among the aristocracy in Paris through the translations of his writings on electricity. He had been granted an audience with King Louis XV in 1767. That had created quite a stir at the time for an American colonist. It was in all the newspapers. However, he didn't imagine that his fame could possibly have extended to the common people of the countryside. He was wrong. As they approached Nantes, the news had preceded them. People lined the road to get a glimpse of the arriving dignitary from America.

When they reached Nantes, a band was playing. The mayor came out to greet them and to tell Ben that a party had been arranged in his honor for that evening. Not feeling especially sociable, but not wanting to make a bad impression, Ben acquiesced and agreed to attend for a short while. He found that he was rejuvenated after a bath at the well-appointed inn.

He also was heartened to see the mountain of mail that awaited him on the desk of his room. Sadly, he didn't have time to read any of it before going to the party. But he did have time to pluck out a letter that was surely from Marianne, addressed to him on fine paper tied with a pink satin ribbon, and smelling delightfully of her perfume. The writing was certainly hers as well, an artistic, flowing script so frustratingly small that even with bifocals, he couldn't make out the words in the failing light.

"Damnation. Why can't she write larger?" he grumbled. "Doesn't she know about my presbyopia?" Then he thought, "Of course not." Never one to highlight his weaknesses, Ben had concealed his difficulty in reading small print as he would naturally conceal any of his failings. He gently put her letter in his pocket to keep it close and resolved to read it as soon as he had better light.

The party was a lively affair, with plenty of food and quite drinkable local wine. The mayor turned out to be a gregarious fellow who took advantage of the occasion to over-imbibe. The townspeople seemed unconcerned about his behavior, leading Ben to conclude that it was not unusual. Many of the prominent local citizens attended to get a glimpse of the eminent Benjamin Franklin. Because of his rusty command of French, Ben listened much and spoke little. To the locals, who were more likely accustomed to famous people acting like conceited blowhards, Ben seemed remarkably down-to-earth and approachable. He wore simple, comfortable clothes that the partygoers might have interpreted as resembling the Quaker fashion. Ben wore a soft fur hat that the women could not resist petting. He had brought it with him from America to keep his head and ears warm during the winter months, but the fashion statement it made in France suggested a rustic, simple way of life. In picking up what he could from the conversations around him, Ben caught the name of "Rousseau" more than once as people apparently compared him, their visiting dignitary, to one of their own legendary philosophers.

Ben recalled Rousseau's treatise *The Social Contract*, first published in 1762, which opened:

Man is born free, and everywhere he is in chains. One man thinks himself the master of others, but remains more of a slave than they.

Rousseau's concepts had helped shape the American Declaration of Independence as well as Ben's personal belief that slavery was immoral. However, he was not so sure that Rousseau was correct in his assertion that man would be better off without society entirely—living instead as the "noble savage." Ben had seen how the American Indians lived and reckoned that he enjoyed the comforts of civilization too much.

Yet, as he looked around the room at these overfed and overdressed country aristocrats, he couldn't help but think of them as somewhat hypocritical. They idolized Rousseau but didn't change their gluttonous behavior. Nonetheless, they seemed to be having a very good time in his honor. So, Ben simply observed, smiled, and delighted in being stationary, on solid ground.

At one point in the evening, a short, wiry man with remarkably shifty eyes approached Ben. He seemed out of place among the fat, jovial aristocrats, and his quick furtive gestures reminded Ben of a weasel. He refused to look directly into Ben's eye, instead glancing around the room as if he might be in imminent danger and ready to flee at any instant. He introduced himself as Pierre Penet. Ben recognized his name from the correspondence he'd had with the Secret Committee.

Monsieur Penet was a merchant from Nantes who had traveled to America and met with General George Washington the year before in hopes of developing a business relationship. He had convinced Washington and members of the Continental Congress that he could supply arms to the revolutionaries. After the Frenchman's departure, the Secret Committee informed Ben that Monsieur Penet and his partner had represented themselves as agents of the French government, an assertion that proved to be false. Penet then claimed there had been a misunderstanding or perhaps an error in translation. Nonetheless, the Secret Committee had advised Ben to proceed cautiously. While it was true that the Revolutionary Army desperately needed armaments and supplies for the troops, Ben recognized that not everyone interested in supplying the necessities of war would be an honest businessman. Based solely on the looks of this man, Ben knew that he could never trust him.

"I hope that we can speak in private. I have important business," Penet hissed. His eyes scanned the room suspiciously.

"This is a party, Monsieur. We will not be conducting any business tonight."

"I understand, Doctor," Penet said quietly. He seemed to relax only a little. "Perhaps in the coach tomorrow. I will be traveling to Paris in the morning as well."

"Great news," Ben replied with more than a hint of sarcasm. Nonetheless, he smiled graciously and turned away, intent on escape.

The interchange might have become uncomfortable except that just at that moment, a pleasingly plump woman approached Ben, intent on petting his cap. Ben seized the opportunity to elude Monsieur Penet by offering to escort her to the *hors d'oeuvres* table. She didn't seem to object in the least to his arm around her waist, and his hand gently tucked under her ample breast. He gave her a little squeeze as he smiled at her pleasant round face. She squealed but did not resist or pull away. In fact, she pushed her hip back against his. It was the closest that Ben had been to a real woman in nearly two months, and he felt a familiar rise in his groin. He yearned to continue to explore the randy feeling. However, once in front of the *hors d'oeuvres* table, his escort quickly lost interest in him. She apparently needed both hands to fill a plate with sumptuous treats.

Ben looked around and noticed that Monsieur Penet had disappeared. The mayor was standing at the bar with a small group, drinking and joking loudly. As Ben approached the group, they quickly moved to adopt him, handing him a glass of red wine. He swirled the wine in the glass and lifted it to his nose—mild oak with a heavenly note of berries and spice. He sipped once and sipped again, savoring every drop.

The following morning Ben arose early and went down to breakfast at the inn. Sitting at the only occupied table in the place was a young gentleman Ben didn't recognize. He appeared to have been up all night. Dressed in fine clothes that were more than a bit rumpled, he was staring blankly into his cup of coffee as Ben entered. Apparently, he'd been waiting for Ben, for he instantly jumped up from his chair and strode across the room to greet him. As he approached, Ben noted that his face looked tired, but under less stressed circumstances would have been cherubic. His eyes were bloodshot, but he did not smell of drink.

"Doctor Franklin?" the man asked in English with a strong French accent. He stuck out his hand.

Ben shook it. He noted a firm, warm grip that was clearly friendly.

"Yes?" Ben said.

"Please let me introduce myself. I am Pierre Beaumarchais."

"I am glad to meet you," Ben replied hesitantly. He remained unsure who this man was.

"As soon as I heard that you had arrived, I came from Le Havre. I had hoped to be able to greet you at the party last evening. Instead, I spent most of the night having a broken axle fixed on my coach. To top it off, when I finally arrived here at the hotel, there was no room for me."

"I'm sorry to hear your tale. Please tell me your name again."

"Beaumarchais, Pierre Beaumarchais."

It finally clicked. Ben lowered his voice even though there was no one yet arriving for breakfast. "Ah, I know your name from our correspondence. You are the founder of *Roderique, Hortalez et cie*, are you not?"

The company that Beaumarchais had secretly founded under the protection of the French and Spanish crowns was intended to provide munitions and other supplies to the American revolutionaries in their fight against the British. Ben also realized that though Beaumarchais might be sympathetic to the American cause, he was an entrepreneur who saw an opportunity for financial gain in the process. Ben was about to become his best customer.

"Yes, that is I," Beaumarchais replied. "Please call me Pierre. I am at your service."

"*Je m'appelle* Ben," Franklin said, switching to French. "I need to practice. My French is terribly rusty. You are also the famous playwright, if I am not mistaken. Hopefully, your play *Le Barbier de Séville* is still running in Paris. I quite look forward to seeing it."

"You flatter me, *mon ami*. I will make sure that you have my box at the theater whenever you like," Beaumarchais replied. He beamed like a proud parent.

A young serving girl in comfortable clothes entered the room with a pot of coffee. As she walked over, Ben noticed that Pierre caressed her with his eyes despite the fact that she was quite plain. Ben thought that it must be a force of habit.

The girl seemed completely oblivious to his attention. She poured Beaumarchais more coffee and gave a slight smile to Ben, asking if he wanted to order something for breakfast. Ben ordered tea with cream and a croissant and thanked the girl.

"I thought that if you were to accompany me on the road from Nantes to Paris that we might be able to speak more privately in my coach," Beaumarchais said. "You will also be considerably more comfortable than in the commercial one."

"What a fine idea. I am in your debt. I met one Monsieur Penet last night at the party, and I would prefer not to have to ride to Paris with him."

"*Belette*," Beaumarchais exclaimed under his breath. But then he seemed embarrassed and went on. "I'm sorry if I appear rude, but this Monsieur Penet is a weasel and is no friend of mine … or yours, I believe."

"I had the same feeling. But will your coach be repaired soon enough?" Ben asked.

"It should already be waiting outside."

The sunlight streamed in as Beaumarchais pulled the curtain back. Ben knew very little about his tablemate other than what he had read from others, some of which wasn't complimentary, but his intuition was that he had found a friend in France.

Pierre Beaumarchais was a well-connected courtier in the confidence of King Louis XVI. He had a reputation for taking risks where others might balk. Ben also knew that Beaumarchais was on his third marriage, and that the first two wives had died prematurely under what some considered to be suspicious circumstances. Both had come from wealthy families. There had been rumors that Beaumarchais might have actually poisoned them to gain control of their fortunes, but nothing formal ever came of it. Ben decided that their first meeting was not a good time to investigate this intriguing but possibly sordid aspect of his new acquaintance's past. Beaumarchais was also an up-and-coming playwright whose characters were witty and irreverent—like the writer himself. Ben thought that might be a better topic for conversation.

"They say that your Figaro in *The Barber* shares many of your characteristics, Pierre. Is that true?"

"Not strictly speaking, but when Figaro says, 'I must force myself to laugh at everything lest I be obliged to weep,' he shares my view of the world at times."

"You don't seem at all melancholy to me." Ben smiled.

They finished breakfast, and Ben went to roust Temple and Benny. He had instructed them to unpack nothing but the necessities, so the preparation to depart was fairly easy.

While Ben was settling his bill with the innkeeper, the mayor entered. He looked more than a little bleary-eyed.

"I wanted to come by and wish you a safe journey," he said.

"I compliment you on your fine stewardship of the beautiful city of Nantes," Ben replied. "Your hospitality has been most remarkable."

The mayor basked in the recognition bestowed upon him by the famous Doctor Franklin. "It will be my utmost pleasure to host a party for you at any time in the future," he said.

Ben wondered if he would ever get the chance.

December 1776

THE ROAD TO PARIS

WITH MORE THAN A LITTLE CURIOSITY, Ben boarded the coach provided by Beaumarchais. It took a small stepladder to enter on account of the large springs, which promised a good suspension. A footman helped Ben up. The interior was quite luxurious compared to the coach in which he had arrived from Auray. Four plush seats were covered in buttery soft, hand-sewn brown leather. It smelled first-rate. Several newspapers were tucked into slots on the sidewall of the coach. The windows were squeaky clean, assuring good light for reading.

The boys, the Reverend, and Monsieur Penet became passengers of the regular commercial coach, all looking somewhat forlorn.

Ben would be happy to dispatch Penet as soon as they arrived in Paris. He would have no pretense to accompany Ben after that. The Reverend would have other work to get done. It would be best if he and Ben did not arrive together. It occurred to Ben that he didn't really know who he could trust in France. He yearned to be once again among trusted folk. Now he would be depending on his intuition alone. Still, he had done this before in his life. It was not as though trusting his instincts and acting on them was anything particularly new to Ben. During his time in England, he had come to form many of his concepts about the need for an independent United States of America based on perceptions of how he was treated. The British had not dealt in good faith with the colonists, and he was marginalized by most in Parliament. Only a handful could he count as friends. He was still contemplating how his perceptions had always guided him well when their small convoy started on its way up the road to Paris.

Nearly as soon as they had left Nantes, Beaumarchais fell fast asleep. The sounds of the town faded rapidly behind them. It was a beautiful morning with the sun gleaming through the half-open windows of the coach. Meadowlarks sang in the grasses alongside the road. Ben reached into his pocket and pulled out Marianne's letter.

The pink ribbon remained tied perfectly around the envelope, although, having been kept in Ben's pocket overnight, it was slightly rumpled. He inhaled the perfumed scent of the paper once again and closed his eyes to savor the memory. But he quickly returned to the letter in his hands. As he unfolded it, a lock of Marianne's soft, strawberry-blonde hair fell into his lap. Ben picked it up and put it to his cheek. This time he sensed not only her perfume but something more profound. Even when she wore no perfume, Ben enjoyed her smell. He would hold her and breathe in what he thought of as her essence. Ben wasn't sure that he could call it a smell at all. He was nonetheless certain he could discern it from that of any other woman. This little lock of hair brought that unmistakable essence rushing back to him—an intoxicating, exhilarating, and exciting sensation coursed through his body.

"That is a powerful natural force," Ben thought. "As strong as wind, or water, or electricity." He looked at the letter in his hands:

October 28
Firenze

Mon Cher,
*I must apologize for my delay in writing to you. The summer
was terribly busy with travel throughout Italy and our never-ending performance schedule. Mama has been merciless in her
pursuit of bigger and more prestigious halls for us to play. While
we have seen many packed houses this year, we seem never to be
able to satisfy her desire for more fame or more fortune. Currently,
we are in Florence, playing at the Teatro della Pergola. We plan
to complete this tour within the next few months, afterwards
traveling by way of Vienna over the winter and Paris in the spring.*
*Yes, I did say Paris in the spring, my love! I have missed you
so very much and only want to be able to hold you in my arms
again. Other than a few headaches and bouts of melancholia
(perhaps from missing you), my health has been fairly good
this summer. I believe that it has been aided by the warm, sunny
weather of Italy. I will try to be a better correspondent. You try
to be a gentleman in France, and don't let too many of those
Parisian ladies flirt with you.*

With All My love,
Marianne

The spring seemed a long way off. Ben put the letter back in his pocket,
feeling a bit dejected. But there was a lot of business to attend to in Paris. Ben
felt sure the time would pass quickly. It was heartening to have something
to look forward to. He smiled contentedly.

"Receiving love letters already?"

The voice came from the other side of the coach. Ben realized that Pierre
was awake and must have observed his reading of the letter.

"What makes you say that?"

"I can smell her perfume all the way over here," Pierre replied. "She must be heavenly."

"Yes," Ben asserted. "She is. Unfortunately, she won't arrive in Paris until the spring."

"Good. That will give us time to get some work done. Besides, I know a lot of French women who would like to get their hands on you first."

"You do?" Ben was more than a little intrigued.

"Oh, yes, my friend. I'm sure you realize that the attainment of great success and fame by a man such as yourself is an aphrodisiac to women everywhere. I doubt that you will lack female companionship—should you desire it."

"You seem to have an eye for the ladies," Ben said.

"I probably have courted more than my share," Pierre replied. He looked a bit smug but then became more serious. "But I've only truly loved one woman," he said.

"And who might that lucky lady be?"

"My lover, Marie-Thérèse. She has a deeper connection to me than any other woman ever has, or ever will, I suspect."

Ben looked perplexed. "Your lover?" he asked. "If you are so close, then why do you not marry her?"

Pierre laughed. "She claims that she dare not because of the fate of my first two wives."

Though Ben had heard the rumors, he gave no sign.

"And what was their fate, pray tell?" he asked.

"I am a widower twice over," Pierre said. "My first wife Madeleine died after only ten months of marriage and my second, Genevieve, two years after we wed. Some ignorant people claimed that the deaths were 'mysterious' because both my brides came from wealthy families and had large dowries. But I can swear to you on my mother's grave that I had no hand in either of their deaths. I was even more heartbroken when my only son, Augustin, died four years ago at the tender age of two. It was a terrible time for me, but

Marie-Thérèse pulled me through. She has been my rock in a stormy sea. I love her with all my heart."

"Losing a young son is a sorrow that I am only too familiar with. Even though it has been forty years since Francis died, I still miss him almost every day."

"Your wife, Deborah, passed away only two years ago, did she not?" Pierre asked. "But she bore you a daughter who lives in Philadelphia, if I am not mistaken."

Ben brightened up immediately. "Yes, that would be my lovely daughter Sally, who is the mother of young Benny traveling with us. She and her husband Richard caretake my home in Philadelphia."

"And you have a son, William?" Pierre said.

"Let's not talk of that bastard," Ben said. He turned a bit flushed. "The only good thing he ever did was to produce my other grandson Temple, who is also with me on this journey. I'm trying to raise that boy right, at least."

"But, *Mon Dieu*! What has your son done to so offend you?"

"As Governor of New Jersey, William continues to be loyal to King George and the English court. He sees the political situation quite differently than I do. In my view, there is no way that we can continue as British colonies, governed from afar by a bunch of idiots who enjoy the tax money they receive but don't care to understand the first thing about the conditions where we live."

"I'll be the first to agree with you there," Pierre said. "I know that our King and most Frenchmen would love to help you Americans if only to stick a poker up King George's royal arse. But I also believe that you have a cause worth fighting for.

"Have you read any of Voltaire's works? I think that we may have a revolution coming in my own country—although you will never hear me say that in public."

"Let's hope for enough stability to get our mission accomplished," Ben said. He worried, not for the first time, about the political situation he was about to enter.

Pierre must have sensed Ben's discomfort because he said reassuringly, "Do not fret, King Louis and the aristocracy are well entrenched."

The two men traveled along, talking of specific suppliers of arms, orders to be placed, methods of shipments, payments, and schedules for quite a while. Beaumarchais scribbled notes on paper that to Ben appeared hopelessly illegible. He thought that would be advantageous if the notes were ever intercepted, but could also be very unfortunate if his new business partner could not decipher the plans they had just spent hours working out. However, Ben felt that he must trust this man, and he sensed that he could.

After a while, Pierre looked up and said, "What is she like?"

Ben could have easily dodged the question or given a superficial response. He first looked perplexed at his coach mate's question, but when Pierre motioned at the letter in Ben's coat pocket, he acquiesced. Beaumarchais warm expression urged Ben to tell all.

"She is the closest thing to perfection that I have ever known. When we are together, I feel that the entire world, the entire universe is peaceful and calm. I become totally immersed in her, and she in me. We mesh together to become almost one being. It's hard to describe in words how wonderful it is ... but I have come to believe that it is a spiritual experience. Do you know that feeling?"

"Oh, yes," Pierre replied. He sighed deeply. "The way you describe it sounds like poetry. You obviously love her. But tell me, what keeps you apart?"

"Schedules, expectations, commitments, you know—the usual things," Ben said. Yet, he couldn't think of a truly good reason why he and Marianne shouldn't be together right now. "She is a musician, with a demanding schedule and a stage mother who keeps her on a tight leash." It sounded as if he was making an apology for her.

"Ah, I know the type," Pierre said. "A beautiful and sensitive woman, but weak, who follows along when mama orders her around."

"Not exactly," Ben replied. "She has her ways of escaping from her mother's clutches."

"So why don't you take her away from all that and marry her?" Pierre asked.

"Until two years ago, that would not have been possible since I was already married to Deborah ... and as you can see from my current situation, I don't exactly have time for a wife," Ben said. His words had a hollow ring to them that Pierre jumped on.

"I don't mean to be presumptuous, but are you sure that is all it is?"

"Alright, there is something else," Ben admitted. He felt his throat tighten a bit. "I've never told anyone this. I'm not even sure that I realized it myself until this moment, but there have been times—when she goes into one of her bouts of melancholia—when I don't truly recognize her. During those times, she doesn't want to be with me. She doesn't respond to me the way I need her to. She doesn't care about me. She doesn't care about anything. I've seen all the life go out of her and it frightens me.

"Earlier in our relationship, I thought that I could pull her out of her gloom—and there were times when I believe that I did. However, the last few years in London, I sensed a change in her. The depth of her spells worsened to the point where she wouldn't eat or leave her bed for days. I couldn't do anything to snap her out of it. She doesn't care for herself during those times. She's like a mannequin. Her sister has to bathe her, dress her, and comb her hair. I think that she wouldn't even get up to go to the toilet if someone didn't make her.

"She has seen the best doctors in Europe, but none have been of any help. They mostly advise various techniques of purging or bleeding to remove the bad humours, but I'm not convinced that does any good. I've offered to try giving her an electrical shock treatment, which I used successfully on a man in Philadelphia to treat his melancholia, but she refused."

"Electrical shock treatment for melancholia, eh? Well, that's a new one on me. The only other new medical treatment for melancholia that I've heard tell of is the '*magnétisme animale*' practiced by Doctor Mesmer of Vienna," Pierre said.

"I'm not aware of him," Ben said.

"I attended a salon recently at Passy. A doctor named D'Eslon spoke of hearing Herr Mesmer discuss his theory of a previously undiscovered force or fluid that can be used to heal. I don't know many details, but apparently, Doctor Mesmer has devised a technique to channel and control this fluid. He calls this force *magnétisme animale* or animal magnetism to distinguish it from the mineral kind. He postulates that, by redirecting or redistributing this fluid in the body, one can heal many ailments. I'm not a scientist, and it was all a bit like Greek to me. Perhaps when we get to Passy, your host Jacques Leray will be able to tell you more, as he heard D'Eslon describe the technique also."

"I'll be sure to ask him when I get the chance," Ben said. Something about Mesmer made Ben uncomfortable. He changed the subject. "Tell me a little more about our host, please."

"I know that Jacques would have preferred to collect you personally in Nantes. It is his hometown. He is adored there. But alas, he was detained by business. This is one of his coaches we are riding in. I am quite sure that the only way I was able to get it repaired so quickly was by using his name. Jacques made his fortune in the shipping business in Nantes but eventually moved his home to Passy in order to be closer to the court of Louis XV. You may also know that he now owns the Château de Chaumont in the Loire valley. Sometimes you will hear his name given as Jacques Leray de Chaumont, a title that he has earned by his fortune and fame. Jacques is a true believer in the cause of American freedom. There have been many dinners at Passy where he has spoken angrily against the British tyranny. I believe that he would single-handedly fund your war effort if he could. But as you know, Jacques has the ear of young King Louis XVI, who will also be a strong advocate for the American war ... of course, he cannot be openly supportive for political reasons."

"Jacques has a son about Temple's age, does he not?" Ben asked.

"Yes, and a lovely wife who dotes on them and who, I'm sure, will spoil you too. I have to love her even more because her name is also Marie-Thérèse, just like my beloved," Pierre replied.

Ben sighed. "I feel as though I could use a little spoiling right now, after over a month at sea, and a week on this road," he said.

That evening by the fire, Ben and Pierre shared a fine Xeres sherry that the innkeeper provided. As the embers glowed, Ben pulled out the letter from Marianne and brought it to his nose one last time. He closed his eyes and breathed in the soft, sweet aroma that reminded him so much of her. The fire and the effect of the sherry enhanced the warm feeling that its fragrance elicited. Ben slowly opened his eyes. He tossed the letter onto the flickering embers. It flared up briefly, causing Pierre to take notice.

"You do not care to save these beautiful letters?" Pierre asked.

Ben glanced over at his new friend. "Long ago, we decided not to save our correspondence. You must understand that I was married to Deborah at the time, and Marianne was an up and coming entertainer. The last thing that we needed was for a blackmailer or the sleazy London tabloids to discover our letters and use our loving words against us. It probably would have been more detrimental to Marianne's budding career than to my reputation, but I painfully agreed. Since then, I have not kept her letters but have instead destroyed them as you just saw. I will always keep her thoughts and feelings close to my heart, even if the vessel that delivered them to me has vanished in a puff of smoke."

"Marvelously spoken," Pierre said. He emptied his glass. "Now, let's get some rest," he said, rising from his chair. "Tomorrow, we will reach Paris."

December 1776

PARIS

AS THEY APPROACHED THE CITY, the road became more crowded, especially after they had passed Versailles. Many fine aristocratic coaches joined them on the road, their professional drivers sitting in uniform, reins in hand, barking out commands to the draft team. But Ben also noted the wider diversity of the coaches they passed now. In America, all of the coaches would be plain working vehicles designed to transport the rider from one place to another in a utilitarian fashion—and attracting as little attention as possible. On this road, there were certainly many unadorned coaches, but Ben marveled at the ostentation of some. It appeared that each one was vying to be more flamboyant than the rest. If one bore plumes of feathers, the next would have plumes twice as high or colorful pennants flying from each corner.

Riders on horseback wove among the coaches on the road, some at a steady saunter while others seemed more intent on their destination. As much as transportation, it seemed that the purpose of the road was business; both sides were dense with vendors hawking their wares and shops catering to the traveler's needs. Out the window, Ben saw everything from sacks of grain and piles of dull green cabbages, to potted plants, to leather goods, even livestock and household items. It seemed one could obtain almost anything along this stretch of road.

Though Ben enjoyed the attention of the passersby, he missed the quiet serenity of the country roads. Now there was little opportunity to think about Marianne. But perhaps that was for the best. Soon enough, he spotted the river Seine. Once they crossed it, Pierre said it would be only a short time to Paris.

The hotel where they first debarked in Paris turned out to be abysmal. Silas Deane had arranged for the Franklins to share the one room available. It was a dark and dreary place with only a small window and two small beds. The cramped, worn accommodations were especially dreary in the cold December mists. Temple and Benny were forced to sleep in one bed. At least that kept them warmer. Ben froze at night.

Because of the lack of space, nearly everything the Franklins had brought with them remained in storage. They took out only a few changes of clothes and the bare necessities. There seemed to be constant noise, both from the neighbors and the street outside. Ben longed for quiet to allow him to think. There was no desk. He longed for a space to write.

Ben had meetings scheduled during the day with his fellow American commissioners, Silas Deane and Arthur Lee, which occupied some of his time. They planned the purchase of munitions and other accoutrements of war from the French entrepreneurs who realized the benefits of trading for tobacco, furs, and other items the Americans had to offer.

But then came night, and the bugs. Ben developed red, itchy marks from his neck to his ankles. He suspected the bed was infested. He inquired at the hotel desk and was informed by the clearly insulted *maître d' hotel* that no one had ever questioned the cleanliness of the hotel before. Ben doubted that was the case but said nothing. He requested fresh bed linens. Despite the change, the bites continued unabated.

As he seemed to be getting no better, one morning, Ben decided to inquire at the front desk if there was a doctor nearby he might consult; he was careful not to mention anything about the suspected etiology.

"*Oui*, there is a physician down the street, to your left as you leave the hotel," the man behind the front desk responded curtly. He turned abruptly away from Ben to continue sorting mail into the slots assigned by room.

Ben crossed the drab lobby. No other hotel guests were up at this hour. He noticed a young woman sitting in the corner of the lobby toward the door, dressed in the typical brightly colored hand-woven scarves of a gypsy. She held a basket in her lap. It bore a sign that read "*Chamomile—six livres.*" She looked up as he approached.

"Chamomile, sir? It helps the itch." She smiled knowingly.

"No, thank you," Ben replied automatically, preoccupied with his mission.

Once he exited the hotel to the dreary street, he became doubly uncomfortable. It was foggy, cold, damp, and foul smelling. A noxious combination of acrid cooking smoke and decomposing human excrement struck his nose. In this section of Paris, there were no sidewalks or sewers. Ben's shoe slipped in the slick mud as soon as he turned left out the doorway, and he nearly fell down. He caught himself. He looked up to observe the driver of an idle carriage for hire giving him a concerned look.

"Coach, sir?" the driver asked.

It would not have been out of the question. In this part of town, aristocrats shopping from one store to the next along the same avenue would often board their coaches to avoid the mud of the street.

"No," Ben replied. It was only a few hundred feet to the doctor's office.

The coachman shrugged. "As you wish," he said.

Ben proceeded carefully, using a combination of sliding and careful stepping through the inch-deep slime. Finally, Ben could see the sign for the doctor's office. He was just beginning to think that he would make it there unscathed when a large carriage came hurtling down the street, spewing mud in all directions. Ben tried to cover up but was badly splattered on one side. He considered turning back to change clothes but decided to press on instead.

After what seemed like an eternity, he reached the door of the doctor's office. His hand slipped as he attempted to turn the doorknob. Ben reached for his handkerchief and wiped his hands and face with it. One more try and the door opened into a small empty waiting room.

A bell attached to the door announced his entry, but no one appeared to receive him. The stark room was barren of furniture other than a few wooden chairs and a small table. A lamp flickered on the table. Ben walked over to it and rubbed his hands in front of the lantern glass. The small fire warmed him a bit.

A stern, dark-haired young woman dressed in a smock appeared at the reception window.

"Yes? May I help you?"

"I would like to consult with the doctor."

"Do you have an appointment?"

Ben looked around the empty waiting room. "Do I need one?"

"The Doctor is very busy."

"I see," Ben said. "Perhaps I should return another day."

"That may not be necessary. I will enquire if the Doctor is able to fit you in today. Please have a seat."

"Thank you."

The receptionist disappeared. Ben sat down in one of the waiting room chairs but found it uncomfortable. He switched to another that was equally bad. The mud on his clothes was beginning to cake. Ben was consternated that the dried mud was flaking off around him when he noticed how dirty the floor already was. There was dirt and dust everywhere. The dim lighting had only hidden the lack of cleanliness previously. Ben itched all the more. After a nearly interminable wait, the woman returned.

"Will you be paying cash for your consultation?"

"What is the fee?"

"It depends on what the Doctor finds that you need. The initial consultation is four louis plus the cost of any medicine he prescribes. If you require additional treatment, it will be more."

Ben suppressed the distinct feeling that he was being fleeced. "I will pay cash."

"That will be four then," she replied, holding out her hand.

"In advance?"

"Yes."

Ben fumbled with his purse. He sorted out four gold louis and gave them to the receptionist.

She accepted the coins, weighing them in her hand. "What is your name?"

"Franklin, Ben Franklin."

"Age?"

"Seventy years."

She wrote his information down in a ledger. Ben wondered if she would recognize his name, but she did not seem to—or if she did, she did not react.

"And your problem?"

"A rash."

She eyed him suspiciously. "Where?"

Ben pondered what types of problems the clientele of this doctor presented with. Given the gritty area of the city in which he practiced, Ben reckoned that bodily rashes should not be so unusual. He wondered if she suspected him of having some form of venereal disease.

"All over," he replied.

"Please take a seat," she said blandly, then disappeared again.

After only a slightly less prolonged delay, she returned.

"The Doctor will see you now," she said. She opened the door next to her reception window and led Ben down a dimly lit hallway lined with empty examining rooms. She pointed him into one. Ben sat on the table there.

"I will let the Doctor know that you are ready to be seen," she said. She closed the door with a stern pull.

Ben looked around the room as he waited once again. A few metal instruments soaked in a jar on the table. Ben recognized them as bloodletting needles, pipettes, and syringes. He resolved that he would not submit to any such treatment for his condition. Charts of human anatomy hung on the walls. Ben spent his time studying them absentmindedly.

Then Ben heard murmured voices in the hall. The door opened, and the doctor entered. He was pulling on his coat as he did so. The coat was probably expensive at one time, but was now stained and tattered. The smell of tobacco and stale alcohol struck Ben immediately. The burly man sported about three days of a beard. A cigarillo dangled from one corner of his mouth, and ash hung precariously from the smoldering tip. His hair looked as if he had just arisen from his bed. His coat collar remained cocked up on one side, adding to his disheveled appearance. He looked Ben up and down with disdain, as he might a leper. The inspection surprised Ben, considering that his own appearance was considerably better kempt, albeit muddier, than the doctor's. There was no formal introduction, no welcome, no smile. The doctor kept his hands in his coat pockets.

"I understand that you have a rash," he said gravely.

"Yes."

"Where?"

"All over."

"Show me. Undress, if you please."

Ben undid the buttons on his shirt. He took the shirt off and unbuckled his trousers, letting them drop. He stood before the doctor naked from his head to his ankles, where his trousers lay in a heap.

The doctor picked up a probe. He poked one of the lesions on Ben's back.

"Ouch," Ben protested.

"How long has the rash been present?"

"Weeks. I believe it might be due to bedbugs in the hotel."

"The hotel on this street?"

"Yes."

"Itchy?"

"Yes, terribly."

"Ummm hmmm."

The doctor turned to leave. Astonished, Ben called out, "What is your opinion, Doctor?"

"Pruritic cutaneous erythema cum excoriation," the physician replied. "My assistant will prepare your prescription." He rapidly disappeared. The door closed behind him.

"I've waited all this time to hear that I have an itchy red skin rash in Latin?" Ben muttered. "I could have told you that." He pulled up his pants and donned his shirt. Luckily, much of the mud stayed behind on the floor. Ben brushed himself off. He didn't feel the least bit concerned about leaving the mud there. He found his way back to the waiting area unescorted. The receptionist sat at her post.

The woman acknowledged that Ben had returned from his consultation. "Please have a seat," she said. "Your prescription will be ready soon."

"And what would that be?"

She appeared annoyed by his question. "I am sure that I wouldn't know. It will be up to the Doctor."

After another long wait, someone who Ben could not see passed a small bundle to the receptionist.

"Your prescription, sir," she announced.

"What is it?" Ben asked.

"What the doctor ordered." She put a notation in her ledger. "That will be two louis."

"Suppose that I no longer want the treatment?"

"Oh my," she exclaimed. Her face showed a look of concern for the first time since Ben had entered the office. "The Doctor would be most displeased if you did not follow his orders. In fact, this prescription cream has been prepared especially for you and is not returnable."

"What if I refuse to pay for it?"

"My dear sir," she replied firmly. "The Doctor insists that you pay for the prescription—or he will be forced to take legal action against you."

"Legal action? This is ridiculous." Ben felt the heat well up under his collar. It made his skin itch even worse. "Where is the *doctor*? I'll speak with him directly."

"Oh no, sir," she replied. It seemed that she had performed this drill many times before. "The Doctor has left to see his many other patients. He will not be back for some time. Please pay the two louis and take your prescription, or I shall be forced to call the *gendarme*."

"The *gendarme*! Oh, this is all too much." Ben grudgingly located two more gold coins in his purse and nearly flung them at the woman. "Here."

She held out the small package. "Thank you, sir." She flashed a counterfeit smile.

Ben stormed onto the street, which was devoid of any commerce in the morning fog. He slipped and slid his way back up the block toward his hotel. When he reached a spot where he could stand without fear of falling, he unwrapped the package to find a small glass jar sealed with wax. Ben pried the top off. It contained a white cream. He dipped a muddy finger inside. He rubbed the greasy cream between his fingers and lifted them toward his nose. The cream had a pungent aroma that overpowered even the stench of the street. It appeared to be lead-based. Ben theorized that the lead in many products caused madness. He knew that lead crystal makers were prone to mental problems as were the miners, smelters, and others who handled lead routinely. He would not be spreading leaden cream over his open sores. He flung the jar into the middle of the street, where it sank into the deeper mud.

Upon reentering his hotel, Ben made a beeline for the gypsy with chamomile for sale. He asked to purchase two packets.

"Yes, sir. That will be twelve livres," she replied demurely. "Dissolve one packet in your bath for relief of the itch." As she handed him the packets, she continued in a hushed voice. "Sir, may I offer further advice and counsel?"

"If you would be so kind."

She beckoned Ben to lean toward her. The smell of chamomile was strong but pleasant about her.

"Replace all your bed linens and your mattress. Thoroughly wash the bed frame. When all this is done, and the new mattress is in place, pour an unbroken ring of powdered mineral borax around your bed. The insects will not cross it and will bother you no more," she whispered.

Ben straightened up and looked at the woman appreciatively.

"Thank you so much. I will do just as you advise," he said.

He located the one last gold coin in his purse and pressed it into her hand. Even though it was more than twice what she asked for her treatment, it seemed like money wisely spent.

Ben followed the gypsy's instructions with his own bed as well as the one the boys shared. The Franklin family had no further trouble with bugs, and Ben made no further visits to the doctor down the street.

January 1777

FLORENCE

MARIANNE SAT IN the doctor's tidy office patiently. She picked up the newspaper a prior patient had left behind. She flipped directly to the society pages. Mother never allowed a newspaper in their apartment, so Marianne was not at all up to date. Feverishly, she read with interest about the couples recently engaged, the socialite balls that had been held, and what the fashionable ladies wore to them. She was quite immersed in a daydream involving dancing at a ball with a dashing young prince when her name was called.

"The Doctor will see you now," the nurse said.

Marianne followed her into the examining room and then was handed a linen gown.

"Undress completely and put this on," the nurse instructed.

Marianne took off her clothes and folded them aside neatly. She donned the plain linen gown, which was stiff and scratchy. Her arms looked like two sausages sticking out of the short sleeves. She couldn't tie it up in the back, so she tucked in the fabric behind her as she sat on the examining table. She waited again, wishing that she had brought the newspaper in with her.

The "doctor" looked like a young boy. Marianne almost laughed when he entered the examining room. He was dressed in a quite formal suit coat and trousers, making him appear more mature to be sure, but the peach fuzz on his face didn't seem that it would even require shaving. He appeared very serious and kept his eyes focused on the paper he held in his hands.

"Are you the student doctor?" she asked.

"No ma'am," he said, not even looking up. "I am *the* doctor."

"How old are you?"

"I'll ask the questions," he said with an irritated tone, which fit poorly with his youthful countenance. "How old are *you*?"

"Thirty-two years."

He cast her a glance as if she were decrepit. "And what brings you to see the doctor today?"

Marianne considered making up some ailment to tell him, such as a cold, so as not to reveal her real reason for the visit since she already had no confidence that he would have anything new to offer her, but instead said, "Melancholia."

"Hmmm," he offered. It seemed as if he had practiced the intonation for effect. "For how long have you been affected by melancholia?"

"All my life."

Marianne went on to describe "the darkness," how it came on and how it dissipated. She told of how she lost interest in everything, how she lost her sense of taste, smell, and vision during these episodes. She told of how she was incapable of caring for herself, how she felt lifeless. Marianne found that at least her young physician was a good listener.

The examination was thorough. Perhaps a bit too thorough, Marianne thought. Of course, he listened to her chest, palpated her abdomen, tested her strength, sensation, reflexes, and every one of her cranial nerves. He made her pee into a cup and dipped his finger in—tasting it for any sign of sugar. Marianne thought that he might have lingered a bit too long when examining her breasts—but if he enjoyed it, he gave no outward indication.

"You seem fairly fit for a woman of your age," he said matter-of-factly at the conclusion of the exam.

Marianne was about to object, but he went on without pausing.

"Modern medical science does not offer an explanation or a cure for melancholia," he went on. He cracked the first hint of a smile that Marianne had seen on him. "Yet, luckily, it is no longer believed that you are haunted by demons.

"Rather, it is now believed that the system of bodily nerves and the nervous fluid is somehow disturbed—leading to the episodes of the darkness that you experience. It is known that bloodletting and purging offer little in the treatment of melancholia. Fresh air and exercise may offer some hope, as may changes in your diet to avoid heavy meats and sauces. Lean meats, fresh eggs, and grapes are thought to be helpful foods."

"I hate exercise and love to eat."

"Hopefully, your episodes will remain manageable, but if the symptoms of melancholia become too profound, or you have no one to care for you when you are incapacitated, then you may have to be committed to an asylum."

"Perhaps I could learn to like exercise," Marianne replied.

"Also, there are now "nerve doctors" practicing in some larger cities— but I would caution you that there are many quacks and empirics. Try to avoid any purported remedies that seem outlandish or odd."

"Thank you. I will follow your advice, Doctor," she said politely.

He scribbled something in her chart, bid her good day, and left the room. Marianne dressed. She pocketed the newspaper as she exited the building. She hadn't received a full explanation or any cure for her melancholia—yet she felt somewhat better, nonetheless.

PART
II

Winter 1777

PARIS TO PASSY

DESPITE THE POOR hotel accommodations, being housed in Paris wasn't without some benefits for Ben. Beaumarchais made good on his promise of an invitation to see *The Barber of Seville* at the opera. Ben laughed so hard that his sides hurt for a day afterward. He also found that he had instantly become the most sought-after guest on everyone's list. He had to turn down invitations to more parties and salons than he could accept. In addition to their business dealings, he and Beaumarchais became closer friends and regular dinner partners. On occasion, Jacques Leray would join them when he was in town. Ben enjoyed the Parisian restaurants and the Bordeaux wine, but he grumbled intermittently to his friends about his living situation.

"Ben," Leray asked at a dinner one day in late January, "would you consider staying with me and my family in Passy? We would like very much to provide you with the space you need."

Ben didn't hesitate but was careful to draw a line between friendship and business. "I accept, with gratitude and pleasure," he said, "but we will have to work out an appropriate lease and schedule of fees."

Jacques laughed. "Of course," he said. And just like that, it was done.

When the boys heard the news that they would be moving out of the shabby hotel, they were ecstatic.

Leray did eventually write out a lease agreement for Ben, but never sent him a bill in all the time that the Franklins stayed at Passy.

On an unseasonably warm February day, Ben and the boys climbed into the Leray coach along with Pierre Beaumarchais and headed for Passy. Temple and Benny were especially excited. Ben had spent the morning arranging to get their wagon, still packed with most of their belongings, out of storage, and outfitted with a team of horses.

They all waved a not-so-fond goodbye to the 'Bedbug Hotel' as it had come to be referred to by the Franklins.

"Good riddance," Ben proclaimed as it receded into the distance.

Crowded boulevards gave way to more sparse and utilitarian buildings toward the city gates. Once outside the gates, they were completely in the country. The trees along the side of the road appeared more randomly than the regimented plantings of the Parisian streets. Nonetheless, the road to Passy was wide and well maintained. They encountered a steady flow of other coaches coming and going in both directions. The boys' anticipation grew as the city faded, and they caught more glimpses of the river. The day had a spring-like quality. Even though it remained too cold, Ben started to think about how wonderful it would feel to be swimming again. When the house came into view, everyone except Pierre let out a gasp. The walls of the Hôtel de Valentinois must have been twenty feet high. From the road leading in, Ben only caught glimpses of the house behind with its green terra cotta roof and limestone walls. Contrasting corner quoins gave the place a regal appearance.

"This place is a palace," Benny said.

Even Ben was not expecting such luxury. His home in Philadelphia was comfortable, but modest. For the past twenty years, Ben had lived mostly in Mrs. Stevenson's townhome in London—which was by no means extravagant. From a view of the exterior, the country home of Jacques Leray promised to be a major step up.

Ben looked toward Pierre. "Are you sure that this is the right place?"

"Welcome home," Beaumarchais said.

The late afternoon sun poured golden light over the walls of the Hôtel de Valentinois as the coach crunched to a stop in the courtyard where even the gravel seemed to glow. Two large oil lamps flanked a huge oak entry door that was swung wide open. Ben noticed fresh cut flowers inside the foyer of the breezeway that connected the two main buildings. With the doors open, Ben could see all the way through to the warm yellow and pink-hued afternoon sky gleaming behind the house. It struck him as the most calming picture he had seen since leaving America. Outside the front door and in the courtyard stood a small army of maids, butlers, footmen, and stable boys waiting expectantly. The little party from Paris exited the coach in awe. As Pierre walked up the front steps with Ben and the stunned boys, the staff descended on the wagon and coach. With military precision, their contents were unloaded and borne off to be put away in the Franklin's new lodgings.

Just as they crossed the threshold, a woman Ben instantly knew must be Marie-Thérèse Leray came gliding over the marble floor of the foyer toward them. She wore a flowered print dress that was neither too countrified nor too formal and fit her slightly matronly figure perfectly. She wore simple jewelry that appeared to be made of shells. Her hair was unpowdered, long, and flowing over her shawl-wrapped shoulders. Her smile radiated a welcome as warm as the afternoon sun. To Ben, she appeared to be the quintessence of comfortable elegance. She curtsied and extended her hand gracefully. Ben accepted her hand in his. He kissed it warmly.

"Welcome to our Hôtel de Valentinois, Dr. Franklin," she said.

"Please call me Ben. And we are eternally grateful for your kindness and generosity in receiving us."

"Please call me Marie-Thérèse." Madame Leray gave another slight curtsey. She didn't withdraw her hand. "Your cause is important to my husband ... and to me, Ben. It is my sincere hope that you will be both comfortable and productive here. I would like to introduce you to my family," she said.

Bustling up behind Madame Leray came four smaller incarnations of her, four young ladies that looked to be between the ages of twelve and twenty-four. They stood in line by height alongside their mother. She pointed successively to the pretty girls from the tallest to smallest.

"I present to you Marie-Elisabeth, Marie-Francoise, Marie-Sophie, and Therese-Elisabeth," she said. "My son, Jacques-Donatien ... Junior we call him ... is down by the river. And my husband, of course, is working. He should be back from Versailles later tonight."

Temple and Benny seemed to have heard only the words "down by the river." They both looked plaintively at their grandfather.

Ben instantly said to Madame Leray, "These are my grandsons Temple and Benny. They have been cooped up in the coach for the better part of the day. May they go find your son?"

Madame Leray smiled warmly at the boys. "Of course," she replied.

Her words were still hanging in the air as the two youths bounded out the back toward the Seine. The girls all watched in various states of amusement, shock, or disappointment to see that these newfound young men were deserting them so quickly. However, their mother just nodded reassuringly. The foyer was suddenly quiet.

"Ben," Madame Leray said. "Marie-Francoise will be in charge of your housekeeping." She nodded toward the second-tallest girl who looked slightly apprehensive but full of youthful enthusiasm. "My eldest daughter Marie-Elisabeth would have had the honor, but she is recently married with a husband and home to care for herself."

"Congratulations," Ben said. He bowed toward the eldest Leray daughter. "Now, if you don't mind, I would like to see our quarters and get freshened up after today's journey."

"By all means, I certainly understand."

Madame Leray looked over toward Beaumarchais and said, "Pierre can escort you to your rooms. We will have a light supper in the dining room at eight o'clock if you and the boys are hungry. Pierre, will you please stay the night as well? Jacques will want to hear the latest from Paris."

Beaumarchais flashed his most charming smile at Madame Leray. "Marie-Thérèse, I didn't relish the prospect of traveling back into Paris at this hour. You are as considerate as you are beautiful."

She blushed. "And you are an incorrigible flirt, but you are always welcome," Madame Leray replied. Something about the manner in which she responded suggested to Ben that she did not get as much attention from her husband as she should.

Beaumarchais led Ben through several hallways, past rooms filled with fine furnishings. The rooms were decorated in a similar style. Even with the cursory tour, Ben recognized several Rembrandt paintings as he walked by. They walked out the back of the main house, and across a well-mani-cured garden, down toward a row of separate buildings closer to the river. The house staff were entering through one door loaded with the Franklin's belongings and leaving through another, empty-handed, to retrieve more. Ben and Beaumarchais walked in the main door and stood in a sitting room furnished in a simple but tasteful French country style.

Ben gazed around his new surroundings. "Charming," he remarked.

"Your bedrooms are upstairs," Beaumarchais said. He motioned toward an oak stairway at the side of the room.

"I am sure that they are well-appointed lodgings," Ben replied. "Is all this space intended for us?"

"Yes, Madame Leray allocated this entire row of buildings to lodge your group. There are similar rooms for Monsieurs Deane and Lee, if they care to join you."

"I wonder if they will be able to resist once they hear of the luxury of our accommodations. What about the other buildings?" Ben asked as he looked at two large empty barn-like structures farther toward the river.

"Madame had those left empty for storage, but I thought that perhaps you would like to have a printing press installed?" Beaumarchais inquired, smiling.

Ben's face lit up immediately at the thought of setting up a press. He realized that he sorely missed the hours of satisfaction he spent setting type since leaving London. He looked forward to once again producing his little books that he liked to call his *bagatelles*.

"Let's go have a look," Ben said. He practically bounded out of the sitting room toward the empty buildings. Beaumarchais had to hurry to keep up with him.

They were just approaching the first building when Ben heard shouts coming up from the river. It sounded like Temple and another male voice yelling for help. Ben's heart started to race. Both he and Beaumarchais sprinted past the second building and across a grassy slope down to a wooden dock along the Seine. Ben could see Temple and Junior standing on the dock, shouting and waving their arms. Temple swung a rope in his hand. In the frigid river, young Benny was floundering about twenty feet from the end of the dock.

"That rope won't nearly reach," Ben yelled before he even got to the dock. Beaumarchais had arrived there first and stood swearing loudly. Ben's feet hit the wooden planks with a rhythmic thud, thud, thud. Temple, Junior, and Beaumarchais all stood at the end of the dock, yelling and waving their arms at Benny in the water.

Ben came barreling through and let out a yell that parted the group. Temple tossed his rope, which fell short, and simultaneously Ben dove off the end of the dock, fully clothed.

As he hit the icy water, Ben thought his heart might stop, but with his leap, he was almost out to Benny. In a few strokes, he reached the boy and grabbed him by the collar. Benny was flailing wildly. Ben saw that the boy was gasping for breath, but at least he was breathing. His face was pale, and his lips blue. He had obviously already taken in some water.

Ben held the boy's head above the water with one arm and reversed direction with the other. At the age of eight, Benny was still small, and Ben was a powerful swimmer. Before long, he was close enough to shore that his feet could touch the muddy bottom. He scrambled up the riverbank, clutching Benny close to him. The boy was wobbly, shaking, and making gurgling noises. Beaumarchais was there and threw his coat over both of them. Ben smacked Benny on the back, hard. Benny coughed out about a cup of river water and then vomited whatever else was in his stomach, which wasn't much.

By this time, the whole house had been alerted to the commotion. Madame Leray, her daughters, and several house staff came running down the slick grassy slope with blankets in their arms. Madame Leray threw a blanket around Ben, and one of the staff threw one around Benny. Finally, able to stand on his own, Benny began to breathe more normally.

"What happened?" Madame Leray asked, glaring at her son.

"We were just playing on the dock, and he fell in," Junior said sheepishly.

"Am I the only one here who knows how to swim?" asked Ben. He looked around. The rest of the group just gazed at each other in shock. No one said a word.

"Let's go up to the house," Madame Leray said.

Sitting by the fireplace in dry clothes and having consumed a hot drink, Ben felt considerably warmer. In fact, he realized that he must have dozed off in the comfortable chair. Beaumarchais and Madame Leray were engaged in a quiet conversation in chairs across from him.

"So that is why I love my own Marie-Thérèse so deeply. She is my soul mate. She is like a bonfire on shore to the lost sailor in me. She inspires me, guides me, provides my *raison d'être*," Beaumarchais was saying in hushed tones as Ben awoke.

"Ah, I remember the passion, the romance, the excitement..." Madame Leray said. She looked wistful.

Ben was beginning to feel uncomfortable that he should be an unwitting part of their intimate conversation. "One word frees us of all the weight and pain of life: That word is love," he said with a yawn.

"Sophocles," Beaumarchais responded.

"Ben, I didn't realize that you were awake," Madame Leray said. She blushed deeply.

"Yes, I had a fine nap," Ben said, trying to appear casual.

"But love is blind, and lovers cannot see the pretty follies that they themselves commit," Beaumarchais said.

"William Shakespeare?" Ben asked.

"Yes ... *The Merchant of Venice*. I only wish that it was I who could claim to have written it."

"You have written words just as true ... and fine," Ben said.

"And you will pen more lines of your wisdom to dazzle us," Madame Leray added.

"Thank you, My Dear," Beaumarchais said.

Spring 1777

VIENNA

MARIANNE DAVIES NEEDED A REST. Mother had arranged for
the series of concert dates in Vienna over the winter—which seemed to be
never-ending, as they were now booked well into the Spring. She had been
practicing all morning under the ever-watchful eye of her mother, who sat
knitting quietly in the corner. Her sister Cecelia seemed to be able to come
and go as she pleased, and it wasn't fair that Mrs. Davies insisted on at least
four hours of musical exercises from Marianne each day. Marianne finished
the sheet of music in front of her and lifted her aching fingers from the glass
bowls of the armonica. She rubbed one hand with the other.

"Mother, I'm tired, and I have a headache," Marianne complained.

"I'm sorry, dear," her mother replied, not even looking up.

"May I stop practicing now?"

At this, her mother looked over from her chair.

"You haven't practiced all the pieces yet for your performance, have you?"

"No, but I don't think that I can do any more just now," Marianne said.

"Alright, my dear, if you must have a break. But you will need to resume your practice this afternoon. It looks like a pleasant day. Perhaps you should take a walk and get some air."

"Thank you, Mother, but I'd prefer a nap."

Marianne was never one to truly enjoy the outdoors. She thought of all the times that Ben had tried, in vain, to talk her into some form of vigorous outdoor exercise. She knew from experience that her body always hurt for days afterwards. So she resisted his attempts to get her to go horseback riding—or God forbid—swimming. The single form of strenuous physical activity that she enjoyed with him, they had not been able to practice for almost two years now. She ached for him to lie with her every night. The thought of his warm muscular hands touching her sent a small thrill across her chest.

"I need to get to Paris," she thought. She closed her bedroom door.

Marianne awoke to a spring breeze rustling the sheer curtain of her bedroom window. The sun seemed high. "It's probably noon," she thought as she looked toward the light. "Mother will not forget that I owe her more practice time." Her headache had subsided somewhat, but a dull ache remained. She splashed her face with cool water from the washbasin.

She was tempted to return to her bed but recalled the doctor's advice and was just thinking that she shouldn't, when she heard the faint sound of music coming from the street. At first, she thought that perhaps it was an organ grinder with a trained monkey. However, as the breeze blew in the window again, the tones seemed too haunting, too familiar. It was definitely the sound of someone playing a glass armonica. Marianne became more intrigued as the music became louder.

"I know of only one other armonica in Vienna," she said out loud to no one but herself.

Marianne donned a simple peach-colored dress. She brushed her unruly hair quickly and placed a straw hat over it. She threw a cape over her shoulders. She left, as was her habit, through the window in order to avoid her mother's watchful eye.

There were many people on the street at this hour. The shops were busy with customers coming and going. No one seemed concerned in the least with Marianne or the music that she was pursuing.

She came to a storefront with no sign above the door. The interiors of the windows were covered with paper as if the store were vacant or for rent. Without a doubt, the music was coming from inside.

Marianne stepped out of the street into the vestibule. The inner door was open a crack, and then, as she watched, it opened wider ... beckoning. Clearly, someone was stationed there to usher in visitors. Marianne took a step into the darkened space. Without speaking, as naturally as though it was a long-established custom, a valet took her cape, hung it carefully on a hook with many other garments, and closed the door.

At first, all she could see were the dancing dust particles in the still air, highlighted by the streaks of sunlight entering the room through the gaps in the paper. Then her eyes began to adjust to the dim light.

The space was filled with people, perhaps a score, both men and women, most dressed in loose linen robes, though others wore customary street clothes. Occupying the middle of the large empty room was a curious object that looked, to Marianne, like an enormous oval wooden bathtub. It was made of smooth oak planks fastened by heavy ropes and appeared to be full of some kind of liquid. Out of the liquid, rose twenty smooth metal rods spaced equally around the rim and bent over the top of the tub.

The rods were phallic, an impression heightened by the behavior of the people in the room. Many of them rubbed against the rods and groaned softly. The whisper of soft flesh against hard, shiny metal was both sensuous and soothing. As Marianne watched, transfixed by this extraordinary scene, it occurred to her that she did not feel threatened or scared. On the contrary, she felt peaceful, even calm. The music seemed to be coming from everywhere and nowhere. Yet she did not see a glass armonica in the room.

As her eyes adjusted further to the darkness, Marianne realized that, in addition to the men and women close to the tub, there were other pairs sitting in chairs around the periphery. Their chairs were drawn close, facing each other. The men sat with their knees outside the women's knees, their feet parallel as if the men contained the women. Each woman had her arms at her sides, but the man had one hand placed below the woman's sternum and the other resting on her thigh. Each pair seemed to be breathing slowly and rhythmically together, locked in this strange embrace.

As Marianne stood watching, one of the couples began breathing faster. The woman's body started to twitch noticeably. Her eyes were closed. She began to smile. No one else in the room paid any attention as these two reached their climax. The woman's twitching became more extreme; her limbs jerked so spasmodically that the man could no longer contain her. She tumbled off the chair and onto the floor, still jerking, and now clutching her arms to her body in a kind of fit or convulsion. Marianne instinctively rushed to help the woman. But before she could get there, two attendants appeared out of nowhere. They gently lifted the fallen woman up and carried her out of the room.

Curious, Marianne followed. The bearers wore dark purple robes, which made them hard to see. The lighter robe of the stricken woman made it appear as if she was floating across the dimly lit space. Marianne followed through a doorway into what looked like a comfortable sitting room. There, the attendants gently placed the woman on a chaise longue. Her limp body no longer twitched, and she appeared to be sleeping peacefully. Marianne watched from the corner as a man dressed in a lavender satin robe embroidered with swirling mystical symbols entered the room with a washbasin of water. It was dark, but the wizard seemed hauntingly familiar to her. Marianne thought that perhaps she recognized him. Was it possible that he was the leader of this strange clan?

The wizard strode over to the reclining woman. From the basin, he pulled a wet cloth, wrung out the excess water, applied the compress to her forehead, then took her hand in his. She made a sweet sound, like a soft sigh, but her eyes remained closed. Marianne took a small step forward.

"Gretchen, can you hear me?" the wizard asked softly. His voice was like honey.

"Yes," she said in a hushed monotone.

"How do you feel?"

"Well."

"Do you remember how you felt when you arrived here today?"

"I was sick."

"In what manner?"

"My stomach hurt all the time. I couldn't eat."

"What is different now?"

"My stomach no longer hurts me."

"Gretchen." The wizard leaned toward her. "I want you to do something. I want you to open your mouth, so that I can place on your tongue a very special morsel of food. You will find that it is the most delicious bite of food that you have ever tasted. You will chew and swallow it slowly, relishing each moment. As the food travels to the back of your mouth and down your throat, I want you to turn your gaze inward so that you can follow it. Do you understand?"

"Yes, I believe so."

As Marianne watched in amazement, Gretchen opened her mouth and stuck out her tongue, waiting for the promised morsel. The wizard reached into his pocket. The room was dim, but Marianne could clearly see that when he brought his hand up to her lips, there was nothing between his thumb and first finger. Nonetheless, when he pulled his hand back from her, she closed her mouth and started chewing. A look of serene pleasure came over her face. Eventually, she swallowed. Her eyes remained closed.

"Now what do you see?" the wizard asked.

"Your wonderful food is being propelled down my throat to my stomach."

"Does everything look as it should?"

"Yes, so far." But then she said, "Oh no." Gretchen sounded frightened for the first time.

"What is it?"

"Once the morsel entered my stomach, I noticed some bleeding."

"Where?"

"From the wall of my stomach, just past the entry."

"Gretchen," he said, more intense now, "it is very important that you closely examine the wall of your stomach. What do you see?"

"Streaks that look like scratches."

"Do you see any growths or tumors? They would be protrusions from the wall of your stomach, perhaps appearing like a mushroom or bump."

"No, just those bleeding scrapes or scratches."

"Good. What do you believe your treatment should be?"

"No excess spice in my diet, whole milk and cream of tartar with each meal," Gretchen said.

"How long will it take for your stomach to heal with this regimen?"

"Around six weeks, I believe."

"Then are you ready to conclude?"

"Yes."

The wizard put his hand on her hypochondrium just below her sternum between her breasts. "When I remove my hand, you will awaken," he said. "You will feel refreshed and rested. You will not recall the images you saw inside your body, but you will recall the prescription required for your cure. You will follow the regimen just as you have outlined. Your stomach will heal within the time you estimated. Now wake up." He removed his hand quickly.

Gretchen opened her eyes. She looked slightly dazed as if awakening from a nap. She straightened herself up on the chaise, looked around, and stiffened a little.

"Oh," she exclaimed.

"No reason to be embarrassed," the wizard said reassuringly. "Remember, I am a doctor. You did very well. How do you feel now?"

"Wonderful—but I'm hungry."

"That is good, yes?"

"Yes, I must go have my dinner now. But first, I must stop at the Apothecary and purchase some cream of tartar."

The wizard stood up.

Gretchen appeared a bit perplexed. She gathered her cloak and left the room. Until this moment, Marianne had felt nearly invisible, observing this remarkable scene without anyone paying the least attention to her. But now she felt like a voyeur caught peeking in a bedroom window. The wizard's penetrating gaze fell on her. She froze as he walked over to her. He lowered the hood of his fanciful robe to reveal a full head of curly brown hair, and an infectious smile. Marianne couldn't help smiling back. He extended his hand. She tentatively extended hers.

"Hello, Marianne," he said. His voice was like silk. "Have you come to begin your treatment?"

Marianne felt the blood rush to her head. His beautiful blue eyes seemed to penetrate her soul.

Suddenly she felt trapped, and panic swept over her.

"No," she cried out. She pushed past him and fled.

She bolted out of the building and didn't look back until she came to her own street. No one was behind her. She slipped back through her bedroom window into her bed, her heart pounding. The room was quiet and warm. Her breathing slowed. She noticed that her headache was completely gone. She felt well for the first time in months, perhaps years. But she wondered just what sort of power this man, this wizard, had over her. Would she be able to resist his spell?

Spring 1777

NEAR PASSY

BEN FLOATED ON HIS BACK in the Seine's chilly water, over six hundred miles away from where Marianne practiced the armonica under her mother's watchful eye. Even though it was still early in the morning, it promised to be an unusually warm spring day. Every once in a while, he gave a small kick of his legs or stroke of his arms. He moved effortlessly through the water, which seemed to caress him. Ben always swam in the nude. It was natural. He was in clear deep water about halfway across the broad river.

Out here, the world seemed incredibly peaceful. The court of Louis XVI was way over in Versailles, and his work for the American Revolution lay waiting for him back on shore. It would be there when he got back. Even Marianne's delay in getting to Paris this spring, which she had promised, seemed less painful. Why did she need to spend extra time in Vienna? Ben didn't know the answer, but it didn't seem to matter quite so much out in the water. He just floated along, listening to the birds, tuning out the distant honking of some geese having a disagreement.

Ben found himself remembering the day in February when they had first arrived at Passy, that day when he had saved Benny from drowning. Benny had not gone back near the river since then. Ben remained intent on teaching Benny to swim, but he knew that if he tried to force his grandson into the water before he was ready, that it would be a lost cause. Ben would bide his time. Benny would be ready when he was ready.

Very few people swam in 1777, let alone in rivers like the Seine. Most people believed that they would catch some disease from the water, or even the air. They understood that diseases were spread by "bad humours," which could result in illness or even death. In Paris, people kept their houses closed up tight and rarely opened their windows.

It had been fewer than one hundred years since the last major outbreak of the bubonic plague in Europe. The very elderly might recall the quarantines imposed to combat the "black death." Smallpox remained rampant, despite the advent of effective inoculation. Consumption and dysentery claimed the lives of many. Medical treatments held little hope of a cure. Bloodletting and purging were the accepted methods to rid the body of these bad humours. In Ben's opinion, these medical treatments rarely, if ever, worked. "Better to not get sick in the first place," he thought.

Since they could afford it, aristocratic Parisians only drank water brought in from pure artesian wells like those in Passy. Most bathed regularly, but only in their own bathtub or at the spa. They would never bathe or swim in a river. Hence Ben had no competition for the waterway other than an occasional cormorant or duck. But Ben believed firmly that the healthful benefits of physical activity, fresh air, and sunshine outweighed the possibility of contagion. Having achieved the ripe old age of seventy-one, he reckoned that he was living proof. While at Passy, Ben either swam or rode horseback daily, weather permitting. If driven inside by snow or ice, he took to climbing the stairways of the Hôtel de Valentinois repeatedly or walking quickly in a circuit through the expansive hallways of the house. Luckily, the climate around Paris was even more temperate than Philadelphia or London. Ben found that he could partake in some form of outdoor activity on most days.

Madame Leray seemed to subscribe in part to his health theory, at least as far as the sunlight and fresh air were concerned. She kept the windows and doors of her house open almost all the time. Perhaps this was the difference between the country air and the city air, Ben speculated. She did not swim or ride horseback herself, and neither did any of her children. This usually left Ben to swim in the Seine or ride by himself, exploring the Passy countryside.

Today, as he floated toward the middle of the river, he felt at one with the universe. "If there is a God," Ben thought, "then this is the closest that I will get to Him, or Her—I should say," as he corrected himself and smiled. The inner peace he was currently experiencing was very much like the feeling he had when he lay with Marianne. It had been too long since he had experienced that feeling with her. The sun was emerging from behind a cloud, sending golden beams of sunlight streaming down toward Ben in his trance-like state.

Just at that moment, he felt a small rush of wind accompanied by a chill. Ben could have sworn that he heard Marianne's voice cry out "no" on the breeze. Instantly he snapped out of his daydream and realized that he had floated farther toward the Paris side of the Seine than he liked. About halfway across, the river became more polluted with human waste. Trash bobbed in the current. The water smelled of urine. Ben turned over just in time to dodge a chunk of human feces floating directly toward him. He spit in the water and descriptively cursed in French, "*Merde.*"

His powerful breaststroke quickly took him back to the clean Passy side of the river, but his placid mood had been broken. Had he imagined Marianne's voice? Was she in danger? What was she trying to tell him? Ben had no answers for any of these questions. He swam briskly back to shore.

Spring 1777

PASSY

THE FOLLOWING MORNING, Ben sat contemplating an intriguing note, delivered early, and written in a masculine, if a bit cavalier, hand. Ben recognized that there were some people he met with whom he formed an instant emotional connection. In his experience, these people seemed to show up naturally just when he needed them. Their integration into his life seemed so natural that he wondered how he had gotten along before knowing them. Though Ben had known Louis Le Veillard for only a short time, the man had quickly become one of those people. The note was from him.

> *Monsieur,*
>
> *I have received a letter from Madame Brillon, to which I can reply only with your help. I have the honor of sending it to you. I shall not second a request that she who has made it renders already as seductive as possible; if you would only grant her Saturday, you would give me great pleasure, because I too would*

have the benefit of spending part of the day with you. I am, with respect, Monsieur, your very humble and obedient servant.

Le Veillard

Le Veillard and his wife owned the spa in Passy. In addition to the usual mineral baths and therapeutic treatments, Le Veillard also bottled the pure water from his spring. He sold the bottles in large quantities at the market in Paris to those who were willing to pay extra for *les eaux minérales de Passy.* This enterprise had made Le Veillard quite a rich man, although the rights to the mineral springs on their property had come to him by way of his wife's dowry.

Madame Leray had informed Ben that Le Veillard had long been infatuated with their neighbor Madame Brillon. "He follows her around like a puppy," she said. "Also ... ." Marie-Thérèse lowered her voice to a whisper. "She is a refined, sophisticated young lady, unfortunately, wedded to a coarse, boorish man more than twenty years her elder."

Ben had further learned that her husband held the position of the receiver-general for the trusts of Parliament, a position that made him a wealthy, if glorified, accountant. In contrast, she was described as possessing the rare combination of striking beauty and true artistic talent. Madame Brillon was an accomplished harpsichordist. She also played the recently invented pianoforte extremely well. She had studied with Johann Schobert and Luigi Boccherini, each of whom had dedicated at least one sonata to her. But her musical performances were reserved for friends and family now. She had neither financial need nor the desire to perform publicly any longer. In the past, however, her performances had achieved an impressive level of critical acclaim.

Needless to say, Madame Brillon intrigued Ben greatly. The note from Le Veillard provided a welcome opportunity to get to know this exceptional woman better.

Saturday next, Ben was having his morning tea on the veranda when Le Veillard unexpectedly rode up on horseback. The man was atop a spirited stallion who looked as though he would love nothing better than to gallop full speed across the lawn. The steed snorted and stamped his foot as his rider reined him in at the edge of the veranda.

"Ben, can you ride with me this fine morning?" Le Veillard asked. From the look on his face, Ben surmised Louis had calculated that Ben would be unable to resist ditching some boring paperwork to cavort across the fields of Passy.

"Louis, I'm not sure that I could keep up with you on that mount," Ben said.

"Diablo? He's really a big baby, not nearly as hot-blooded as he appears. One gallop across the field, and he will be content to canter the rest of the way."

In some ways, Le Veillard reminded Ben of Pierre Beaumarchais. Both men were handsome philanderers to be sure. However, to Ben, Louis epitomized the idle rich. While Pierre, like Ben, was always busy doing something productive, Louis appeared to relish spending his time getting absolutely nothing accomplished. But then again, Louis was a hedonist after Ben's own heart. As far as Ben could tell, he spent most of his days at the spa, exercising, eating, drinking, or socializing. He joked constantly and seemed never to talk about any serious subject other than the science of water purity. This was, of course, his business interest. Nonetheless, he seemed to have a lot of free time on his hands.

Today Le Veillard sported leather pants, gloves, boots, and crop. A billowy, white silk shirt open to the waist showed off his thick chest hair. His wavy sun-streaked light brown hair fell around his shoulders. He looked like a tanned Adonis. Clearly, the outfit had been chosen not to impress Ben, but rather in case they encountered any of the local ladies on their ride. In fact, Ben assumed he'd been invited along simply to provide a convenient alibi.

"I'll be ready to ride in five minutes," Ben said. He headed off to change clothes and tell Temple that their correspondence could wait until tomorrow.

Ben and Louis lit out from the Hôtel de Valentinois. On the first truly warm day of spring, the trees and fields of Passy were intensely green. In the sunlight, the verdant color was almost overwhelming.

"Did you know that my esteemed colleague, Dr. Priestley, recently described the process whereby plants rejuvenate the air?" Ben asked. "And that your own countryman Lavoisier postulates that a newly discovered element he calls 'oxygen' is produced by plants?"

"No," Louis said. He seemed only politely interested. "How does that work?"

Ben began to explain the basis of the elements that Antoine-Laurent Lavoisier had recently expounded, including his proposed periodic table.

Le Veillard looked completely lost. "How many so-called elements does he think there are?" he asked.

"I don't know, but I can tell you that water is not one of them."

"What do you mean?" Le Veillard looked shocked. Since time immemorial, water had been considered one of the basic elements.

"My friend and colleague, Joseph Priestley, has broken down your precious water into smaller elements, one called hydrogen and one that Lavoisier now calls oxygen," Ben said. "Using electricity."

"Impossible!" cried Le Veillard.

"Oh, no, my friend, it is not only quite possible, but it is expected, from prior experiments that have been done. One thing that you must know, good science is a process of discovery that builds upon a solid foundation of experimentally supported evidence and should continue indefinitely."

Le Veillard appeared to be making some kind of mental calculation. "So ... do you mean to say ... that people will have to buy more of my water to convert it into these new elements of hydrogen and oxygen?"

Ben laughed out loud. "Louis," he said. "People will continue to need water, and if need be, they can convert water from the Seine into its basic elements."

Le Veillard looked hopeful. "But my pure water would produce much more pure elements than that filthy river water, *n'est pas?*" he asked.

"I suppose that might be true," Ben admitted. He really didn't know if Le Veillard's pure spring water might be any better than the water from the Seine for this purpose.

The two men rode along without talking for only a short while before Ben brought up the subject of Madame Brillon.

"Do you remember the first time I visited her house?" Ben asked.

"Yes, that was a fiasco," Le Veillard replied.

Ben and Le Veillard had been invited to a luncheon at the Brillon home almost two months before. On that occasion, the invitation had come from her husband. Ben had accepted, having made the mistaken assumption that there was better communication between the man and his wife. He only found out later that she was completely unaware that she would be meeting the illustrious Doctor Franklin that day. And then it had been Le Veillard who informed her on the very morning of their visit. She had no time to prepare. Nonetheless, she joined the party just as they sat down to the table.

Ben thought that she looked beautiful, if tense. She hardly spoke. Possibly, this was because her husband completely dominated the conversation. He was expounding on some tedious aspect of the financial markets in excruciating detail when Ben felt her gaze land like a soft breath on his neck. He instinctively turned his attention toward her. She held a spoon full of soup in her hand. She was just lifting it toward her lush, full lips. Her chestnut hair fell in ringlets over soft alabaster shoulders. Ben's eyes met hers with a jolt. The spoon leapt out of her hand, spilling soup down the front of her dress. Embarrassed and agitated, she quickly excused herself and ran out of the room.

Ben recalled that her husband hadn't even noticed the exchange. He continued to discuss the connection between political events and bank lending rates as though nothing had happened. He glanced up at his wife only as she was leaving the table. And even then, he kept right on talking.

The sound of her footsteps receded quickly up the stairs. A door slammed. To Ben's great dismay, she did not return for the remainder of the visit. As the coach had pulled away, Ben thought he saw her looking out an upstairs window.

Today, Ben would get another chance to be with her. He wondered if their connection would be as strong.

Soon they approached the outskirts of Paris. Just beyond the tollhouse on the Paris side, they came upon a row of buildings that housed several disreputable taverns. Ben noted that a straggle of Friday night revelers still celebrating out front, even at this late hour on a Saturday morning. As they drew closer, Ben thought that he recognized one of the men outside the closest saloon. The man wore a clerical robe and held a sign in large bold letters that Ben translated roughly as "Repent, ye sinners!"

"Well, well," Ben exclaimed.

"Do you know that man?" Le Veillard asked.

"That is the Reverend Smith, an Anglican minister and . . ." Ben lowered his voice, "a spy."

"He also seems to possess *le desir de morte*," Le Veillard observed wryly.

As the two riders approached, several more drunken men spilled out of the tavern into the early morning sunlight, squinting from the brightness. However, as their eyes adjusted, they caught sight of the Reverend Smith admonishing their intemperance with his haughty pose and Biblical verse. Boisterous from a long evening of drinking, they soon surrounded the Reverend. Several women joined them, barmaids finishing their shift or barflies abandoning the chase for the night.

One man stumbling out of the tavern caught Ben's attention. He was dressed in a more refined suit of clothing, clearly not that of a tradesman or worker, although rumpled after a long night of drinking.

"That looks like Monsieur Penet — 'The Weasel,'" Ben exclaimed.

Le Veillard looked impressed. "You know that man also?" he asked.

"Yes, both accompanied me on my trip from Nantes to Paris a few months ago. Penet rode in a coach with the Reverend. I thought that they might come to blows."

"It seems that time may still come."

Penet must have recognized the Reverend because he bounded toward him, yelling obscenities and waving his fists in the air.

Le Veillard smacked Diablo sharply with his crop, and the large horse bolted toward the altercation. Ben's horse followed only a few paces behind as they pulled up among the rowdy drunks confronting the clearly frightened minister. By this time, the Reverend's nose had been bloodied, yet he kept his hands at his sides. Penet was about to take another crack at the Reverend when Le Veillard separated the two by riding between them. He planted his right foot on Penet's chest and sent him sprawling. A shrill whistle sounded down the street. Ben looked up to see several *gendarmes* running toward the fracas.

Ben dismounted at the Reverend's side, his horse shielding them from the mob. He placed one arm around the shaking minister's shoulders. With the other hand, Ben pulled out his handkerchief and applied pressure to the Reverend's nose. At the same time, Penet scrambled to his feet, intent on attacking Le Veillard. But Le Veillard had anticipated this response. He held his riding crop at his side until just the instant that Penet grabbed his leg. Then he let the crop loose with a blow to the Weasel's head so severe that blood from the wound spattered his white silk shirt. He jumped off his mount just as the gendarmes arrived. As they grabbed Penet and hauled him up from the dirt, he had a wild look in his eye as if he wanted to murder them all.

Spitting and shouting obscenities, Penet was taken into custody. The *gendarmes* quickly dispersed the remainder of the crowd, who went tottering off, up the street, and back to their homes. On the far sidewalk, Ben sat the Reverend down. As the street became quiet, a pretty barmaid approached Le Veillard. She placed her hand on his chest, heaving from the conflict.

"Your shirt will be ruined if you don't get it off and into cool water," she said. She gave him a seductive smile.

Le Veillard looked over at Ben sheepishly. "I must have my shirt attended to by this lovely young lady," he said.

Ben nodded. "I can take care of the Reverend."

"I'll come by this afternoon and collect you at your lodgings, alright?"

"I'll be waiting for you." Ben smiled.

Le Veillard quickly tied up his horse and disappeared through a walkway leading to rooms above the tavern.

"I thank you for coming to my aid," the Reverend said. He held Ben's handkerchief to his face.

"My dear sir, if men are so wicked with religion, what would we be without it," Ben said.

As the Reverend closed his eyes, he relaxed his posture. "How true," he said. Then he added, "But we should not be seen together, Doctor Franklin."

Ben glanced up the road in the direction of Paris. A coach was approaching them rapidly. Ben pulled his hood over his head so as not to be recognized. As the coach pulled to a halt in front of him and the Reverend, Ben confirmed the British embassy's ambassadorial seal on the door. An armed coachman jumped down and ran over to collect the Reverend. Without saying a word, the guard assisted the clergyman into the coach. When the door opened, Ben caught a glimpse of the British ambassador, Lord Stormont, sitting stone-faced inside the coach's shadows. The driver cracked his whip, and the coach quickly turned around, heading back toward Paris as swiftly as it had arrived.

Ben stood for a moment, watching the coach disappear. He silently hoped that the Reverend's mission spying for the American cause was proceeding more successfully than his proselytizing. The street was empty. Ben mounted his horse and rode back to Passy alone.

Spring 1777

PASSY

THAT AFTERNOON, Le Veillard showed up at Ben's lodgings just in time to get to their appointment with Madame Brillon. If he had been any later, Ben would have taken his own coach to visit his vivacious neighbor.

"Difficult and taxing work?" Ben asked. His friend looked a bit the worse for wear as he climbed into the coach.

"At least my shirt will survive," Le Veillard said. He flashed a tired smile. "If anyone asks, I've been with you all day."

"Of course," Ben replied. "But who do you think will be more concerned with your whereabouts? Your wife or Madame Brillon?"

"Oh, Anne Louise, to be sure, for she thinks of me as her personal possession, expected to be at her beck and call, always. Not that she has bestowed any of her considerable affections upon me," Le Veillard said.

"Well, that is heartening," Ben replied. "I'm encouraged to hear that any woman can play 'cat and mouse' with you, especially our Madame Brillon."

Le Veillard laughed. "I am sure that you will have more success with 'The Ice Princess.'"

"Why do you call her that?"

"Because even before we met, I was forewarned of her reputation. I had heard that she did not take any lovers. I had difficulty believing it, given the countenance of her husband and also the word of Madame Leray that Monsieur Brillon carries on an affair with the family *au pair*."

"Does everyone in France have a lover?" Ben said. He had been celibate, if not by choice, since his arrival in the country. He must have sounded a bit exasperated.

Le Veillard laughed. "Everyone except you, my friend," he said. "But perhaps it is your turn."

Le Veillard's coach came to a halt at the front door of the Brillon estate. The butler escorted Ben and Louis inside. They walked through a marble foyer into a fashionable parlor where, on the previous visit, they had met Monsieur Brillon. Today, beautiful music filled the house. Where before, Ben had found the place ostentatious yet drab, today it looked more alive. Fresh cut flowers had been arranged in well-placed vases. The windows sparkled as the afternoon sun shone through. The music paused but still seemed to echo through the halls of the mansion. Ben and Louis were standing where the butler had left them when the rear door of the parlor opened, and Madame Brillon entered. She looked first at Louis.

"Louis, how good of you to come and bring with you Doctor Franklin," she said. She held out her hand to him. Louis bowed deeply and kissed the top of her hand. He held on to it for a moment too long—or so she must have thought because she pulled her hand away.

"Doctor Franklin," she said. She turned to Ben and extended her hand toward him. "I am so glad that we finally get to meet appropriately."

"*Enchanté*," Ben replied. He tried to make it sound as if they were being introduced for the first time. Ben held a lovely delicate hand with fine bones and the smoothest alabaster skin that he could ever recall. He leaned forward and put his lips gently on the back of her hand, drinking in her wonderful fragrance. She made no move to withdraw it. Warmth ran through his body, from his lips down to the tips of his toes. Madame Brillon tensed almost imperceptibly as if she had felt the sensation as well. Then she relaxed and smiled. She breathed a small exhalation that might have been a full sigh had they been alone, Ben thought.

She wasn't ready to forget their first embarrassing encounter just yet.

"I must apologize for our first meeting, Doctor Franklin," she said in a more businesslike manner. "I was unprepared for your visit." She shot a look at Le Veillard that was more than a bit icy. He flinched.

"I completely understand," Ben said. "Please call me Ben."

"Anne Louise." She curtsied slightly, keeping her hand in his.

"Were you the one playing that beautiful music when we arrived?" Ben asked. He lifted her left hand, looking down at them as if to examine them both. "You have marvelous hands."

Madame Brillon blushed slightly. "Thank you, Ben. Would you like me to play for you?"

"Indeed," he said.

She led them out of the parlor with Le Veillard trailing along, lost in adoration.

"Where were you this morning?" she asked over her shoulder to Louis as they walked down the long hall. "I was expecting you."

"I was out riding with Ben, and time just slipped away," Le Veillard said.

Madame Brillon glanced over at Ben for confirmation. "Yes, we rode together this morning," he quickly offered. Luckily, she let the inquiry drop because Ben doubted that if she probed deeper, he'd have been able to cover for his friend.

The house was well furnished with elegant furniture and works of art that struck Ben as harsh or cold, at least as compared to the Hôtel de Valentinois. Perhaps, it was simply that Madame Leray used more color, or warmer colors. Most of the Brillon house reminded Ben of a museum. He couldn't imagine children playing here.

Their footsteps echoed as they toured the sparsely decorated hallways.

In contrast, when they entered the music room, it was bright, alive, and cheery. The room was large enough to accommodate a chamber orchestra and a small audience. There was an immense gilded harp near center stage. Sheet music was strewn on several music stands arranged in a small grouping, with hard wooden chairs, around the harp. Anne Louise bypassed this area and went to a sunlit corner where two comfortable chairs were positioned in a grouping with a pianoforte.

"Will your husband not be joining us?" Ben asked.

"No, he is at the Treasury all day," she replied.

Ben turned toward the piano so as not to reveal his pleasure at this news. The instrument was a true work of art. The wood had a rich dark finish that shone in the afternoon sun. It was a rectangular box set horizontally on delicate legs with a keyboard at one end. The name *Sébastien Érard* was inscribed above the keyboard. The top was propped open slightly.

"It looks like an English *Zumpe*, only larger and more beautifully made," Ben commented.

"You are clearly a man who knows pianos," Anne Louise said. She looked impressed.

"Nonetheless, I am unfamiliar with yours, Madame."

"Monsieur Érard delivered it to me only last month. It is the first piano that he has made in his own Paris shop. Even Marie Antoinette has not had hers delivered yet." She flashed a look of smug satisfaction.

Le Veillard moved toward a small table between the two chairs. He poured out two snifters of cognac from the decanter placed there. He offered one to Madame Brillon, who waved her hand, declining it. He then offered a glass to Ben, who took it.

"Anne Louise, before you sit down to play, may I please have a look at the mechanism?" Ben asked.

His hostess laughed. "Of course. I have not looked inside there at all. Perhaps you can explain to me how this invention works."

Le Veillard sat down in one of the comfortable chairs. He took a large sip of the cognac and yawned. Ben and Anne Louise walked around toward the open side of the piano. Ben propped up the top. He leaned over to marvel at the intricate works inside. As Ben was concentrating on the craftsmanship of Monsieur Érard, he felt Madame Brillon close at his side. He turned his head to find that their lips were an inch apart.

"Do you like what you see?" she whispered.

Ben straightened up slightly so that he could see the outline of her figure bending over the piano. Her dress accentuated her slim waist. In this position, its silky fabric clung over her derriere just enough to give him a sense of what lay underneath. She was standing on tiptoe in delicate, lacy shoes open at the back. Her finely turned ankles were revealed as her dress pulled up.

"Yes, I do."

Just at that moment, Le Veillard snored loudly. Ben and Anne Louise both laughed.

Ben was about to begin expounding on the unique double-escapement action that Érard had incorporated into her piano when Anne Louise took his hand and led him to the empty comfortable chair.

"I want to play for you," she said sweetly. She turned to the snoring Le Veillard and kicked his shin with the heel of her shoe.

He awoke with a yelp. "I must have dozed off," he apologized.

When Anne Louise began to play, Ben was transported into a heavenly place. Le Veillard returned to his slumber, but at least he quit his snoring. She played the piano with such beauty and skill that Ben felt tears well up in his eyes. She played some pieces that Ben recognized, but also some he had never heard before. Occasionally, she sang or hummed along with the tune. She had a wonderful voice. At the conclusion of each song, Ben clapped. The music was so beautiful that it was hard for him to speak.

After quite some time, she stopped, and Ben rose to his feet, applauding. He tried to cry "Bravo", but his voice cracked with emotion. She came over to him, and they embraced.

"Thank you so much," he finally said.

"You are quite welcome. You are obviously a man who appreciates music.

I am glad that my playing pleases you. Is there anything that you would like to hear?"

Ben had thought that the concert was over. He was elated to find that she would be willing to continue.

"Do you know any of the Scottish dances?" Ben asked, hopefully.

"No," she cooed, "but won't you teach me?" They sat down on the piano bench. He could feel the warmth of her thigh through the many layers of fabric. He pecked out the first Scottish reel that came into his mind, a jaunty, yet haunting, melody like many of his favorite traditional songs.

Anne Louise picked up the tune and started playing harmony.

"This is beautiful," she whispered. "What is it called?"

Ben thought for a moment. "*Kissing is the Best of All*," he replied.

"Do you mean like this?"

She turned and kissed his neck. A long-absent, much-missed, tingle of electricity raced through Ben's body. He turned toward his beautiful companion, a bit surprised by the swiftness of her affectionate move and looked deeply into her chestnut brown eyes flecked with green. Ben wrapped his arms around her. He took a slight breath in, closed his eyes, and pressed his lips toward hers. But at just that critical moment, Le Veillard let out a loud snort. Anne Louise stiffened, pulling away from Ben.

"Oh, Doctor," she said, blushing, "we have barely met. You must think me quite forward."

"That is not what I was thinking at all," Ben said softly. He was desperately trying to reclaim the prior moment. It was gone. He silently cursed Le Veillard as Anne Louise turned back to the piano and started to play a sonata.

Le Veillard eventually woke up, hungry, of course. Anne Louise had small portions of meats, cheeses, and fruits served. Elegantly, even artfully, presented, the exquisite preparations seemed completely lost on Le Veillard, who dove in voraciously. Ben complimented his hostess on her cuisine. They discussed a wide range of topics over the course of the afternoon from the goals of Ben's mission in France for the America cause, to their love of music, and even recent political events. Ben and Anne Louise tried a game of chess, but she had no talent for it, and he quickly checkmated her. She took her loss well though, exclaiming, "My husband is the better chess player in our house." It was the first time she had mentioned Monsieur Brillon since their arrival.

Ben decided to quickly change the subject. "Has either of you heard of the work of Doctor Franz Anton Mesmer from Vienna?" he asked.

Le Veillard shook his head, looking bored.

"Yes, I have heard his name," Anne Louise said. "I've heard that he is attempting to restore the sight of a blind pianist by the name of Maria Theresa Paradis. I heard her play last year at a salon in Vienna. She was a gifted child prodigy. Still no more than eighteen years old now, I would think. The Empress, Maria Theresa of Austria, the namesake of young Mademoiselle Paradis, is also her patron.

"Marie Antoinette's mother?" Le Veillard piped up. He looked more interested in their conversation.

"The very same, but you're missing my point," Anne Louise said. "The Empress provides Mademoiselle Paradis with a pension to compose and play music. This Doctor Mesmer is playing with fire if she regains her sight but loses her ability to play."

"Why would that happen?" Ben asked.

"I'm sure that you recognize that the ability to play a musical instrument often comes more easily to one who has lost their sight," she explained. "The other senses, especially hearing and touch, must become accentuated to compensate for the loss of eyesight. If one were to regain sight after many years of darkness, could it not be disconcerting, even detrimental, to a musician who has come to rely on sensations to which they have adapted over time?"

Ben put his hand to his chin in his pose as the great thinker. "I suppose you have a viable theory," he said.

"I'll take that as high praise from the master." Anne Louise curtsied demurely in a way that made Ben want to sweep her into his arms.

He resisted the temptation, asking instead, "Do you know anything else about this curious doctor? I've heard that he also treats melancholia."

"I wouldn't know about that, but they say that he plays the glass armonica."

A look of shock swept over Ben's face. "The glass armonica I invented?"

"Oh my dear, I had no idea that was your invention," Anne Louise said. "You are a marvelous and talented man. You must tell me all about yourself."

Ben wasn't ready to be diverted. "Have you heard him play?" he asked.

"No, I've only heard mention of him in musical circles. But I have heard others play your glass armonica. It has a haunting, mystical quality that many find soothing. Not to offend you, but I find that its tones make me feel uneasy. It's difficult to explain, but there is something about the music that makes me feel I am losing control of myself. Once, after a concert by Glück, I had to douse my head with cold water to clear the feeling of drunken stupor that his music produced. Since that time, I prefer the harp or pianoforte."

"I know that the tones can be disconcerting in the wrong hands," Ben said. He realized that he sounded a bit defensive, "but you should hear Handel play. His glass armonica music sounds heavenly, never discordant or cloying."

"And I am sure that you must play it divinely yourself, Monsieur Inventor." Anne Louise smiled.

Ben smiled back. "If you will indulge me, I will obtain an instrument and play for you at our very next meeting."

"I will look forward to it."

The sun had already set when Ben and Le Veillard boarded their coach. They spoke little, as both men were tired from the eventful day. As Ben settled into his bed, he could still smell the perfume of Anne Louise Brillon on his neck. He resolved to avoid washing it off for as long as he could. Would he ever be allowed to know more of the pleasures she hinted at today? But Ben was also concerned. How did Herr Mesmer come to own a glass armonica?

Since inventing the first instrument for Marianne sixteen years ago, Ben knew of only a few in existence—mostly in the hands of musicians. What would a medical doctor want with one?

Spring 1777

SOMEWHERE NEAR KINGSWOOD

NEAR PASSY, the dense forests of the Kingswood, an ancient hunting ground, opened into a series of gently rolling hills covered with knee-high grass and accented by a few sturdy oaks. Ben's horse followed the trails left by countless deer through the grass down the meandering shallow valleys and over the small hills. The path was rocky in spots, a good workout for both horse and rider. On this bright morning, the sky was a cobalt blue with a few high wispy clouds. Ben was just observing the clouds when he spotted a flock of small black birds on the horizon. The birds were flying in tightly coordinated formation, known as a murmuration, making a figure-eight pattern. As Ben crested a small hill, he noted that they seemed to be repeatedly circling the same area, but from his position, he could not make out why.

He admired the precision of their mass movement and was fascinated by how they kept to their tight formation. From a distance, the murmuration appeared to be a single animate being rather than a swarm of individuals.

Intrigued, he nudged his horse in their direction. "Does one bird lead?" he wondered. "And if so, how does he, or she, communicate with the others?" He was thinking of an experiment that might be set up to probe this question when he topped a small rise and saw what the birds were circling.

A majestic oak stood alone on a grassy meadow. Even from across the valley, Ben could see that its canopy was lush and full. The flock continued to make a figure eight above and around it. As his gaze followed the shape of the tree toward the ground, he noted something else odd. It appeared as though appendages radiated from the trunk. From this distance, the base of the tree looked unnaturally thick. The appendages reminded Ben of the aerial prop roots of a Banyan tree he had seen on his travels, but he'd not been aware that such trees existed in France. He was further surprised to see that the appendages appeared to be moving rhythmically around the tree in a direction opposite to that of the flock of birds circling above. Curious, Ben rode closer.

Sixteen human figures were attached at the waist by thinner ropes to one thick rope girding the trunk of the giant oak. They wore flowing robes with hoods that hindered Ben from telling if they were men or women. They shuffled their feet in unison to the beat of an unheard rhythm. As Ben approached, he heard a low moaning or chanting coming from the group. The sound was punctuated by an occasional shriek or cry that at first curdled Ben's blood.

As he drew closer, the cries sounded more ecstatic than painful. Ben pulled up alongside this strange group under the awning of the huge tree. No one paid any attention to him. The air was eerily electric, but there was no wind. All Ben could hear was the patting of bare feet on the mossy ground and the chanting. Ben dismounted. Up close, Ben could tell that there seemed to be an equal number of men and women in the group, spaced evenly around the trunk of the tree. He walked over to one of the female figures, who was undulating slowly, rhythmically. She was a tall young woman with thick sandy brown hair under the hood of her robe. She stared straight ahead, mumbling the same chant as the rest of the group. They seemed to be reaching a crescendo. Ben reached out to touch her shoulder. Just at that moment, the sun slipped behind a cloud, and the scene suddenly darkened. Above, a tremendous fluttering caused Ben to look up, but a sudden loud outcry from the group brought his attention quickly back.

The woman he had just tried to touch now writhed on the ground, panting and groaning. The other members of the group were in contortions as well. Some were lying on their sides, some leaning over, some stood, but all clutched themselves and groaned ecstatically.

The woman at Ben's feet seemed to come around. Her breathing slowed. Ben knelt down. As she composed herself, she became aware of Ben's presence. She sat up and straightened her robe. Her face was mildly flushed, and she appeared a bit breathless. She did not seem at all embarrassed. Her hood had come down, and her hair fell around her shoulders in a most natural cascade. She had skin like fine porcelain, now blushed around her high cheekbones. Her eyes were clear and bright. Ben thought she looked serenely beautiful.

"Are you alright?" Ben said. He must have looked concerned.

"Yes, I feel wonderful," she replied. "Why do you ask?"

"You seemed to be immersed in some form of ritual." While he couldn't pinpoint why he was concerned, given her current apparently satisfactory condition, he remembered that a moment ago she had been thrashing about wildly on the ground.

"For weeks, I have been terribly sick," she confided to him as though Ben was her dearest friend. "My head throbbed constantly, I was anxious, and had difficulty breathing. I had intermittent sweats. I tried the usual purging and bleeding prescribed by the doctors. Nothing helped in the least. Finally, I consulted with Doctor D'Eslon. He suggested that I try a new treatment he had learned in Vienna to channel the fluid called *magnétisme animale*. I did not understand the science he explained behind this new treatment, but what did I have to lose?"

"And your symptoms?" Ben asked.

"Completely gone," she said. "I hope this feeling will last." She took

Ben's hand and placed it inside her robe on her bare sternum. "Do I feel hot to you?"

"A little." Ben gulped. He could feel his own temperature rise. He gently removed his hand. Always the scientist, he asked, "Do you remember the process of your cure?"

"Not entirely. I do remember sleeping very poorly last night. I had been instructed to bathe and don this linen robe before meeting the group at the office of Doctor D'Eslon at sunrise. We all boarded a wagon that brought us to this spot. We found the ropes already affixed to the tree, exactly the same in number as members of the group. Doctor D'Eslon told us to tie the ropes to our waists. He started a chant and showed us the proper direction to move. Then he left with the wagon. At first, I felt stupid, a grown woman tied by a rope to a tree in the middle of nowhere, wearing nothing but a hooded robe. But after a few minutes, everything changed.

"I remember that I felt as though I was a bird soaring through the air. I was flying in tight formation with countless other birds. I watched their wings. When they dipped, I dipped. When they pivoted, I pivoted. What they knew, I knew. The result was that we moved as one. It felt wonderful. The movement increased in tempo until I could no longer see individual birds in the flock. It didn't matter; I instinctively knew when to turn. It was as if I was one with the Universe.

"I felt the strength of the entire flock course through my muscles. I could look up and see the stars in the sky. I saw faint lines coming down from the sun and the stars, connecting each bird in the flock. The lines also connected through me. I understood in that instant how we are all connected. I remember thinking that I must truly be seeing the fluid of which Doctor D'Eslon spoke.

"Then the beating of our collective wings became faster and faster until finally, there was a bright explosion. The sensation was absolutely exquisite. It caused every muscle in my body to contract and then relax. I felt weightless. I realized that I had separated from the flock. But still, I felt them with me. I knew that they had conferred upon me the good health of the group.

When I awoke, I was human again. You were standing in front of me, looking concerned as if something was wrong. But I knew I was completely cured."

"Truly amazing," was all that Ben could say. By this point, the rest of the group was starting to mobilize. Ben looked around. Some were untying their ropes; some were stretching, while a few huddled together. They rubbed various parts of their bodies. Ben started to overhear some of the other conversations.

"How do you feel?"

"Better."

"You?"

"Wonderful, but a bit sore."

As if on cue, the wagon arrived at the far side of the tree from where Ben stood. Ben saw a man that he assumed to be Doctor D'Eslon jump off and start walking over to speak with members of the group.

Ben looked back to see that his young woman had untied herself from the tree. She had raised her hood and begun walking toward D'Eslon. She would have been hard to recognize among all the linen robed figures except for her statuesque height and a delicious saunter when viewed from behind. Ben felt a wave of panic.

"What's your name?" he called after her plaintively.

She turned briefly and whispered back at him, "Antoinette." Then the group subsumed her.

Fall & Winter 1777

VIENNA

MARIANNE HURRIED THROUGH the deserted early morning streets. Her mother and sister slept as she'd exited through her bedroom window. By now, she knew the way to the storefront well. Mesmer would be waiting for her when she arrived, always seeming to know when she was coming. Moreover, she would be his only patient. When she had started these treatments, other clients had been there. But as the treatments became more intimate, he told her there was a need for greater privacy, and Marianne found herself inexplicably glad to have his undivided attention.

Six weeks earlier, Mesmer had arrived at the door of Marianne's lodgings bearing a package wrapped in brown paper. Mrs. Davies had answered the ring; Marianne listened from the hall to their conversation. Mrs. Davies knew who he was—everyone in Vienna knew Franz Anton Mesmer. He was married to Anna Maria von Posch, a wealthy widow of the late Colonel von Posch. His rich wife's money had not only given his nascent medical career a boost, but also allowed him to be a major supporter of the arts in Vienna. He was a personal friend of the Mozart family.

Mrs. Davies resented never having been invited to the Mesmer villa, Marianne knew. Regular concerts there included the likes of young Wolfgang Mozart and Joseph Haydn. Nonetheless, she would have put on her best false smile.

"May I help you?" Mrs. Davies asked suspiciously.

"I believe this belongs to one of your daughters."

"What is it?"

"Her cape."

"And how did you obtain it?"

"I believe that she left it at the opera."

Marianne and Cecelia had attended the opera the previous weekend, but Mrs. Davies would not recall either one of them reporting having left a wrap.

"How do you know that it belongs to us?" she asked.

"Mrs. Davies, I recognized your lovely daughters in the audience that evening," Mesmer continued. "As the crowd dispersed, I tarried to speak with a colleague. I found this cape as I left the theater." He patted his package and continued. "I believe that it belongs to your daughter Marianne. The initials 'M.D.' are embroidered inside."

"Thank you for returning it," she said. She held out her hands.

"With your permission, I would like to return it to Marianne personally," Mesmer said firmly. He held on to the package.

Mrs. Davies crossed her arms on her chest and frowned.

"Also, I would like to speak with you about a late-summer series of concerts that I am giving in my garden. I was hoping that your daughters might be available to play."

The promise of money would soften Mrs. Davies considerably. "I believe Marianne is at home," she said. The door swung open. "Please do come in then, Doctor." Her voice was suddenly sweet as syrup.

The Davies' parlor showed none of the opulence to which Mesmer was accustomed. Most of the threadbare furnishings didn't even belong to the family, though they owned the multitude of musical instruments placed around the room, including Marianne's lovely glass armonica.

"You must excuse our disarray," Mrs. Davies said apologetically. "We were not expecting guests. Have a seat, and I'll fetch Marianne."

As soon as she left the room, Mesmer opened the top of the armonica case. He put his foot on the treadle. The glass bowls started spinning. He touched a rim of one of the bowls gently. A haunting sound emerged.

"Please," Marianne urged as she entered the parlor. "Stop." Mesmer stood immediately.

"Hello, Marianne," he said, "I was just appreciating what a fine instrument you possess. My poor copy is no match for this fine workmanship."

"Doctor Franklin had it made especially for me," she said, immediately defensive.

"Yes, I know."

The ringlets of his brown hair framed a cherubic face with the smoothest complexion that Marianne had ever seen on a man. She could barely look at his piercing blue eyes for fear that she would fall into his arms. Marianne steeled herself.

"Franz, our relationship was different five years ago. We can't return to that place again."

"I am not asking you to," he said softly. "I am merely returning your cape."

Marianne felt stupid. Why did this man have such power over her?

During the summer of 1772, she had left England with her family for a tour of the continent, stopping in Vienna for only a few weeks en route to Italy. Her fling with the young doctor had been as brief as it was passionate. He was a music lover. She was a music lover. He complimented her armonica playing after a concert. He had never seen an armonica before. He romanced her. He wined and dined her. He was rich. But he was married. Marianne knew that there was no future in her affair with him back then—and there certainly was none now. But among the many favors, she had allowed him as a result of their brief intimacy was that she had let him borrow her armonica to copy it. She had never told Ben anything about that summer. What he didn't know couldn't hurt him, she reckoned. However, the copy of the armonica stood out as the one remaining piece of evidence of their affair. She wished now that she had never consented to any of it.

"But I also wanted to ask if you would like to attend another of my séances?" he said. "I have discovered a new fluid that heals."

"What makes you believe that I am sick?"

"I don't think that you are sick, but my technique is particularly effective with common maladies I know you to be vexed by—such as headaches." He looked at her and paused as if to measure her reaction. "And melancholia."

Marianne wasn't entirely sure that this wasn't a ploy designed to end up with her back in his bed. But she couldn't help being intrigued after having witnessed the demonstration of healing at the storefront with her own eyes.

"All right," she said with slight reservation, "but only in a group."

"Of course," he capitulated. "There is a group every Wednesday at noon."

Mrs. Davies reappeared with a tray of tea.

"Doctor Mesmer would like you and your sister to perform at one of his concerts," she announced.

Marianne looked over at Mesmer, who shrugged ever so slightly. She recognized that this subterfuge had gotten him past the front door.

She looked back to her mother, now holding their calendar. "We might already be booked," Marianne said. It also occurred to her that more bookings in Vienna would further delay their departure for Paris, already overdue.

"Our bookings are tight now," Mrs. Davies said. She scrutinized the nearly empty calendar but was careful not to let the doctor see the pages. "Hmm, we could possibly fit you in ... we'd have to charge you two hundred florins," she offered matter-of-factly.

"Two hundred florins!" he protested. "Madame, I can only pay one hundred."

"We can book it for no less than one seventy-five," she said icily. She had the practiced calculation of many years of experience. Marianne wished that her mother was not quite so good at this. Mrs. Davies waited silently, holding the teapot but not yet pouring.

"All right, one fifty then, but no more, and the girls must sing and play for at least an hour," Mesmer said at last.

"Agreed," replied Mrs. Davies coolly, "but the florins must be in silver—no paper money." She poured tea into three cups.

"Agreed." Mesmer stirred a spoon of sugar into his tea.

And just like that, the bargain was struck. Reflecting on the transaction afterwards, Marianne felt slightly seedy, as if she had been sold to the highest bidder. But she realized that her mother managed a business, selling the musical talents of her daughters, and had done so successfully for many years, with the result that they always ate decently, slept in a warm bed at night, and had clothes to wear. "Perhaps that is the same bargain that the well-managed prostitute ultimately accepts," she recalled thinking to herself at the time. Yet, she had come to appreciate her mother for her business acumen. Marianne doubted that they would do as well if she or Cecelia were put in charge of the family business.

At the Wednesday séances, Marianne took her treatments around the baquet—the large wooden tub she had previously seen—with the others. She learned to apply the iron rod to her head and neck, which seemed to help ease the painful throbbing of her headaches. A few times, when no one was looking, she tried applying the rod to her nipples or between her legs, but she found that stimulation of these parts only increased her longing for coupling. If Ben were here it would be different, she thought. But she promised herself she was not going to get back in bed with Mesmer.

Mesmer hardly paid any attention to her at the séances initially, other than through the most basic of instructions. However, she found several of his male assistants quite attentive to her. Once, she caught Mesmer glaring at her as she opened her blouse to let a strapping young man place his hand on her hypochondrium. "It serves that old lecher right," she thought. She closed her eyes and tried to feel the *magnétisme animale* flow through her body.

As time went on, Marianne's resolve softened. Perhaps it was that she ultimately felt she was getting mere titillation from his assistants. Perhaps it was that she wondered if he really had something to offer her.

Mesmer came to her one autumn day when she was fully relaxed in a trance. He sat in front of her, his knees flanking hers.

"Marianne, can you hear me?" he asked soothingly.

"Yes."

"I would like to try guiding your inner vision today. Will you agree?"

"Yes."

"What are you seeing right now?"

"I can see you—I can see me—I see the room where we are sitting, but it is as though I am looking down at us from outside my body. I am observing our interaction from over there." Marianne pointed slowly to a spot in the corner of the room near the ceiling.

"Good, you are already outside your body, then?"

"Yes."

Marianne noted that a low chanting had started up. It was rhythmic, infectious, irresistible. It seemed to come from everywhere and nowhere. She looked at Mesmer. His eyes began to glow like bright blue iridescent pools. The room faded away.

"Let the flock guide you," he whispered.

A shimmering image of a flock of birds emerged from behind him. They flew around him and toward her. Quickly she was surrounded. She heard the rhythmic beating of their wings and was surprised that this apparition did not seem unusual or frightening. It seemed perfectly natural that she had left her body behind and looked back to observe that she still sat *en rapport* with Mesmer.

She found that it was quite effortless to fly. Her perspective changed as she left the storefront. Rather than being at ground level, she found herself hovering at some distance over the street. She could see people moving around below, but no one seemed to notice her. It should have been very bright outside, being around noon, but the sunlight appeared to be strangely dark—as if she was peering through a deep blue glass.

"Look up," Mesmer instructed.

She gazed up in awe as he pointed to faint lines streaking from the shimmering sun, moon, and stars above. Marianne saw the birds climbing higher toward the cosmos. The faint lines connected each bird in the flock. She looked back down at Mesmer to see that the lines connected to him too.

"May I join them?" she asked.

"Next time," he said gently. "This is enough for your first flight."

Other flights followed. Marianne learned to soar with the flock. The leaves on the trees were turning bright colors below. She loved to follow the swirling air currents with the birds. Marianne found she could speak to the birds without talking, could hear without listening. She understood that she enjoyed the health of the flock. Each time she came back from a flight, she felt wonderful—at peace with the world. She didn't suffer a headache or feel even the least melancholy for months. In fact, she felt energized, alive. It was the first time that she ever felt this way in her life.

Mesmer taught her how to use her special vision to see inside other people as well. Most people, he said, couldn't develop the inner sight that she had developed effortlessly. For them, he had found an alternate way to get the information about their maladies. That was to magnetize a surrogate who would relay the information to him. Mesmer had only a few people he trusted to do this. When she described her "findings" to him, he knew just what to prescribe to make someone feel better. Marianne wondered why he didn't examine them himself. Mesmer explained that his role was more of a conduit for the fluid—like a lightning rod.

When she asked him once to explain how *magnétisme animale* worked, she got a dissertation on planetary influences, molecules, and elasticity theory that was so incomprehensible that she had to ask him to stop before her brain exploded. Nonetheless, however it worked—she found that she enjoyed helping other people heal.

Marianne and Antoine, Mesmer's valet, became his prized assistants, using their inner vision to diagnose those patients who could not develop the special sight themselves. Sometimes they would examine a patient simultaneously. They found it interesting to compare their findings. It astounded Marianne how often they found identical abnormalities. Marianne also found it odd that Antoine could magnetize as quickly and effectively as the great doctor himself, without the least education in or understanding of planetary influences, molecules, elasticity, etc. etc.

Mesmer got her back in his bed, of course. But it was completely different this time. Where before he had been passionate, even bordering on brutish at times, now he was only gentle and caring. More odd, she thought, was that he now seemed content just to lie naked in bed with her, massaging and stroking parts of her body until she reached a powerful climax. His own member, that she recalled from the past as being smallish (compared to Ben) but at least effective, now never became sufficiently erect. She'd tried stimulating him with her hands, her mouth, even her breasts, but to no avail. When she complained that she didn't seem to please him anymore, he attributed his lack of response to overwork. However, Marianne also knew that the case of Mademoiselle Paradis must have been weighing on his mind.

The case was the sensation of the Viennese tabloids that summer and fall. The blind eighteen-year-old pianist had come under Mesmer's care. His treatment had initially seemed to be promising, where all prior treatments had failed. She had begun to be able to recognize light and dark as well as some shapes. Yet the newfound sight had proved detrimental to her piano playing. The visual signals confused her to the point that she lost her ability to play at a professional level. Apparently, being able to see her fingers move caused her to try to anticipate the movements—rather than to simply feel them as she had done before. Yet Mesmer had insisted on continuing her treatments. He felt that she would adapt with time.

At one point, Mesmer was nearly accused of kidnapping her. Her family, being fearful that she might lose her pension from the Empress if no longer able to play, started a veritable war in the tabloids. They spread rumors that the doctor might be taking sexual liberties with this visually handicapped young woman. The mind of the Viennese populace turned against him. Marianne herself occasionally wondered if the rumors were true, if Mesmer might be more aroused by a nubile teenager than by her more mature body. And now the medical community of Vienna seemed outraged by the possibility that his techniques could cure those they had deemed incurable. Mesmer was assaulted from all sides.

The early morning sun came streaming through sheer curtains into the bedroom. The November light had a cold quality that Marianne knew heralded the upcoming winter months. Her pre-dawn walks from her lodgings to the apartment Mesmer kept above his storefront clinic were becoming more brisk, but his bed was warm. Marianne was relaxing in the glow of the good work from his marvelous hands.

"I'm leaving Vienna," he announced without the slightest warning.

She sat bolt upright.

"What?" she exclaimed. "When?"

"As soon as I can arrange it," he said flatly.

"Where will you go?"

"Paris. I plan to move my practice there."

"Ah, Paris. I love Paris," she said. She relaxed a bit, settling back into the down pillows and pulling the soft white comforter up to her shoulders. "I should have been there months ago." She thought about Ben waiting and felt a twinge of guilt that quickly passed. "What about your wife?"

"She will stay here in Vienna, at the villa. There are still a few patients who require ongoing care."

"Good," she said smugly. Not that Mesmer's wife ever interfered with his attention to her. Still, Marianne felt it would be better to have her in another country and completely out of the way.

"I have a colleague in Paris, Doctor D'Eslon, who has arranged for my introductions. It seems the Queen herself is interested in my technique."

Marianne pouted, not enjoying the thought of a royal competitor for his attention—especially not one with the formidable reputation of Marie Antoinette. Mesmer must have caught her drift as he put his arm around her.

"Only business," he said soothingly. "Only business."

She pulled away from him. "I'm sure that is what you tell your wife about me, too."

"My dear, she doesn't even know you exist," he replied. Then he smiled eerily. "But what have you told your friend Doctor Franklin about me?"

Marianne felt her stomach knot up. She tried to keep a serene exterior, but her mind raced. She hadn't realized before this moment that Mesmer knew anything more about her relationship with Ben than his gift of the glass armonica. Perhaps he was guessing.

"Nothing. Why would I tell him such private information?" she said as calmly as she could. She started to get dressed.

"Oh, I was just wondering," he said.

As Marianne slipped back through the window to her own bedroom, she thought that perhaps she had been right ... that nothing good would come from her renewed relationship with Mesmer. "Yet, some good has come of it," she corrected herself. "I have been rid of my headaches. I can now help other people heal. And I have not felt melancholy in months." She looked forward to being in Paris, but she wondered how she would balance her relationships with these two powerful men—all the while keeping her mother in the dark about her affairs.

All Hallows Eve, 1777

PASSY

BEN HAD LONG LOOKED FORWARD to this evening—an elegant party at the Hôtel de Valentinois with the promised attendance of a special royal guest. After several days spent tending to tedious ambassadorial business, he was anticipating an enjoyable night. He recalled the revelry of Hallowe'en in England but knew that tonight would be different. In France, there would be no costumes, no bands of rowdy tricksters arriving at the door to demand money or treats, no games designed to find out who would marry in the next year. The grand house was splendidly decked out for the occasion. Colorful gourds, bundles of golden wheat, and other harvest decorations were placed strategically about. The floors and windows sparkled in the glow of bright candlelight. The smell of mulled wine invited Ben in.

Hostess Madame Leray and her neighbor Madame Le Veillard were stationed near the entranceway, greeting guests. Each was dressed in a gown laced with golden fall colors. Jacques Leray moved quickly through the large rooms, alternately mingling with revelers and supervising the serving staff. Several guests had already made their way over to meet the famous Doctor

Franklin. After nearly a year in France, he was getting to be less of a novelty, but he always drew a crowd wherever he went, and he enjoyed the attention. The evening wore on in pleasant, if tame, revelry.

The moment she entered, a ripple of excitement and anticipation swept through the crowd. It was as if lightning had just struck nearby, and the air became suddenly electrified. Marie-Thérèse took her wrap, handed it to a butler, and the two began talking excitedly. The new arrival tossed her sandy brown tresses in an effortless and carefree way. People continued to talk and laugh, carrying on their normal conversations, but a hush fell over the room as she moved through. She appeared oblivious to the reaction she created, but Ben could keenly see that she knew the effect she had. Luckily, he was well positioned to observe, not close enough that he would be among the first she greeted. In fact, from the crowd's response, he believed it would take her some time to work her way to where he stood.

Ben had forgotten his talk with Le Veillard and was now completely besotted, soaking in everything that he could about her from afar. She was, without a doubt, the most beautiful creature that Ben had ever seen. Yet he couldn't help thinking that she looked familiar. She was young and full of energy; she carried herself with an aristocratic posture but seemed not at all haughty. She greeted the other party guests enthusiastically with a smile that lit up the room. Her skin was like porcelain, radiant, and flawless. She was thin, not in a consumptive way, but rather in a sensual, athletic way that was evident despite the extravagances of her evening gown. "Unlikely that she has any use for a corset," Ben thought. She moved with a fluid motion synchronized to an unheard symphony. Her body was just the perfect size for a woman, Ben estimated. Not too short, but not too tall either, statuesque. Ben imagined that if she stood directly in front of him, her pert breasts would touch his chest. She would have to look up only so slightly to kiss his lips.

"Daydreaming?" Le Veillard said. He snapped Ben out of the progressively more erotic fantasy he was having. "She is quite a captivating creature, is she not?"

"Am I so obviously smitten?" pleaded Ben.

"Oh yes, we all are, my friend." Le Veillard said. He smiled and sighed.

Jacques Leray came up, bearing a tray. "Have you seen my new Champagne glasses?" he said. He offered one to each man.

Ben thought that his host must be trying to distract him, but his brief moment of infatuation was already lost. The young woman had stepped into a crowd of revelers, disappearing from view. Ben accepted a glass of Champagne held not in a traditional flute but rather a shallow bowl on a short stem.

"My, this is a most pleasing and interesting shape," Ben said. He took a sip. "And, of course, a great Champagne as well, my friend. Where did you find these glasses?"

"Marie-Thérèse bought a whole set from the artist who makes them. They are becoming quite the rage. I thought you might be interested to know that the artist is said to have modeled the shapely bowl from a cast of Marie Antoinette's breast."

"Which one? Left or right?" Ben asked, looking across the room to where the lovely young woman had reappeared.

Jacques laughed. "Well, if I ever get the chance to conduct the research and find out empirically, I shall let you know," he said and then moved off.

"Our young Queen is headed this way," Le Veillard said excitedly.

Ben could see that the young woman he had just been admiring had now spotted him as well. It was clear that she was purposefully making her way across the room, intermittently hindered by acquaintances trying to engage her. Ben noted that she was polite but didn't say more than a few words to each one. She arrived to them at the fireplace gracefully. Ben thought that she looked even more stunning up close. And then he realized why she had seemed so familiar—it had been she, cloaked and hooded, under the oak tree in Kingswood.

Le Veillard addressed her first. "Your Majesty," he said as he lightly kissed the back of her hand. "May I introduce my good friend, Doctor Benjamin Franklin?"

"*Enchanté*," said Ben. He took her delicate hand in his. "Please call me Ben."

"It is my pleasure to finally meet you properly, Ben," she replied. She glanced at the Champagne glass in his other hand. Ben thought that she blushed slightly. Le Veillard must have noticed her reaction too.

"We were just hearing the story behind these unique Champagne glasses," Le Veillard blurted out.

"It is despicable. Such fabrications some people will make up to sell their wares," she replied. Her icy look shut Le Veillard up quickly. She turned to Ben, leaning in close to his ear and softly whispered, "But you could easily have discovered by the old oak tree that my breasts could not be contained by such a small bowl."

"I am absolutely sure of it, your Majesty," Ben said out loud. His tone gave nothing away.

Le Veillard put on his most injured expression. It had no effect on her. Her royal composure remained completely intact.

"I was expecting to find Doctor D'Eslon here," she said. She looked around at the crowd. "Oh, there he is talking with Jacques Leray. Come. You must meet him." Marie Antoinette took Ben's hand and led him through the crowded room.

As they drew close, Ben surmised that the doctor was expounding on the healing properties of *magnétisme animale* to a small group, including their host.

"New fluid ... effect of the heavenly bodies ... cure without potions or drugs . . ." Ben could only catch snippets of what he was saying because of the noise in the room. But then he heard the doctor say "Mesmer . . ." as they joined the small group.

"When is he arriving?" Marie Antoinette asked.

"Hello, my dear Antoinette," the doctor said. D'Eslon looked genuinely happy to see her although he didn't answer her question. He greeted his Queen with what appeared to Ben to be less than appropriate formality, but she didn't seem to notice or care.

"I want you to meet Doctor Benjamin Franklin," she said. Immediately, there was a chill. The smile vanished from D'Eslon's face and was quickly replaced by an uncomfortable expression.

Ben extended his hand. "*Bon soir*," he said as cordially as he could.

"How do you do?" D'Eslon replied flatly. His handshake was limp and brief.

"I am very well—thank you. I would like to hear more about Doctor Mesmer's techniques. I understand that you have studied with him."

"Yes," D'Eslon said warily. He eyed Ben as if he were a criminal trying to decide how much information he could give the police without incriminating himself. "Perhaps another time." He very quickly excused himself.

Marie Antoinette looked at Ben apologetically. She followed D'Eslon onto the patio and spoke to him outside the door for a few minutes before rejoining the party.

When she got back to where Ben and Le Veillard had re-established themselves by the fire, she said, "I am sorry that he was so rude. I don't know what came over him."

"Perhaps he fears that our Doctor Franklin might become a better Mesmerizer than he?" Le Veillard said.

"I doubt that," Ben replied. "More likely, he feels threatened by a challenge to the scientific basis of his method."

"But you have seen the results with your own eyes," Marie Antoinette said. "Does not that convince you of the value of this new discovery?"

"What I have seen is intriguing, but science demands proof," Ben replied. "If Doctor Mesmer has discovered a new fluid, we should be able to touch it, see it, or measure its effects. Also, it seems odd to me that only certain people can channel or direct it. I don't understand why only a chosen few people are in on the 'secret.'"

"Well, I have seen it—and I know that it works," Marie Antoinette said. She sounded a bit miffed. "I hope that you will keep an open mind to this wonderful treatment. Doctor Mesmer should be arriving in Paris soon. I am sure that he will be able to explain his discovery to you."

She motioned almost imperceptibly to a clique of young men and women standing nearby. The entourage swiftly engulfed her. Someone threw her wrap around her shoulders. Talking and laughing gaily, the group left without even a goodbye to their host or hostess. Ben looked around to note that Le Veillard was missing as well, presumably swept away with the young Queen and her band of revelers. Her aura lingered briefly in the air, but soon the room became much quieter in the aftermath.

"I guess the party is over," Madame Leray said to Ben. There was a tinge of sadness as she looked around at the older crowd left behind.

Ben gave her a warm smile. "But what a remarkable affair it has been," he replied.

Winter 1777

VIENNA

THE LATE AFTERNOON SUN cast a cool blue hue on the streets covered with fresh snow. Marianne decided just to walk down to the *Christkindlmarkt*.

The time leading up to Christmas in Austria was always a magical time. Vendors came from all over the country to sell everything from hot-spiced wine to handmade wooden ornaments. Rows of booths filled the square, forming a sort of maze. The winter air was laced with the smell of freshly cut pine boughs and meats roasting on small fires in some of the booths. Marianne found the warmth of these grills mixed with the chilly air delightful. The ringing of small bells by some of the vendors combined with the friendly banter of sellers and buyers added to the festive atmosphere. Marianne smiled as she observed some good-spirited haggling going on in one of the booths she passed. She tried on—and then bought—a pair of Tyrolean hiking boots. They were not stylish by any means but were very comfortable and rugged.

She had just stopped to examine some brightly colored blown glass globes when she heard a familiar voice. Marianne froze. She instinctively drew her hood more tightly around her face, checking to be sure that none of her hair was visible. The voice came from a booth in the next row over. Marianne could see Mesmer's silhouette through the back of the stall where she stood. She took a step to the side just to be sure that he couldn't see her. As she did, she saw a finely dressed but extraordinarily fat woman at his side. Marianne took a good look at Anna Maria von Posch. She seemed almost as wide as she was tall. Marianne stifled a laugh. To complete the ridiculous picture, Mesmer's wife was talking incessantly, her small head jerking back and forth with each gush of words from her small round mouth. From where she watched, Marianne could only pick up snippets of what she was saying.

"Oh, I love this ... this one is no good ... Franz, I must have this," she babbled on and on.

Marianne snuck a glance back at Mesmer, who appeared extremely bored. Every once in a while, he would produce a coin from his pocket and exchange it for a wrapped package as directed by his spouse. He already carried a stack of bags and packages under his left arm, a beast of burden. Von Posch carried nothing but a small shoulder bag. Marianne followed their shopping spree surreptitiously from the adjoining row. She had a fleeting temptation to swing around and confront the doctor and his wife.

"Hello, Frau Mesmer," she could almost hear herself saying. "I am your husband's lover." She quickly put the idea out of her head. "If she sits on me, I'm done for," she thought and laughed out loud.

Marianne didn't quite see what happened next, but suddenly she heard shouts in the row where the Mesmers shopped. The man was clearly drunk, and he was swearing.

"And you keep your filthy hands off the young girls," the man bellowed.

Marianne tried to peek through the back of a booth to get a better view of the commotion. She could just see Mesmer from behind. He now clutched his parcels in both arms. His wife stood in front of him, confronting the drunkard. She was swinging her bag at the man ineffectively. Several bystanders tried to hold the man back. A guard was bustling toward the fracas.

"Evil sorcerer," the drunkard howled. "Wizard of debauchery." A torrent of expletives followed.

Anna Maria von Posch was also yelling something in return that Marianne could not understand. Mesmer seemed to be trembling. His knees looked as if they might buckle.

"At least she makes a good shield," Marianne thought as she pondered the situation. This man Mesmer, who she could find so intimidating at times, hid behind the fat wife who ordered him to carry her packages.

Just as soon as the guard had nabbed the drunken man by the collar, Mesmer barked at his wife, "Let's go!"

Marianne tried to pull away from her peephole, but Mesmer whirled around too quickly. He looked directly at where she hid. Marianne could not tell if he had spotted her, but his icy expression caused her to shiver all the way back home.

"I must get out of Vienna," Mesmer said, looking up from his newspaper. He and Marianne sat at a table in his apartment above the storefront. Nearly a week had passed since the incident at the *Christkindlmarkt*. Marianne nodded matter-of-factly as she sipped from her bowl of hot chocolate milk.

"Do you know that I had to fight off a man in the *Christkindlmarkt* the other day? I was doing some Christmas shopping there last week when this giant of a man recognized me in the crowd." He didn't mention anything about his wife being there, Marianne noted. "Well, there I was, minding my own business, when this ogre approaches me, swearing up a storm."

"What was he upset about?" Marianne asked. She wondered how Mesmer would tell the tale.

"Something about my techniques ... I suppose. You know, the lies and innuendo published in these scandal sheets nearly every day." He tossed the crumpled newspaper on the floor. "Marianne, I have been terribly misunderstood by the Viennese people."

"I know, I know," she replied as consolingly as she could. "What happened in the market?"

"He came running at me, swinging his fists."

Mesmer gestured wildly with his arms. Marianne almost had to laugh—he really did look something like the deranged drunkard she had observed. She put her hand up to her mouth to stifle it.

"Whatever did you do?"

"I flattened him with one punch."

Marianne was indeed glad that her hand was perched in front of her mouth. She nearly choked as Mesmer demonstrated his right hook in the air above the table.

"You flattened him?" she managed to squeak out.

"Yes," Mesmer said confidently. "I laid him out on the ground."

Marianne tried to sound impressed. "Then what happened?" she asked.

"The guard came, grabbed the ogre by the collar, and led him away."

"Well, at least that part rings true," Marianne thought.

"What did your wife think of your heroism?" she said, baiting him.

Mesmer gave her a puzzled look. "What makes you think that she was there?"

"She wasn't?"

"No," he said. There was not so much as a subtle hint of his dishonesty.

"I just thought that perhaps you protected her from the ogre," Marianne proposed. All the while, she was recalling how it had been very much the other way around.

"No."

Walking home through the nearly empty streets of Vienna, Marianne contemplated how easily Mesmer had lied about the incident at the *Christkindlmarkt*. She wondered if there were other lies that he had told her—and gotten away with.

January 1778

PASSY

THE WEATHER WAS FOUL, chilly, and damp, with gusty winds and intermittent snow and rain, a good time to huddle by a fire. Ben stayed inside most of the month nursing his gouty foot. He had regular visits from the other two American commissioners, Silas Deane and Arthur Lee, but few other visitors came all the way out from Paris. Madame Brillon had written a note at the turn of the year to wish Ben a happy 1778, but also to inform him that she was suffering from a severe cold. His usual Wednesday evening visits would have to be postponed until they were both feeling better. The young, brash American naval captain, John Paul Jones, made a short visit to the Hôtel de Valentinois early in the month to meet with the commissioners, which created a stir with the females of the household. Ben had to admit that he cut quite a dashing figure.

Pierre Beaumarchais remained in Paris nursing an injury he had suffered in December. He had been rushing home with news of the American victory over the British at Saratoga when he was thrown from his horse, dislocating his shoulder. When Ben got word of the mishap, he sent Beaumarchais a bottle of his best cognac to help ease the pain. Ben also heard news that Madame Brillon was composing a triumphal "*Marche des Insurgents*" to celebrate the American victory. He would have a hard time waiting to hear it. A Paris newspaper reported an unfounded story that Ben had discovered a cure for dropsy, or swelling of the extremities, using tobacco ash. Ben wrote the editor asking that a correction be printed.

Ben also received the sad news that the ship that had carried him to France, the Reprisal, had sunk off the coast of Newfoundland. All hands were reported lost with the sole exception of the cook. Ben envisioned Tom adrift in the icy Atlantic waters and wondered if he had recovered. He silently said a prayer for the brave American sailors he had come to know during his passage over a year before. Especially he remembered Captain Wickes, the man who had never taken a wife because he assumed that one day he would not come home. "How accurate was that prophecy?" Ben thought.

The morning of Thursday, January 29th, a letter arrived by special courier. Temple brought it directly to his grandfather as the bearer was instructed to wait for his reply. What he read made Ben jump up out of his chair, momentarily forgetting his gouty foot until it reminded him by throbbing. The letter was from Cecelia Davies, Marianne's sister. It was sent from a hotel on the Left Bank—in Paris!

Paris January. 29th, 1778. Grand Hôtel de Londres Rûe Dauphine.

Sir.

I hope you will Excuse the liberty I take in troubling you with this line but being come to Paris with my Mother and Sister on account of the latter's health, should think myself guilty of an unpardonable neglect were I not to take an opportunity of waiting on the ingenious Inventor of the Divine Armonica. My Sister continually expresses her infinite Obligations to You Sir, and as She is just at present able to go out is extremely desirous to have the pleasure of seeing you; but lest we might happen to call at an inconvenient time I should Esteem it a particular favour could you let me know by the Bearer any moment tomorrow when you are at leisure, as we are very impatient to have the happiness of waiting on you. If not tomorrow, any other Day Except Saturday or Monday next. My Mother and Sister desire their most respectful Compliments, and I have the honour to be Sir Your most Obliged and most Humble Servant.

Davies Inglesina

La Inglesina was Cecelia's stage name. Beyond that revelation, the letter offered up more questions than answers. Why was Cecelia writing to him and not Marianne? Ben had been fruitlessly watching the daily post for her perfumed letter since the previous spring when he had expected her to arrive in Paris. Through the summer, fall, and early winter, he had been deprived of that pleasure. Now the Davies family apparently had finally arrived, and he still had no direct word from Marianne. This worried Ben, as did Cecelia's report that they had come to Paris on account of Marianne's health.

However, he decided that he would never find the answers to his questions unless he responded to Cecelia's request. Tomorrow was impossible; he had a full day of meetings scheduled. Either of the upcoming weekend days would be fine—but Cecelia had requested not Saturday. Ben quickly dashed off a note for Temple to give to the courier:

Dinner Sunday, Hôtel de Valentinois, Passy

B.F.

128

The following day, Ben received this response:

Paris January. 30th, 1778.

Sir.

I should have been happy to the greatest degree in the honour of Dining with you Sunday, but to my misfortune since my Sister's late Illness she does not Dine from home; but I shall have the honour of waiting on you with my Mother and Sister Sunday afternoon if you will give us leave. They desire their most sincere Compliments with a thousand thanks for the kind Invitation, please too accept mine likewise. I have the honour to be with the greatest respect and Attachment Sir.

> *Your most obliged and*
> *most Humble Servant*
> *Davies Inglesina.*

Ben gave Temple the letter to file. He walked up to the main house to find Madame Leray.

Ben found her in the kitchen. "What kind of illness does not allow one to dine from home?" he asked.

"Perhaps an intestinal problem? Why?" she replied. "I have no idea. And you should not be asking me such questions. You're the doctor."

"But I'm not a medical doctor," Ben said. "Do you remember my invitation to the Davies sisters and their mother to dine on Sunday?"

"Ah," Madame Leray said. "Thank you for reminding me. I will need to order something special."

"No need. I have just been informed by her sister that Marianne Davies does not dine from home ... on account of her illness," Ben said.

Madame Leray looked slightly alarmed. "What kind of illness can she have?"

"My dear, that is exactly what I have asked you! I have not seen Marianne in over three years—but I believe she suffered only from headaches and melancholia."

"Doesn't everyone?" she said. She put her fingers up as if to rub her temples. "I could probably accommodate any dietary restrictions that she has."

"I am sure that you could—and thank you—but there is no need now, as they will only be visiting in the afternoon."

"Then we will certainly have to plan an activity. The sisters are both gifted musicians, am I not correct?"

"Yes, I had the very first glass armonica made for Marianne." Ben smiled.

"She holds a special place in your heart, I believe," she said. Her smile tempted him to reveal all.

"You are very intuitive. Yes, we have been very close." Ben tried to change the subject before she pried the whole story out of him. "If we are going to have an impromptu concert, perhaps we should invite a few friends to make an audience."

Madame Leray seemed willing to let the nature of Ben's relationship drop for the moment. "Well, Jacques should be here—unless he is working, of course—as well as my children and your grandsons. We could invite our neighbors the Le Veillards and the Brillon's."

Ben wasn't fond of the idea of having Madame Brillon in the same room with Marianne Davies. Even given the platonic relationship he had with the Ice Princess; it didn't seem like a good idea. He shook his head as if dismayed. "I'm afraid she has a bad cold," he said.

"All right, it will just be our families and the Le Veillards then," Madame Leray said. "But what about Beaumarchais? He is a music lover."

"Good idea." Ben was thinking that having a few people available to occupy Cecelia and Mrs. Davies might be welcome. He was hoping to get Marianne alone—if only to find out how she really was.

Beaumarchais arrived at the Hôtel de Valentinois on Sunday, just before the appointed 1:00 p.m. dinnertime, with his arm in a sling. He gingerly got out of his carriage and walked into the house. Madame Leray greeted him with a kiss on both cheeks. The weather was chilly, but at least it was sunny that day. Ben's gouty foot was recovering well. He had gone out for a short horseback ride earlier with Le Veillard, who stayed for dinner, of course. Madame Le Veillard visited with Madame Leray, helping her prepare the house for the afternoon guests. The music room sparkled; new bunches of dried wild-flowers tied up with red ribbons adorned the house. The staff bustled with activity. Jacques Leray was inexplicably home, not at work. He joined the jovial group at the dinner table, sitting in his usually empty seat at the head.

"We have a special treat in store this afternoon," Jacques said. He held up a wine goblet towards Ben. "Our esteemed colleague, Doctor Franklin, has arranged for a visit by the talented Davies sisters. We are hoping that we can prevail upon them to play something for us."

"Without incurring a fee from Mrs. Davies?" Le Veillard asked, deadpan.

Everyone laughed. Mrs. Davies's tight-fisted reputation had become legendary everywhere—even at the Hôtel de Valentinois.

Ben tried to put a different emphasis on it. "I hope that they will enjoy simply spending an afternoon in the country with our families," he said. "If some lovely music happens along the way, then so be it."

"*Oui, oui!*" A cheer of approbation went up from the table.

After dinner, the men retired to the library to talk business. There was news from Nantes of shipments bound for the revolutionary army in America. The American navy was apparently wreaking havoc with British shipping all along the coastline of Europe and into the English Channel. They all hoped that the victories at Yorktown might herald a turning point in the war.

"At the very least, it should allow King Louis to show his backing for your American cause more openly," Jacques Leray opined.

The women and children had gone to the music room to prepare for their special visitors. Ben could hear them laughing and singing. Someone was playing the pianoforte rather badly. He suspected Junior was the culprit.

When the carriage pulled up, it was nearly 3:00 p.m. Ben heard Madame Leray bustle toward the door. He went to the library window to see if he could catch a glimpse of the Davies disembarking, but the view was obscured. It seemed like an eternity before Madame Leray and Madame Le Veillard arrived in the library, escorting Mrs. Davies and her two daughters. Cecelia looked thin, but Marianne appeared radiant and healthy. Her long strawberry-blonde hair shone like a beacon. She looked even more trim and fit than Ben had remembered. "So much for a mysterious illness," he thought.

The moment she saw Ben, Marianne dashed across the room, practically tripping her mother, who tsked in disapproval. The frail Mrs. Davies had to grab hold of Cecelia to catch her balance.

Marianne embraced Ben. "I have missed you so much, darling," she whispered.

Ben soaked up the smell of her hair. He responded passionately, "And I you."

Monsieur Leray cleared his throat. The two separated, although Ben would have been much happier to hold her in his arms all day. Marianne secretly pressed a small note into Ben's hand, which he pocketed quickly.

As Madame Leray began the introductions, a server appeared with a tray of refreshments. The children joined the adults and were introduced. The Leray girls were especially full of questions about music, the theater, where the sisters had played, and on and on. Ben observed that Junior, Le Veillard, and Beaumarchais had encircled Cecelia, who seemed to enjoy the male attention. Her mother finally interposed herself, dispersing the would-be suitors. Madame Le Veillard enlisted her husband's help in moving some chairs in the music room, a clever ploy designed, Ben surmised, to pull him away from temptation. "Unfortunately, she can't chaperone him twenty-four hours a day," he thought. Le Veillard wore a forlorn expression as he was led away.

The afternoon passed quickly. The expected impromptu concert was ostensibly organized by the children, and its announcement raised not even a word of protest from Mrs. Davies.

The Leray children acted as ushers.

When they were finally all seated in the music room, Ben whispered to Jacques Leray, "Perhaps she expected as much."

With Marianne playing the harpsichord and Cecelia singing, Ben was instantly transported. If he closed his eyes, he could have easily imagined himself in heaven. The melodies these two talented young women produced were strong, yet sweet, haunting, and ethereal, at times evoking a vision of misty Celtic fields. At other times, the melodies were more down-to-earth, reminiscent of familiar folk tunes. Their harmony was perfect. Ben felt the emotion rise in his chest. He kept his handkerchief close to dab the tears welling up in his eyes, and he was not the only one so affected in the audience.

He never did get the chance to be alone with Marianne that afternoon. At the end of the concert, after only one encore, Mrs. Davies announced that they soon had to depart. She explained that they had a busy schedule and that the girls needed their beauty sleep, deftly directing her statement to Madame Leray, who had no choice but to acknowledge that she understood. All too soon, their coach was departing from the circle drive of the Hôtel de Valentinois.

Beaumarchais, too, soon begged his hostess's forgiveness, claiming renewed shoulder pain, and boarded his coach back to Paris. Their special guests gone, Madame Leray and Madame Le Veillard adjourned to the sewing room. Monsieur Leray also disappeared, claiming to need to get some work done. The children dispersed for more exciting pursuits.

Ben and Le Veillard sat alone in the now quiet study, sipping cognac and listening to the clock tick.

"So, what does her note say?" Le Veillard asked.

"What note?"

"The one she passed you when you two embraced."

Apparently, Le Veillard had observed the transfer. "I don't know. I haven't opened it yet," Ben replied. He pulled out the small envelope from his pocket. Like all the rest of her letters, it came tied with a pretty bow. He held it up to his nose, inhaling deeply. Instantly, her essence once again filled his senses. He imagined burying his face in her hair, being fully immersed in her. Ben quickly opened his eyes and untied the bow, tossing the ribbon into the fire where it flared up briefly. He tore open the envelope and put on his bifocals. Even over by the window, he could barely read the small script.

Mon Cher,

I hope that you are not angry with me. My delay has been unavoidable. Please meet me at the Cheval Sauvage—Tuesday, 3 February, at 7 a.m. I assure you that I will make the wait worth your while.

As always, yours,

M

"She wants me to meet her at the *Cheval Sauvage* on Tuesday morning," Ben said. "Where is that?"

"You know where it is, Ben," Le Veillard said with a smirk. "The Wild Horse is that seedy bar and hotel on the outskirts of Paris, near where we rescued your friend the Reverend. I think that the lady has some disreputable behavior on her mind if she wants to meet you at that place. No one goes to the *Cheval Sauvage* unless they wish to get into trouble."

"Is it safe?" Ben asked, concerned.

"Of course not," Le Veillard continued. "The *Cheval Sauvage* is a den of iniquity. I love it. I do happen to know a handsome barmaid there. Do you remember the one who washed my shirt?"

"You have kept in touch with her?" Ben said, incredulous.

"Why in the world would I not?"

"I thought that was perhaps a one-time affair."

"It's only a one-time affair if she wants it so. I'm always ready to give a 'repeat performance.'" He laughed. "Ben, since Marianne has invited you, I'm assuming that she will have procured a room."

"I would assume so. Could we find out?"

"I'll find out. On a Tuesday morning, there shouldn't be anyone occupying the upstairs rooms of the *Cheval Sauvage,* save perhaps a few drunkards sleeping it off. I doubt that anything the two of you do will roust them. Out of curiosity, why does she want to meet you so early in the morning?"

"She often leaves the house before her mother and sister awaken."

"Is this the way you two always arranged things?" Le Veillard asked.

"More or less," Ben replied. "In London, she could always feign a headache or some other illness, lock herself in her room, then sneak out to meet me. While she occasionally could manage other times of day to rendezvous, the early morning hours ultimately became easiest for her. Besides, I'm always up early anyway."

"Do you want me to go with you?"

"Louis, after seventy-one years, I don't think that I will need any help with this," Ben said.

"No, I was thinking more of providing some security for you—just in case."

"Thank you, *mon ami*, I would appreciate that."

Just after 6:00 a.m. on the following Tuesday, Ben heard Diablo snorting outside his window. The early morning February light was still quite dim. Ben was, of course, already dressed and ready to go. He estimated that the ride to the outskirts of Paris would take no more than thirty minutes. Nonetheless, if Le Veillard was already here—why not get to the *Cheval Sauvage* early to reconnoiter? They rode in silence until they approached the outskirts of town, and then Le Veillard spoke.

"My friend improved your room reservation. You were originally booked into a small, stuffy room with no window, but she has arranged for you to have a better room at the front of the building. I will give you the key when we get there."

"Thank you, Louis. I appreciate it." Ben was surprised to find himself a bit nervous, but he relaxed when they rounded the final corner to find no one else on the street.

"I hope that she didn't forget," Le Veillard said.

"She wouldn't," Ben said.

He took the key from Le Veillard, handed him the reins, and dismounted. Ben ascended the well-worn wooden stairs to the rooms above the tavern. He heard loud snoring down the hall, but nothing else. The hallway smelled of stale beer and urine. Ben looked at the key. It bore the number 11. He opened the door to the room with that number. The door made an eerie creak on closing. The room was empty. There was a plain wooden bed, chair, and dresser. A lamp flickered on the bedside table. The furniture appeared well worn but clean. A colorful patchwork quilt on the bed imparted a more comfortable feel. Ben noticed a washbasin with fresh water and towels. Ben checked his watch. It was about ten minutes before seven. He went to the window and looked out. Le Veillard had crossed the street and tied the horses to the hitching post. He sat under a cape with his back against the building across from the *Cheval Sauvage*. As Ben watched, a dark-haired young woman left the building beneath his window and crossed the street to where Le Veillard was encamped. He opened up his cape to let her in. She snuggled up next to him in the cold morning air.

Ben sat on the chair. After a few minutes, he heard the unmistakable sound of soft footfalls on the stairs, though he had heard no horse or carriage approach on the street. Marianne must have arrived by foot. He sat up, alert. A key entered the door of Room 11. The door pushed open. Ben strained to see the figure wrapped in a dark cloak as she entered the room. She closed the door behind her with a creak and threw back the hood of her cloak.

Ben was standing now. Marianne smiled at him. She always had the most beautiful smile. Perhaps a few more lines etched her face than the days back in London. Ben took a step forward. He held her firmly, appreciating her body pressed up against his. Her hands and nose were cold, but her body was warm. Ben stroked his hands over her back and hips. She felt divine. He pulled her even closer to him as they kissed. Her tongue darted everywhere. His lips burned. Her essence filled his senses as they fell into bed.

As Ben awoke to the noise of a horse in the street, he realized that he must have dozed off. He reached over to the space next to him in the warm bed, but Marianne was gone. The morning light was rapidly brightening. Ben threw on his clothes and went to the window. Le Veillard and the barmaid had also vanished. Only the two solitary horses remained tied up across the street. The only person around was a shopkeeper sweeping off his porch farther down. Out of habit, he checked the room to make sure that he left nothing behind. He closed the creaky door and headed downstairs. As he walked past the bar, he heard soft voices.

"Ben?" he heard Le Veillard say.

Ben entered the dimly lit bar to observe his friend and the barmaid sitting at a table. Le Veillard took a sip from a steaming tankard.

"Ben, this is my friend Maggie." LeVeillard smiled as he introduced a sweet-looking young woman with mousy dark brown hair, loads of freckles, and penetrating green eyes. Her appearance was more Celtic than French.

"It's a pleasure to meet you. Thank you for upgrading the accommodations," Ben said a little sheepishly.

"You are welcome," she replied as if it were an everyday occurrence. It struck Ben that perhaps it was. "I have some hot coffee ready," she offered.

"No, thank you, but I would take tea if it is not too much trouble," Ben said.

"Of course not." She responded with the countenance of a woman who, though regularly ordered to fetch drinks for a living, appreciated being asked politely.

"You hail from Brittany, do you not?" Ben guessed.

"Yes," she said. "How did you know?"

"You look wonderfully Celtic; however, it is your beautiful accent that gives you away."

"Thank you," she replied, blushing slightly. "I grew up in a little fishing village north of Brest. All I recall is that it was cold and desolate all winter. Paris suits me much better." She left the table to fetch Ben's tea.

"She's delightful," Ben said to Le Veillard.

"Yes," Le Veillard replied. His smile intimated he held a much deeper knowledge of her charms. Ben detected a hint of sadness hidden there as well.

The two men left the *Cheval Sauvage* just as the first of the laborers started to arrive for their morning drinks.

"It is incredible to me that those men can start drinking heavily this early in the morning," Ben remarked as they climbed upon their mounts. He looked back to see Maggie pouring drinks at the bar, flirting with the customers. Le Veillard had turned his back already and was proceeding out of town toward Passy.

After riding quietly for a while, Le Veillard spoke. "So?" he asked expectantly.

"So what?"

"So, how was it?"

"That's a very personal question," Ben replied. Le Veillard and he had become close friends, and Ben was accustomed to Le Veillard asking him personal questions. But he didn't always feel obliged to answer.

"Don't tell me if you don't want to," Le Veillard said with resignation when he saw the look on Ben's face.

"It was different."

"That is not at all what I expected you would say," Le Veillard replied. "I thought that you would say 'heavenly', or 'wonderful', or something pat like that—but not 'different.' What does that mean?"

"I'm mulling it over—but it was not the same."

"So, what has changed?"

"As I said, I am not entirely sure. She responded in almost exactly the same way as she had when we were in London. But somehow, she was not the same. Does that make any sense? There was something almost imperceptibly different, and yet I perceived it. It was as if she was not entirely there. As if she was not completely with me. As if something else—or someone else—was on her mind."

"Do you suspect there is someone else?"

"I have no hold on her. She is free to bed whomever she wishes. I have always enjoyed that same freedom myself."

"I'm sure that is true," Le Veillard said. He winked. Then he quickly became serious again. "But when she is with you, she should be with you only, don't you agree?"

"Yes, and vice versa. I did not have Madame Brillon on my mind this morning when I was with Marianne."

"Ah, the lovely and unattainable Anne Louise," Le Veillard sighed.

"You bear the look of unrequited love," Ben said jokingly.

"And you, my friend, do not wear such a forlorn look. So, I must assume that you have been able to melt the Ice Princess. You must have convinced her to avenge through you, her philandering husband, where I was never successful."

Ben laughed. "Don't give me more credit than I am due," he said. "The woman likes to flirt, to be sure, but I will tell you honestly that I have not bedded her to this day, and doubt that I ever will. However, as you have told me many times, French women have a hundred ways of showing their affection. I believe that I may just have to be content within the ninety-nine ways."

"Well, that is ninety-nine more than I'll ever know!" Le Veillard cried. He spurred Diablo for the final stretch home.

Ben considered what Louis had said. Perhaps there was someone else now in Marianne's life. But who?

April 1778

PARIS

MARIANNE HURRIED TOWARD the *Tuileries Jardin*. Mother would not sleep late today, she knew, but Marianne felt compelled to take the risk. She did not want to miss this morning's event. The shops bustled with early trade as she whisked along. The smell of fresh coffee tempted her. Outside one café she saw a troupe of musicians setting up, preparing to entertain the customers. They tuned their instruments and joked with each other. There was magic in the spring air. They played a sonata. Marianne paused to enjoy the music and the warm early morning sun on her face. Her stomach grumbled.

"Mesmer can wait a few minutes," she said to no one. She sat down at an empty table nearby.

A waiter brought her coffee. Marianne inhaled deeply to savor the aroma. She took a sip. She watched a *thimblerigger* attempting to get passersby interested in buying into his shell game. Some of the people on the street looked, but none tarried. They just went on about their business.

Marianne's thoughts turned to Ben. She had seen him only a few times since her return to Paris. Their rendezvous at the *Cheval Sauvage* had left her confused. Before going there that day in February, she had thought that she might get completely lost in Ben's arms; that he might sweep her off her feet as he had once done in London; that afterwards, she might forget Mesmer and live only for Ben once again. But things had not turned out that way. Marianne discovered that day that she thought about Mesmer even when she was with Ben. That made her uncomfortable. She had never before thought about another man when she had been with Ben. She was deep in contemplation when she heard a woman's voice from the next table.

Marianne glanced over to observe a woman intently watching the shell game. The *thimblerigger* weaved his arms seductively over the shells, sliding them across a smooth board. Occasionally he lifted a shell to reveal a small gold coin underneath. The aristocratic woman sat alone, a small colorful fan in one hand and a cup of coffee in the other. She wore gaudily colored makeup as if she might be able to paint her youth back on.

"Isn't it confusing?" the woman asked.

"Yes, it most certainly is," Marianne replied, but she was thinking of her own situation.

"I am obsessed with it. I feel I should be able to figure out the puzzle. The truth must be hidden there somewhere."

"Do you think so?"

"Do you want to know how I pick?" the woman asked.

"Tell me," Marianne said.

"I follow my heart."

"Have you ever discovered where the coin is hidden?"

"No." The woman looked sad.

"Why do you continue to play?"

There was no answer. Marianne paid the waiter and bid the woman *adieu*. She headed off again toward the *Tuileries Jardin*. She couldn't help thinking that an unseen hand played a sort of twisted shell game with her. In it, the gold coin was her happiness, and the shells of Franklin and Mesmer swirled around, sometimes partially revealing it, but most often concealing the prize. As she rushed through the city, Marianne wondered if she would ever discover it.

Marianne turned the final corner to gaze upon a wondrous sight. A throng of several hundred people congregated on the lawn of the *Tuileries Jardin*. They had all come to be treated by Mesmer. She recognized him in the center of the crowd. He was hard to miss. He stood on a pedestal wearing his long lavender silk robe. His ringlets of wavy brown hair glowed in the sunlight. His eyes were cast down, and his arms encircled in front of him. He held a shiny metallic object in his hands. Marianne turned her attention to Antoine, Mesmer's valet, passing out ropes to the people in the crowd. He wore a white linen robe. He was instructing the people to tie the ropes around their waists and then to each other. Marianne could see that several long rope leaders led back to Mesmer like the spokes of a wheel. The crowd was utterly silent. In fact, even the noise of the city disappeared behind her as Marianne stepped into the throng.

She approached the pedestal from the right. At the same time, Antoine approached from the left. Mesmer opened up his arms in both directions as if to welcome them but kept his gaze toward the ground. Marianne noted that there was a small step to each side of the pedestal. She and Antoine simultaneously stepped up, flanking Mesmer. Antoine handed her a white linen robe, which she donned. Mesmer began slowly chanting and tapping his bare feet on the pedestal. It acted like a drum, sending out a rhythmic sound. The crowd began mimicking his actions. Marianne heard their ecstatic moans followed by the flapping of wings. She sensed the sky darken as a huge flock of small black birds appeared, flying in tight formation. No one looked up except Mesmer, who slowly brought his eyes to the horizon. The flock encircled the throng of supplicants. Their chanting increased in intensity. More and more birds began darting along the rope lines, creating a breeze toward the center where Marianne stood. Once they got to Mesmer, the murmuration would shoot skyward only to loop back once again, faster and faster. Soon Marianne could no longer see individual faces in the crowd as the air was so thick with birds. Mesmer's hair stood straight up in the wind.

The beating of wings and feet and voices quickly reached its crescendo. Time seemed to stop.

A single bird hovered directly in front of her. She stared into its eye. It provided a window into her soul. She knew that she was one with the flock. There was a loud crack, which sounded like a peal of thunder. A flash of light. The birds vanished.

Marianne looked out at the crowd. Many had dropped to the ground. Also, their canes, crutches, and other aids lay strewn around them. They started to move, get up, look at each other, talk. Marianne could hear individuals closer to the pedestal, commenting on how well they felt. She looked back toward Mesmer. His arms were held out slightly in front of him, palms up. He reminded Marianne of a painting she had once seen of Jesus healing the sick. Mesmer wore the same expression of divine placidity. His eyes were open but not focused on anything or anyone in particular. Marianne became aware of Antoine's hand on her shoulder. She locked arms with him behind Mesmer.

"Everything all right?" Antoine asked.

"Yes. You?"

"Good. I should get the doctor home. He will be tired."

"Of course."

Marianne looked around. The crowd was dispersing. Several volunteers had collected all the ropes. Mesmer's coach appeared. The coachman jumped down and opened the door. Mesmer sighed heavily. He slumped down onto Marianne and Antoine. They assisted him off the pedestal and into the coach. He sunk back into the cushion and appeared to be asleep. Marianne kissed him on the nose. He smiled and then started to snore loudly.

"Will he be all right?" Marianne asked Antoine.

"Yes, the process of channeling the *magnétisme animale* is taxing, but he will be fully recovered after a good nap."

Marianne felt wonderful. She skipped all the way back to her hotel, wondering if, by chance, she had discovered the golden coin.

May 24th, 1778

THE ROYAL SCIENTIFIC LABORATORY

THE *Château de la Muette* sat at the edge of the Kingswood, a short ride from Passy. Ben knew the site well as he often explored the area on horseback. Whenever he had the time, Ben enjoyed stopping in to visit his friend and colleague, Jean-Baptiste Le Roy, director of the Royal Scientific Laboratory, which was housed in a wing of the château. Le Roy, a distinguished member of the Academy of Sciences in Paris had not only presented, but vigorously defended, Ben's theories on electricity more than twenty years earlier—and they had remained good friends ever since.

Today, the occasion was a dinner that Madame Le Roy had arranged. When Ben arrived early for dinner but only slightly late for yet another tour of the laboratory, his friend was already expounding on its history to his other guests.

Le Roy looked up to welcome Ben. "Ah, here is the illustrious Doctor Franklin, just in time for our tour," he said. He glanced at his watch as if to give Ben a gentle reproach for his tardiness and started walking through the laboratory.

"The original mansion was constructed in the 16th century on the site of an even older hunting lodge. It was built for Henry the Fourth's wife, Marguerite de Valois. The origin of the name 'Muette' is not fully known—but since the word literally means 'silent or dumb woman'—we think that she must have been either a very quiet or not so smart lady." A few of the guests chuckled, but Ben had heard the anecdote before. He gazed around to see what new equipment his friend had installed.

Le Roy went on. "Our building was significantly expanded and updated by old King Louis XV prior to the wedding of his grandson and Marie Antoinette in 1770. The wing that houses our Laboratory was added during that expansion. After their marriage, the future King and Queen of France lived in the other part of the château. And even after young Louis assumed the throne in 1774, they continued to stay here when not at court in Versailles. Until last year."

"The royal family does not come here anymore?" one of the guests asked.

"No, the place is a lot quieter with only a small caretaking staff left behind," Le Roy said.

In the early afternoon light, the massive scientific equipment gleamed in the large open laboratory. There were machines everywhere. Many had shiny metal or glass parts. Some were moving, some still. Some appeared to be in various stages of completion, their parts were strewn on the massive oak workbenches. Two technicians worked on a machine, which Ben recognized, a long-spark electrical apparatus designed by Le Roy himself. It consisted of a large glass disk, rotated by means of a metal crank. The disk was sandwiched between a pair of cushions at one side and two collecting combs at the other. The cushions and the collectors were each connected to a large upright brass conductor, supported by two thin twisted glass rods. Just as the group walked up to the machine, a large spark flew between the conductors, creating a flash of light, a crackling sound, and the smell of electrified air that Ben recognized instantly. The guests made appropriate sounds of amazement.

Ben looked over at Le Roy, who was smiling smugly. "Merely a parlor trick," he said, passing close enough to his host so that no one else could hear.

After a few more scientific demonstrations, the group left the laboratory for their meal. Madame Le Roy had arranged the table so that Ben could sit between her husband and one of the guests who Ben did not know. He was an abbé and a physicist, a specialist in magnets, according to Le Roy. The topic of conversation soon turned to his area of expertise.

"Do you know the work of Maximilian Hell?" he asked Ben.

"The Jesuit priest and astronomer from Vienna?"

"There could not be more than one of him," came the reply. "He has been experimenting extensively with the healing qualities of magnets."

"He has found evidence of true physical healing using magnets?" Ben asked incredulously.

"I believe that he has. Not only that, but the Viennese physician Franz Anton Mesmer has taken his work even further. However, Father Hell disputes that Mesmer discovered anything new with his technique."

"I have often observed the effects of magnets on iron objects but never on the human body," Ben replied. "In fact, I once tried applying a magnet to my own gouty foot without any success in eliminating the pain or swelling. That small test discouraged me from further experimentation in this realm, but I would be happy if you would enlighten me."

"Father Hell believes that the flow of blood fluid is intensified by the application of a magnet to the body, thereby improving the removal of bad humours."

"I suppose that theory might be plausible, but I would like to see some evidence that it is true."

"I'm not sure how one would go about testing that. Doctor Mesmer now claims that he does not need a magnet to effect the same cure. He claims that he can channel the same healing fluid using only his hands."

"I was recently made aware of that claim by your fair Queen. I will be anxiously awaiting a more thorough demonstration and proof. If it is true that there is a new fluid that will cure our human ills, I will be happy to embrace it," Ben replied.

Madame Le Roy beckoned for dinner to be served. Ben wondered what the fare would be. His host was considerably more famous than wealthy, living on a pension provided by the King and a few royalties from his inventions. Le Roy's father had been a celebrated and successful horologist, but that fortune had passed on to his older brother, who kept the watchmaking company going. Nonetheless, Ben had never left hungry from his friend's home. The Le Roy family had a frugal way of doing more with less. Tonight was no exception. The first course was piping hot wild mushroom soup with leeks. Next, a haunch of venison appeared. The Le Roy's benefited from the fact that the caretakers of the mansion had been allowed to continue hunting in Kingswoods. However, the *piece d' resistance* was a large steaming casserole that smelled wonderful. Its ingredients had Ben puzzled. His host must have seen the strange look on his face as he passed the casserole.

"Do you know what this is?" Le Roy asked.

Ben spoke tentatively in a low voice so as not to be overheard. "*Pomme de terre?*" he ventured.

"We call the dish '*hachis parmentier*'. It is the favorite of our neighbor, Monsieur Parmentier, who grows these potatoes nearby."

"I have eaten many a potato in Ireland, but are they not outlawed here in France?" Ben asked. He knew that they had been banned as it was thought that they carried leprosy.

Le Roy laughed. "No," he said. "They became legal five years ago. While a prisoner of the Seven Years' War in Prussia, Monsieur Parmentier lived on potatoes, and he attributes his survival to the eating of them. He has made it his mission to re-introduce this much-maligned vegetable to the French people. The King granted him a plot of land near here to grow them. He had been bringing his produce to the château for so long that he has continued to do so even after the royal family moved to Versailles. We are always glad to see him."

"It never ceases to amaze me how you do so much with so little, my friend," Ben said.

The dinner concluded with a flaming dessert, which was so sweet that it hurt Ben's teeth. It was delicious. He finished his portion contentedly.

Ben, Le Roy, and the Abbé retired to the fireplace in the study, each with a large snifter of inexpensive brandy.

"Ben, you have done some experimentation on the healing properties of electrical fluid, have you not?" Le Roy asked.

"Yes, many years ago, I noted that I could make the arm of a man, having been previously paralyzed by a stroke, move once again by applying an electrical charge over his nerves. While the subject was quite overjoyed to see his useless limb move, the treatment did not result in any permanent recovery. He was no more able to move the arm voluntarily after several treatments than before them. I eventually gave up on the utility of this approach."

"As a physicist," the Abbé commented, "I don't know much about medicine, but it seems to me unlikely that this electrical fluid could have any beneficial effect on the human body."

"Why do you say that?" Le Roy asked. "You seem inclined to believe in the effects of magnets."

"Well, I have seen how you can make your mechanical inventions move by using this force, but the human body is the creation of God. It moves by the will of the person as governed by His laws," the Abbé replied.

Ben couldn't resist. "But Father, from the time of Descartes we have known that in many ways, the human body does work like a machine that our inner workings follow physical principles and laws. Wouldn't it make sense that the electrical fluid could have effects within the body as well? For example, even though I was unsuccessful at curing paralysis by my method, I was able to cure a man of his melancholia by a strong electrical shock."

At that Le Roy jumped in. "But Ben, that effect might be the same as any sudden, strong physical or emotional shock could have on the melancholic—it either cures them or sends them into a catatonic state from which they may never return. I'm not sure that I'm convinced of the utility of the electrical fluid for this purpose."

Ben frowned. "Neither was I," he replied. "But I think that it does demonstrate that there is an effect."

"Perhaps," said the Abbé. "But by that logic, any known physical force would have an effect. For example, a fire warms the body—or in excess causes burns." He looked into the fireplace. "Water soothes—or in excess drowns, et cetera."

"And what about Mesmer's *magnétisme animale*?" Ben asked. "Do you believe that it is a true physical force that can be used to heal?"

"I think that someone who wants to believe that they are going to be healed will sometimes be so—at least temporarily. The powers of suggestion, imagination, and imitation can be strong. Physicians have always used these powers at least to comfort, if not to cure," the Abbé said thoughtfully.

"Well spoken," Ben said, "and charlatans with good track records abound."

"I am not convinced that this Doctor Mesmer is a charlatan," Le Roy said. "I will reserve judgment until I have seen a demonstration with my own eyes. I understand that he has recently arrived in Paris."

At that moment, as if on cue, Madame Le Roy entered the study. She bustled over to the group briskly. She gave her husband a wink and turned to the Abbé.

"Come, Father, my guests would like to hear tales of your travels," she said as she took him by the arm. The Abbé cast an apologetic glance at Le Roy and Ben as she led him away but did not resist at all.

"Ben, I want to show you something," Le Roy said as soon as the study door was closed.

"It sounds very confidential," Ben said, alluding to the staged exit of the Abbé.

"Not terribly so. But it did occur to me that the Church should not be made aware of this little experiment quite yet. The Abbé will be quizzed by his superiors as to what he has seen here as soon as he returns home, I am sure."

"You are always the soul of discretion, my friend."

"Perhaps it's a trait, learned the hard way, from years of keeping my father's watchmaking trade secrets."

He walked Ben toward a bookcase. With the push of a concealed button, the bookcase swung open to reveal a hidden passageway.

"Very mysterious," Ben marveled.

Le Roy pushed the door closed behind them. The two men walked silently along the dim, damp corridor. If Ben's sense of direction was correct, they were flanking the laboratory they had toured as a group earlier. At the far end of the corridor, they came to a locked door on the left. Le Roy fumbled for his keys. Ben noted an unlit hallway to his right.

"Where does this lead?"

"Secret exit," Le Roy replied matter-of-factly. "As a precaution, the royal family had several of these tunnels built so that they would have an escape route in the event of an emergency. I have not explored them all, but this one leads to a small hunting cabin in Kingswoods." He found the proper key and opened the heavy door silently.

Ben followed his host into a small laboratory. It was as dimly lit as the hallway but gratefully warmer. On a central workbench was an astounding sight. Ben gasped as he took it in. Standing on the workbench was a tall glass aquarium enclosing the largest electric eel that Ben had ever seen. It must have been at least six feet long from end to end, Ben estimated. The creature wriggled with an undulating motion, diving down and then returning to the surface of the water to gulp air.

Ben's jaw dropped at the sight. "Truly amazing," he said.

"I probably should have warned you, but I couldn't resist surprising the unflappable Doctor Franklin," Le Roy said.

"Where did you get her? A female of the torporific eel family ... unless I miss my guess."

"Ah, I see that you know your eels," Le Roy said. He bore the expression of a proud father. "I acquired her from Doctor Edward Bancroft. He brought her back from a voyage to Guiana where she was captured. The King paid a small fortune for her. I suspect that he believes she might be useful as a weapon, but I'm not so sure."

Ben walked over closer to the tank. He noted several metal rods leading to instruments placed around the aquarium. Nearby on the floor was a group of Leyden jars wired in series.

"Be careful," Le Roy warned. "Her shock can kill a man."

"Have you measured the strength of it?"

"My technicians are still trying. She destroyed the first two electrometers that we attached. They are building a more robust one now. However, today I would like to try holding her electrical fluid in these Leyden jars, if you will assist me."

"Of course," Ben replied.

"Good. I believe that the preparations are in order. All we need is a shock. Stand back." Le Roy said. He proceeded to run towards the tank waving his arms at the giant eel.

There was a loud, crackling electrical sound followed immediately by the shattering of glass. Sparks flew from the Leyden jars. At first, Ben thought that perhaps the aquarium had cracked, but he was relieved to see that it remained intact. All but two of the Leyden jars were completely obliterated. There was glass everywhere. Le Roy was lying flat on his back, covered with glass shards. Ben rushed over to him. He looked dazed but quickly came around. Three young technicians, having heard the commotion, entered from the main laboratory side through a door that was previously hidden. They helped Ben get Le Roy to his feet. One grabbed a broom. He started sweeping up the mess as if this was an everyday occurrence. It occurred to Ben that it probably was.

"What happened?" Le Roy asked sheepishly.

"She apparently packs quite a punch," Ben said.

"Did any of the jars remain intact?"

"The last two, I believe."

"Let's have a look."

The huge eel had reverted to undulating slowly in her enclosure, apparently none the worse for wear. Ben walked over to the remaining intact Leyden jars sitting amid the rubble on the floor. Le Roy brought an electrometer from a nearby workbench and attached the leads to one of the jars. A ball floated up between two hearty gold leaves.

Le Roy seemed pleased. "Fully charged," he said.

As the two walked back through the damp secret corridor to the study, they vigorously discussed the technical aspects of the electrical demonstration that Ben had just witnessed. However, once back by the fireplace, Le Roy became more somber and contemplative.

"Here is a question for you to consider," Le Roy said. He folded his arms as if working up a theory to go before the Royal Academy of Science. "I don't really want an answer right now. In fact, I'm not sure that there is an answer. I just want you to ponder it. If a creature such as that eel may not only contain but also voluntarily apply the kind of electrical force that we have just seen, why would a man not be able to wield a similar power?"

Ben gave his host a puzzled look.

"I am referring to *magnétisme animale*," Le Roy added.

"I believe that you may be laboring under a misconception, my friend. Do you truly believe that there is a physical force that Doctor Mesmer and his disciples are able to control and apply? Are you suggesting that such a force might be similar to the way your eel uses her power to hunt and defend herself? If so, I would like a chance to measure it in the manner we just observed with your charged Leyden jars."

"I'm not sure exactly what I'm suggesting at this point," Le Roy replied. He scratched his head and looked a bit befuddled. "I agree that I would like an opportunity to measure this new fluid, if it exists. However, I also recognize that some forces remain unmeasurable—even by our advanced methods of today. Consider light. We both know that it exists; yet we cannot measure it. The best that we can do is to compare differing levels of light with our eye."

Ben chuckled. "Yes, I must admit that we remain in the dark about light," he said. "But light has some very measurable and reproducible effects, my friend. If I stay out in the bright sunlight too long, my skin will burn. If the light gets too dim, I must put on my bifocal glasses to read."

"Could we not measure the effects of *magnétisme animale*? Certainly, there have been some remarkable cures described," Le Roy said.

"I would leave that for the physicians to decide."

"There is not much science behind what those quacks do," Le Roy said, frowning.

"I must agree with you there," Ben replied. "But hopefully, someday even our medical doctors will be forced to demonstrate efficacy or else suffer abandonment of their techniques."

Le Roy wasn't quite ready to concede. "Ben," he almost whispered, "what about the healing power of the mind? We've both seen examples of people returned to health who kept a positive countenance, while others, convinced that they would succumb, in fact, did so. It seems to me that in both cases, these people had their expectations fulfilled. Could that not represent a power that we currently cannot measure?"

"Jean-Baptiste, there I agree with you up to a point ... but you and I have both lost sons to illness, despite all our hopes and prayers for a different outcome. I believe that there comes a time when the disease becomes overwhelming. You must admit that we are still mortal. We will all eventually succumb to something, despite any powers of our mind to temporarily believe otherwise. Don't misunderstand me; you know that I am a strong advocate of maintaining a positive attitude toward life and health as well as practicing a vigorous lifestyle. As I observe the populace of Paris, I see a great number who seem never to be in good health or good cheer. They are fond of medicines, always taking something for some ailment or another. If these people could only be persuaded to forbear their drugs and potions, they would do much better. If they were to become convinced that, instead of these poisons, simply the touch of a hand or the pressing of an iron rod cured them, they might attain good effects though they mistake the cause."

"I see what you mean," Le Roy replied. "One's state of mind can be a powerful force in both sickness and in health."

"Perhaps I'll go ask your friend the Abbé what he thinks about individual will, as compared to God's will, in sickness and in health," Ben said.

"Oh, no, you don't," Le Roy exclaimed. He put his hand on Ben's arm as if to restrain him. "If I encourage you to debate religion with that man, we will be here all night," he said.

As he refilled Ben's snifter, Ben wondered what kind of a punch Mesmer might possess.

PART III

Summer 1778

PASSY

IT WAS NOT LIKE BEN to get angry, but a letter in his morning mail had incensed him. It was from Richard Bache, Ben's son-in-law, and Benny's father. As he read and reread it, Ben felt the heat build up in his neck and face. He kicked the post at the bottom of his stairs and yowled.

British soldiers, led by the notorious Captain Andre, had ransacked Ben's Philadelphia home. The soldiers had been encamped there over the past winter, causing his daughter Sally and her family to flee to the country. Upon their retreat, the soldiers had stolen some of his scientific and musical instruments, rummaged through his papers, and generally left a mess for Richard and Sally to clean up. Worst of all, they had made away with a portrait of Ben that was hung next to one of his late wife Deborah.

Luckily, it sounded as if there had been nothing worse than property damage. Sally had remained in hiding with Ben's new granddaughter. At least his family was safe. Ben contemplated how hard the past winter must have been for his daughter, displaced from her familiar surroundings and home, in her delicate condition, with no assurance of what the future would hold for her and her unborn child. He thought about her giving birth in a farm-house. He wondered who had attended to her. The war usually seemed so far away, but now it felt very close and personal. Ben decided he needed a swim.

Normally Ben swam against the flow as he headed upstream, a habit that afforded him the advantage of working his muscles until he got tired, then drifting back effortlessly as he cooled down. Today, it took him longer than usual to fatigue due to his anger. By the time he decided that he'd had enough, Ben looked over to see the town of Auteuil, much farther upriver than he had ever gone before. He turned over to float on his back for a while. Large white clouds seemed to mirror his calm floatation as they drifted across the blue sky. Ben could hear the songs of a few birds in the distance but nothing else. He focused on his own breathing as it now slowed after his exertion. The current gently pushed him toward home. He felt much better. "Things will work out," he told himself.

He was deep in this meditation when he felt a pronounced ripple in the water, jolting him out of his relaxation. It was not unusual for small fish or birds to share his waterway, but whatever had caused this ripple was too big. Ben's first thought was of Le Roy's electric eel. "Ridiculous," he scolded himself. "That eel is safely contained in the royal laboratory, and even if it were to somehow escape, it could not end up in the Seine." He wished that he had his glasses as he treaded the water, scanning in all directions. He saw nothing unusual. Occasionally, in the past, he had encountered stray dogs swimming across the Seine. Whether they did it to escape from some danger or to find new hunting grounds, he did not know. Perhaps that was it. He returned to floating on his back, contemplating the clouds. No sooner had he done so than he collided with something.

Ben nearly jumped out of the water. He yelled. Whatever he'd collided with yelled too. His heart was racing. He quickly rubbed the water from his eyes, prepared to defend himself. Instead, Ben found himself face-to-face with a woman. A woman in the middle of the Seine. A woman *swimming* in the middle of the Seine. A woman *swimming nude* in the middle of the Seine. Ben was in shock.

"Hello," was all he could muster. They were about a foot and a half apart. The river seemed to stop. Both were treading water. Nothing moved except the clouds floating by.

"Hello," she replied, almost as if nothing out of the ordinary was happening. "Are you hurt?"

"No. You surprised me, but I'm fine. Did I injure you?" Ben asked. He made note of her long silvery-gray hair, tied back in a ponytail, wet and fragrant of flowers. She had more than a few lines on her thin, tanned face. Ben noted that they were mostly smile lines. The sun glimmered on her wet shoulders, dotted with freckles. She smiled warmly, and all the lines on her face vanished.

"I seem alright too," she said. Ben watched her hands move down over her athletic body. He followed as far as the murky water would let him see.

"Do you swim here often?" she asked, ignoring his gaze.

"No, first time," he stammered. He forced himself to look directly into her eyes. "You?"

"Every day the weather allows."

Ben was about to explain that he usually did not get this far upstream and that it was not his usual time of the day for a swim when, to his astonishment, another swimmer approached.

"Ah, finally, the Abbé has caught up," she said.

"The Abbé?" Ben asked.

"Yes, he is my swimming partner. It is not safe to swim alone, you know, Monsieur?" She gave him a look of disapproval. The lines on her face reappeared.

"Yes," Ben said. Once again, this remarkable woman had caught him completely off guard. He was about to remind her that he had just encountered her swimming alone too, but thought better of it.

"My name is Ben ... and yours?" he said, trying to establish some equilibrium.

"Minette," she replied. The other swimmer arrived. He was a stocky man in his early thirties, Ben assessed. He was breathing heavily but appeared fit. From what Ben could see, he was nearly hairless save for two brushy brown eyebrows that looked like wooly caterpillars. It crossed Ben's mind that the Abbé might be a eunuch. He certainly hoped this was the case since he was swimming with an attractive nude woman. As soon as the man spoke, that theory was dispelled.

"Madame Helvétius," the Abbé exclaimed in a deep male voice. "You didn't wait for me." He sounded exasperated.

"I'm sorry, Martin," she replied. "I thought that you would catch up. It is a good thing that I ran into Ben here."

The Abbé looked back and forth between the other two swimmers.

"Ben ... Ben Franklin?" he said excitedly.

"I am he," Ben said. Ben was not entirely sure that he was so happy to be recognized, being as he was *sans* clothes, in the middle of the Seine.

"Ah, so you are my famous neighbor," she said. She held out her hand. "You must attend one of my salons."

Ben took her hand, planting a kiss on its back. The downward motion of his gaze afforded him a peek underwater to observe that her nipples reacted to his affection.

"I'll try to dress more appropriately for the occasion," Ben said.

She laughed with a hearty tone that was as radiant as the sun on Ben's face. "You are a friend of Monsieur Turgot, are you not?" she asked.

"Yes," Ben replied. "He and Monsieur Vergennes have been most helpful in our cause. They have both been a great aid to the American war effort."

"I will make sure that he invites you then. Now we must go. *Bonjour.*" She nodded at the Abbé, who appeared nearly fully recovered. Then she smiled at Ben, who, once again, found himself speechless. He could only watch as they swam back toward shore. At least Ben got a tantalizing view of her backside as she retreated.

Alone again, he noticed that his legs were burning from treading water for so long. He turned over on his back, found his favorite river current, and floated towards Passy. By the time he got back to the Hôtel de Valentinois, Ben had forgotten all about the troubles in Philadelphia. He resolved that he must find out more about the remarkable Madame Helvétius.

The afternoon was mostly filled with dry ambassadorial business. After the events of the morning, Ben had fantasized that the *Poste* might contain a word from Monsieur Turgot, but it did not. Instead, he got more than his fill of the usual deluge of letters requesting introductions from French nobility wishing to become officers in the Continental Army. These idle gentlemen usually inquired as to the stipend they would be offered. Ben would write back politely that there were no stipends available. If he had as many Frenchmen volunteering to be infantrymen as he had erstwhile officers, the Continental army would be in even better shape. In other business, there were the same tedious financial matters to be addressed. Shipments of supplies, prizes held for ransom by the American privateers, talks of hostage exchanges, and the like. Temple filed the letters, dutifully cataloging each according to his grandfather's instructions.

The one potential bright spot, as his day wore on, was a scheduled meeting with John Paul Jones. The young captain was currently staying at the Hôtel de Valentinois between naval missions. Ben had taken a liking to the brash young man since first they'd met. The hopes of the American navy lay in men such as Jones, Ben been known to declare in public on more than one occasion.

But Jones was also a hothead, famous for his short temper. He had fled to the American colonies from England in 1773 after supposedly killing a mutinous member of his own crew. In his interactions with other American naval officers, Jones had had more than his share of skirmishes. These altercations were mostly generated by his perfectionism, Ben surmised. Jones expected no less than maximal effort from himself and everyone else around him. This quality made him a naval officer without equal, but also a difficult person to deal with at times. Nonetheless, Ben always found him to be both trustworthy and capable—two attributes that endeared him.

In France, Jones had quite a reputation as a ladies' man because of his rakish good looks and swashbuckling nature. Louis Le Veillard, an equal womanizer in Ben's opinion, could hardly tolerate being in the same room with the man. Once Ben had mentioned Jones's name in conversation with Le Veillard and without the slightest hesitation, his neighbor had hissed enviously, "If I pranced around in that naval uniform, I'd have twice the women falling over me as he does." Ben was determined to do everything in his power to keep the two men separated in conversation and location after that, as he fancied both and didn't want to encourage discord.

Just before the appointed hour of his meeting with Jones, Ben felt the need to stretch his legs. He told Temple to take a break. The lad sprinted down toward the river. Ben walked out of his lodgings and up the lawn toward the main house, aiming for the kitchen. The staff would be busily preparing supper, he knew. He might be able to divert a piece of fruit headed for a tart to have as a snack, he thought. But as he passed the root cellar, Ben noted that the door was slightly ajar. It occurred to him that it would not be suitable for the stored vegetables on such a warm day. As he came within earshot, Ben heard the unmistakable sounds of coupling. Soft moans accompanied by the slightly wet slapping of flesh on flesh caused Ben to pause at the entrance to the dark cellar. For a moment, he wondered if he should just keep walking to the kitchen, leaving the lovers to complete their delicious task. "But Madame Leray runs a tight household," he thought. "Perhaps it would be better to discover these lovers, allowing her to discipline them according to her wishes."

Ben entered the darkened room and cleared his throat loudly.

Two figures jumped up from the corner where they had been locked in an embrace. They both set about arranging their clothes, which were severely out of place. Ben's eyes adjusted to the dim light quickly. The first thing that he noticed was the naval uniform. While Ben had been fully expecting to discover two frisky members of the house staff, he was not entirely surprised to identify the male lover as none other than John Paul Jones. He was, however, entirely taken aback when the woman who pushed past him, running out the cellar door, was Madame Leray.

"Ben," Jones said apologetically. "You have caught me with my pants down."

"If I had known that it was you in here, John Paul, I would have kept about my own business." Ben laughed. "I thought perhaps I had discovered the house staff dilly-dallying on company time," he explained.

"I hope that I can count on your discretion," John Paul said sheepishly.

Ben thought for a moment. "On one condition," he proposed.

"And what would that be?"

"That you desist from any further intimacies with our fair hostess. I realize that she is a beautiful woman and sorely neglected by her husband, but I don't see any good coming out of this relationship."

"You are a wise man, Ben. I agree to your terms and thank you."

"Now, I believe that you are late for a meeting with me, young man," Ben chided.

Jones grinned. "I can't be late if you are here with me," he said.

Ben chuckled. "*Touché*," he replied. The two men left the cellar, heading toward Ben's quarters.

At supper, Ben made a point of sitting next to Madame Leray. She appeared tense. They made small talk for a while but mostly ate in silence. Only a small group was present at supper, the others at the table being Temple and the Leray children. Monsieur Leray's place was set, but he remained at work, as usual. John Paul Jones understandably had decided to dine out.

"Ben, may we talk after supper?" Madame Leray asked.

"Of course. Le Veillard and I are planning on riding together later, but we will have time as the sun will set quite late this evening."

After the staff had cleared the table, and the rest of the family departed to their quarters, Madame Leray and Ben sat.

"Ben, I am truly sorry for what happened today," she said. "John Paul told me that you are willing to be discrete. For that, I am eternally grateful."

"Did he tell you that my one condition is that he desist in his advances toward you?"

She laughed. "No," she said, "but most likely, this is because it was I who made the advances, not he."

"Oh, then I will require the same condition of you. I don't see that any good can come from your relationship."

"Yes, and I will comply, of course. But may I ask you a question?"

"By all means."

"You are aware of my husband's work schedule, I believe. You are aware that he is rarely home. However, I doubt that you are aware of how little intimacy we truly share, even on the few occasions when he is here. Over the past few years, I have felt him lose interest in me. My question is this: How does one keep the passion alive over the many years of marriage?"

"First, let me say that I am not the best one to answer your question," Ben said. "The latter years of my marriage to Deborah, I was mostly absent—across the ocean in England. In fact, I was overseas when she passed away. But even before that, our relationship had cooled, changing from its early passionate form, to what seemed more like a friendship."

Ben stopped short of confessing what he felt that she already knew—that he had carried on an affair with Marianne. He went on. "After a while, Deborah and I were more like two housemates than lovers. We didn't fight ... but we really didn't communicate, either."

"That is exactly what I mean. I know that Jacques is a good man. He works hard to provide our family a life that few others enjoy. Yet some days I would trade all this ..." she said, motioning at the splendid trappings around her, "for the closeness that we shared when we first married."

"I understand. Wealth can provide both a blessing and a curse. Particularly if, with the acquisition of material things, a couple loses their sense of togetherness. You know, that 'just the two of us against the world' sense that we felt when we were young and poor. When all we had in the world was each other. The one bit of advice that I can share, is that you need to find a way of keeping the passion alive inside you. It might be that you live through your children, your hobbies, or your charity work. I don't know what truly excites or motivates you. I know for me, it has been my devotion to science, the American cause, and physical fitness that keep me going."

"I have outside interests ... and they do keep me going to some extent." She frowned. "But sometimes they are not enough. I have thought a lot about why I needed John Paul. It wasn't just about physical gratification. Although I must say, I enjoyed that." She blushed slightly. "There was an emptiness in my life that he filled. I will miss that feeling of fulfillment even more than the coupling. But I know that ultimately it is I who must address that emptiness. I cannot rely on anyone else to do it for me."

"I understand completely." Ben smiled. A few tears streaked Madame Leray's face, but she looked resolute. "You are a strong person and will be fine," he said.

They were hugging as Louis Le Veillard entered.

"Ah-ha," he bellowed. "I knew that you two were up to something."

"Louis, you flatter me. I have begged Madame Leray to be my lover so many times I cannot count them anymore, but she has steadfastly refused me. She says that she will only consider you."

"Oh, if only it were so. But I'm afraid the lady shall remain an icy monument to monogamy."

"How right you are, my friend," Ben said. He gave Madame Leray a subtle wink. She returned the most adoring look he had seen in quite a while.

"Are you ready to ride?" Le Veillard asked.

"Absolutely. Let us be off before the sun sets any lower."

Summer 1778

PASSY

LE VEILLARD SET OUT from Passy on Diablo with Ben barely keeping pace on his mount. The sun was already sinking in the western sky as they took the road toward Paris.

"Where are we headed?" Ben asked, despite the fact that he really didn't care. He was just glad to be outside riding on such a beautiful early evening.

"I need to go into Paris to collect a small debt," Le Veillard confessed.

"Oh, wonderful," Ben replied sarcastically. "I won't provide much protection for you. You should have brought one of your men."

Le Veillard laughed. "No, it is not like that at all. It is more of a favor for a man who runs a small shop on the *Place Vendôme*. He was a good friend of my father-in-law, one of our first customers for bottled spring water in Paris. He finds it difficult to get all the way out to Passy due to his health and the long hours he keeps at his shop. He does not trust anyone to bring the money to me, so I ride in every month or so, and we settle up his account. He feels more comfortable with the personal service, and I like the exercise. Besides, it gives me a convenient excuse to get into Paris."

They rode hard until they reached the outskirts of Paris. The riders slowed down as they approached the familiar row of gritty bars, including the *Cheval Sauvage*, now filling with fatigued workers winding down after their day with a pint. Ben secretly wished to join them. They rode on. As they approached the center of Paris, the streets became more crowded. Ben didn't mind slowing down as it gave him a better chance to observe the people around him. Some recognized him and waved. The late sun raked across the *Tuileries Jardin* casting long shadows of the people strolling through the gardens.

During earlier trips to Paris, before he was quite so recognizable, Ben had enjoyed sitting near one of the kiosks here. Everywhere flowers were in full bloom, an explosion of red, blue, and yellow. On the far side of these orderly gardens designed by Le Nôtre a century earlier stood the Royal Palace. Today, the sun's low angle bathed the already impressive façade with pure golden light, accenting its beauty. After stopping to appreciate the scene for a moment, Le Veillard led his horse north into the *Place Vendôme* where tall buildings surrounded the square.

Where only one moment before Ben's world had been bathed in abundant warm sunlight, inside the square only the cold blue light of the early evening sky was able to filter down, cooling the gray limestone façades and obscuring by shadow the openings to the shops and apartments under the colonnade. Ben observed a few people walking through the openings onto the square, but they seemed featureless, ghostlike.

"Would you prefer to join me or to stay out here?" Le Veillard asked.

"I'll tend to the horses," Ben replied. "Will you be long?"

"No, just a few minutes," Le Veillard said. He handed over Diablo's reins as he dismounted.

Ben dismounted also. He tied the reins to a hitching ring near the entrance of the shop Le Veillard entered. He felt a slight chill. A boy approached with two buckets of water and a brush. Ben nodded at him.

The boy placed a bucket of fresh water in front of each horse and proceeded to brush Diablo. "Good lad," Ben said.

"This is a big horse," the boy exclaimed. "I don't think I can even reach the top of him."

"Just do what you can," Ben replied. "He'll be fully groomed when we get back home."

Ben felt another chill. He looked around. Something seemed amiss, yet it was nothing Ben could identify. Just then, he caught a brief splash of color from across the square out of the corner of his eye. A flash of peach-colored fabric darted out of a portico. Just as quickly, it was gone. But Ben knew that color. It was Marianne's. Instinctively his gaze tracked the projected path that someone walking in the shadow of the colonnade would take.

"Watch the horses, will you, boy?" Ben said. Not waiting for a response, he strode briskly across the square to intercept the apparition.

He got to the place where she should have been but saw nothing. Ben looked in both directions. He popped his head into the closest store. No sign of Marianne, or anyone else, wearing a peach-colored dress.

"Damn," he said. Maybe his mind was playing tricks on him. It had been a very long day. He was about to head back over to where he had left the horses when one of the nameplates on the door leading to the apartments upstairs caught his eye. Being newer, brighter, shinier than the others, it stood out from the patinaed ones. Ben walked over to inspect it. He tilted up his bifocal glasses. To his astonishment, it read:

Franz Anton Mesmer
Physician

Ben considered for a moment ringing the bell. But what would he say to Mesmer? Even if he found Marianne were here, what business was it of his? Ben walked back across the square in a daze. Le Veillard returned to the horses almost simultaneously with Ben. The boy handed each of them a set of reins. Louis tossed him a coin.

As they rode out of the *Place Vendôme*, Le Veillard said, "Ben, you look as if you've seen a ghost. Are you alright?"

The sun was waning even more as they rode toward the Seine, but it was still much warmer than inside the square. The warmth fortified Ben a bit.

"Yes, I'm alright. I thought I saw Marianne, but I must have been mistaken."

"Tell me about it."

Ben recounted the whole encounter as they rode back to Passy. When he had finished, Le Veillard was quiet for a few minutes. Then he spoke.

"Ben, do you love her?"

"If you had asked me that question five years ago, I would have said yes unequivocally and condemned you for asking, but today I don't know. We have been together only a few times since she returned to Paris. Our relationship is not the same as it once was. She has changed."

"You know my theory. I believe that she has taken another lover."

"I'm afraid that you may be correct," Ben said. A profound sadness swept over him.

The next morning, a letter arrived. Ben knew instantly that it was from Marianne. Tied in pink ribbon, it smelled heavenly. As tempting as it was to open it immediately, he hid it away until after the tedious business of the morning was done. Then he strode out into the garden to stretch his legs. He sat on a bench and read:

August 15th
Paris

Mon Cher,

Once again, I find that I must apologize for my poor correspondence. I have no excuse other than a busy performance schedule. I hope that you are not angry with me. I assure you that we will be together again soon.

As always, yours,
M

Ben sat in the morning sun amid the lush flowers. The droning of the bees was the only sound other than the distant rush of the Seine. Madame Leray appeared with a tray of tea. Ben pocketed the letter. She sat down next to him.

"How is she?" Madame Leray asked softly.

"Who?"

"Marianne, of course," she went on. "What kind of a hostess doesn't try to keep track of her guests' affairs?"

"One that does not meddle?"

"Alright," she said, "if you think I'm being meddlesome, I'll leave you alone to brood." She started to get up.

"No, stay," Ben pleaded. "I would appreciate your counsel."

"If you insist," she said with a smile. She sat back down next to him, folding her hands in her lap and sat erect, ready to listen intently.

After swearing his hostess to secrecy, Ben proceeded to confess the entire story of how he and Marianne had met in London so many years ago, how they had managed to carry on their clandestine affair for years, despite the watchful eye of Mrs. Davies. He confessed his long-standing love for her, but also told of his concerns about her melancholia.

"Is that the 'illness' that keeps her from dining out?" Madame Leray asked.

"I suppose so, although she also suffers from headaches. She wrote to me last year that she was undergoing some new form of treatment. I assumed that there might be restrictions on her diet. She is definitely more lean than I have ever seen her."

"Why don't you simply ask her about the nature of the treatments?"

"We haven't had much time to talk when we get together." Ben gave a sly smile.

Madame Leray blushed slightly. "Oh, I understand."

"But that is not really the explanation, either," he went on. "I am not sure that I want to know the full account of her treatments. Yesterday I could swear that I saw her near the quarters of Doctor Franz Mesmer."

Madame Leray looked slightly shocked. "The Doctor from Vienna?" she asked. "But he is all the rage of Paris, don't you know?" Her expression became more reflective. "Perhaps she is having a consultation. Many of my lady friends have. There is nothing sinister about consulting a physician—although from what I have heard, I will grant you that his techniques sound unorthodox."

"It has also occurred to me that they both arrived from Vienna at about the same time earlier this year."

"Most likely, a coincidence."

"I want to tell you about a dream I had." Ben relayed to her the dream that had first haunted him on the Reprisal in the Quiberon Bay. "I have thought about that dream many times since. I am convinced that it was Mesmer standing in the shadows. It was as if he was controlling her movements."

"So, you believe that the connection between your Marianne and this Mesmer is something more than the usual doctor-patient relationship?"

"Le Veillard thinks that they are having an affair."

"Louis thinks everyone is having an affair," she said.

Confiding in Marie-Thérèse made Ben feel slightly better but no less confused about the direction his relationship with Marianne was headed. They were moving apart as clearly as the Leray's. Perhaps it was natural, but it bothered Ben.

October 10th, 1778

PASSY

ALL SUMMER, Ben had anxiously awaited an invitation from Madame Helvétius after his chance encounter with her in the middle of the Seine. He had swum back to the spot of their meeting several times, but had never found her again—perhaps, he thought because she, like Madame Brillon, spent her summers in the country.

But on Sunday, October 3rd, the letter Ben had long awaited finally arrived. Written by Monsieur Turgot, it invited Ben to accompany Madame Helvétius to the home of Jean François de Saint-Lambert, the poet and philosopher, on the following Sunday, October 10th. Ben surmised that she had now returned to Auteuil. Maybe she believed her own house would be unsuitable for entertaining after the long vacancy of the summer; either that, or she wished to meet him on more neutral ground. Whichever was the case, Ben would be glad to finally make the formal acquaintance of his captivating neighbor. He quickly accepted Turgot's invitation, arranging to call for Madame Helvétius after dinner on the appointed day. He would borrow a coach from his host, and the ride into Paris would give him and Madame Helvétius time to get acquainted.

In order to prepare for the encounter, Ben enlisted the aid of Madame Leray. He had come to trust her appraisal of people, and she had previously divulged much about Madame Helvétius to him. The rest he would have to find out for himself.

Ben found her alone in the kitchen. "What can you tell me about Monsieur de Saint-Lambert?" he asked.

"Jean François de Saint-Lambert? Why?"

"I will be visiting him next Sunday."

"Well, I know he was a military man before he became a natural philosopher. I would expect that you are aware of his writings in the *Encyclopédie*."

"Yes, I am familiar with his published works. I was hoping that you knew something about his personal life, perhaps." Ben smiled.

"Oh, I see. You want the scandal," Madame Leray said with an arched eyebrow. She reveled in her role as a gossip. "Our dear Monsieur de Saint-Lambert is, of course, most notorious for having led to the death of Voltaire's Émilie."

Ben took a step back. He looked shocked but said nothing.

"No, no!" Madame Leray exclaimed. Collecting herself, she continued on calmly in a hushed voice. "Not a direct role in her death, you understand. She died of an embolism a few days after bearing him a child. They were lovers."

"Voltaire and Émilie?" Ben looked a bit lost.

"Yes, but also Émilie and your Saint-Lambert."

"But wasn't she married to the Marquis du Chastellet?"

"Yes, of course. But they had arranged to live separate lives after she bore him three children. She is my personal heroine—if you know what I mean."

"I think I do," Ben replied. He remained somewhat confused, however. "But, you lost me with Voltaire and Saint-Lambert."

"I will try to explain. About thirty years ago, Voltaire arrived in Lunéville, quite a fashionable town, with his lover Émilie, who was, by then, already an accomplished mathematician. Apparently, while at Lunéville, Émilie became infatuated with the dashing young military man and courtier, Monsieur Saint-Lambert. Despite the fact that she was already into her forties, they conceived a child together. Unfortunately, she met her death from complications after giving birth."

"What did Voltaire think of this situation—let alone her husband?"

"I have no idea what the Marquis thought. He and his wife were living quite separate lives by that time. But Voltaire had not a jealous bone in his body. While in his writings, he mourned her loss—as we all did—he knew that the affair with Saint-Lambert had finally made his Émilie happy. As you may know, she finished translating Newton's *Principia Mathematica* into French while pregnant with the child that would ultimately cause her death."

"She had a remarkable scientific mind," Ben said solemnly. "I am aware of her brilliant observations on fire and heat. Also, she significantly extended Newton's theories on the energies of moving objects. Her passing was a loss to all humanity."

"As was the passing of Voltaire last May." Madame Leray looked at him appraisingly. "But Ben," she said, "I do not think this is really what you want to know. And I'm sorry to say that I know little about the relationship between Saint-Lambert and Helvétius—either the late Monsieur, or your recent—shall we say 'obsession'—the '*Notre-Dame d'Auteuil*'."

Ben sensed a twinge of jealousy in her voice. "Why do you call her that?" he asked.

"Oh, I don't mean to be malicious or cruel, *mon cher*, it's just that she carries herself with such a detached air."

"But is she not descended from the royal family of Empress Maria Theresa of Austria?"

"Yes, she is a distant cousin to Marie Antoinette, I believe."

"Well, I would think that would allow one some social distinction."

"Granted, but then her husband had the decency to die young, leaving her everything. And now she lives a life of leisure in a house with three men, free to follow her intellectual pursuits in her weekly salons."

"Now I really do sense some jealousy in your voice, my dear ... but three? I had heard only of Abbé de la Roche and Abbé Morellet, and they are men of the cloth."

"But she has recently taken in a strapping young medical student named Cabanis, I am told." Madame Leray let the thinly veiled accusation hang in the air for a moment. "*Mon Dieu*, I despise that woman," she said. She slammed her fist on the kitchen table for effect.

"Don't be spiteful," Ben admonished. "You have everything that you need, and then some."

He put his arm around her and gave her a friendly hug. He decided that he had better change the subject. "What can you tell me about Voltaire and Helvétius?"

Madame Leray softened under Ben's touch. "Him or her?" she asked. "I was thinking of the late Monsieur, but is there something I should know about her, too?"

"No, nothing that I know of."

Ben breathed a small sigh of relief that did not go unnoticed by his hostess.

"You know that Monsieur Helvétius and Voltaire were rivals in philosophical circles. I doubt that Madame Helvétius, considering how devoted she was to her late husband, would have anything to do with Voltaire."

"I seem to recall Voltaire saying, 'I detest what you write, but I would give my life to make it possible for you to continue to write.' Wasn't that quote in reference to Monsieur Helvétius?" Ben asked.

"Yes, I believe so. But Monsieur Helvétius wasn't the only one in the household who felt the lash of Voltaire's sharp tongue. He often referred to Abbé Morellet as '*Abbé Mords-les*' because of his often-acerbic disposition."

When Ben looked puzzled, Madame Leray added, "*Abbé Mords-les*— roughly translated into English—is Father-bite-them."

Ben laughed. "I've known Abbé Morellet since he visited England many years ago. I have never known him to be overly bitter, but I agree that his wit can be savage." Ben wanted still more information. "But tell me about this medical student. What was his name?"

"Cabanis, Pierre Jean Georges Cabanis," Madame Leray said. She wore a dreamy look that Ben had not seen since her affair with John Paul Jones.

"Please, my dear, take hold of yourself," Ben chided. "Where did this Monsieur Cabanis come from?"

"Apparently your Madame Helvétius took him in, at the request of his patron, Turgot. He hails from the south, Corrèze, I believe, where his parents live. He recently started medical school in Paris at the age of twenty-one. Prior to that, he traveled around the continent and spent some time as a tutor in Poland. He also writes poetry. I understand that he submitted a new translation of Homer's *Odyssey* for a recent competition but did not win the prize. A truly remarkable young man by all accounts."

"It never ceases to amaze me how much information you know about people you have never even met," Ben remarked admiringly.

She pouted. "But I would surely *like* to meet the young man."

"You are incorrigible," Ben said. He laughed. "Let's have some tea."

Madame Leray put the kettle on the stove and stoked up the fire.

"What can you tell me about Turgot and Madame Helvétius?" Ben asked. He was not satisfied that he had learned all that he needed to know about the household at Auteuil.

"You think that *I'm* incorrigible? I know that Turgot has proposed marriage to her several times, dating back even to before she married Monsieur Helvétius, and that she has rebuffed each attempt."

"Why do you think she has refused him?"

"I don't know for certain, but I can tell you I don't believe it's out of respect for her dead husband."

"Why not?"

"Look at it this way, Ben. Here is a nearly sixty-year-old woman who has managed to remain healthy and beautiful."

Ben recalled her glistening lithe body in the Seine. "Truly," Ben responded with a smile.

"Now, you simmer down," Madame Leray teased. She went on. "So her rich husband passes away while she is still young, leaving her financially well-off. She marries her two daughters to men of their own choosing, each one given a château as a dowry—where she, the vibrant *grand-mère,* can visit and be doted upon. When back home at Auteuil, she continues her late husband's fashionable and popular salon, collecting ideas from the best minds in Europe. And now to top it all off, she lives with three men. If I were in her situation, I wouldn't remarry either."

Ben wore a resigned look. "When you put it that way . . ." he sighed.

Though a brisk autumn walk from Passy to Auteuil would probably have taken Ben no more than twenty minutes, for this trip, Ben needed to borrow the coach of Jacques Leray to pick up Madame Helvétius and escort her to the poetry reading at the house of Monsieur de Saint-Lambert in Paris. They would meet Turgot there. "Much to his chagrin," Ben mused as he relaxed in a warm, fragrant bath. "I am sure he would rather ride in the coach to separate us. He has managed to keep the lady and me apart all summer. But today, in spite of him, we shall meet, nonetheless."

From Auteuil, the coach ride back through Passy and on to the home of Saint-Lambert would last about an hour, Ben estimated, with perhaps another hour for the return trip. "Too short a time to fully get to know her, but at least I will have her undivided attention," he thought.

He dressed in his finest worsted wool pants and a textured silk shirt. The fabrics felt smooth against his skin. He attached a gold pocket watch by its chain to his contrasting vest. It was the only jewelry he thought he should wear today.

Itself a potential conversation piece, the watch had been beautifully crafted by Julien Le Roy, the father of Jean-Baptiste Le Roy, Ben's good friend and director of the Royal Scientific Laboratory. The elder Le Roy had been appointed royal clockmaker to King Louis XV in 1739. Unfortunately, the unrivaled horologist had died in 1759. Ben was glad that he had been able to acquire one of Le Roy's fine watches prior to his death.

Ben checked the time against his dressing room clock—perfect. He snapped the cover closed. He tucked it into his vest pocket. He grabbed his deep red fur-trimmed cloak as he whisked out the front door. The elegant coach sparkled in the early afternoon light flooding the courtyard outside the Hôtel de Valentinois. The coachman attentively hopped down from his perch on the box seat, opened the coach door, and slightly bowed as Ben stepped up into the comfortable cabin. Ben settled back in the plush leather seat with a sigh.

When the coach came to a stop a few minutes later in Auteuil, Ben thought that the coachman must have erred. In fact, if he hadn't known better, Ben would have guessed that he had arrived in front of an English country home instead of a French château. Out his coach window, he saw a profusion of flowers growing over and through a low fence around the yard. The garden was certainly not in the French style. There were no tightly manicured hedges, no geometric patterns, no small delicate flowers arranged according to color. Instead, there was an explosion of unkempt, unruly, and untamed flowers and plants with barely enough organization to differentiate the garden from the wild. Ben could see only the garden path as he entered through the gate. The house was nowhere in sight.

The gate closed behind him with a smack. The delicious scent of hibiscus tantalized him. Several cats ran up to his feet, greeting him with plaintive meows. Ben chuckled when he noticed that each was dressed in a brightly colored velvet and satin jacket. Each cat wore a different color scheme with a contrasting ruffled collar. The outfits were obviously customized to the size and coloring of the wearer. The cats followed him in procession, like an entourage for a king. Their bells lightly tinkled as they walked.

Within a few minutes, the house came into view. Again, it was not at all what Ben had imagined. A low, unassuming two-story façade of white stucco punctuated by blue shutters gave it the appearance of a country cottage. Ben checked his pocket watch. It read a minute before two o'clock. "I will be right on time," he thought as he walked up to the door.

As Ben rang the doorbell, the cats scattered. One ran inside through the doorway, which was partly open. No one answered his ring. "This is odd," Ben thought. It was certainly a different reception than one would get at the Hôtel de Valentinois. There, a doorman would have been waiting to take his wrap and announce his arrival. Ben knocked on the heavy door. Curiously, no response came. He decided to go in.

"*Bonjour,*" he called out as he entered. It was slightly cooler inside the house. Ben stood in the foyer for a moment to allow his eyes to adjust to the diminished light. It was still and quiet. He heard the wall clock ticking. The clock chimed twice. Ben was just beginning to wonder if anyone was at home when he heard voices from down the hall. He moved slowly toward the back of the house to investigate, past a large parlor with a huge stone fireplace and comfortable chairs arranged in a semicircle. It appeared to be a good place to hold a salon. He peered in briefly to observe that the room was empty. He passed a dining room that looked as if it could easily accommodate twenty for a meal. Along his way, he noted that the interior decoration of the house was considerably less formal than others around Paris that he had visited. The décor gave Ben a peaceful, relaxed feeling that he suddenly realized he'd missed since leaving Philadelphia. It felt like he was at home.

As Ben entered the kitchen, a pungent smell hung in the air, like sautéed onions and smoked bacon. Two men sat at a large farm table in the middle of the room. Both wore what appeared to be bedclothes. There were dirty pots left over from the recent meal everywhere. A large orange tabby cat in courtier's attire sat on top of the table. The cat begged for a morsel from the man Ben recognized by his bushy eyebrows. It was the abbé whom Ben had met swimming with Madame Helvétius in the middle of the Seine.

"Giacomo ... up ... up!" the clergyman commanded, attempting to entice the courtier cat to stand on its hind legs with what appeared to be a piece of bacon that he held just out of reach.

The other man was a lanky young fellow who Ben concluded must be the medical student Cabanis. He did not see Abbé Morellet—or Madame Helvétius, for that matter. As soon as Ben entered the kitchen, the Abbé jumped up, dropping the piece of meat. Giacomo pounced on it.

"Dr. Franklin," the Abbé exclaimed. "We were not expecting you."

"I can see that," Ben observed wryly. "I believe that I am supposed to collect Madame Helvétius at two o'clock for a poetry reading in Paris." He pulled out his watch, which now showed three minutes past the appointed hour.

"Hopefully, she remembered that you were coming today," the Abbé said apologetically. "She is upstairs. I will let her know that you have arrived."

"Thank you. Monsieur Turgot is expecting us to meet him in Paris around three at the home of Monsieur de Saint-Lambert," Ben explained.

The Abbé hustled toward the door. "Pierre, introduce yourself to Doctor Franklin while I fetch Minette, would you?" he called back.

The gangly young man looked more than slightly intimidated by their illustrious unexpected guest. "I am Pierre Cabanis, Doctor Franklin," he said. He stood tentatively to shake hands with the famous man standing in his kitchen.

Ben embraced his waiting hand warmly. "Please call me Ben. I understand that you have recently begun medical school. Medicine is an important profession."

"I hope that I will have something to contribute," Cabanis said with sincere humility. He seemed to relax a little.

"I am sure that you will," Ben replied. "May I ask, where is my friend Abbé Morellet?"

"Oh, he is around somewhere ... most likely in the library."

Ben hadn't noticed a library on his brief unguided tour of the house. "I would like to see him before we have to leave, if we have the time."

"I am sure that you will have time," Cabanis replied. He bore a smile that made Ben think that he might know something Ben did not. Ben was about to inquire as to what he meant when the bushy-eyebrowed Abbé reappeared.

"She knows that you are here—and she knew of the appointment this afternoon. Apparently, she simply forgot to let any of us know," he said with a look of consternation. "I believe that you have by now acquainted yourself with our most recent houseguest, the aspiring young doctor Cabanis, but I don't know that you and I have ever been properly introduced." He stuck out his hand, which Ben shook enthusiastically. "I am Martin de la Roche, Doctor Franklin."

"Please call me Ben. It is good to meet you where my feet can touch bottom."

"Yes, and at least one of us is properly clothed this time," the Abbé said.

Ben laughed. "Tell me, Martin, how did you come to live here in Auteuil with Madame Helvétius?"

"I was a close colleague of Monsieur Helvétius. When he passed away in '71, Minette asked if I would assist her with the cataloging of his works. I have been here at Auteuil ever since. His works are voluminous. He was a prolific writer. I believe one of the greatest minds of our age."

"I would certainly agree."

"Last year, we published his *Treatise on Man: His Intellectual Faculties and His Education*. Have you read it?"

"Not yet. I have been kept busy organizing a war of independence for America," Ben said.

"Understood," the Abbé continued. "Anyway, it didn't create the furor that his *De l'Esprit,* published during his lifetime, caused. Perhaps because he was already dead, or perhaps because it was seen as less controversial—whatever the reason, it seems to have been more widely accepted."

"I understand that the public outcry over the first book caused him to retire from public life, giving up his lucrative post as a farmer-general, collecting taxes for Louis XV."

"You know, I believe that he was really already prepared to retire at that point. He had made his fortune."

"Yes, and as it turned out, not so much time left on this earth."

"He spent the last several years of his life traveling with Minette and living a peaceful existence at his château near Rémalard."

"A fortunate man."

"I would say so, in many ways."

Ben checked his watch. It was now a quarter past the hour. Abbé de la Roche noticed Ben's impatience.

"Do you think that she will be long?" Ben asked, somehow already knowing the answer.

"What if I find Abbé Morellet for you?" de la Roche offered. He directed

Ben out of the kitchen. "Young *doctor* Cabanis has some dishes to do, and I should get dressed. Minette has many wonderful qualities, but punctuality is not among them—especially when she is preparing herself to go out. However, the most wondrous aspect of all is that, whenever you arrive at your destination with her, everyone will be happy to greet you despite the hour. Might I be so bold as to suggest that you keep your watch in your pocket for the remainder of the afternoon?"

"Of course, you are right," Ben said with resignation. It had been a long while since he had waited on a woman dressing for an event. Ben had forgotten the ritual.

Martin led Ben to the library, where he found Abbé Morellet deep in contemplation of a huge tome. He knocked on the open door. When the Abbé recognized Ben, he practically leapt up to greet him.

"Ben, Ben Franklin, what are you doing here? I had no idea that you were coming."

"André, my old friend, apparently, my visit was unintentionally kept a secret by your ladyship. She and I have been invited to a poetry reading in Paris. I have come to collect her and escort her there."

"How remarkable," the Abbé said. He directed his attention back to the ancient book on his desk. "As usual, Ben, you have impeccable timing. I could use some help with this text. It is written in some form of old English that is confusing to me."

"Do you think that we will have time?"

"Oh yes, we will have time," the Abbé said. Once again, Ben sensed that the members of the Helvétius household were in on some kind of secret joke.

"So, what are you studying so intently?"

"It's an old book by Paracelsus I found in Helvétius's collection."

Ben eyed the dusty, moth-eaten tome. "Paracelsus wrote over 200 years ago. From the looks of your book, it is a first edition," he said, meaning it as a joke.

The Abbé missed the humor entirely. "Yes, I think that it might be," he replied quite in earnest. He carefully turned the yellowed pages.

"And why, pray tell, are you spending your time studying Paracelsus? I would think that you might leave that to young Cabanis, for his training on the history of medicine."

"I am interested in determining if there is any historical, scientific background to *animale magnétisme*."

"Not you too," Ben moaned. "Has everyone in Paris gone Mesmer crazy?"

"I am certainly not 'Mesmer crazy,' as you say. In fact, I'm looking for some ammunition to refute an assertion that I heard expressed by your friend Le Roy."

"And what was that?"

"Le Roy seems convinced that Mesmer may have discovered a new physical fluid emanating from the stars. I recall a similar concept having been described by Paracelsus, but in much more mystical terms. Something about a fluid or vapor emanating from the heavens affecting health. I believe that this may be the passage I am looking for." He pointed to a paragraph on the darkened page.

Ben adjusted his bifocals. The book looked like it might have been printed on Gutenberg's original press. The font was archaic, full of flourishes.

"Which passage has vexed you so?" Ben asked.

"This one," the Abbé said, pointing.

The vertue of the Spirit of Life is extended, or enlarged by the Stars, and all the Influences of the whole Heaven, by which the firmament is manifefted, and 'tis like a coeleftial, invifible Vapour, with which it is united, even as Cold & Heat are, when a temperature is conftituted and made from them: But if haply the Stars of the Members do at any time run crofs, corrupt, and caufe Fits, then alfo that member of the body is vanqifhed, and either ftops the Spirits of Life, or doth vitiate and corrupt it in the fame Place.

"Yes," Ben said, "the old English is troublesome to read. The letter 'f' can be an 'f' but it can also be an 's' or even an 'st'—you have to interpret it in context."

Ben finished roughly translating the passage of text into French for the Abbé.

Morellet looked perplexed. "What do you think it means?" he asked.

"I'm not entirely sure," Ben replied. "These old tomes contain many unsubstantiated theories put forth by perceptive men to explain their observations of natural occurrences in the world around them. Unfortunately, like many before and since him, Paracelsus offers no evidence for anything that he conjectures."

"I agree. We must have proof. Nonetheless, I can now debate Le Roy more effectively—thanks to your kind assistance."

"I am only too happy to oblige."

"How about a game of chess?" André asked. He put the book aside.

Ben was about to ask if they would have the time—but thought better of it.

He had just handily checkmated the Abbé Morellet when Martin rushed into the study. "Minette is coming downstairs," he said.

Ben resisted the impulse to take out his pocket watch and observe how late they would be for the reading. Instead, he smiled and simply said, "I must go now."

Light streamed in from the open doorway into the foyer at the bottom of the stairs. A menagerie of cats gathered, along with Ben and Martin, as if they all were awaiting a royal audience. The very first thing Ben noticed about Madame Helvétius was her hair, a slightly unruly thick silvery-gray mane of it, beautifully natural and unpowdered, that flowed over her bare shoulders. Large curls bounced jauntily with each step she took. She looked absolutely stunning as she descended. She wore a simple flowing white dress that was neither too formal, nor too casual. Bangles worn on both wrists jingled, echoing the bells of the courtier cats, who were becoming increasingly excited as their ladyship approached. Her whole appearance was one of pure casual grace. It occurred to Ben that, if he had not just waited what seemed like an eternity for her appearance, he would have assumed that she'd simply thrown on what she had available. On reconsideration, Ben recognized that creating the perfect picture he now enjoyed probably took more preparation than he'd initially thought.

"I hope that I have not kept you waiting," she said. Her smile was alluring and playful.

"Of course not, Minette," Ben replied. His next words instantly erased any feeling of inconvenience that he might have been harboring. "It is wonderful to see you. You look enticing."

"Thank you, and you too," she said. She looked him up and down.

Ben realized that she had just appraised him in a manner that might have made him slightly uncomfortable—had the look come from anyone else. But Minette could get away with it easily. As she descended the last stair, she walked briskly over to where he stood. She held out her hand. Ben kissed it. Her hand felt perfect in his. It was soft, warm, supple. She offered him the other hand to hold, as well. They looked into each other's eyes as if they had known each other forever. The courtier cats encircled them. The abbés, and everything else for that matter, disappeared. Ben was smitten, and he knew it instantly. After much too short a time, his enchantress broke the spell.

"Shall we go?" she asked softly.

Ben turned to face the door. Her arm fell so naturally into the space between his elbow and his wrist that she seemed made for him. The courtier cats escorted them out through the garden to the waiting coach. Ben almost hated to release her arm as the coachman assisted her up the stair, but the thought of sitting right beside her for the next hour fortified him.

Martin came running out of the house with her coat, handing it off to Ben just as he entered the coach. "Have a good time," he said. Ben noted a slightly forlorn tinge to his voice.

Minette fell back into the coach seat with a delicious laugh. She kicked off her dainty pumps, exposing her shapely legs from the knee down. Ben caught a tantalizing glimpse of her athletic calves previously hidden by the ruffles of her long dress. Ben took his seat beside her. She then threw her legs over into his lap as naturally as if they were two childhood sweethearts.

"Is that alright?" she asked. And then, as if she needed any further explanation for her action, she added, "I hate wearing shoes." She flashed a flirtatious pout.

Ben looked down at the two lovely feet now resting in his lap. He immediately perceived a stiffening in his groin. His breathing quickened. "You have marvelous feet," he said, slightly breathlessly.

She must have noticed his reaction. She said, "Oh, I shouldn't tease you, should I? What shall we talk about on our way to Monsieur Saint-Lambert's house?" She started to pull her legs away. Ben held them firm.

"No, it's fine—really." She left them there. "What is the poem that we will hear tonight?" Ben asked.

She looked piqued. "I believe that Jean François will be reading something from his *Les Saisons* that he published now almost a decade ago. *Mon Dieu,* I wish that man would come up with some new material," she exclaimed.

"So, you did not want to go to the poetry reading today?"

"Oh, please forgive me—of course, I do—with you. It seemed that this was the only way I could get Turgot to invite you. He is so jealous. He would only have us meet at a neutral site."

"Turgot, eh?" Ben had reckoned that he was the fellow responsible for the long delay in his seeing Minette again. "So, why then, did he allow me to pick you up and have you alone for a full hour each way?"

"It appears that when you suggested picking me up, he could not refuse the request of the eminent Doctor Franklin. He is too much of a lifelong courtier to offend—even if his wicked plan to come between us was foiled."

"But you could simply have invited me yourself. You did not have to wait for Turgot. Or we could have met in the middle of the Seine once again—that is neutral territory, is it not?" Ben said.

"I would love to swim with you again—and we will do so," she said. "But you must also understand my situation. I am a single woman in a man's world. As you probably have surmised, I do pretty much as I please and don't care what anyone thinks, but I continue to require the protection of the royal court to keep the property owned by my late husband. And though Turgot is no longer officially in any capacity in Versailles, he remains very well connected there. The last thing I need is to have some magistrate challenge my claim to the Helvétius properties. For this reason, I need Turgot."

"But didn't he also propose marriage to you?" Ben realized that she might consider this too personal a question. He quickly added, "If it is not too impertinent for me to ask, of course."

"*Mon cher*, I want you to know everything about me," she replied. "Of course, he proposed—many times, so many times. He proposed before I chose to marry Claude, and he proposed after I became a widow. I think that he has proposed on almost every occasion that we have met since." She giggled. "Perhaps he is even planning to propose again tonight." She suddenly looked pensive. "But I always refuse—and I always will refuse."

"Why is that, if I may ask?"

"The official response to your question is 'out of respect for my dearly departed husband' but between you and me . . ." She almost whispered, as she pulled closer. "I don't really believe that a woman *needs* to be married. Let's face it, marriage is about children, it's about property. Marriage is a legal, social, and religious bond between two people. Well, I've had my children—my daughters are grown and have families of their own. I enjoy the protection of Monsieur Turgot without having to give over all my property to him as my husband. What does he need more money or land for anyway? He has plenty of his own. And finally, as you may know, I spent a good part of my young life locked away in a monastery, so I definitely don't need any more religion. My aunt, Françoise de Graffigny, saved me from that place. Do you know that her husband, a respected chamberlain in the house of the duke of Lorraine, drank heavily and beat her unmercifully? She finally extricated herself from that abusive marriage and moved to Paris. Auntie Françoise told me some men believe that marriage means their wives belong to them, like their horses or their cows. Women are treated like chattel. Some men feel that marriage gives them the right to treat their wives as they wish—not my dear husband, mind you. But why would any woman expose herself to that risk unless she absolutely must for childbearing, property, or religious reasons?

"There," she took a breath. "That is why I refuse."

Ben looked at her adoringly. "I certainly agree with what you say and respect you for your decision to remain single—but what about love?"

"Oh, Ben," she cooed. Minette looked at him with such tenderness that he thought he would melt. "I'm not saying that people shouldn't marry for love—my own two daughters both married wonderful men who they love dearly. I believe them both to be blissfully happy. I'm saying that love and marriage don't necessarily go together. I'm saying that one doesn't necessarily need to marry to be in a loving relationship ... and that two people certainly don't need to be married to enjoy the pleasures of love." She pressed her bare feet down lightly on his lap.

They rode on in nervous silence. Ben knew what he wanted and was relatively sure that Minette wanted the same thing. But he was also a bit apprehensive. It would be only a few more minutes until they arrived at the home of Monsieur Saint-Lambert. How would it appear if the coach door opened on the two distinguished guests rolling on the floor?

The coach arrived in front of the home of Monsieur de Saint-Lambert much later than the appointed hour. Minette and Ben were still flirting like a couple of school kids. Ben could see from his side of the coach that Turgot stood outside the townhouse, waiting nervously, tapping his foot. He was looking at his pocket watch as the coach pulled up. He appeared to be cold as if he had been standing outside for some time. Ben held up Minette's coat for her as she slipped her arms into the sleeves. She put her shoes back on. She tried to be more serious. Ben lustily watched as she bent over to fasten the delicate straps around her ankles. The coachman jumped down and opened the door.

Minette took his hand and alighted. Turgot practically bounded over to escort her. Ben descended as well. Turgot greeted them both warmly, although he was clearly chilly from exposure to the brisk fall air. They entered the home to find a party already well in progress. However, it was clear that the poetry reading had been delayed, awaiting the guests of honor. A tall, distinguished-looking gentleman who Ben could only assume was Saint-Lambert was the first to greet them. He took Minette's hand with a deep bow, lightly kissing the back.

"My dear Minette, so wonderful of you to come," he said. He spoke in such a rich baritone voice that Ben instantly knew why women swooned over him. He turned his attention to Ben. "And Doctor Franklin, I am so glad that you could attend. You are in for a real treat. Wouldn't you say so, Minette?"

She shot a quick glance at Ben and almost burst out laughing, but somehow maintained her composure.

"Oh yes, *mon cher*," she replied. "A real treat."

"Please call me Ben," Ben replied as flatly as he could. He squeezed Minette's hand for support. The glaring conceit of this aging, elegant, honey-voiced courtier started to sink in. "Perhaps he writes good poetry," Ben thought, allowing his host the benefit of the doubt. However, he glanced over at Minette, who was shaking her head in the negative—as if she had just read his mind.

They entered the house packed with aristocrats and courtiers. The ladies all wore the latest fashions of the day. Their hairstyles seemed designed to be more extravagant than whatever had come before. Ben wondered where it would all end, if someday some unfortunate woman would topple over from the weight of her hairdo. He whispered that supposition to Minette, who slapped him playfully—but hard.

"I'm trying to be serious now," she whispered back to him. She continued to greet Viscount this or that.

"Alright, I shall behave," Ben said.

Minette cast him a mischievous look. "Only just for now."

As Ben looked around the crowded room, he recognized many of the powdered heads of Paris. He seriously doubted that Saint-Lambert attracted this crowd to his regular poetry readings. They were here to see Ben—and Minette. When placed in this position before, mixing with a throng of well-wishers, each of whom wanted his undivided attention, Ben developed a strategy. He had taken the tack of listening intently—but only for a limited time with each one so as not to offend anyone. Because Ben was physically taller than most of the French, he could survey the crowd over their heads. When he felt that his time listening to one aristocrat drone on had expired, he would make eye contact with another, excuse himself—and move on. Minette apparently had a different strategy. She talked only with a small group who gathered around her tightly—like a glove. From what Ben observed, Minette threw her entire spirit into the conversation. He could hear her laugh across the room, her beautiful head thrown back with delight. She pressed a finger to her lips as she listened intently. She touched people. She put her arm on someone's shoulder. She hugged a woman. She frowned when someone must have informed her of bad news. She wasn't working the room as he was, she was living it.

A bell rang, informing the guests that the poetry reading was about to begin. The guests slowly took their seats in the parlor. Ben sat on one side of Minette, Turgot on the other. The lights dimmed. A hush came over the crowd. Saint-Lambert had changed from the fashions of a courtier into a green velvet robe. He stood behind a table that appeared to have been chosen because it resembled an altar. He lifted up his arms. The crowd went silent. He began to speak.

"*The Seasons*, by Jean François de Saint-Lambert," he intoned in that deep baritone voice. He was quiet for a moment—pausing for dramatic effect.

Summer—the Farmer.
O thou whose flowering art most needed,
Friend's innocence, honest farmer,

It is easy and gentle, your happiness!
Ah! If only he did not fear an unfair power
A junior tyrant or greedy financer,
If the law protects him, he is happy without charge
With nature, who has sent all her benefits.

Ben looked at Minette, sniggering softly. She started to giggle. Saint-Lambert continued, completely oblivious.

He may love what he loves tomorrow today
And the peace of his heart is never bored.
You make it happy, fresh and pure delight,
Committed to the hymen, the knots of nature;
Wife chooses shared work,
From a friend of his heart it softens the pain.

Ben looked at her again. She stifled a chortle. She got up and headed for the door. Ben followed. Turgot looked at them, aghast. Saint-Lambert, if he noticed at all, certainly was not inclined to stop reading his poem. All of the guests remained glued to their seats, even Turgot. Ben and Minette ran from the parlor through the unfamiliar house, laughing uncontrollably. The house staff leapt out of their way. Ben spied a door leading out to the garden. He pulled Minette in that direction.

As soon as they entered the garden, all was calm. Ben sat her down on a secluded bench. A portico of hanging vines sheltered their retreat. While chilly out, it was warm and cozy in their hideaway. A fountain trickled somewhere nearby.

"Was it simply my poor translation, or is that the worst poem ever written?" Ben asked breathlessly. They snuggled up on the cool stone surface of the bench.

"It is truly the worst. Didn't I warn you? But I thought that I was going to be able to keep my composure until you looked at me."

"Oh well, now what will the aristocrats think?"

"I'll tell them that I got sick and that you assisted me."

"How long does that poem take to read?"

"Probably about twenty minutes, although it seems like an eternity."

"And we lasted, what about the first minute only?"

Minette looked at him. "What is going through your mind, Ben?" she asked.

"Well, by my calculation, we currently have roughly nineteen minutes for you to be ill and for me to be taking care of you. I can do a lot to cure you in that time."

"Alright, put your hand here then," she said. Minette took his hand and directed it underneath her dress, between her legs. Ben noted instantly, much to his delight, that she wore no undergarments. His fingers gently explored the moist, warm area. His fingers became wet. She moaned softly. She opened up his shirt and put her hands on his chest. He pulled her down with him behind the bench. The soft ground cover made a perfect bed.

They walked back through the house, hands locked together. "I wanted to scream," she said.

"Me too."

"I can't wait to get you in my bed where you can make all the noise you want."

"Won't the abbés' mind?"

She laughed. "I doubt it," she said.

Ben plucked a leaf out of her hair affectionately, marveling at how so many men revolved around her.

The sound of polite clapping came from the parlor. Ben and Minette rejoined the party just as the poetry reading was ending. The crowd was standing, starting to mill about. Ben and Minette slipped in unnoticed by everyone except Turgot. He must have been on the lookout for the two fugitives,

Ben thought. Minette immediately went over to him. Ben couldn't hear what she said, but he surmised she was telling him that she had become ill. Turgot looked concerned. She reassured him that she was better now. He seemed satisfied.

Saint-Lambert cornered Ben. "What did you think of my poem?" he asked.

It seemed completely incongruous to Ben that the dashing young military officer Madame Leray had described as winning the heart of Émilie, would have become transformed over time into this pompous conceited old windbag.

"*Magnifique*," Ben said.

"What was your favorite part?"

"Oh, there were so many," he replied, scrambling.

But Saint-Lambert was not letting him off the hook so easily.

"Yes," the poet replied conceitedly, "but which part did you enjoy the best?"

Before he could respond, Minette appeared, as if by magic, at his side.

"Ben, didn't you tell me that the deer hunting scene particularly moved you?" she said.

"Yes, of course. I think that was certainly my favorite part of all."

"Ah yes, the deer hunting moves everyone," Saint-Lambert said smugly. He seemed satisfied and moved off to collect the congratulations of some others nearby.

As soon as Saint-Lambert was out of earshot, Ben whispered to Minette, "You saved me."

"Thank you for curing me," she cooed.

"My pleasure. That was only a first consultation, I hope."

"Me too," she replied. She gave his hand a squeeze.

November 28th, 1778

LOGE DES NEUF SŒURS, PARIS

AS BEN ENTERED the Masonic Lodge of the Nine Sisters, he was almost bowled over by apprentices dashing around carrying every form of decoration for the ceremony. Golden compasses, swords, aprons, and amulets came out of their storage bins. These would be placed prominently to honor a great man tonight. Ben walked briskly across the expansive carpet of black and white squares toward the kitchen, seeking a glass of Madeira. He patted his inside coat pocket to reassure himself that he had not forgotten his notes for the eulogy he would deliver this evening. Under his left arm, he carried a satchel containing his black trousers and shirt, leather apron, and cap. Ben entered the kitchen to find John Paul Jones and another man he recognized as Antoine Court de Gébelin sitting at a huge wooden table. De Gébelin was a gaunt, sickly appearing fellow with a complexion the color of gray clay. Both men were already dressed completely in black for the occasion. Jones wore his naval cap, but De Gébelin sported a dark red fez embroidered with the traditional compass and square motif. In front of the two men lay an array of Tarot cards.

"You possess many *batons*, my friend, which foretell success, advantage, and fortune," de Gébelin was expounding as Ben approached. The young naval officer appeared to be enthralled.

"Superstitious nonsense," Ben said.

John Paul jumped up as if Ben had caught him with his pants down once again.

"Hello, Ben," he said sheepishly.

"Brother Jones, you should know better than to believe in such mystical fabrications," Ben admonished.

"I resent that, Brother Franklin," de Gébelin said. A pained look came over his face. "I have gone to great lengths to document the ancient Egyptian knowledge locked in these cards."

"Excuse me, Brother de Gébelin," Ben said. He was only slightly apologetic. "I do not mean to impugn your character or your work, but I am unconvinced of the scientific basis of these cards—especially any ability you might claim for them to foresee the future." Ben walked over to the cupboard, withdrew a crystal snifter, and poured a good measure of Madeira from the decanter on the table. The vessel was already more than half empty. "However, if you two drink any more of this, I can foretell your future," Ben said. He put his fingers to his forehead and closed his eyes. "I predict that you will be retching up your guts before supper."

The three men had a brief laugh. De Gébelin began coughing at the end of it and spit into a cup. Ben bid them *adieu*, retreating to work on his speech. Despite the frenetic activity in the rest of the Lodge, he found the study to be empty and quiet. Many other members were arriving early, but they were either put to work decorating or otherwise occupied. Ben sat down in a large comfortable chair near the fireplace. He took the notes from his pocket, adjusted his bifocals, and began reading.

Ben had penned the words several months before, more to satisfy himself than because he believed he would deliver them as an organized eulogy after the death of Voltaire. He had begun with one of his favorite quotes from the man himself:

Satire lies about literary men while they live, and eulogy lies about them when they die.

Ben resolved that he would not tell any lies about the great man today—if possible. Yet he knew that there would be plenty of hyperbole among the other speakers at the Lodge. Other than the King and clergy, who despised him, most Parisians had held the aged philosopher in the highest esteem for his fierce defense of social justice, his biting wit, and his irreverence. This admiration transcended his twenty-eight-year forced exile to the country town of Ferney near the Swiss border.

Voltaire had finally returned to Paris only this past February to attend the premiere of his play *Irene* at the *Comédie Française*. Despite his attempt to appear incognito so as not to incur the wrath of the King, Voltaire was quickly recognized, to thunderous applause. And King Louis XVI lacked his grandfather's resolve. It was even rumored that Marie Antoinette herself had taken a liking to Voltaire's comedic writing, going so far as to request a short *divertissement*. Voltaire opined that no one in Paris had the heart to throw an octogenarian out of the city, even a revolutionary one.

Whatever the reason for his reprieve, Voltaire found himself once again to be the toast of every fashionable salon in town. Ben had assisted with his induction into the Masonic Lodge early in April. The two men had sat in this very room discussing topics ranging from religion to freedom, to their love of the printed word. While both deists, Voltaire was clearly more antagonistic to the Catholic Church than Ben. Yet, they agreed that all people should follow altruistic principles. They also agreed that all men should be free to enjoy life, liberty and the pursuit of happiness. This made Voltaire an enemy of the *ancien regime* but endeared him to Franklin. They'd become instant friends.

But Voltaire was not well, and he succumbed to pneumonia in May. It was reported that he had been approached on his deathbed by a local priest and asked to forswear Satan. His last words reportedly were, 'This is no time to make new enemies.' The Catholic Church quickly denied him a proper burial, but Voltaire's close friends had anticipated their move and had him buried privately. That left only the many public occasions, such as the one on this day, to eulogize him.

As Ben sat sipping his Madeira, he thought back to his last meeting with the great man at the Academy of Science in late April—only weeks before his death. The old philosopher appeared increasingly frail to Ben. Lines etched his gaunt face. He walked slowly and was noticeably stooped. Though only a decade younger, Ben was in much better physical shape. They greeted each other warmly and shook hands. Someone in the crowd cried out, asking for a 'proper French greeting'—meaning a hug and kiss on both cheeks. The two great men acquiesced, and a roar went up from the two hundred Academy members in attendance. Ben recalled that not until they hugged had he fully appreciated the emaciated state of his colleague. Voltaire's breathing caused a rattle in his chest that gave Ben pause. Ben recalled thinking that the old heretic wouldn't be long for this earth.

As Ben penned a few more lines on the paper from his pocket, John Paul Jones entered the study. The band was starting to tune up some musical instruments in the hall. "How is the eulogy coming along?" Jones asked.

"I believe I will have to improvise," Ben said. He frowned at the jumble of random thoughts he had managed to scribble on the paper in his hand.

"I'm sure that you will impress us all with your eloquence."

"Did you tire of having your fortune told?" Ben asked.

"I didn't find out anything that I didn't already know ... if that's what you mean. Why do you not believe in the Tarot?"

"I am willing to believe as soon as I'm shown proof that the predictions are any more accurate than simple chance alone. I'm sure you realize that in our lives, many good and bad things will happen," Ben said.

"Of course."

"Well, I assert that if someone tells you that something good will happen to you—you will capture many prizes, for example—and the event subsequently happens, then you may well feel that the prediction has come true. But I believe that you will probably forget and hence discount the predictions that don't come true—which, I postulate, are equally as likely as those that do. You simply give more credence to the predictions that seem to come true, making them stick in your memory."

"I understand ... I think," John Paul said, but he appeared uncertain.

"Furthermore, any good fortune teller will read subtle clues from his subject. If de Gébelin draws a card for you that could be interpreted as associated with naval success on the one hand or matrimonial success on the other, which interpretation do you think he will offer?"

Jones cringed. "Not matrimonial, I certainly hope."

"Do you see what I mean, then?"

"Yes, but still, I enjoy having my cards read."

"Then, my advice to you is simply to enjoy it for the entertainment, but put no stock in the predictions, my friend."

The door to the study swung open again. Ben recognized two of his fellow freemasons, Jean Bailly and the Marquis de Condorcet, engaged in a heated discussion as they entered. Bailly, an accomplished astronomer, was most famous for describing the orbit of the comet discovered in the previous century by the Englishman Edmund Halley. Condorcet, unarguably the finest mathematician in France, seemed to be badgering the older Bailly.

"What do you mean 'no astronomical basis for the fluid'?" Ben overheard Condorcet say. Bailly didn't get a chance to answer.

"Good afternoon, Brother Franklin," they said upon seeing Ben.

"What were you two arguing about?" Ben asked.

The pair of scientists looked at each other like two Catholic schoolboys caught debating whether God exists.

"We weren't arguing," Bailly offered sheepishly. "Merely having a discussion."

"Your 'discussion' sounded interesting. May I inquire as to your topic?"

"*Magnétisme animale*," Condorcet replied.

"And what of it?" Ben asked. He rose from his chair to stand with the two scientists and John Paul Jones.

"Mesmer's medical dissertation was entitled '*Dissertatio Physico-Medica de Planetarum Influxu*'," Condorcet explained.

John Paul Jones looked lost as the words rolled across the room. "Excuse me?"

"I apologize for the Latin," Condorcet said. "'*A Dissertation on Physical Healing by the Influence of the Planets*.' I was just asking our esteemed astronomer if he agreed with Mesmer on these planetary forces as the source of his fluid."

Ben looked toward Bailly. "And?"

"First, let me say that Mesmer's dissertation is not even an original work," Bailly said. "I believe it was largely copied from a book by Richard Mead, personal physician to Sir Isaac Newton."

"An Englishman influenced our Viennese wizard now dazzling the French?" Ben said. He laughed, but no one else seemed to get the joke.

"Even before Mead, there were other physicians who noted the relationship between planetary bodies and human conditions," Bailly continued. "The effects of the phases of the moon on cycles of female menstruation or the increased likelihood of seizures in epileptics have been well described by Bartholin and have been postulated since the time of Galen. We know that changes in the barometric pressure may lead to bodily aches and joint pain in susceptible arthritics and that some diseases are more likely to be associated with certain seasons, like pleurisy in the colder months. These may all be examples of the planetary influence on the human body."

"So, you think that Mesmer is correct?" Ben asked.

"No, not at all," Bailly responded. "While I grant that there may be certain planetary influences on the body, I do not believe that Mesmer—or anyone else for that matter—can control them."

John Paul Jones, who had been listening attentively, spoke up. "Brother Bailly, I am no scientist to be sure, but I must ask you a question."

"Yes?" the astronomer said. He peered over his glasses.

"Modern man now controls a great number of universal fluids that were previously untamed and wild. Our colleague, Brother Franklin here," Jones said, placing a hand on Ben's shoulder, "has made great strides in taming the electrical fluid. What leads you to believe that we will not learn to use more of Nature's energies, harnessing them to do Man's bidding?"

Before Bailly could answer, Ben interjected. "You will recall that I did not harness the electrical fluid alone. I stood on the shoulders of many before me who had described features of the electrical fluid. Many important scientists communicated with me, replicated my electrical experiments, and verified my findings. Not only that, even once the findings had been reproduced consistently, some remained unwilling to accept the veracity of the work. I know that you older gentlemen will recall that one of your own countrymen, the Abbé Nollet, God rest his soul, continued to expound his theory that there existed two electrical fluids—one positive and one negative—even after my theory had been proven that a single electrical fluid was present but with positive and negative states." Ben took a breath and a sip of Madeira.

"John Paul," Bailly said kindly. "I have no doubt that in the future, Man will learn to harness more of the forces of Nature. Wouldn't it be grand to learn how to control Gravity, the light of the Sun, or even Time—as we have Fire, Water, and soon Electricity? My point is this—the method of science requires that experiments be performed to prove a theory. It requires that the results be consistently reproducible."

John Paul Jones gave him a blank stare. "Sorry, you've lost me again, Professor."

Bailly smiled. "Each time the experiment is repeated, it should yield the same result. Different scientists, using the same technique, should be able to obtain the same findings. If they are not able to do so, then there is a problem," he said. "Mesmer has steadfastly refused to publish his theory in a form that can be tested. Further, he claims that only by paying him a large fee and submitting to his tutelage may one learn to harness this mysterious fluid."

"Even more mysterious," Condorcet interjected, "is that Mesmer's technique seems to work best on beautiful young women."

Jones perked up. "I should learn this technique," he said.

The three older men laughed.

"All you need to do is to don your naval officer's uniform, and you will have more than enough beautiful women, young and old, swooning over you," Ben chided.

Jones looked like he might respond—but thought better of it and remained silent.

The door opened to allow other freemasons into the study as the hour drew nearer to the start of the ceremony. Through the door to the hall, Ben caught a glimpse of Marie Antoinette's favorite composer, Niccolò Piccinni, standing in front of the orchestra's violin section, emphatically giving last-minute instructions to the players. Ben wondered if she would be attending tonight. He knew that the King would not be present, given his rancorous relationship with the honoree. But Royal disapproval had never before stopped the impetuous Queen.

One of those to enter the study was Cabanis, who made his way toward the illustrious foursome. As the young medical student approached, Ben had the opportunity to observe that he still seemed undernourished, but less so than the first time they'd met. It appeared that living in Auteuil was agreeing with him. Although Cabanis clearly had the intention of joining their group, several other members distracted him as he approached. Being only an apprentice, he was expected to serve the older freemasons. And so, along the way, Cabanis detoured to fetch a cognac for Brother Leland, and a glass of Bordeaux for Brother Montgolfier. He took his duties in stride, without any apparent disdain for the orders he received. He finally arrived at the group talking by the fireplace and addressed Ben first.

"Brother Franklin," Cabanis said. "May I refill your glass?"

"No, thank you, Pierre. I have already had just enough Madeira to allow me to deliver my eulogy with passion, but any more and I will blubber."

Ben went on. "May I introduce you to my distinguished colleagues? Professor Bailly, the Marquis de Condorcet, and of course, the illustrious captain John Paul Jones." All three men greeted the new apprentice cordially. "We were just discussing medical history, a field that I believe you have recently been studying."

"I can't say that I have become an expert just yet," Cabanis said. "Was there something that you seek to understand?"

"Not specifically, but earlier, we were discussing the effects of planetary forces on the human body. Professor Bailly mentioned a few examples, but that left me wondering if we knew all of the effects."

"I'm sure that we do not," Cabanis said thoughtfully, "but I will attempt to find out for you what is known on this subject."

Ben laughed. "You have plenty of work to do with your medical studies. There is no need to prepare anything extra for me."

"It is no trouble," Cabanis said. "I am becoming interested in this area of medicine as well. It will be instructive for me. For if we don't study the past, we will be destined to repeat old mistakes."

"You are wise beyond your years, my young friend," Ben said. He put his arm around the apprentice's shoulders. "You seem to be filling in. Is Madame Helvétius feeding you well?"

"Oh yes," he exclaimed, "and even if she forgets, the Abbé de la Roche always looks after my nutrition."

"Good. You can't learn on an empty stomach—but you must eat to live, not live to eat, my friend."

"Thank you, Ben, I'll remember that," Cabanis said.

Piccinni struck up the orchestra in a jaunty fanfare clearly meant to indicate that the festivities were about to begin. The freemasons filed out of the study to take their places in the audience. Ben took his seat next to de Gébelin on the stage alongside others who would speak today in honor of Brother Voltaire. The wooden chair was small and uncomfortable, and, for the sake of his backside, Ben hoped the ceremony wouldn't drone on too long.

The brightly lit hall was packed with Lodge members and guests. Ben looked out over a curious collection of scientists, academics, and the many aristocrats of Parisian society. At first, he was disconcerted that he could not find Minette as he surveyed the crowded room. They had been seeing quite a lot of each other since the evening of poetry. But then he noted that Cabanis had reserved an empty seat between himself and Monsieur Turgot. Ben had no doubt that she would arrive late.

The Queen and her clique, including Louis Le Veillard, were just now filing into reserved seats in the front row. Le Veillard looked more than a bit haggard, as if he had been out partying all night and most of the day as well. In contrast, Marie Antoinette looked as fresh as if she had just stepped from a bath. She waddled slightly under a fecund belly, yet she was luminous as usual. The King and his ministers, as well as most members of the clergy, were conspicuous in their absence. Because of that, Ben was even more pleased to see the Queen. It was technically illegal to eulogize a heretic such as Voltaire. Ben had pondered, until he spotted her, if some overzealous *gendarme* might consider raiding the gathering.

As he perused the crowd, Ben did not find Marianne, but then again, he had not been expecting to see her. Mrs. Davies would never allow such an event to interfere with her daughter's practice schedule. But then, Mesmer wasn't there either, and Ben couldn't help wondering if they were together. He tried to quickly banish the thought from his mind.

On stage, alongside the speakers, a large easel stood, draped by a cloth embroidered with emblems of the Masonic Lodge. As the orchestra concluded playing, a hush came over the crowd. Brother de Gébelin rose from his chair and walked over toward the easel. He cleared his throat.

"Brothers—and Sisters," he started. "We have gathered here today to celebrate the life of our dear departed Brother Voltaire. The Lodge of the Nine Sisters is exceedingly proud of our fallen Brother. We have taken the opportunity to have this painting commissioned to mark the occasion."

With a flourish, de Gébelin pulled on the cloth. The crowd gasped and then erupted into applause. "The Apotheosis of Voltaire" was a masterful rendering of the philosopher ascending to heaven astride a winged horse. The artist Dardel had portrayed Voltaire trampling injustice—a figure which bore a striking resemblance to the King of France.

Ben glanced back at the audience to see that Minette was now in her seat between Turgot and Cabanis. Somehow, he had missed her arrival. However, from that point on, Ben only partially heard de Gébelin, as he concentrated more on her lovely face. She winked at him.

When de Gébelin finally concluded, Ben rose to speak. The audience looked slightly dazed, but Ben felt their attention on him as he strode to the lectern. "Ladies and gentlemen ... my dear Brothers and Sisters," Ben said solemnly in a clear deep voice. He paused to adjust his ceremonial leather apron, the symbol of the Masonic Lodge, then peered out through his bifocals across the rapt audience.

"If you would not be forgotten as soon as you are dead, either write things worth reading—or do things worth writing. Our Brother Voltaire had the fortunate experience of accomplishing both of these in the rich life that we celebrate today . . ."

Ben went on to highlight some of the philosopher's more notable accomplishments. He tried carefully to avoid highlighting Voltaire's more heretical and revolutionary ideas in hopes of keeping his eulogy as non-controversial as possible. He spoke of his last meeting with the great man, where he had discovered both the strength and the frailty Voltaire possessed.

"Brother Voltaire stood for reason. He did not believe or follow blindly. He questioned everything, bowing only to Truth. He fought injustice as long as he lived. For those qualities, we honor the man. For those qualities, we should emulate him."

When Ben put down his bifocals at the conclusion of his remarks, the audience rose with thunderous applause.

De Gébelin stood again somewhat sheepishly, the former pastor having just been seriously out-orated by the former printer. He went on to introduce each of the other speakers on the stage—who were mercifully brief in their remarks.

De Gébelin's concluding remarks were once again too long-winded, yet he was generously well received by the audience when he finally pointed toward the banquet hall and declared, "It is now time to eat!"

December 3rd, 1778

PASSY

BEN SAT COMFORTABLY in the study of the Hôtel de Valentinois. His tired feet rested on a well-cushioned footstool covered with heavily patterned Turkish fabric; Madame Leray called it her 'Ottoman.' Ben fanned his toes toward the fire crackling in the fireplace. Dusk was approaching, wrapping a chilly dark cloak over the countryside of Passy.

A maid entered the room to light the lamps, but Ben barely noticed. The chessboard in front of him looked like a battlefield with black and white chessmen engaged in combat from one side to the other. More than a few captives lay on their sides off the board. Jacques Leray sat across from Ben, contemplating his next move. Ben thought perhaps he should urge his host on, but he decided against it; he was enjoying the calm of the moment after a hectic afternoon.

Temple had been released from his secretarial duties to go fraternize with Junior, and the two had merrily headed off into town in search of local girls. Benny was home from school and had been only too happy to assist the printers working at Ben's press until supper. The evening meal would not be ready for a few hours, leaving plenty of time to finish this game—and perhaps even start another.

But Ben's idyllic mood was broken by Benny's cries as he ran into the house. "Grandpa, Grandpa!" the boy called urgently.

Ben and Jacques jumped from their chairs, running to intercept him in the front hall.

"Benny, what is it, my boy?" Ben said, instinctively checking the panting nine-year-old for bleeding. He was relieved to see none. The rest of the Leray family quickly assembled in the hall as well, having heard the commotion.

"Grandpa, you must come outside and see," he said breathlessly.

Madame Leray grabbed several cloaks from hooks in the hall, handing one to each person as they filed out the front door. Benny ran to the center of the courtyard and pointed to the northern sky.

"Look," he exclaimed.

There were gasps all around as the Leray family gazed upward at an astonishing display of the Northern Lights.

Ban's panic subsided. It sunk in that there had been no calamity. "Ah, the Aurora Borealis," Ben said.

Glimmering sheets of purple, green, pink, and blue streaked down toward the horizon, undulating like fabric in the breeze against the dark blue background of the winter sky.

"Where does it come from?" Benny asked. He snuggled up to his grandfather.

Ben put his arm around the boy. "No one really knows, but I have a theory that the display represents electrical discharges in the atmosphere."

Benny seemed perplexed. "Then why don't we see it every night?" he asked.

"I think it has to do with the way the electrical fluid is affected by warm and cold air currents. It's a bit complicated, but I believe that the atmosphere becomes overcharged when warm air above cannot release the electrical fluid. The air reaches out, but the frigid earth turns a cold shoulder. The electrical fluid must then stay in the air, where small discharges result in the colors that we see. It's like winter lightning."

Benny looked a bit lost but seemed satisfied enough not to ask any further.

"It's dazzling," Madame Leray exclaimed. She stared up at the show. "As are your words Ben; you should publish your theory. I don't think that I have ever heard as clear an explanation of the Northern Lights as you just gave us."

"I've published parts of my theory before—but you are correct—over the years, there have been many ridiculous postulations. It would be refreshing to have a more credible explanation published. I only wish I had the time."

"You will only have the time if you decide to do it. It is all a matter of setting your priorities," Madame Leray said.

"Yes, of course, you are right as always," Ben said. He smiled. "I will do it."

Marianne had retired to her room before supper, feigning a headache. She needed some time to herself. As it was Thursday, there was no performance scheduled tonight. Her mother sat knitting in the parlor of their suite at the *Grand Hôtel de Londres*. Cecelia was working on her correspondence. Marianne had told them both that she couldn't eat any supper. They would not expect her to emerge before morning.

Since the time when they had lived in London, she had insisted that their lodgings be at ground level if at all possible, and now Marianne's room faced the garden offering access to the street. Ostensibly, this was due to her fear of heights—but in actuality, Marianne enjoyed the freedom that this arrangement allowed. For similar reasons, she had always insisted on having a window or door that led directly outside. To her mother and sister, this request was explained by her claustrophobia and frequent need for fresh air. This was at least half true, for Marianne thought that she might truly have gone mad long ago if she'd been cooped up in a windowless room. Nonetheless, the latitude to escape unnoticed was just as much the reason for her request.

After nearly a year in Paris, Marianne had become quite proficient in her nighttime escapades. She kept a hooded ankle-length black cape in her room at all times. Her thick Tyrolean boots made little noise as she dashed through the dark streets. Marianne knew the locations and patrol routes of every *gendarme* for miles. She knew especially well the short walking distance from her hotel on the *Rûe Dauphine* to the *Place Vendôme* across the river. Late at night, she felt most vulnerable crossing the *Pont Neuf* alone. More than once, she had hidden in the wooded shadows on the *Ile de la Cité*, the ancient island in the middle of the Seine, until she felt safe to proceed. Once on the opposite bank, she wove her way through the backstreets and alleys, carefully threading between the watchful lookouts of *Palais Royal* guards and the shady characters frequenting the *Jardin des Tuileries* at night.

On this particular evening however, there were many people walking or sitting outside despite the chilly weather. The Northern Lights were spectacular. Lovers huddled along the *Pont Neuf* paid no attention to Marianne as she whisked by. She wondered what Mesmer would make of the glittering atmospheric display. When she arrived at his lodgings in the *Place Vendôme*, a séance was in full swing.

Several people sat around the baquet. She quickly recognized Doctor D'Eslon and Marie Antoinette sitting *en rapport* outside on the deck with a blanket over their legs. The Queen appeared to be in a deep trance, her eyes closed, her porcelain skin slightly flushed, her breathing slow, peaceful, and rhythmic. She did not see Mesmer but felt that he must be here. She sat down at her regular place on the deck.

The chill made her glad that she wore her cloak. The Northern Lights scintillated in the sky in front of her. Was she imagining it, or could she see a flock of birds flying in the dancing rays?

Mesmer's valet, Antoine, appeared at her side with a pewter mug steaming with fragrant tea. Marianne took a deep drink. The warmth of the tea relaxed her even further.

"Would you like some assistance, Mademoiselle Davies?" he asked.

"I doubt I will need much help tonight, Antoine. These lights are spectacular." Marianne smiled. "But I always appreciate your guidance."

Antoine sat across from her with his knees flanking hers. The sparkling

Northern Lights formed a halo around his head. She pulled the string that tied her cloak in the front. He rubbed his hands together briskly in an attempt to warm them. Despite that, when he placed his right hand on her sternum she gasped slightly.

"I am sorry," he said.

"It is nothing," she replied.

Very soon, her breathing slowed. She felt her spirit leave her body and hover above the deck. Marianne noticed the shimmering image of Marie Antoinette also floating a few feet above the shell of her body. Her translucent image seemed divinely serene. She sat cross-legged with her arms resting on her knees, her palms facing the sky, connected to faint lines streaming down. Her eyes were closed. She must have sensed that Marianne had joined her because the young Queen tensed ever so slightly, turned, and opened her eyes.

"Marianne," Marie Antoinette said calmly. "I am so pleased that you could join me tonight. I have missed seeing you these past months."

"I am glad to be here," Marianne replied. Despite her one-time fear that the young Queen might be a rival, Marianne had found instead that they had bonded in friendship. She wished that their paths crossed more frequently.

"I have something to show you. Let's fly," Marie Antoinette said.

The birds Marianne had seen before were clearly beckoning now. The two women joined hands and were swept away with the flock. Marianne had flown many times since Vienna, but never had there been a night like this.

The air was clear over the gleaming streets of Paris as they flew. The Northern Lights shimmered down with all the hues of the rainbow. The Man-in-the-Moon beamed, his smiling face hovering over the two women in their flight. Faint white lines connected many of the stars into constellations of animals or mythological human figures. Marianne watched in awe as the figures came to life in the dark blue background of the sky above her. Orion let loose an arrow in the form of a comet. Ursa bellowed to her cub to catch up.

The throne of Cassiopeia stood empty before them as they flew higher above Paris and the Earth. Marie Antoinette approached the bejeweled chair and sat down as naturally as if she were in the palace at Versailles. Marianne paused in front of the young Queen and genuflected.

"Rise, fair Marianne," Marie Antoinette commanded.

As Marianne brought her eyes up, she realized, for the first time, that they were not the only two spirits present. Marianne stared in amazement at the Queen's womb. Perhaps she had not noticed before, or perhaps it had been hidden from her view.

"Oh, my heavens," Marianne exclaimed. "You're pregnant!"

"Yes," Marie Antoinette said serenely. "Thanks to you."

"So, how did this little miracle occur?"

"In the usual way, I suppose."

"But I thought that he couldn't?" Marianne looked perplexed.

"We were very young when we married," Marie Antoinette explained. "Neither of us had any experience in these matters. If anything, I had more worldly experience than he did." She blushed slightly, then continued. "But you know how men are. I didn't feel it would be appropriate that I should be his 'teacher,' lest he wonder where I had gained such knowledge. So we bumbled along, ineffective for many years. I secretly hoped that perhaps some serving girl would show him the ropes, but apparently no other woman ever tempted him. I even enlisted my brother Joseph to investigate the cause of Louis's inability to let loose of his seed. His report would have been comical if it hadn't been so sad. He found out only what I already knew—that my husband was physically normal but had no idea how to consummate the act of coupling. Unfortunately, Joseph couldn't describe what he should do to solve the problem. Do you remember our first séance together?"

"Of course. It was early in the spring," Marianne said. "I had not seen you in many years. Not since I gave you childhood music lessons back in Vienna at the royal palace. My, what a beautiful woman and Queen you had become."

"Thank you," Marie Antoinette said.

"Mesmer asked if I would guide your trance that day. Using your inner vision, we found that you were perfectly healthy and intact. We turned our attention to your husband—finding him healthy as well."

"Do you remember what you then described to me?"

"We talked about a lot of things that day, your Majesty. I don't recall saying anything that was new or unique."

"You described for me a technique that you had used with your man—who was that?"

"I believe that I did not say."

"Yes, of course—no matter." Marie Antoinette looked slightly disappointed that Marianne was keeping her secret. "You told me how you had learned to contract and relax your pelvic muscles rhythmically during coupling to enhance his pleasure—whoever the lucky devil is." The Queen smiled.

Marianne smiled back but remained silent.

"You suggested I practice tightening these muscles, as if I was stopping my pee, and then releasing them again. I must admit that I was skeptical at first, but I tried it. I practiced every day."

"And you think that this simple technique did the trick?" Marianne asked. She was now feeling just a bit proud.

"Absolutely. The very next time that we coupled, I held him using these muscles. It took a little while, and I got tired, but for the first time, I was able to extract his juices. We both wept with joy afterwards. And now look at me just eight months later." She patted her bulging stomach.

"She is beautiful," Marianne replied, "and healthy too. Motherhood becomes you."

"She?" Marie Antoinette looked slightly disappointed.

"Yes."

"It is no matter. I now know how to conceive a child with His Majesty. An heir should not be a problem. But what of you, Marianne? You never had children?" the Queen asked. Her voice was tinged with sadness.

"I often wondered when I was younger why I didn't get pregnant. But I have found through my own inner vision that my female organs never properly formed," Marianne confided. "On the brighter side, my anatomy has left me free to follow my musical career, unfettered by pregnancy, and yet enjoy the baby-making process all these years."

"Yes. And you will never get these ugly stretch marks on your skin," the Queen said.

The sparkling lights of the Aurora started to diminish around the two women.

"We should get back," Marie Antoinette said at last.

The flock returned to collect them.

On Mesmer's deck, the shimmering Northern Lights were now even more subdued. The warm glow of several lamps flickered softly. Doctor D'Eslon remained huddled *en rapport* with the corporal figure of the Queen, but Marianne was surprised to discover that Mesmer himself had replaced Antoine in that position with her. She effortlessly rejoined her body. His supple hands felt good, topping her thigh and pressed against her sternum.

"How was your flight?" he asked.

Marianne stretched her arms over her head. "Wonderful," she replied dreamily. "The Queen is pregnant."

Mesmer laughed. "You have not been keeping up with the newspapers, have you? It has been the talk of Paris these last months."

"No," she replied, slightly miffed at his criticism. "You know that Mother won't allow them."

"How is the baby?"

"She is beautiful and healthy. She will be born within the month, I would think."

"Would you care to give me the exact date? I could make some money in the betting pool."

"You are incorrigible. I wouldn't tell you if I knew."

Marie Antoinette stretched also. Marianne watched Doctor D'Eslon assist her up. She held onto his arm as she made her way over to where Marianne sat with Mesmer.

"I must go now," the young Queen announced. Marianne rose to give her a hug.

She heard the synchronized hoofbeats of the team of draft horses bringing the royal carriage through the *Place Vendôme*. They came to a stop just below the deck. As their party walked through Mesmer's clinic, Marianne observed that the baquet was now empty. Antoine was tidying up, dousing the lamps as he proceeded through the rooms. The two doctors and Marianne escorted Marie Antoinette to her coach. D'Eslon assisted her up, and then followed her in.

"I will be dropping the doctor off at his lodgings," Marie Antoinette called back to Marianne. "Would you like a ride too?"

Marianne could just imagine the consternation it would cause if the royal carriage were to discharge her at the door of the *Grand Hôtel de Londres*.

"No thank you. I prefer the walk," she replied, which was also true.

"Good night, then."

The carriage left the square as gracefully as it had entered. Marianne and Mesmer stood alone on the colonnade at the entrance to his suite.

"Must you leave right away?" Mesmer asked. She looked at him for a moment, knowing exactly what he proposed. "You could stay for a while if you want to ... I meant to say."

Marianne found that she enjoyed making the powerful doctor dangle on the hook a while. He said nothing but gave her a pleading look with his deep blue, piercing eyes.

"All right," she finally said. "But you'll have to feed me first—I'm famished. I hope that you have a steak to fry up."

"I'm sure I can find you something in my kitchen," he said, pulling her back inside the building.

Later that night, fully satiated in every way, Marianne walked home through the nearly empty streets of Paris. The Northern Lights had completely disappeared, and the moon had waned, leaving only the inky black sky punctuated by a few stars twinkling coldly. Despite her heavy cape, Marianne felt a chill as she started across the *Pont Neuf*. The *Ile de la Cité* appeared completely deserted at this late hour. She hesitated halfway across just to be sure. The clanking of the rigging on the barges and houseboats below produced an eerie melody. A large rat eyed her suspiciously from atop a garbage heap down by the river. Nothing else was moving.

Marianne thought perhaps she heard the faint cries of patients interned at the *Hôtel Dieu,* but it could have been waterfowl just as easily. The bells of *Notre-Dame* cathedral struck one o'clock, startling her. She hurried on toward the Left Bank. The strains of a lone street violinist, perhaps hoping to capture a coin from late-night revelers, caught her ear as she traversed the *Rue Dauphine.* Soon enough, though, Marianne was safely tucked into her warm bed, remembering the marvelous events of the night.

To her surprise, she found her thoughts turning to Ben. She wondered if he had seen the Northern Lights. She wondered if they had affected him as they had her. If he had experienced the mystical wondrousness of them. Clearly, this could not be true. Most likely, if he observed them, all he saw was twinkling light in the sky. Surely Ben would have some dull scientific explanation for them.

Early Spring 1779

THE TUILERIES JARDIN, PARIS

SPRING HAD ARRIVED in Paris early. The trees and flowers were all starting to bud, but Marianne didn't notice. Instead, she gave herself a stern lecture as she raced across the expansive gardens. The soft breath of a warm spring breeze had awoken her. Without meaning to, she had fallen asleep at Mesmer's apartment the evening before, satiated by his healing hands and a few glasses of his fine Madeira.

Awakening with a start as the first pale light of morning crept through the window, Marianne knew that mother would be up with the sun. She had to be safely tucked into her bed by that time. The tall, immaculately trimmed hedges of the *Tuileries Jardin* provided good cover for her flight. She was making good progress until she saw the two men.

Marianne's first instinct was to alter her path to avoid them, as no upstanding citizens would be found there at this hour. She strained to perceive what the huddled figures were doing. They stood alongside a boxwood tree across a small glade from her. She might not have noticed them at all had they not exchanged a piece of white paper that caught her eye. Fascinated, she crept closer to hear their conversation.

They spoke in hushed tones. The man who had passed the note was of a wiry aristocratic build. He wore dark, exquisitely well-tailored clothes. His black hair was thick but tidy. The other was a taller man. Marianne was startled to see that he wore the attire of a minister.

"Why would a man of the cloth be having a clandestine meeting in the *Tuileries Jardin* before dawn?" she asked herself.

Her curiosity quickly overwhelmed her desire to race home. As she crept closer, she began to be able to distinguish what they were saying.

"Is this what must get to him so urgently?" the Reverend asked. He shook the small piece of paper in his hand. He seemed peeved at being called out at this hour of the morning.

"Yes."

"Written in your invisible ink between the lines, as usual, I suppose?"

"Of course."

"Does Stormont have enough of the fluid to develop it, Edward?"

"How would I know that?" the smaller man replied. He now sounded irritated himself. "If not, have him contact me again, and I'll prepare some. Good day."

With that, he walked off, leaving the Reverend standing by the tree. He shrugged slightly, turned, and strode in the opposite direction. The strange meeting concluded, Marianne judged that it was now safe for her to proceed as well. She once again slipped silently through the pre-dawn shadows toward the *Palais Royal* and home. She pondered what kind of business a man named Edward and a Reverend could be conducting in the early morning hours, passing papers with invisible writing for Lord Stormont, the British ambassador. She resolved to ask Ben as soon as she got the chance. The sun was just rising as she deftly entered her bedroom window. She snuggled up in her bed to escape the morning chill.

Ben made the Tuesday morning reservation to meet Marianne at the *Cheval Sauvage* through Le Veillard. When Louis arrived early, Ben was ready to go. Le Veillard reined Diablo in, still panting from his brisk morning trot across Passy. Ben must have looked glum because Louis became serious quickly.

"Why so morose on this fine spring morning?" Louis asked.

"I'm alright," Ben said unconvincingly.

Le Veillard looked at him. "No, you are not."

Ben mounted his horse. They rode toward Paris.

"I'm concerned about my relationship with Marianne," Ben confided when the two friends were alone on the road.

"What is there to be concerned about? She calls, you come, no problem."

"Don't be so flippant," Ben admonished. He became quiet. They rode without speaking for a small stretch.

Le Veillard finally broke the silence. "All right, please tell me what is bothering you," he said.

"You know I told you that I felt she and I were growing apart?"

"Yes."

"Well, I have also been growing much closer to Minette."

"So?"

"So, that presents a problem for me. While I think that you and I are very similar in our appreciation of women, I suspect that we differ in our approach to them. When I love a woman, I want to be with her exclusively."

"And you love Minette?"

"Yes."

"And you no longer love Marianne?"

"I did not say that. I still have loving feelings for her. However, they have faded as my feelings for Minette have strengthened."

"And what exactly is the nature of your problem? Didn't you once write 'as in the dark all cats are gray' in reference to the interchangeability of female partners?"

Ben laughed. "Ouch, you would use my own words against me," he said. He made a motion as if to thrust a dagger into his chest. "That quote is from a bagatelle I composed over thirty-five years ago—and contained my advice to a fictitious younger man about taking an older mistress. I am surprised that you remember it."

"It is one of my personal favorites," Louis said. "Besides, I think that it fits the current situation, do you not?"

"No, of course not," Ben said. "I wrote that a young man should consider marriage as the best resolution of his natural desires, but that if he would not accept my best advice, he should seek an older woman as a paramour."

"I am all for marriage."

"Yes, and for the pursuit of liaisons outside of that holy union as well, I suspect."

"Of course, it is only natural."

The ride back to Passy seemed significantly warmer to Ben. The air temperature had gone up, but he also enjoyed the warm flush of his recent intimacy with Marianne.

"So?" Le Veillard asked impertinently. It seemed as if he expected a full report.

"So what?" replied Ben.

"How was the *chat gris*?"

Ben laughed. "She's fine. Louis, as I told you on the way here, she and I have been growing apart, yet it doesn't stop us from being close when we are together. We have known each other for a very long time."

"Did you talk?"

"She now mostly espouses the virtues of *magnétisme animale*, of which you know I am not a believer. We've become more and more separated in our philosophies. But she also told me of a meeting she witnessed between two spies."

"Spies?" Le Veillard said, perking up.

"Apparently, she overheard a conversation between the Reverend

Smith and a man I believe to be Edward Bancroft."

"The Reverend who we saved from Monsieur Penet last year?"

"One and the same."

"And Doctor Bancroft, secretary to Silas Deane of your American commission?"

"Yes."

"Ben, you told me that you suspected the Reverend of spying, but Bancroft—were you aware of his complicity?"

"Not fully. However, I have sent him on a few missions to England over the years and expected that, while there, he might meet with British agents. I long entertained the belief that he could be convinced by them to act as a double agent. The British can be quite persuasive—especially to someone who enjoys money as much as Bancroft. Therefore, he is only given such information that I anticipate would not jeopardize the war effort."

"What do you think the meeting was about?"

"I recently invited Doctor Bancroft to a dinner where certain details about a shipment of French wine bound for England were discussed with Monsieurs Leray and Beaumarchais. Bancroft was instructed to proceed to Calais and meet the ship there. Nothing clandestine about this shipment, mind you, merely commerce. But I did insert an encoded message into the passport requested by the ship's captain. I entrusted this passport to Bancroft. My suspicion is that he decoded the message and passed the information to Reverend Smith."

"So, the information is in British hands now?"

Ben was pensive for a moment. "Yes, but it is not of any consequence. As I said, I have not allowed Bancroft access to any truly useful information for some time. The information he receives now merely serves only to satisfy his British handlers sufficiently that they will continue to trust him."

"How do you keep all these agents and counteragents straight? How do you know who to trust?" Le Veillard asked with a look of consternation.

"It is not easy, my friend. A shortage of trust is only one small part of the price of war. There has never been a good war or a bad peace."

Back in his lodging at the Hôtel de Valentinois, Ben searched for an old letter in his files. Upon locating the yellowed paper, he spread the sheets out on his desk and reread the old writing his friend Le Veillard had referred to earlier in the day. He chuckled at his own witticism, penned when he was but a young man himself:

25 June 1745
Why A Young Man Should Choose An Old Mistress.

My Dear Friend:

I know of no medicine fit to diminish the violent natural inclinations you mention; and if I did, I think I should not communicate it to you.

Marriage is the proper Remedy. It is the most natural state of Man, and therefore the State in which you are most likely to find solid Happiness.

Your reasons against entering into it at present appear to me not well founded. The circumstantial Advantages you have in view by postponing it are not only uncertain, but they are small in comparison with that of the Thing itself, the being married and settled. It is the Man and Woman united that make the compleat human Being.

Separate, she wants his Force of Body and Strength of Reason; he, her Softness, Sensibility, and acute Discernment. Together they are more likely to succeed in the World. A single Man has not nearly the value he would have in the State of Union. He is an incomplete Animal. He resembles the odd half of a pair of Scissors.

If you get a prudent, healthy Wife, your Industry in your Profession, with her good Economy, will be a fortune sufficient.

But if you will not take this Counsel and persist in thinking a Commerce with the Sex inevitable, then I repeat my former Advice, that in all your Amours you should prefer old Women to young ones.

You call this a Paradox and demand my Reasons. They are these:

1. *Because they have more Knowledge of the World, and their Minds are better stored with Observations. Their Conversation is more improving, and more lastingly agreeable.*

2. *Because when Women cease to be handsome they study to be good. To maintain their Influence over Men, they supply the Diminution of Beauty by an Augmentation of Utility. They learn to do a thousand Services small and great, and are the most tender and useful of Friends when you are sick. Thus they continue amiable. And hence there is hardly such a thing to be found as an old Woman who is not a good Woman.*

3. *Because there is no Hazard of Children, which irregularly produced may be attended with much Inconvenience.*

4. *Because through more Experience they are more prudent and discreet in conducting an Intrigue to prevent Suspicion. The Commerce with them is therefore safer with regard to your Reputation. And with regard to theirs, if the Affair should happen to be known, considerate People might be rather inclined to excuse an old Woman, who would kindly take care of a young Man, form his Manners by her good counsels and prevent his ruining his Health and Fortune among mercenary Prostitutes.*

5. *Because in every Animal that walks upright, the Deficiency of the Fluids that fill the Muscles appears first in the highest Part. The Face first grows lank and wrinkled; then the Neck; then the Breast and Arms; the lower Parts*

continuing to the Last as plump as ever: so that covering
all above with a Basket, and regarding only what is below
the Girdle, it is impossible of two Women to tell an old one
from a young one. And as in the dark all Cats are grey,
the Pleasure of Corporal Enjoyment with an old Woman
is at least equal, and frequently superior; every Knack
being, by Practice, capable of Improvement.

6. *Because the Sin is less. The debauching a Virgin may be*
her Ruin, and make her for Life unhappy.

7. *Because the Compunction is less. The having made*
a young Girl miserable may give you frequent bitter
Reflection; none of which can attend the making an old
Woman happy.

8th & lastly. They are so grateful!

Thus much for my Paradox. But still I advise you to marry
directly; being sincerely

Your Affectionate Friend,
Benjamin Franklin

Ben poured himself a generous draught of cognac. He contemplated the 'older woman' Minette, and the younger Marianne. He recognized that he had also become a great many years older, and hopefully a dram more mature, than when he had penned this humorous piece at the age of thirty-nine. He wondered what advice he would give a seventy-three-year-old who still struggled with his relationships with women. He wondered if there would ever come a time when he would learn to heed his own advice. He wondered if the war, and the need for spies, would ever end.

Summer 1779

PASSY

BEN WAS SLEEPING FITFULLY; it was too hot and stuffy. Even with his bedroom window wide open, there was no breeze. The humidity was oppressive, unusual for Passy in summer, except just before it rained. An owl hooted outside, awakening him. "I can't close the window," he thought, "or I'll suffocate." Instead, he threw off his sheet.

Ben walked to the window and yelled breathily, "Get away." He waved his arms and heard the flapping of large wings as the owl flew off to hunt elsewhere. Wearily, he poured some water into his washbasin and splashed his face. He wet a washcloth and slapped it on his sweaty neck and chest. He returned to his bed and flopped down with a thud. Before long, he dozed off.

In his dream, steam rose from the wet streets in the early morning light. The buildings skirting the streets were neat and clean, tidy storefronts with apartments above as always.

Ben recognized the setting. He'd been on this street in his dreams before, and yet he didn't know where he was.

It was silent. Other than Ben, no one appeared to be out at this hour.

The glistening cobblestones had been laid with precision. Despite the soft light, all of the buildings' angles were sharp, crisp, and clean.

"Perhaps Austrian workmanship," he thought. Before Ben had much time to ponder his location, a male figure approached through the fog. The sun was just now rising behind the man. He appeared to float over the cobblestones toward Ben. He wore a robe of lavender silk embroidered with swirls, comets, suns, and crescent moons. Ben had seen that robe before, and he strained to identify the wearer, but the sun's position kept the man's face in shadow. Then a reflection from a storefront window briefly lit up the man's face. Ben could see that it was Mesmer. He instinctively tried to move away but could not; he was stuck, paralyzed. And though the wizard approached calmly, his appearance seemed both haughty and menacing to Ben. He wished that he could simply retreat into the buildings' shadows.

"*Guten tag*, Doctor Franklin—or should I say *bonjour*?"

"Where are we?"

"This is my *straße* in Vienna," Mesmer said. He swept his hand to the side dramatically as he gazed around at the tidy shops bordering the street.

"And why are we here?"

"I would hope to convince you, more than any man, of my power," Mesmer replied. His penetrating blue eyes focused directly at Ben. They seemed to glow.

"Then show me proof," Ben said courageously, not entirely sure that he desired a full demonstration in his current immobilized state.

"The proof is in my cures."

"Suggestion, Imagination, and Imitation could account for the results."

"No. I control a force of Nature that heals."

"I have no doubt that Nature, or God, or whatever you choose to call the force of Divine Intervention, heals people." Ben decided that he should stop short of calling Mesmer a liar.

"And so ... ?"

Ben became aware that he should proceed cautiously. "As a scientist, I need to see proof that man can control any of Nature's forces—including this healing fluid of which you speak," he said.

"You want proof? I'll show you proof." The wizard raised his arms angrily.

Ben could do nothing but watch as a flash of brilliant blue-white light crossed the short distance between them, striking Ben squarely in the chest. He was hurled backwards. The world disappeared.

Ben awoke with a gasp to hear the remains of a loud cascade of thunder. His bedroom was pitch black. He smelled the unmistakable acrid odor of a lightning strike nearby. Rain started to pour outside his bedroom window. He touched his own chest to assure himself that he was not injured. He seemed intact though his heart was racing. A refreshingly cool breeze accompanied the downpour. He got up to close the window a little, lest it rain in.

Benny came running into Ben's room, terrified by the storm. "Grandpa, Grandpa," he cried.

"There, there—it's all right, it's just a thunderstorm," Ben said soothingly. He realized that, after his dream, he needed the reassurance as much as his grandson. They curled up together in Ben's bed. Benny fell asleep almost instantly, but Ben lay in the dark listening to the rain until his heart slowed to its normal pace, and he, too, fell back asleep.

October 1779

PARIS

IN TENSE SILENCE, Ben and Anne Louise Brillon rode in the carriage through the outskirts of Paris. She fidgeted. He stared out the window. They held hands for part of the way. It was cold and gray outside, the sort of autumn weather that cast a pall over the city. When Anne Louise sighed as she frequently did, Ben looked at her beautiful face and tried to smile reassuringly. But he was nervous too.

When Mesmer's letter had arrived requesting his presence, Ben's first impulse was to decline. He could have made any one of a thousand excuses. Indeed, he was not sure that it set a good precedent to be meeting with the man, for some might view it as Ben's tacit endorsement of Mesmer's techniques.

In the end, it was Anne Louise, the music lover, who had convinced Ben to accept the invitation. Among the women at her salon earlier in the year, Mesmer's armonica playing had been described as hauntingly beautiful, transporting the listener to a peaceful, ethereal place. Anne Louise had studied with many famous musicians, some who had even dedicated their sonatas to her, and now she wished to find out what music this man could produce.

Anne Louise said that she was glad that Ben would be there when she met Mesmer, for she had been warned that Mesmer possessed a presence that could make a woman feel uncomfortable. She seemed deep in thought when they pulled up to their destination in the *Place Vendôme*.

Mesmer's valet, Antoine, met them at the door. Ben observed that the nameplate was no longer so shiny, so new—as it had been when he first saw it. Anne Louise squeezed Ben's hand tightly as they followed Antoine up the stairs and down the dark hall. They entered Mesmer's study. The wizard sat in a chair by the fire, wearing a lavender robe. He didn't immediately get up. He appeared to be absorbed in his book. Antoine cleared his throat. Mesmer looked up and slowly put his book aside.

"Very apathetic," whispered Ben.

Anne Louise whispered back, "Very rude."

Mesmer spoke softly, in a monotone, "Ah, Doctor Franklin and Madame Brillon. So good of you to come."

Anne Louise gazed around the room, apparently looking for the glass armonica, but the room held only a harpsichord. Mesmer also noticed her search. "My glass armonica is out for repairs presently," he said. "I am sorry to disappoint you. I know that you are a music lover."

"I am sure that Ben could fix it. He invented it ... Were you not aware?" Anne Louise replied.

Mesmer looked right past her at Franklin and replied, "Yes, I know. I had mine reproduced from the original that Mademoiselle Davies brought to Vienna many years ago. Unfortunately, I don't think that even the great Doctor Franklin could have replaced a broken bowl today."

Ben tried to sound conciliatory. "Yes, that is a job for a trained technician," he said. But it struck him that he did not recall Marianne ever mentioning that the instrument he had constructed for her alone had been copied—especially not by Mesmer.

Mesmer rose from his chair. Though a smaller man than Ben, he carried himself proudly—making the most of his stature. He approached Madame Brillon first, taking her hand in his, and kissing it. She didn't resist at all, Ben noted. In fact, she let out a small sigh. He then turned to Ben.

"You like to heal people, do you not, Doctor Franklin?" Mesmer asked.

He left Ben no time for further contemplation of the effect the Wizard had on The Ice Princess. And although he was caught off guard by the revelation of the copying of his glass armonica, Ben did not want to ask Mesmer any more about his relationship with Marianne. Pursuing that path made Ben very uncomfortable.

"My doctorate is honorary. I am not a medical doctor trained in the healing arts as you are," Ben said, trying to regain his composure.

"Ah, yes, but I have read of your experiments with electrical fluid. Is it not true that you attempted to cure certain conditions?" Mesmer seemed to be luring Ben into a debate.

Anne Louise leaned toward Mesmer as though she anticipated getting more of his attention. She sat down at the harpsichord glumly when it became clear that she would not. She touched the keys, producing pleasant tones.

"Yes, I found that a strong electrical shock could cure the melancholy for a period of time," Ben said. "But when I tried to restore movement to those with a paralyzed limb, I was not successful. So, I eventually abandoned the use of electrical fluid as a way to restore lost physical functioning. However, many other scientists are working in this area, even today."

"Did not you try it for conditions of the heart organ?"

"Most men don't survive a lightning strike."

"Yes, but in smaller doses, perhaps?"

"Perhaps. I am yet to be convinced. I'll need proof."

Anne Louise started playing a soft, slow melody of her own design, which served as incongruous background music to the increasingly tense discussion.

"All right, Doctor Franklin. What if you could cure almost any condition, not through the use of electrical fluid but rather through a totally new and previously undiscovered one?" Mesmer said.

Ben raised his eyebrow. "And you have discovered this new fluid?" he asked.

"Not only have I discovered it, I can control it, and I can use it to cure many illnesses previously deemed 'incurable' by modern medical techniques," Mesmer replied. He looked like a proud father. "I have named this force *magnétisme animale* because it has many of the properties of mineral magnetism but exerts its effects on living beings rather than metal or rocks. I theorize that there is an unseen, immeasurable force that flows through all creatures, and within this energy is the power to heal."

"I have heard testimony from some of your subjects. Of course, many afflictions pass with 'tincture of time' alone. Didn't Moliere write, 'The role of the physician is to entertain the patient whilst the disease runs its natural course'?"

For the first time, Mesmer showed a hint of a smile. "And Hippocrates instructed us to 'First, do no harm.' Physicians of today, with their constant bloodletting, purging, and toxic medications, have certainly killed more patients than they have cured."

"I must agree with you there. Physicians are not the most progressive or open-minded lot. But how do you know that your force produces the effect that you claim?"

"By my observations," Mesmer replied. He became more animated and appeared a bit defensive. "I have treated hundreds, nay thousands, who have benefited greatly from this force, eliminating a tremendous amount of suffering."

"And created a lucrative practice in the process," Ben said.

Mesmer's face tightened. He hissed, "I treat all who arrive at my door."

Ben wasn't letting go, however. "Yes, but some get more attention than others in your practice, do they not?"

"Only limited by my interest in their condition," Mesmer said. "Unlike you, I must make a living from my work, but I don't see myself as catering only to those who can pay for treatment."

"*Touché*," Ben said. "But where is the measurement of your force? I can use a Leyden jar to store electrical fluid and discharge it at will, each time with a reproducible effect."

"I am the storage vessel for *magnétisme animale,* and I can assure you that the effect is equally reproducible in my hands," Mesmer said, back on the defensive. "Do you not believe that there may exist forces we cannot measure with modern scientific instruments? Can you measure the power of love?"

Ben paused a moment, because this was, of course, the chink in the armor of his argument. He couldn't take anything on faith. He always wanted proof.

"No," Ben said with some resignation. "I cannot measure love."

Mesmer turned to Anne Louise. She rose from the harpsichord to stand with him. He took both her hands and gazed into her eyes.

"So beautiful," he said.

Ben pulled the watch from his pocket. "It is time that we go," he said.

Anne Louise seemed reluctant but followed Ben out.

As they rode in the coach back to Passy, Ben related the dream he'd had about Mesmer. Anne Louise intently listened until he finished.

"What do you think it means?" she asked. Then she added, "Not that all dreams have meaning."

"Oh, I believe that it has a meaning. My interpretation is that Mesmer wields a certain power, not a physical force or fluid, but rather a power over the mind in a state of dreaming or unconsciousness."

"He does have wonderful eyes," she said dreamily.

"Snap out of it," Ben replied with some irritation.

Anne Louise slapped her own cheek. "I am sorry," she said. "But why would his power work on some and not all?"

"My theory is that one has to be open to it. In the dream state, our mind is open to all kinds of fanciful things. Haven't you ever been able to fly like a bird or done things that you could never really do while awake?"

"Yes, I frequently dream of doing certain things that I cannot do in real life," she sighed and smiled coquettishly.

"Perhaps only because you limit yourself, my dear," Ben replied. His expression turned to a sad smile. He decided to drop the subject of their platonic relationship. "My dreaming mind is open to believing that Mesmer may have special powers—based on what I allowed him in my dream. However, my mind, when fully awake, will not allow it. If one believes that *magnétisme animale* is capable of curing ills, then it is quite possible that it may seem so. My belief is that many of these illnesses would have resolved spontaneously—or with the standard cures and medicines that Mesmer also provides to his patients. However, in combination with his suggestion that wellness will be the result, those who achieve it will ascribe their cure to his powers. If I were to truly believe that Mesmer was able to control me, then the outcome of our meeting today might have ended up more like my dream."

"I'm glad that you came out unscathed."

"Yes, I as well."

Anne Louise looked a bit perplexed. "But don't all doctors use this technique to some extent?" she asked. "When my doctor prescribes something for me and tells me that it will help, I feel better even before the treatment has had time to work."

"As always, you are very perceptive, my dear. Yes, of course, the doctor's reassurance that we will heal, like the mother's kiss, contains the power to make one feel better."

Ben contemplated the power that Mesmer seemed to have over these two women in his life—Marianne, and now Anne Louise. He squirmed in his seat but said nothing. He wondered if there would ever come a time when he would have to fully confront the wizard. Their meeting today seemed only to be a prelude to such a showdown. Neither man would, nor even could, step back, to be sure. Ben wondered what confrontation was coming and what the outcome might be.

Late Fall 1779

AUTEUIL

BEN RODE ALONE to the home of Madame Helvétius for the Friday afternoon salon. His stomach grumbled as he thought of the hearty seasonal supper that would surely follow the discussions of the salon. It promised to be an entertaining soiree, as always. In addition to the good company of the abbés, he looked forward to catching up on how student doctor Cabanis was progressing. And then there was always the promise of stealing a little time with the *Notre-Dame d'Auteuil* herself. However, an event such as this evening would undoubtedly not allow him to capture her full attention. He resolved to simply enjoy himself after a long week. If he stole a kiss or two from her over the course of the evening, that would have to satisfy him for today, or so he resigned.

Ben tied up his horse at the front gate. He appeared to be the first guest to arrive. He was escorted up the garden path by the courtier cats, bells jingling as they paraded along. When he arrived at the house, he found it abuzz with activity. Rented staff scurried in and out of various rooms bearing chairs, cut flowers, linens, and other objects. The Abbé de La Roche appeared to be directing traffic when Ben entered the front foyer.

"Ben," de la Roche said. "Welcome."

"Thank you, Martin. Am I the first to arrive?"

"Yes, and the house is nearly readied. Now we lack only the remaining guests."

"Who is expected?"

"I can not tell you all of them, but I recall at least Bailly, Lavoisier, Guillotin, Le Roy, and Condorcet."

"A fine assortment of intellect."

"Yes, and we will have a special guest today."

"And who might that be, pray tell?"

"I am sworn to secrecy, but I will give you a hint." The Abbé cracked a sardonic smile as he began twitching and scratching himself grotesquely. He headed off to continue his preparation before Ben could answer.

"Oh, no!" Ben exclaimed. "Not Marat."

"You guessed," Martin replied. He glanced over his shoulder with a look of exasperation, and he was gone.

Jean-Paul Marat was a physician and minor scientist known to Ben from his writings and a few experiments with optics that Ben had witnessed. Ben judged the man's scientific work as not very original. He broke no new ground in his theories. However, he had a decent writing style and could summarize the work of others well. Sometimes, Ben reckoned, people with the talent to collect and present the works of others could play an important role in science. The difficulty, as Ben perceived it, was that Marat also carried a giant chip on his shoulder. He often publicly declared himself to be persecuted when immediate praise from the scientific community did not follow the printing of his works. His pamphlets were often scathing.

The Royal Academy had turned down Marat's admission several times, infuriating the man, who saw himself as a much more important figure in the scientific world than he was given credit for. Ben questioned Minette's decision to invite into her salon a man who had superciliously dealt with the theories promulgated by her late husband. Marat's insensitivity in lambasting the theories of Helvétius had even caught the attention of Voltaire, who derided the young man stingingly in a review. This, of course, infuriated Marat, who henceforth counted Voltaire among his "enemies." Such was his nature. His pruritic skin condition only added to the general feeling of discomfort most people sensed around him.

Ben resolved to remain neutral in what were sure to become the heated discussions of the afternoon. He ambled freely around the first floor of the house. Not finding Minette anywhere, he guessed that she must be upstairs preparing herself for her debut. He wouldn't disturb her. While it was still relatively peaceful, he decided to seek out the Abbé Morellet. Ben found him just where he thought he would be—in the library. Also, true to form, the Abbé was huddled with medical student Cabanis, passionately discussing something Ben could not glean as he entered the room.

"Good afternoon, gentlemen," Ben announced.

The two broke off their discussion immediately.

"Ah Ben," Morellet said. "Are you here for Madame's salon?"

"Yes, but apparently, I am the first of her guests to arrive."

"Good, then you must join our discussion," Morellet said.

Cabanis appeared a bit exasperated and seemed all too happy to have Ben join in.

"I would be glad to," Ben replied. He gave Cabanis a pat on the back. "What are we discussing?"

"Miracles," the Abbé and Cabanis replied simultaneously.

"Miracles?" Ben asked. It quickly sunk in why the young medical student might be frustrated with the old man of the cloth.

"Yes, do you believe in them?" Morellet asked.

"I try to make it a policy not to place belief in things that I don't understand."

"A very diplomatic response," the Abbé said. He smiled and went on. "Just when you entered, we were discussing John 2:6, the events at Cana of Galilee. You are, of course, familiar."

"Yes," Ben replied. He nodded solemnly. "The turning of water into wine."

"Do you understand how it happened?" the Abbé asked. He seemed to be baiting Ben a bit.

"I am not sure that I completely understand the process, but I will give you my interpretation." Ben paused for effect.

"Please, go on," the Abbé said.

"First, let me say that in order to understand this or any other event described in the Bible, one must avoid the trap of taking the written words too literally."

"What do you mean by that?" the Abbé asked.

"Don't be shocked, my old friend," Ben replied. "I am only saying that I believe the Great Book was given to humanity to guide us through parables. These teachings should provide mankind with the proper general direction in which to proceed with our lives, not the detailed instructions of how to live our lives on a daily basis. In fact, in my opinion, if we take these words too literally, we run the risk of debasing the importance of this great work. We will not see the forest for the trees. I believe that God would intend for us to interpret the meaning of any Biblical event—such as the miracle at Cana—within the context of our own experience with the world and with divine provenance."

"All very well and good," the Abbé said. He seemed to grow a bit more agitated. "But do you believe that God turned the water into wine?"

"My dear Abbé," Ben replied. "I see, with my own eyes, this miracle every day."

"You do?" Morellet asked incredulously.

Just then, the light streaming into the room caught Ben's attention. He turned to gaze out the window of the study. The sun had just broken through the clouds between light rain showers. He motioned quickly to Cabanis and put his arm around the shoulder of the Abbé Morellet.

"Follow me," Ben commanded.

The three men walked out a back door of the house into the gardens. Ben led them through the flowers, now well past their prime, to a small vineyard at the back. They walked under a dripping pergola. In the vineyard, the cool rain glimmered on twisted vines tied to their posts. The fruit was now gone, but yellow-brown leaves clung to the branches. Ben breathed in the earthy smell of rainwater mixed with soil. Sunlight streamed down in golden beams upon the vineyard through transient openings in the dark clouds. The three men stood among the rows of vines. There was not a sound save for the distant songs of birds.

"Open your eyes and look carefully at this scene as I do, my friends," Ben said to the two perplexed men. He looked around, pointing to the vines.

"See how the rain falls from the heavens upon this vineyard." His hand lowered to point toward the base of the plants. "Look there as the water enters the roots of these vines to be changed into fruit. Note that the fruit, now harvested, has been crushed, fermented, and made into wine." He paused again, smiling broadly.

"When you observe this, you will understand as I do that God turns the water into wine constantly." He inhaled another deep breath of the rain-refreshed air and exhaled with a soft sigh. "The wine so produced is evidence that God loves us and wants us to be happy."

"Yes, I see now what you mean," the Abbé said.

"I hope that you will agree with me that this is a much more important, complex, and deep understanding of the power of God than the literal telling of the story could ever impart."

"Well spoken, Ben," Cabanis said with a grin.

The classically trained Catholic abbé, the young agnostic medical student, and the old deist stood there in the vineyard for some time, as if in a church, experiencing God's work all around them.

They remained deep in contemplation when Martin burst out of the house and ran toward them. "Oh, there you are!" he exclaimed as he reached them. "The salon has started—and it is already getting ugly." He made a contorted face.

"We had better get in there," Morellet said. He moved toward the house.

Cabanis bounded past the abbés. Ben decided to take up the rear. He followed the others inside. Even from down the hall, the sounds of raised voices heralded an acrimonious debate.

As he entered the salon, Ben recognized Jean-Paul Marat standing in the center of a throng of eminent scientists. His posture was defensive. The French language was flying so fast that Ben caught only snippets.

"Newton was wrong . . ." Ben caught Marat saying as he walked up to the group. The scientists parted to let Ben join the inner circle but kept up their verbal offensive with Marat. Ben decided not to speak just yet. Besides, he could not get a word in edgewise.

"I believe that there exists a nervous fluid that connects the body with the soul," Marat postulated at one point.

"And what is your proof," someone shouted back at him.

"I am conducting experiments now," came the reply.

And so the rancorous testimony went on. For some time, Ben listened quietly. During one lull, he thought it might be constructive to request that Marat explain his recent experiments with the solar microscope. This piece of equipment directed the intense light of the sun through a series of lenses to illuminate small objects and project their greatly magnified images onto the wall. Most scientists used the device to examine the details of small everyday objects. While interesting, the findings were not unexpected. However, Marat was the first scientist to examine physical manifestations, such as a flame or electrical spark. Ben knew Marat believed that he had been able to observe what he called his "igneous fluid" by this method.

"Jean-Paul, would you be so kind as to enlighten this group regarding your observations with the solar microscope?" Ben said.

"Thank you, Ben," Marat said. It was as if he felt that he had found at least one friend in the room. "I'll be happy to explain my observations to the best of my ability."

But Marat's explanations only prompted another onslaught of

questioning and criticism by the group of scientists. Ben knew that this was all part of the scientific method—that to be a good scientist, one must be able to fend off such attacks against one's theories without taking them personally. As the debate raged on, Ben recalled his ongoing parries of years past with the Abbé Nollet regarding his theories of electrical fluid. While they had been taxing and sometimes exasperating, Ben had never taken the attacks personally. Perhaps it also helped that Ben's theories had ultimately been borne out regarding the dual nature of electricity, positive and negative combined in the same force. Ben wondered if even he would be so magnanimous had he ultimately been proved wrong.

Nonetheless, he observed in Marat, a man who did not appear to take criticism well. He became only more defensive as the arguments continued. As he became more agitated, he twitched and scratched at his irritating skin condition, which further inflamed him. Marat glared at some of the eminent scientists in the room with an icy stare. At one juncture, he asked the name of one of his inquisitors as if he were preparing a mental list for retribution. The young man shrank back into the throng, but the Marquis de Condorcet stepped forward.

"You can take my name, if you like," Condorcet said. He appeared not the least bit intimidated.

"I know who you are," Marat said, scowling. "You shall all pay for your contempt." He stormed out of the house, slamming the door behind him. A great roar of laughter went up from the group. Ben thought that perhaps he should say something, but before he could do so, Doctor Guillotin took the floor.

"That Jean-Paul Marat does not seem a man to be trifled with," Guillotin observed.

"He seems harmless enough to me," Condorcet said. "Besides, he should learn to tolerate criticism better."

"Yes, perhaps he should," Guillotin replied. "But will he?"

Madame Helvétius entered the salon looking as ravishing as usual, but with a perplexed expression on her face. A hush fell over the room. Ben had positioned himself near the door to be closest to her when she arrived. Minette came over to him directly. Ben took her hand and kissed it. She blushed ever so slightly at the warmth of his kiss. Then she stiffened up.

"Ben," she said in a reproachful tone. "What happened to my salon guest?"

"We are all your guests, Madame," Ben replied, playing dumb. He pointed around the room at the other scientists, now looking slightly abashed.

"No Ben … I am speaking of Jean-Paul Marat." She wasn't letting any of them off the hook quite so easily.

"Oh, *that* guest," Ben replied. "He left." A ripple of sniggering crossed the room.

"And why did he leave? Were you boys mean to him?" She looked directly at Condorcet, who avoided her gaze.

"Madame," Ben replied. "John-Paul Marat is not a scientist of the same caliber as these men."

"Nonetheless, there is no excuse to torment my guest."

The men gathered around her mostly looked grim or sheepish, although there were one or two who seemed proud of themselves.

"You are right," Ben said. "We should always behave honorably as gentlemen. It will not happen again." The last of the smiles faded. His statement was accompanied by much earnest nodding on the part of the scientists.

Minette's expression changed immediately to a warm smile.

"Thank you, Ben."

She gave him a glance that promised a suitable reward for his gallantry later. Then she addressed the rest of the group. "*Le Salon de Helvétius* will now officially begin. Who has the first topic of discussion?"

Condorcet, most likely trying to redeem himself, stepped forward. "I do, Madame," he said.

"Then please, present your item, Professor Condorcet," she replied. It seemed that all his prior transgressions were forgiven.

"Today, we are discussing the lifting abilities of heated air and hydrogen vapor."

As the salon got back underway in earnest, the room was once again engulfed in debate. Ben pulled Madame Helvétius aside, unnoticed.

"Minette, I realize that this is your salon, and it is, of course, your privilege to invite anyone you choose. I am simply wondering what led you to invite John-Paul Marat today? He was no friend of your late husband." Ben's voice was hushed as the discussions carried on around them.

"No, of course, he was not," she replied. "But you know, Ben, I believe that man may have something to offer. If not in his science, then perhaps in his ideology."

"As a scientist, he is a minor figure. I know nothing of his ideology."

"I believe he has been inspired by your American Revolution," she said.

"Minette," Ben said. A slightly shocked look crossed his face as her meaning sunk in. "Do you think that Marat has designs to topple the existing government of France?"

"I don't know, but I believe that he does not see the existing monarchy as the only way—as I am sure that you, of all people, will understand."

"I only have an issue with King George, not King Louis."

"Oh, I see. So, you only object to an oppressive monarchy when it affects you personally. Is that it, you big hypocrite?" She smiled and gave Ben a playful shove on the chest.

"You know that is not true," he said.

Yet Ben had to concede—at least to himself—that she was partially right. While the French monarchy was supporting his goal of an independent United States by aiding the American war effort, Ben recognized that it exerted as tight a control over its subjects as the British did over the Colonists, perhaps even more so. Oppressive censorship and intolerance of even the slightest criticism characterized the *ancien regime.*

Ben realized, looking at her right then, that there was nothing more alluring than an intelligent woman. He knew that Minette could keep up with him, both mentally and physically. He wanted to take her in his arms right there.

She must have read his mind because she took his hand.

"Let us escape. No one will miss us," Ben whispered.

She blushed. "Behave yourself," she said and squeezed his hand. "But, could you stay after supper?"

PART
IV

New Year's Eve, 1779

PASSY

ALL DAY BEN had been restless, agitated, and discontent. For a while, he'd attempted to attend to business, writing a few letters, but he soon grew bored and half-heartedly attended a small party hosted by Madame Leray. There, he drank a sip of Champagne and listened to Monsieur Leray animatedly retell the story of how the glassmaker had shaped the glasses in the form of Marie Antoinette's breast. The group of older men and women from Paris seemed to have heard the story before too. The pretty Leray girls were busily helping their mother with the party, and for a while, Ben observed them as they skillfully attended to the guests.

He missed Minette. He thought of her bright smile, her careless laugh, her silvery hair fragrant with flowers. The night before, when they had been together, Ben had proposed marriage to her, and she had rebuffed him. Not in a mean or condescending way, of course, but in her usual jovial way—as if he couldn't be serious. Yet Ben thought that he *was* serious.

"Perhaps, I am destined to follow the fate of Turgot," he thought and sighed. As soon as he determined that he had stayed long enough at the party, Ben found his hostess and kissed her cheek.

"Are you alright?" Madame Leray asked. She must have noted his subdued demeanor. "It is not midnight yet."

"Yes," Ben managed to reply. He wanted to spill everything out to her, but this was not the time or place. He donned his cape and strode across the lawn to his lodgings. The night was cold. The newly frozen grass crunched under his feet. The temperature in his parlor was not much warmer than outside. He lit a lamp just inside the door. "It will be warmer upstairs," he thought as he ascended. The small stove in his bedroom needed stoking but soon elevated the temperature to the point where he could shed his cape.

Ben settled in to write a bagatelle for Minette. The idea had come to him from a dream he had had after her rejection.

"I need a new strategy," he said out loud. Then he picked up his pen and wrote:

The Elysian Fields by B.F.

Saddened by your barbarous resolution, stated so positively last night, to remain single the rest of your life, I went home, fell on my bed, believing myself dead, and found myself in the Elysian Fields. I was asked if I had a wish to see some Important Persons.

Take me to the Philosophers.

There are two who reside quite near here, in this Garden. They are very good neighbors and very good friends of each other. Who are they? Socrates and Helvétius.

I have prodigious esteem for both of them; but let me see H. first, for I understand some French and not a word of Greek.

He received me with great courtesy, having known me by reputation, he said, for some time. He asked me a thousand questions on war, and on the present state of religion, of liberty, and of the government in France. — But you are not enquiring at all about your dear friend Madame H.; yet, she is excessively in love with you, and I was with her but an hour ago.

Ah said he, you are bringing back to my mind my former felicity. But one must forget, in order to be happy in this place. For several of the first years, I thought of nobody but her. Well, now, I am consoled. I have taken another wife. One as similar to her as I could find. She is not, to be sure, quite as beautiful, but she has just as much common sense, a little more wisdom, and she loves me infinitely. Her continuous endeavor is to please me, and she has gone out right now to search for the best nectar and ambrosia to regale me with tonight, stay with me and you shall see her.

I notice, said I, that your former companion is more faithful than you: for several matches have been offered her, and she has turned them all down. I confess that I, for one, loved her madly, but she was harsh towards me and rejected me absolutely for the love of you.

I pity you, said he, for your misfortune, for she is truly a good and lovely woman, and most amiable. But Abbé de la Roche and Abbé Morellet, aren't they anymore in her home, every now and then?

Yes, of course, for she has not lost a single one of your friends.

Now, if you had won over Abbé M. (with coffee and cream) and got him to plead your cause, you might have met with success; for he is as subtle a debater as Duns Scotus or St. Thomas; he puts his arguments in such good order that they become almost irresistible. Or, better still, if you had convinced Abbé de la R. (by the gift of some fine edition of an old classic) to argue against you: for I have always observed that when he advises something, she has a strong tendency to do the exact opposite.

As he was saying this, the new Madame H. came in with

the nectar. I recognized her instantly as Madame F., my former
American housemate. I claimed her as my spouse. But she said
coldly, I have been a good wife to you for forty-nine years and
four months, almost half a century; be content with that. I have
formed a new connection here, that will last for eternity.

Grieved by this rebuke from my Eurydice, I resolved there
and then to abandon those ungrateful spirits, and to come back
to this good world, to see the sun again, and you. Here I am.

Let us avenge ourselves!

Ben went downstairs and out to the print shop. There he spent the rest
of the night and much of New Year's Day painstakingly setting the type to
print his work. By the time he had a copy in hand that pleased him, it was
mid-afternoon. He arranged for the bagatelle to be dispatched by courier to
the home of Madame Helvétius in Auteuil and went off to bed.

The following morning Ben slept in late—for him. In fact, he was awakened by a commotion in his parlor well after the winter sun was up. Temple's
voice was calling him from downstairs.

"Granddad, granddad ... are you awake?"

Ben threw on a robe and walked to the top of the stairs. "I am now,"
he replied.

"Oh ... I am sorry. You have a visitor at the main house."

"Who is it?"

The Abbé Martin de la Roche."

"Go back up and tell him that I will be there in five minutes."

"Alright, Granddad."

Ben hurriedly threw on some clothes. When he arrived at the main
house, Martin was pacing the floor. His bushy eyebrows writhed.

"Martin," Ben exclaimed, "what is the matter?"

"My goodness Ben, your bagatelle has our whole house in a frenzy since
last night. I had to come tell you."

"Did Minette enjoy it?" Ben asked a bit apprehensively.

The Abbé seemed to relax a little. "When Minette received your beautifully printed pamphlet, she almost discarded it, thinking it most likely some proselytizing religious material. But the initials B.F. caught her eye—so she opened it. As she read, she started to giggle. These then turned to chortles, followed soon by big guffaws so violent I thought that she was going to have a fit. Ben, she was practically rolling on the floor. I have never seen her so."

"I thought that my words might amuse her, but I'm not sure that it was intended to be all that funny."

"I read it ... Morellet too. We thought that the bagatelle was just like you—witty, amusing, and intelligent. You must publish it."

"Thank you, Martin."

"The part about our Monsieur Helvétius being wed in heaven to your dearly departed Deborah was a stroke of genius."

"Thank you."

"And the part where she does everything the opposite of my advice, I hope is not really so true?" He looked slightly hurt.

"Of course not."

The Abbé then took on a more sedate tone and serious expression. "But Ben, may I confide in you?"

"Of course."

"While I hope that you will never give up trying, I doubt that Madame will ever marry again."

"Why is that, Martin?"

"Because she loves her freedom too much."

"I know," Ben replied wistfully. He thought for a moment, then smiled. "How about a spot of brandy?"

"If you insist," the Abbé beamed as they walked toward the study.

Ben knew in his heart that Minette would never marry him—or any other. But he secretly hoped that she would accompany him back to Philadelphia someday. He found himself wondering if he would be able to take her home with him to America when the time came.

January 2nd, 1779

PASSY

BEN DECIDED TO READ the morning's mail. One piece stood out among the routine correspondence. It was from Beaumarchais. As was typical when the topic was secret, it was in code.

> *Mr De Beaumarchais a l'honneur de présenter Son respectueux hommage a Monsieur franklin. Il le prie de vouloir bien remettre au porteur de la présente les 56 lettres acceptées. Un peu de dérangement dans la Santé de Mr De Beaumarchais l'empéche d'aller lui même. renouveller a Monsieur Franklin les assurances du respect avec lequel il est le très dévoué Serviteur du noble ministre des Etats unis.*

Literally translated, it read:

Mr. Beaumarchais is pleased to present his respects to Mr. Franklin. He asks kindly remit to this bearer the fifty-six accepted letters. A little disturbance in the health of Mr. Beaumarchais prevents him from going himself.

Renew the assurances, Mr. Franklin, of the respect with which he is the very devoted servant of the noble ambassador of the United States.

Ben knew that there were no fifty-six letters; rather, this was code for fifty-six British merchant seamen recently captured by the American Navy and now held being for ransom. He decoded that Beaumarchais was not sick, but rather was worried about the transaction. Beaumarchais always worried. At the very least, Ben thought, fifty-six captive British subjects will bring a much-needed swap for American prisoners of war, even if no financial remuneration. He decided that he should meet with the Reverend as soon as possible.

The gaunt figure appeared from behind a boxwood tree in the Tuileries as if he could see Ben approaching.

"Beaumarchais is concerned about these prisoners," Ben said.

"He worries too much. He will make himself sick."

"You are not concerned?"

"No, Lord Stormont has already given the order to ensure their release. It seems that one of the seamen is a distant relation. These men will soon be returned home in exchange for several Americans held by the British, and a fair ransom—to spend as you wish. John Paul Jones will complete the transaction within a fortnight."

"And what of Bancroft?"

"If you will continue to supply me a few morsels of misinformation, I will keep him occupied."

"Thank you," Ben said. Thinking his business with the Reverend done, he turned to leave.

"But Ben, I must tell you something else about Bancroft," the Reverend almost whispered.

Ben froze. "What is it?"

"I found out that he recently sold some of his poison to Herr Mesmer."

"What would Mesmer want with poison?"

"I do not know." The Reverend disappeared behind the boxwood and was gone.

Early Spring 1780

PARIS

THE EARLY AFTERNOON LIGHT filtered down through the canopy of trees heavy with buds announcing the imminent arrival of spring. Ben knocked on the green door of the row house on the *Rue Jacob* in the quiet *arrondissement*. The woman he recognized as Marie-Thérèse, lover and housemate of Pierre Beaumarchais, answered the door. She wore her hair tied up with a handkerchief, and her smock bore splashes of flour. Clearly, she was a woman interrupted while baking. She wore a blue-checked cotton blouse, arrestingly unbuttoned at the neck, with the collar nonchalantly flipped up. She portrayed the crisp seductiveness of a Parisian housewife, which held many a husband in conjugal bliss. Marie-Thérèse wiped her hands with a cloth.

"Oh, *bonjour*, Doctor Franklin." She greeted Ben with a warm smile.

"*Bonjour*, Marie-Thérèse," Ben replied with a small bow. He took her hand and kissed it on the back. It tasted like flour. "Is Monsieur available?"

"Yes, I believe Pierre is expecting you this morning. Come in."

She led Ben through the tidy house to a small room toward the back.

There they found Beaumarchais sitting by the fireplace huddled over his writing desk. Papers were scattered everywhere. He looked as though he had been up all night. He wore a dark red silk robe over his pajamas. His hair was a mess. A musty mixture of stale tobacco smoke, coffee, and cognac hit Ben's nose as soon as he entered the room.

Marie-Thérèse looked at Ben. She rolled her eyes.

"Pierre, Doctor Franklin has arrived," she announced. She bustled off toward her kitchen.

Beaumarchais jumped up. "Oh my, Doctor Franklin," he exclaimed. "Is it that time already?"

"My friend, you look as though you are in the midst of a creative frenzy. I can come back another time," Ben offered.

"No, no. Please sit down," Beaumarchais said. He cleared a chair of crumpled papers. "I need your counsel."

"How may I be of service?"

Beaumarchais wrung his hands in exasperation. "I am re-writing *The Marriage of Figaro once again*," he said.

"And why would you be doing that, my friend? I have heard that it is wickedly funny, just like *The Barber of Seville*," Ben said. "Although I have not been invited to any of the readings yet."

"At present, I am confined to granting only private performances as it has not yet passed the King's censor. However, I will make sure that you have an opportunity to see my work performed. Marie Antoinette plays the Countess to perfection."

"Ah, your sharp tongue displeases His Majesty, methinks," Ben observed.

"It must be easy for you to be so blasé. You simply declared outright war on your sovereign."

"*Touché*," Ben said. He pressed his hand over his heart.

"But I want my work seen by a larger audience. I have been racking my brain all night. I must tone down the parts that the censor finds offensive and yet keep the wit intact."

"I understand your challenge only too well," Ben said. "I too have had to use wit to make palatable my critiques of injustice. But there is great satisfaction to be gained in working to craft a piece to achieve your goal without being offensive or crass."

"Yes, I particularly remember '*An Edict by the King of Prussia*'."

Ben smiled. "My point in that bagatelle was that it made about as much sense for England to attempt to restrain the trade of our colonies as it would for the King of Prussia to claim jurisdiction over many things made by the English."

"Do you think that King George got your point?"

"I doubt it. It didn't stop the British attempts at enforcement of their unjust controls and tariffs."

"Ben, that is why I must try to move this country away from the tyranny of the *ancien regime*. The will of the people should rule."

Revolutionary talk made Ben uneasy. He still very much needed the assistance of the French government with his American war effort, and he found that the current French regime suited this purpose. He quickly changed the subject.

"Marie Antoinette plays the Countess?" Ben asked. "She was delicious as Rosine in *The Barber of Seville*."

"Yes, and she plays this part very well also. You shall see her at our earliest opportunity."

"It will be my pleasure," Ben said.

However, he wondered if the French monarchy would survive long beyond the American Revolution.

Summer 1780

PARIS

BEAUMARCHAIS'S PROMISED reading could not come quickly enough, as far as Ben was concerned. His diplomatic mission had seemed especially grueling of late. The French resolve for the backing of his effort to win the war seemed to be waning, and he had to admit there was not as much success as he would have liked to show for their support to date.

Much of Ben's time and energy had been consumed recently by attempting to mitigate a feud between the always-hotheaded John-Paul Jones and another American naval captain by the name of Landais. The two men seemed locked in increasing episodes of one-upmanship that threatened to do damage to the American cause. On more than one occasion, Landais had actually fired on Jones's ship. His defense had been that it was an inadvertent fire in the heat of a battle with the British. Madame Leray, however, held another view. Since her husband personally sponsored Captain Landais, she believed there was a plot afoot to assassinate her former lover. The whole situation put Ben in a most difficult position. He desperately needed his naval officers fighting the British, not each other, as well as his host's continued financial and ideological support. Ben tried to straddle the diplomatic fence as best he could.

If the marine battlefront had its share of difficulty, at least at sea, there were some victories to be celebrated. The war on land appeared to be going badly. In May, British Forces had taken Charleston, South Carolina. While the capture of that beautiful city was not pleasant to contemplate, the Waxhaws massacre weighed even more heavily on Ben's mind. In that incident, loyalist cavalry and British dragoons led by Banastre Tarleton had cut down a revolutionary insurgent force of nearly two hundred men while they were attempting to surrender near Lancaster, South Carolina.

Ben wished for the war to be over. He longed for a diversion, and there were precious few to be had. Both Madame Helvétius and Madame Brillon had fled the summer heat of Paris for their respective country homes. Marianne seemed perpetually unavailable, preoccupied with her career—or so she said. On the brighter side, Benny was back from boarding school for the summer. He had finally agreed to let Ben teach him to swim. Benny had also developed an interest in learning to operate Ben's printing press. These occupations engaged the precocious eleven-year-old and his delighted grandfather on many evenings as long as the sun stayed up.

But, at last, the invitation from Beaumarchais arrived. Ben accepted immediately. He and a guest were to be welcomed for the private reading of Beaumarchais's new play at the home of Pierre Samuel du Pont, the Inspector General of Commerce, the successor to Monsieur Turgot. Ben knew Monsieur du Pont through his business dealings, of course. More than that, he held in utmost respect this son of a watchmaker who had risen from humble surroundings to become a successful physician, scientist, and member of the inner circle of the French court.

Du Pont had a lovely family, made up of his wife Nicole and their two boys, roughly the same ages as Temple and Benny. They shared many interests with the Franklin's—science, commerce, the arts, and literature—to name a few. Du Pont's book entitled *Physiocrasy,* published in 1767, advocating for low tariffs and free trade among nations, resonated strongly with Ben's own beliefs. Only the distance between their lodgings—du Pont lived in the southeastern quarter of Paris, referred to as Nemours—kept them from being even closer friends.

Ben dashed off a note to Madame Helvétius, inviting her to accompany him to the reading. He sealed the note with candle wax embossed by his stamp. "I hope this will tempt my Minette away from her peaceful country life, even if only briefly," he thought. He hiked up the hill to the main house to catch the express post.

Her response came the very next day. She would be pleased to go with him. As he read her short letter, obviously done in haste, and with her usual misspellings, he could almost feel the longing she had for him. Ben missed her all the more. It was difficult to concentrate on his ambassadorial duties the week leading up to the reading. Ben swam daily to work out some of his tension, but as the date approached, he felt increasingly restless with anticipation.

The day before the reading, a hand-delivered note came from Auteuil. It read:

> *Demain, mon amour, s'il vous plaît arriver tôt si*
> *mai que nous nous rassasier pour le long voyage à Nemours.*

> *Minette*

As usual, her choice of words intrigued Ben. She asked that he arrive early enough at her home tomorrow so that they would have time to "satiate" themselves prior to the long ride to Nemours. He could think of at least two ways to interpret her words. He hoped that she was not inviting him to join her for a meal.

The day of the reading arrived with the morning sun promising robust warmth as it quickly burned through the misty coolness. Ben dressed in crisp linen. He left his pocket watch at home. A few wisps of fog hugged the lowest dales as he passed in the coach on the way to Auteuil.

The courtier cats escorted Ben up the garden path. A male voice was singing opera inside. Handel's *Rodrigo* ... in Italian, Ben recognized. He pulled the doorbell. The singing stopped. Martin appeared and welcomed Ben inside. He was wearing what looked like a smock. Ben gave him a puzzled look.

"I am presently painting the library," the Abbé said by way of explanation. "Neither Cabanis nor the Abbé Morellet are at home. They found other things to occupy themselves as soon as I started on this project."

"No doubt," Ben said. He smiled, amused by the appearance of the burly abbé in a smock, a few splatters of paint on his bushy eyebrows.

"I understand that you and Madame will be attending a private reading of *The Marriage of Figaro*. Is that correct?"

"Yes," Ben replied, "at the home of Monsieur du Pont. Marie Antoinette will play the Countess."

"Ah, I would love to see that. She was wonderful as Rosine."

"Yes, she was."

"Do you know when *The Marriage of Figaro* will be publicly performed?"

"No, it still has to pass the King's censor."

"Yes, of course." The Abbé looked disappointed. "I hope that will be soon."

"Me also, my friend," Ben replied. "Madame asked that I send you upstairs," he said. Martin seemed the epitome of discretion.

The two separated, the Abbé back toward the library, while Ben ascended the stairs.

It was slightly warmer upstairs, although there was a breeze through the hallway. It carried the distinct fragrance of Minette's perfume. Ben could faintly hear the Abbé, who had resumed singing opera in Italian, as he continued to follow his nose to Minette's boudoir.

Minette sat in front of an oval mirror at her dressing table with her back to the door. She was nude from the waist up. Her back was tanned. She was combing her long silvery-gray hair. Each stroke of her arms caused the muscles of her upper back to tense, defining her lithe physique. Ben could have enjoyed the view a good while longer, but she noticed him in the mirror.

"Oh, Ben," she exclaimed. Yet, she didn't make the slightest move to cover up. "You *are* here early."

"Just as you ordered, my lady."

"Thank you. You can assist me," she purred.

"I was hoping that I might. Do you require another cure?"

"You are incorrigible. No, truly, I need your opinion. Do you like my hair better down as it is ... or up?"

Ben tried to be diplomatic. "I like it either way," he said.

"You are no help," she complained. "Let me show you. This is down." She put her arms out to the side with palms up. "And this is up." She took her long hair and folded it masterfully in a knot, lifting both arms above her head. When she did, her breasts rose just enough for Ben to savor a wonderful view in the mirror from behind. Her nipples, which had been angled slightly down until that maneuver, now pointed straight toward the mirror. The muscular line of her shoulder, upper arm, and axilla gracefully blended into the slight bulge of her pectoral muscle, leading Ben's eye directly to the lovely pair.

It was impossible for him to keep his attention on her hair.

"Umm," was all that Ben could manage to say. He walked up close behind her. She kept her arms raised as he gently reached around her and cradled her breasts. They felt incredibly soft, smooth. Just the ideal weight and size to fill his large hands. She moaned softly. Her nipples hardened immediately. She stood and turned around. As she dropped her arms, her silvery tresses cascaded around them, filling the space with her fragrance. She pulled Ben's crisp linen shirt off over his head. Then she wrapped her arms around his muscular back at the waist. She squeezed, pressing her bare chest into his. She looked up at him. Their lips embraced in a kiss that took Ben's breath away. He felt it to his toes.

At some point, Ben came up for air. He looked over at her bed, an unmade mess of white linen sheets covered in an explosion of brightly colored pillows. Minette must have caught his glance because she released him and bounded for the bed, ditching her loose skirt in the process. She giggled as she dove in, sending pillows flying. Ben wasn't very far behind.

The long coach ride to the city home of Monsieur du Pont was made exceedingly more pleasant by the morning's adventure. Relaxed, happy, and filled with a sense of well-being, Ben and Minette talked of science, of art, of war, and of independence. The mundane route that might otherwise have been nearly intolerably boring to Ben came to an end almost too soon—except that he had the return trip to look forward to.

Nicole du Pont met them at the door of the largest home in Nemours. The street was lined with the coaches of those who had already arrived. This quarter of Paris itself was decidedly working class, Ben observed. The du Ponts were the upper crust of their neighborhood, and many at court might wonder why they stayed here. The family, though, had roots in the area where Pierre du Pont had grown up. The family shop still operated in the area despite Pierre having exited the family watchmaking business. Although Nicole hailed from a minor noble family, she seemed to fit into the neighborhood perfectly. Ben could imagine her shopping at the local market with the other housewives just as easily as rubbing elbows with the elite in Versailles.

She smiled as her famous guests walked up the steps. "Pierre would have met you personally, but he has gone to *le cave*."

"*Le cave?*" Ben and Minette asked simultaneously.

"Yes, you know, the family wine cellar. We call it *le cave* because it is literally a tunnel dug into the side of a hill near here. It has been in the du Pont family for so many generations that I suspect Pierre's ancestors once called it their home. Now it is simply where our wine rests."

As they stood at the front door, a wagon bearing two men in frumpy hats approached. Ben noticed a wine cask strapped in the cargo area.

"Oh, here is Pierre now," Madame du Pont said. She waved.

The wagon pulled up at the front door. One of the men jumped down from the wagon and bounded over toward Ben and Minette. He took his frumpy hat in hand and proceeded to present himself to the astonished guests with a deep bow. His pants and boots were splattered with mud, there were sweat stains on his shirt, but now that he was closer, Ben could see that it was indeed Pierre du Pont. He looked not at all like a courtier and certainly not like the Inspector General, but instead like a common workingman who might be delivering wine to the home of a nobleman.

"Pierre, you reek," his wife exclaimed. She pinched her nose, feigning disgust.

"Sorry," he said. He took a step back. "Gustav and I had to move some casks to a drier area of *le cave.*" He nodded over at the man driving the wagon, who Ben noticed was even muddier than his host.

Ben laughed. "I am glad to see that your success has not spoiled you for hard work."

"That it has not," Pierre replied. He wiped his mud-splattered brow with his hat. "Nicole, while I get cleaned up, would you be so kind as to show our guests to the theater?"

"Of course, my dearest, I was just about to do so when you pulled up. You had best hurry along, though. We don't want to start the play too late."

Monsieur du Pont bounded back up on the wagon, grabbed the reins, and gave them a crack. "Yaaaa," he bellowed. The draught horse clopped slowly forward.

"Follow me," Madame du Pont said.

Ben and Minette entered the foyer. The house was much more lavish inside than the plain exterior let on. Chandeliers hung heavy with candles in every room. The parquet floors were exquisite, the rugs Oriental, and the furniture finely turned and expertly arranged. Ben and Minette followed Madame du Pont through the elegant home to a garden in the back. A professional-looking stage had been set up there with about thirty chairs arranged in front. An equal number of guests milled around the lawn, chatting.

The sun was starting to lower in the west. Large white painted reflector panels had been placed strategically off the back of the house to illuminate the stage as the sun set. Ben could see that a stagehand perched in a crow's nest manned each panel. Ben surmised that the amount of reflected sunlight directed at the stage could be tuned by adjusting the angle of the panel. At present, the stage was fully lit. A slight young man with wild auburn hair played the pianoforte at one side. Ben thought he recognized the lad.

"Is that Wolfgang Mozart?" he asked.

"Yes, doesn't he play divinely?" Madame du Pont said.

She was motioned aside by one of the house staff, who whispered something in her ear. "I'm sorry, I must go," she said to Ben and Minette. She whisked off toward the house to deal with whatever minor problem had arisen.

Ben and Minette each scanned the party to see if they knew anyone else in attendance. Ben pointed out Doctor D'Eslon sitting down front near the stage by himself.

"The Mesmerist?" she asked.

"Yes."

"You don't believe in his *magnétisme animale* fluid, do you, Ben?"

"No."

"But, our Queen does."

"Apparently so, for D'Eslon seems to always show up where she is."

"Perhaps he is infatuated with her. Many men are, you know. Your friend, Monsieur Le Veillard would be her lap dog if he could." She laughed.

"D'Eslon doesn't impress me as a man prone to infatuation."

"Shall we go say hello to him? He looks lonely," she said.

"I suspect that he would rather sit alone than have a visit from me."

"And why is that?"

"For the simple reason that I have challenged him to show me the evidence that Mesmer's fluid has the effects that he claims it does."

"He should not hold that against you. He should want to prove his theories."

"They are Mesmer's theories. Regardless, I have found in D'Eslon a man who seems willing to believe blindly in them since it suits his purpose."

"And what would that be?"

"Money, prestige, and power over others."

"Strong inducements, indeed. Let's *not* go say hello just now."

Ben looked around. "No Monsieur Turgot?"

"He won't be coming."

"And why is that?" Ben asked.

Minette lowered her voice to a whisper. "You are aware that he was removed from the post of Inspector General of Commerce?"

"Yes."

"Well, Monsieur du Pont replaced him."

"So?"

"It is not that Monsieur du Pont had any part in the scheme, but still, it left a bitter aftertaste for my patron. I have not seen the two men together since that time."

"And Turgot won't mind you being here tonight?"

"Ben, I am your guest. If he has any qualms, it would more likely be that we are together ... rather than that I visit the home of Monsieur du Pont to see a play."

Ben was reminded of why they were there. "Do you see Beaumarchais?" he asked.

"No, he is most likely backstage. What do you know about this play?"

"I know that it's a continuation of the previous storyline he started in *The Barber of Seville*. Do you recall how Figaro rescued Rosine, the young page of the old lecherous Doctor Bartholo—how Figaro connived to have her marry her true love Count Almaviva instead?"

"Yes, it was masterful how Figaro set up the events so that no other outcome was possible."

"Well, *The Marriage of Figaro* takes place a few years later. Rosine is now the Countess, unhappy and ignored by her husband, Count Almaviva. In an ironic turn of events, the Count now plots to seduce young Suzanne, personal maid to the Countess, but betrothed to Figaro. I don't know how it all ends up, but knowing Beaumarchais, I am sure that it will be wickedly funny."

263

"It sounds so. But I didn't hear you say anything that should keep it from passing the censor."

"I am not sure about that either. I know that Beaumarchais has been working diligently to tone this play down without losing his bite. He enjoys poking fun at the nobility, but they are usually the ones laughing the hardest at the *Comédie Française*."

"Everyone gets the joke except the King and his censor, I guess."

"I suppose."

Mozart finished a beautiful sonata to scattered applause. Monsieur du Pont, looking much cleaner in a white silk jacket, ruffled shirt, and trousers, bounded on stage from behind a side curtain.

"*Mesdames et Messieurs*," he announced. "Please take your seats ... in order that our performance may begin."

A curtain dropped just behind him as he bounded off the stage. Everyone quickly found a seat. Ben and Minette were in the first row, center. She squeezed his hand as the curtain went up. A server delivered a glass of the house red wine to Ben. He smelled French oak, blackberries, and a little sage. One sip told him that he would enjoy this night. He looked over to where his host sat, catching his eye. Du Pont raised his glass. Ben answered by raising his also, in a salute to the fine vintage recently liberated from *le cave*.

The stage was set as a large room, mostly barren of furniture with the exception of one large chair and a dressing mirror. Figaro was on his hands and knees, measuring the room with a long ruler. Suzanne stood in front of a mirror, fixing a bridal garland in her hair.

The actor portraying Figaro spoke first.

FIGARO. *Nineteen foot by twenty-six.*
SUAZANNE. *Figaro, look at my wedding bonnet. Do you like it better like this? (She adjusts it.)*
FIGARO. *(Taking her hands.) My darling, it is perfect. What sight could be better calculated to enslave a bridegroom than that dainty, virginal garland on the head of my pretty wife-to-be,*

on the very morning that we are to be married?

SUZANNE. (Shrugs) What are you measuring, my love?

FIGARO. I'm trying to calculate, my dear Suzanne, if the grand bed his Lordship has given us will fit in here.

SUZANNE. In here? In this room?

FIGARO. In this very room. He is letting us have it.

SUZANNE. I don't want it.

FIGARO. Why not?

SUZANNE. I just don't want it.

FIGARO. And why not?

SUZANNE. I don't like it.

FIGARO. Usually one would give a reason . . .

SUZANNE. And what if I don't want to?

FIGARO. (aside) The minute women get you in their pocket . . .

A titter rippled through the audience upon Figaro's observation.

SUZANNE. Having to prove I am right means admitting that I might be wrong. Are you or are you not my slave?

The actor playing Figaro paused just there, looking furtively at the audience. Ben, and everyone else, immediately burst into boisterous laughter.

Later in the first Act, The Countess Rosine made her first appearance. The audience reacted with a small thrill as they recognized Marie Antoinette. Ben recalled a quite similar reaction upon her entrance to the party at the Hôtel de Valentinois. Though all eyes were instantly on her, she didn't seem to notice. She was statuesque, impeccably dressed in what, for her, would be rather plain everyday attire, Ben thought, yet she carried herself with regal charm and grace. When she spoke her first line, Ben was entranced along with the rest of the audience. Her voice was clear and soothing, yet she enunciated perfectly. She appeared calm, natural, completely in character. It was as if she really were the Countess.

"Probably easy for her to play royalty," Ben whispered to Minette. She poked him in the ribs.

By Act Five, those same ribs ached from laughing so much. But just in the nick of time, Beaumarchais got more serious. Count Almaviva had seemed to have successfully tempted Suzanne into agreeing to his advances. The other characters did not know, however, that Suzanne and the Countess had plotted to switch places at the critical moment.

> FIGARO. (pacing alone, gloomy) ... No Count, you won't have her, you shall not have her! You think that because you are a great lord that you are a great genius! Nobility, wealth, rank, high position ... such things make a man proud. But what did you ever do to earn these? Choose your parents carefully, that is all. Take away that and what have you got? You are an average man.

"I can see how the King might take exception to those words," whispered Ben. He received another poke.

In the climactic scene, which took place at night in an outdoor pavilion, the Countess was dressed in disguise as Suzanne. In the dark, the Count mistakenly believed that he was seducing his prize, when actually it was his own wife. Figaro and the "real" Suzanne observed the interaction from opposite wings.

> COUNT. (Taking his wife's hand) Such skin! So soft, so silky! The Countess's hand isn't half as smooth to the touch!
> COUNTESS. (Aside) What would you know?
> COUNT. Or her arms as firm, as shapely. Or her fingers as pretty and elegant ... and teasing.
> COUNTESS. (Imitating Suzanne's voice) And love ... ?
> COUNT. Ah, love is a tale of the heart and pleasure drives its

story. It's pleasure that has brought me here to worship at your feet...

COUNTESS. Don't you love her any more?

COUNT. I love her a great deal. But after these years of marriage, it becomes so respectable.

COUNTESS. What did you look for in her?

COUNT. (stroking her hand) What I find in you, my sweet.

COUNTESS. But what exactly?

COUNT. I'm not sure. More variety perhaps, more spice in our life, a whiff of excitement, for her to say no sometimes, who knows? Wives think that they've done all they need do once they've decided they love us. Once they've said they're in love, deeply in love – they become so endlessly accommodating, so eternally relentlessly agreeable, that one fine day a man is startled to find that he has achieved boredom – not the happiness he was looking for.

COUNTESS. (Aside) I never knew!

COUNT. The fact is, Suzanne, I've often thought that if husbands look outside marriage for pleasures which they don't find inside it, it's because wives don't think enough about how to keep our love alive, how to renew theirs, how to--what's the word?--rejuvenate its pleasures by varying them.

COUNTESS. (Indignant) So wives must do it all?

COUNT. (Laughing) And husbands nothing? Should we try to change our nature? Our function is to catch them; theirs ...

COUNTESS. Theirs?

COUNT.... . is to keep us. People forget that.

COUNTESS. I won't.

COUNT. Nor me.

FIGARO. (Aside) Nor me.

SUZANNE. (Aside) Nor me.

"Nor me," Ben whispered. "Ouch." He received another jab in his rib. Ben took Minette's hand and held it lest she be tempted to poke him once again.

"Nor me," Minette said. She gave his hand a squeeze.

The play concluded with the substitution revealed; the plot to seduce Suzanne foiled, her honor intact; Figaro and Suzanne married; the Count and Countess reconciled—at least for now; and the whole cast singing a happy song accompanied by the wild-haired young pianist named Mozart. The entire audience stood clapping as the cast took repeated bows. Beaumarchais joined the cast for their last one. Ben watched the stagehands direct the final rays of the setting sun onto the stage just as the curtain came down to thunderous ovation.

As the audience was now all standing, the staff swiftly moved all the unoccupied chairs to the sides—opening up a large grassy area in the middle. Paper lanterns were lit in the trees, giving the garden a most festive appearance in the twilight. Conversations began. The host and hostess mingled with the guests on the far side. More wine and many trays of hors d'oeuvres appeared, served by white-gloved house staff. A small throng of well-wishers surrounded Minette and Ben. They were all people that Ben either couldn't recall the name of … or didn't recognize at all. But Minette knew some of them, leaving Ben free merely to shake hands, smile affably, and listen to their banter. The couple remained the center of attention only briefly though, for as soon as the cast appeared, their entourage abandoned them as quickly as it had arrived. However, Pierre and Nicole du Pont came over.

"What did you think of the play?" Pierre asked.

"*Magnifique*," Ben replied.

"It has so much more depth than *The Barber of Seville*," Minette observed. "The characters, while mostly continuations from the former play, all seem to have grown, developed."

"I am glad that Beaumarchais has kept his bite," Ben said.

"Hopefully, this version will pass the censor," Pierre du Pont observed. "That is him over there." He motioned to a dour-looking man sitting by the side of the garden.

"He doesn't appear overly happy," Ben said.

"That is his job," Nicole du Pont said. "Your job, Doctor Franklin, is to enjoy yourself tonight." She raised her hand and a server hustled over with a tray of delicious looking *hors d'oeuvres*.

"I'll do my very best," Ben replied. He popped a tasty pastry covered morsel into his mouth.

The throng seemed to be moving in their direction once again, but Ben could see that it was being driven from inside this time. As the larger group enveloped the foursome, Ben realized that Marie Antoinette, or Beaumarchais, or both, had been maneuvering the crowd toward their position. Once surrounded by the throng again, Ben and Minette stood face-to-face with the playwright and Marie Antoinette. Ben took her hand just as Beaumarchais reached for Minette's.

"*Enchanté*," each whispered as they bowed, savoring a fragranced hand.

As the two men came up from their enjoyable greeting, Beaumarchais spoke first.

"Ben," he said, "I'm so glad you could come tonight and that you were so thoughtful to bring the captivating Madame Helvétius."

"Flatterer," Minette said. She blushed slightly.

"And you, my dear friend, I knew that your play would be wickedly funny, but your casting of our fair Queen as the Countess was a stroke of genius," Ben said. He was still holding her hand in his.

Marie Antoinette curtsied. "Thank you, Doctor," she said.

"Ben, I can't keep her away from the set. She was a born actress—missed her calling by becoming a Queen, if you ask me," Beaumarchais said. He laughed, but it quickly turned to a yelp. Marie Antoinette must have given him a whack on his foot with her heel.

"But probably a bit better off financially because of it," Ben said. Everyone in the vicinity laughed heartily except Doctor D'Eslon, hovering just behind the Queen. He wore the same scowl that Ben had noted earlier.

"Yes, I'm strictly amateur," she said.

"Ah, a perfect choice of words, my dear, for it literally means 'one who does something just for the love of it,'" Ben replied.

"Sometimes it seems that I'm strictly amateur too," Beaumarchais said. He turned his pockets inside out to show they contained no money. "If it were not for the du Ponts, this reading would never have happened."

"Speaking of our hosts, we must find them and thank them before I have to leave," Marie Antoinette said, looking around.

"They were just with us," Ben said. Pierre du Pont tapped him on the shoulder from behind. "Oh, there you are," Ben exclaimed.

Ben and Minette quickly traded places with the du Ponts. Ben snatched a handful of hors d'oeuvres as he and Minette made their way toward the coach. He looked forward to the long ride back to Auteuil. He decided it best to avoid bringing up the topic of marriage tonight—or anytime soon.

Summer 1780

PARIS

THE QUEEN'S COACH entered the *Place Vendôme* near midnight. Marianne watched from the balcony as she stepped down.

"Did you see Ben?" Marianne asked as soon as she and Marie Antoinette were with the flock, perched among the stars. She had long ago admitted to the Queen that she and Ben were lovers and confessed to her confusion over their relationship. The air was crisp, clear. Dark iridescent blue surrounded them. The zodiac constellations spread overhead, rippled gray clouds below. The Queen sat upon the sparkling, translucent throne of Cassiopeia, a scepter shimmering in her right hand. She seemed slightly distracted as she flicked the wand, releasing a small comet across the sky. Marianne sat on her usual stool at the Queen's side. She wasn't sure she had been heard. She waited.

"Marianne, I probably shouldn't tell you," Marie Antoinette said at last. "You could have come to the play yourself."

"You know I couldn't ... Mother ..." Marianne started to protest.

Marie Antoinette abruptly glanced at her with a look that stopped her mid-sentence.

"Alright, I could have come. But did you see him?" she asked pleadingly.

"Yes."

"How did he look?"

"Fine, Marianne, he looked fine."

"What do you mean, 'fine'?"

"I mean fine—all right, he was big, strong, handsome, virile—I wanted to have him right there on the grassy lawn of the du Pont's garden."

"Now, you are making light of me!"

"No, I'm not. *I've* never actually had the pleasure. You know that you can couple with him any time that you want. Ben will always come when you call. All you have to do is escape from Mother … and Herr Mesmer."

"Mesmer has no power over me."

"Then why have you not seen Ben in months?"

"I've been busy." Marianne was quiet for a moment. "Was he with someone?"

"I'm not telling you."

"Was it that Madame Brillon?"

"She's a haughty bitch. Do you know that she owns the first piano made by Érard in Paris?"

"My Queen," Marianne exclaimed. "Don't be spiteful. You must have twenty pianos in the palace."

Marie Antoinette laughed. "I'd like to find an excuse to slap her in irons," she said.

Marianne went on, "Most likely, your cousin then, the carefree widow Helvétius."

"At least she is sensible … and she shall never marry him."

"A small consolation. She's probably bedding him tonight."

"Perhaps, but just remember what I've said to you many times before. He would be with you if only you asked."

"I know."

"So why don't you claim him? His wife has been dead seven years now."

"I am not sure that I could hold him. You know what happens when you marry a man who strays from his wife, don't you?" Marianne asked.

"Yes." Then they answered in unison, "You get a husband who strays from his wife . . ." They looked at each other, and both laughed.

"Now, let's get the work done that we came here for," Marie Antoinette said as they recovered from laughing.

"Alright," Marianne said. She felt a slight churning in her stomach. She knew that she had no hold on Ben, but still abhorred the idea of another woman having him.

"Do you see that man way over there?" Marie Antoinette asked.

Marianne squinted into the inky darkness in the direction the Queen pointed.

"No. I don't see anyone."

"I'll bring his image closer."

Marie Antoinette flicked a comet toward the constellation Leo. The shimmering ball soared out across the sky. Then slowly, it came floating back toward them. As it returned, Marianne could see that it held within it an image of a man sitting on a chair. He was holding his chest. Closer up, Marianne could see the look of pain on his face. He appeared frightened. His breathing was labored. The Queen brought the glistening image to rest right in front of them. He was full size now. Marianne could see the beads of sweat on his brow. His right fist was clenched tight to his chest.

"It is Monsieur de Gébelin, is it not?" Marianne asked. "He appears to be in pain."

"Yes, it is de Gébelin. Can you see what is wrong with him?"

Marianne peered into the iridescent spherical image. She had to move around his side to get a better view of what was under his clenched fist. She saw his heart pumping the blood fluid throughout his body.

"I can't quite ... Wait just a minute . . ."

As Marianne looked closer, she noted that one particular wall of de Gébelin's heart did not seem to be working in harmony with the rest. It lay motionless while the other walls moved rhythmically in and out. "It appears that his heart organ is not working properly."

"Good ... I mean—not good for him, but good that you can see what is wrong."

"Yes, it appears that a part of his heart muscle has died. That can't be good. He needs his blood fluid pumping around his body. What was he doing just before this happened?"

"Climbing the stairs to his room at the Lodge of the Nine Sisters."

"As Ben says, the heat of the activity is directly related to the amount of exertion. Perhaps Monsieur de Gébelin has exceeded the capability of his heart organ to keep up with the activity he was trying to perform?"

"Perhaps. What would you recommend he do in this situation? Doctor D'Eslon is treating him."

Marianne said, "I know of no treatment that will bring the dead heart muscle back to life. My only suggestion is that he tries to live within his limitations. Take the stairs one at a time, resting halfway up or any time he has these pains in his chest. Avoid excessive heat or cold, other stresses on the heart organ. Eat small meals, avoid red meat, and take plenty of water. Walk daily, but only below the level of exertion that results in chest pain. With time he may find that he can tolerate more activity. That, I believe, is all that he can do for his condition."

"Thank you, Marianne," Marie Antoinette said.

"Limit his activities! I could have told you that," Marianne heard D'Eslon mutter under his breath to Marie Antoinette as they sat *en rapport* across the patio. Her sense of hearing remained very much heightened after her flight. The Queen cast her a knowing look.

"What an idiot," Marianne said out loud.

"Who?" Mesmer asked. He looked up from where he had been sitting with his knees locked outside hers, his warm hands on her left thigh and sternum.

"Nevermind."

The rhythmic hoofbeats of the royal team stopping just below on the

Place Vendôme heralded the end of their time together for the night. It was past two a.m.

"Walking?" the Queen asked.

"Yes, it will do me good," Marianne replied. She threw on her dark cape despite the warm evening.

Mesmer's pleadings for her to stay would fall on deaf ears tonight. She pushed him aside and headed toward home.

Midnight October 22nd, 1780

PASSY

"OUCH, OH, OUCH," Ben groaned. He awoke with a searing pain in his great toe. He immediately knew that his old nemesis, Madame Gout, had decided to pay him a visit. He tried the usual remedy. He thrust his throbbing foot out from under the covers. There was no relief. After some further suffering, Ben quit his bed. He lit the oil lamp on his bedside table, grumbling to himself about his misfortune. He hobbled over to the washbasin, placed it on the floor, and covered his foot with cool water. It helped for a moment. Then the throbbing returned. He dried off his foot and hobbled next to his medicine chest. There he dissolved a heaping spoonful of willow bark powder in a cup of water and drank. It tasted bitter. By now, Ben was completely awake.

He decided to write. Sitting at his writing desk, pounding foot propped up on a pillow, the flickering yellow lamplight illuminating a small sphere of his space, he picked up his pen.

B.F. and The Gout

Franklin. Ouch, oh, ouch! What have I done to merit these cruel sufferings?

Gout. Many things. You ate and drank too freely, and too much indulged your legs in indolence.

F. Who is it that speaks to me?

Gout. It is I, the Gout.

F. My enemy in person!

Gout. No, not your enemy.

F. Yes, my enemy; for you would not only torment my body to death, but ruin my good name; you reproach me as a glutton and a tippler.

Gout. The world may think as it pleases. But I know very well the amount of meat and drink proper for a man who takes a reasonable amount of exercise, yet would be too much for another who never takes any.

F. I take—oh, ouch—as much exercise as I can, Madame Gout. You know the reasons for my sedentary state; the work that I do. It would seem that you might spare me a little, seeing that it is not altogether my fault.

Gout. Not a jot; your rhetoric and politeness are discarded. If your occupation is a sedentary one, then your amusements, your recreations, at least should be active. You ought to walk or ride on horseback instead of taking the carriage. But let us further examine your course of life. While the sun is up well before breakfast, when you have leisure to go out, what do you do? Why, instead of gaining an appetite by exercise, you sit and read books, pamphlets and newspapers—most of which are not worth the trouble. Next you eat a large breakfast; four cups of tea with cream, one or two pieces of buttered toast with slices of dried beef, which I fancy are not things the most easily digested. Immediately afterwards you sit down to write at your desk or talk with people who apply to you on business. Thus the time passes until one o'clock without any form of bodily exercise. But this I will pardon you because, as you say, of your sedentary occupation. But after dinner what do you do? Instead of walking in the beautiful gardens of the friends with whom you have dined as men of sense would, you sit down to chess where you may be found for two or three hours. This is your perpetual recreation, which is the least fit for any sedentary man; because instead of accelerating the motion of the fluids, the attention it requires only retards the circulation and obstructs internal secretions. Rapt in the speculations of this wretched game, you destroy your constitution. What can be expected from such a course of living, but a body replete with stagnant humours, ready to fall prey to all kinds of dangerous maladies, if I, the Gout, did not occasionally bring you relief by agitating those bad humours – purifying and dissipating them? If it were in some nook or alley in Paris, deprived of walks, that you played a while at chess after dinner, this might be excusable. But it is the same with you in Passy, Auteuil, Montmartre, Epinay or Sanoy, where there are the finest gardens and walks, the purest air, beautiful women, and the most agreeable and instructive conversation, all of which you might have in walking. But these are all neglected for this abominable game of chess. Alas, amidst my instructions I almost forgot to administer your punishment. Take that twinge, and that!

The arguments flowed from Ben's pen onto the paper for some time. Ben closed his eyes, listening to the sound of birds starting their day in the steel gray of autumn, his leg propped up on a pillow with the foot thrust out of the covers.

"It's going to be a long winter," he groaned, to no one but himself.

Early Spring, 1781

PASSY

OVER THE WINTER, Ben's gouty foot had slowly healed. Minette came to Passy frequently to nurse him, and Ben enjoyed the attention. Nonetheless, he decided to take the earliest opportunity to fulfill his promise to Madame Gout by going for a swim. "Perhaps a bit too early," he thought as he dove off the dock at the back of the Hôtel de Valentinois into the chilly water of the Seine. However, he warmed up quickly after a few muscular strokes in the direction of Auteuil. As he swam, he contemplated the events of the past winter.

In November, he had received word that the British captain John Andre—the man who had once occupied his home in Philadelphia and stolen his portrait—had been hanged. Andre had been caught attempting to aid a plot by the American General Benedict Arnold to surrender the fort at West Point to the British. Apparently, Andre had been discovered, dressed as a civilian, in an area controlled by the Americans. He was found with papers written by Arnold, detailing access to the fort. Andre was tried as a spy and quickly executed.

Ben swam on his back in the Seine, contemplating the captain's ignoble end. Although he never wished harm on any man, he did feel vindicated in his bitter dislike of Andre. General Arnold had narrowly escaped down the Hudson River and was believed to have rendezvoused with the British navy. The plot was foiled, but the whole business still worried Ben. Arnold would surely reveal any American secrets that he knew. Ben hoped that General Washington had taken appropriate action to guard against this. Trusting Washington as he did, Ben felt sure he would take Benedict Arnold's knowledge into account when planning his future strategy.

In more promising news, Ben had recently learned that the Green Dragoon—Banastre Tarleton—the man who had led the Waxhaws massacre—had been defeated in South Carolina. Even better, Tarleton had been captured along with over six hundred of his men in the battle at Cowpens. Ben sincerely hoped that this might be the turning point in the war.

He observed a flock of geese flying north. Their formation looked like a "V," Ben thought, "for victory … perhaps this will be our year." He turned over to practice his breaststroke.

The water of the Seine was clear and cool. The sun felt warm on Ben's back. He lifted up his head from time to time to check his bearings. About halfway through his usual distance, he caught a glimpse of something on the water ahead. As he drew closer, Ben could distinguish three objects bobbing on the surface. They could easily have been detritus left over from the winter, but Ben couldn't help but hope that they were, in fact, swimmers, and that he would meet up with Minette here again. He pushed ahead with big strokes.

As he approached, Ben saw that his hope would be realized. As he pulled up to the lead swimmer, he recognized the silvery-gray hair, wet and shimmering in the sun. Minette's fresh smile warmed Ben to his toes. Close behind her were the Abbé de la Roche and medical student Cabanis. Cabanis and de le Roche seemed out of breath as the four of them greeted one another.

"Martin … Pierre," she ordered. "Head back home. I'll catch up with you shortly."

The other two receded with a cheerful farewell. Ben embraced Minette. She felt firm but soft and slippery in his arms.

"It's so good to see you, Ben," she purred. "How is your foot?"

"Much better, thanks to your kind ministrations."

"So, you will quit your sick bed at the Hôtel de Valentinois to dine with me soon?"

"Yes, of course, at your earliest invitation, my lady." Ben did his best formal bow while treading water.

She laughed. "Then, I shall swim home and post a perfumed invitation as soon as I dry off."

"I will be anxiously awaiting it."

He held her a little longer, but much too soon, she said, "I must go catch those boys. They are out of shape after the long winter, but their youthful vigor will negate my advantage before long."

"I doubt that," Ben replied with a smile. He reluctantly let her go. She swam off back toward Auteuil, kicking up her legs as she disappeared.

Ben returned to the solitude of his swim. He listened to the sounds of the river birds in their spring mating rituals. Ben could almost decode many of their cries as they defended their turf, advertised their availability, or jousted to prove themselves worthy of a mate.

"How little different we are from them," Ben thought.

As he drew close to home, Ben noted a sizable flock of small black birds flying in murmuration. From this distance, their synchronization gave the appearance of one large organism. Only occasionally did an individual bird stray from the pack to dissolve the illusion of a large body in the sky.

"Just how does each of those little creatures know which way to turn?" Ben wondered.

Late Summer, 1781

PASSY, FRANCE &
SPA, BELGIUM

LE VEILLARD ARRIVED before the first light. Diablo whinnied outside Ben's window, alerting him to his friend's appearance. Ben had been expecting him. He knew that Louis needed to talk. His son, known to everyone by the nickname *Le jeune,* had boarded a ship earlier that summer on what had promised to be an adventure. He was supposed to have made contact with people Ben knew in America and to have started a job there. But instead, the ship had been captured by the British. Diverted to England, *Le jeune* was now held captive—as a prisoner of war.

Ben was already dressed in his riding clothes. "I'll be right down," he called quietly out the window. He did not want to disturb his grandsons, still fast asleep. He grabbed a light cape on his way out the door.

The air was crisp. Ben stood on the lawn, looking up at the last twinkling of the disappearing stars. Diablo snorted. A few wisps of the enormous beast's hot breath swirled in the tranquil air. The ground was wet with dew.

"It should be a pleasant morning to ride," Ben remarked. He started hiking up the hill toward the stable. Le Veillard rode ahead to roust the stable hand.

Ben entered the stable to observe the boy, his unruly mop of hair littered with more than a few bits of straw, yawning as he led a stout horse out of her stall. The air, considerably warmer inside, smelled earthy. The boy appeared half-asleep as he stumbled over to hoist Ben's saddle up on the horse's back. He cinched the straps, yawning again. Ben thanked the boy and mounted. Back outside the stable, Ben noted the first violet rays of dawn to the east.

"*Taïaut*," Ben barked. He smacked the rump of his horse with his crop. She bolted toward the road.

Le Veillard quickly caught up.

Ben glanced over at his friend. Despite Le Veillard's impeccable dress, he appeared not to have slept in days. He had dark circles under his eyes.

"You look dreadful."

"I know," Le Veillard replied. "You should see my poor wife. She has worried herself sick. Have you heard anything new about *Le jeune*?"

"No," Ben replied. He tried to be as sensitive as possible. "I recently wrote my friend William Hodgson in London explaining the situation. I authorized him to pay any ransom demanded and provide your son with money to get home."

"Thank you, Ben." Le Veillard looked a little relieved. "I will most certainly reimburse you." Then he looked more anxious again. "Do you think that he will be all right? They wouldn't harm him, would they?"

"Louis, trust me, they only want the ransom money or to exchange him for some British subject whom we have captured. The British won't harm him. When he is back home safe, he will have a tale to tell. Once he has returned, we will find him another ship to take him to America."

"No, Ben. We've discovered through this recent experience that his mother can not bear for *Le jeune* to be on the other side of the world."

Ben was slightly surprised, but he acquiesced. "As you wish," he said.

"His mother has family in Bordeaux who will provide him with a position," Le Veillard continued.

"It sounds settled then."

"Yes, I believe it is," Le Veillard said. But he looked unsettled.

"So, what is the matter?"

Le Veillard was quiet for a moment. Ben waited. The first rays of brilliant sunlight raked across the field, bathing the two riders in a warm yellow glow.

"Ben, she's getting married," he blurted.

"Who?"

"Maggie."

Ben was now quite sure that he had missed something. "*Who?*" he asked again.

"You know, Maggie, my friend at the *Cheval Sauvage*."

"Oh," Ben said. His recollection of the pretty barmaid who hailed from Brittany was quickly rekindled. "I never knew of such an encumbrance deterring you before," he said.

Le Veillard's eyes flashed with pain.

"I'm sorry," Ben quickly added. He resolved to be sensitive to his friend's feelings.

"Ben, the situation is terrible," Le Veillard continued. "Not only does she plan to marry this other man and move far away . . ." He paused briefly, then almost wailed. "He ... he ... he is a *pig farmer*!"

Ben felt an almost irrepressible laugh well up inside his chest, but the expression on Le Veillard's face sobered him.

"I am truly sorry, Louis," he replied. "Is there anything to be done?"

"I don't believe so. I have offered her money, offered to buy the bar and give it to her, showered her with jewelry, perfume, flowers, love notes. Nothing worked. She told me the only offering that might make her reconsider would be a proposal of marriage from me."

"But you are already married."

"Yes, Ben. Believe me. I know that ... and so does she."

"Louis, I can tell by the look on your face that you have struggled with your decision."

"Ben, it has been the most difficult one of my life. I must let her go."

"I see."

"Think about it, Ben. I enjoy a most enviable position in Passy. However, the mineral springs from which I derive my fortune came to me as my wife's dowry. The property would most likely revert to her family in the event of an annulment—even if I could get the Church to grant me one. And what reason would I give? Impotence on my part? I think not! Non-consummation of the marriage? No, our grown children would be strong evidence against it. Consanguinity? Impossible." Le Veillard sighed. "No, I am trapped."

"I am encouraged, at least, that you recognize how fortunate you are," Ben said.

"Yes, but a gilded cage is still a cage, my friend."

The two men rode on a while, the early morning colors brightening slowly into late summer daylight. They passed fields of lavender, the perfume so fragrant that it saturated Ben to his core. They passed fields of sunflowers. The huge yellow heads now bowed under the weight of their seeds. The smell of a nearby barn wafted over their path.

Ben chuckled, "A pig farmer, eh? Somehow, I can picture her covered in mud, tending to the little oinkers."

"Don't torture me, please," Le Veillard pleaded. He quickly changed the subject. "And what of Marianne?"

"Oh, now you would torture me?" Ben replied.

"No, I am simply making conversation," Le Veillard protested.

"If it must be told, I don't know where she is."

"Oh, Ben, now I am sorry. I had no idea. Do you believe that she is with him?"

"It is certainly possible. As far as I can tell, they each quit Paris earlier this month. Madame Leray showed me the open letter Mesmer wrote to Marie Antoinette, threatening to leave the city unless his demands were met. He left for Spa. Marianne also vanished about the same time."

"It could be a coincidence."

"Madame Leray said the same thing."

"But you don't believe it to be so?"

"No."

They rode on in silence toward home.

The warm mineral water of the deep Roman bath swirled around Marianne's torso. A distinctly salty, slightly sulfurous smell tickled her nose. She almost sneezed. The late summer sun streamed through rectangular windows strategically positioned high enough on the walls to let light in while maintaining a general dimness so that the bathers were not inhibited from shedding their clothes while taking in the healing waters. The strains of a string concerto floated in through the same windows. Currently, only Marianne and Mesmer shared the large pool.

Marianne pouted. "What are we doing here, Franz?" she asked.

"Enjoying the waters," Mesmer replied flatly. "Do you know that people have been coming here for hundreds of years to do the same?"

"That is not what I was asking. Why are we not in Paris? I miss it." She sounded whiny, even to herself.

"You are giving a series of concerts with your sister, cleverly arranged by *moi* to avoid Mother's suspicion of you traveling with me."

"She makes you pay far too much, you know."

Mesmer smirked. "Oh, I think it's worth it." He reached out and placed his hand on her hip.

Marianne moved slightly out of his reach.

He shrugged. "I have heard an interesting theory that the name of this lovely Belgian town is actually an acronym for Emperor Nero's famous statement: *Sanitas Per Aquas* ... Health Through Water."

"You didn't answer my question."

"Peter, the Great Czar of Russia, was cured of his indigestion by drinking the water here."

Marianne pouted again. "I want to go back."

"And so we will, my dear, in good time. To answer your question, I needed to get away from Paris, from the clamor of so many sick people seeking my healing powers. Perhaps I needed to heal a bit myself."

Marianne turned back toward him. "Are you sick?" she asked. She looked over at the man she had known intimately for over nine years. He looked generally healthy. True, he had a more protuberant belly—and considerably less hair now than before, but he didn't look ill.

"No, not physically," he replied. "Marianne, I feel that I have been given a great gift in the discovery of *magnétisme animale,* and yet, it is also a burden."

"In what way?"

"I know that my discovery helps people heal. It makes them feel better. Droves of the sick and injured, many of them incurable, come to my door. After my treatment, they leave, feeling some relief, having some hope. If not cured, then at the very least, they are helped along the road to recovery. And yet, I can't convince the Ben Franklins of the world."

Hearing Mesmer speak Ben's name made Marianne flinch. She hoped she gave no outward sign. "Men of science will always want proof," she replied.

"I understand that." He paused, looking more serious than she had ever seen him. "But you believe that it works, don't you?"

For the first time, Marianne sensed that there might be doubt in Mesmer's mind. She could almost feel his vulnerability.

"Yes, Franz," she said. She moved closer to him. "I do believe that you have discovered something powerful. I don't know anything about the science of it. I'm not sure that I want to. I couldn't tell you if it is a new fluid, a mystical spell, or something in between. But I have flown with the flock.

"I have experienced their power, channeled through you, to understand without speaking, to hear without listening. I have sat with the Queen among the stars. I have peered into the bodies of men. My observations have assisted you in your diagnosis and treatment of many. I, myself, since we began this treatment, have not experienced the depths of melancholia that forever tormented me. I *do* believe that your discovery works."

"Thank you," was all he said, but the look in his eyes said so much more.

Later that afternoon, they made love. Not the insipid, one-sided plea-suring of Paris, but the inspired interplay of their first summer in Vienna. Mesmer surprised her with his passion, his potency, his renewed hunger for her. Marianne lost herself in his arms.

"These really must be healing waters," she said. She smiled as she reluc-tantly dressed. The hour was getting late. Mother's knitting would not occupy her forever. Marianne kissed Mesmer softly on his bald head.

"Yes, I believe that they must be. *Sanitas per aquas,*" he said.

"Franz, let's go back to Paris."

"In due time, my dear ... in due time."

February 1782

PASSY

THE LETTER FROM Madame Brillon was addressed "*Mon Cher Papa*" ... "That sums up our relationship fairly well," Ben thought to himself glumly as he read the long letter she'd written from Nice. "She considers me a father figure." Ben had long ago given up any hopes of a more carnal relationship with the Ice Princess.

Along with her news from the south of France, the letter also served to introduce one Lord Cholmondely—an Englishman, previously unknown to Ben—who apparently wanted to meet the famous Doctor.

There was nothing unusual in that. Since the Americans had won the battle at Yorktown, Ben had received a steady stream of correspondence from friends in England, urging reconciliation. It seemed that British public opinion was finally turning away from war—even in the imperious Parliament. "It only took a sound thrashing and the surrender of their General Cornwallis to convince them," he mused.

One sentence in her letter caught Ben's eye. She warned that Cholmondely might well be more than he appeared to be. She raised the concern that he might be a spy.

Le Veillard knocked on Ben's door well before sunrise. As he entered, he shook a light dusting of snow from the shoulders of his heavy cape.

"I hope we are taking the carriage this morning," he said. "I'm half frozen."

"Of course," Ben said. "How about some hot tea?"

"What, no coffee?" Le Veillard asked. He feigned annoyance, even though he knew full well that Ben kept no coffee in the house. "I'll have to go roust Madame Leray's kitchen staff."

"You will do no such thing," Ben said. "After our business this morning, we can visit the coffee house ... if you must."

"Ben, I was joking. I am fine for now. What *is* our business this morning?"

"We are going to meet a spy."

Le Veillard looked slightly taken aback. "Ben, I have not known you to partake in this cloak and dagger activity yourself. Why not send Edward Bancroft?"

"Bancroft might do for this job, but he is presently in London ... selling short his shares of munitions stock."

"I should do so too," Le Veillard said. Noting the exasperated look on Ben's face, he added, "If I had any to sell, that is."

"Let's go," Ben said. He threw Le Veillard's heavy wet cape back at him, then went over to the fireplace and used some tongs to extract two good-sized stones from the fire, placing them in a cast iron "carriage warmer." Ben hauled the heavy device toward the door.

"I'll take that," Le Veillard said.

Ben donned his cape. The two men marched up the hill toward the stable, grass crunching under their thick boots.

Once settled into the carriage, Le Veillard spoke again. "Ben, do you really believe that the war will soon be over?"

"Yes, Louis, I do. The victory at Yorktown last October was decisive by all accounts. Over eight thousand British and Hessian troops, two hundred artillery pieces, thousands of muskets, many transport ships, wagons, and horses were captured in that battle by our General Washington and your Comte de Rochambeau. I do not believe that the British army or navy will soon recover from that event."

"I hope that you are correct. Americans and French standing side by side to defeat the British; it must have been quite a sight."

"When this war is over, Louis, the American people will owe an eternal debt to the French for our freedom." Ben gave a slightly awkward bow, the best he could do sitting on the plush seat.

The winter sun was just starting to brighten the sky as the carriage entered the *Tuileries Jardin*. No one seemed to be about. The carriage stopped in front of a large boxwood tree. From behind it, a gaunt figure emerged.

"The Reverend," Le Veillard whispered.

"Louis, let me do the talking," Ben said.

The door to their coach opened, and the lanky man climbed in.

"It is colder than a witch's tit out there," the Reverend exclaimed. He put his bony hands by the heater, rubbing them together.

"Thank you for coming," Ben said. "I realize that you will be leaving for home soon."

"Yes, back to Maryland, and family." The Reverend looked wistful as he went on. "And I hope, one day, back to Philadelphia."

"It will happen," Ben said. He put his hand on the shoulder of the clergyman.

Le Veillard wore a perplexed expression, but he kept silent.

Ben went on. "Did you meet with Lord Cholmondely?"

"Yes."

"And?"

"He is no spy."

"How do you know?"

"Doctor Franklin, I have been spying for you and the American cause since before we both arrived in France six years ago. I have made innumerable trips to England—ostensibly on church business—when in reality, I went to collect information as the Secret Committee instructed. Trust me.

In London, as here in Paris, I have met up with all sorts of seedy characters. Included among them, of course, is your man Bancroft who spies for both you and the British ... and who has become quite rich in doing so. I believe that I have become a good judge of character over these years."

"Yes," Ben replied. "Of course. I was simply hoping for something more specific."

"Well," the Reverend said. He rubbed his hands again. "He is a close friend of Lord Shelburne, the one Englishman who has been your strongest ally in Parliament these many years."

"Yes, and hopefully will be vindicated for having done so."

"As we all pray," the Reverend replied pensively. "Also, he carries a Sevres medallion of you. A present from Marie Antoinette."

"Clearly, he is a man of discerning taste," Ben replied.

"All right, mock me if you must," the Reverend replied. He appeared annoyed at Ben's attempt at humor, but he quickly returned to business. "The only request that he has of you is that you provide him with a letter—of your own composition—that he may carry back to Lord Shelburne."

"That sounds safe enough. I'm never at a loss for words." Ben laughed once again at his own joke.

The Reverend remained stone-faced. "Is there any other service that will be needed of me at this time?" he asked.

Ben looked at the drawn face of this man. Through his own moral conviction that the American Revolution had been the right thing to do, he had risked his life, risked alienating his Anglican Church, sacrificed precious time away from his family, and suffered travels that would severely test much younger men. He looked tired.

"No. Go home now, my friend. Your work here is done. I sincerely believe that it was what God meant for you to do. Lord Stormont has been recalled to London. The war should soon be over," Ben said. He thought for a moment and then added, "I thank you with all my heart."

The Reverend climbed down from the carriage. He walked away from them, across the gardens still empty of any vegetation save a few evergreen trees. A light snow fell. Ben hoped that the next time they met, it would be on the streets of Philadelphia.

Ben ordered tea with cream to the slightly puzzled look of a young waiter at the coffee house. The pungent smell of fresh coffee filled the air of the shop on this cold morning. Men sat at long tables with pots of steaming brew in front of them. He and Le Veillard chose a table for two at one side. With the lively conversations all around, they would not be overheard. Nonetheless, Le Veillard spoke in hushed tones.

"So, Ben, please help me understand. This Reverend, the man we saved from the Weasel several years ago, has been working for you all these years?" Le Veillard asked. He looked incredulous.

"Yes, for the American cause," Ben replied smugly. "Not that he worked entirely in Paris, mind you. As he said, he has traveled to England many times—and back to Maryland, where he currently makes his home with his wife and seven children."

"And Lord Stormont never suspected?"

"Not that I am aware of. Who would suspect an Anglican priest of being a spy?"

"Remarkable," Le Veillard said. "You have let me see a side of you today that I suspect few others know."

"What is that?" Ben asked.

"Spymaster," Le Veillard said.

"Louis, sometimes the simplest plans are the best. I discovered in the Reverend, a man who strongly believed in the ideal of American freedom but was trapped by his oath to support the King and his Church. His only option was to work behind the scenes to effect change. In that role, he has played an important, if unsung, part in the founding of our country—and there are many more men and women like him. If I, during my time here in France, have enabled any of them to be more effective in their work, then that will satisfy me."

"Spoken like a true statesman," Le Veillard said. He poured the syrupy coffee from the pot into his cup, adding steamed milk.

"Tell me of *Le jeune*," Ben said.

"The boy made it safely to Bordeaux, thanks to your kind intervention on his behalf in London. Yet we have not heard from him directly."

"Oh?" Ben said.

"No, I suspect he feels that by withholding his correspondence, he is punishing his mother and me for "banishing" him to the backcountry in Bordeaux."

"I wouldn't describe that lovely region as backcountry."

"Neither would I, but I am sure that is the way he sees it. We've heard, by way of Madame Leray, that he is busily chasing the local farmer's daughters with gusto. It never ceases to amaze me how wide a net that woman throws and what a wealth of gossip she collects."

"Yes, she does seem to know everyone's business. It is a rare talent. Still, I am heartened to hear that young Monsieur Le Veillard has not lost his taste for the fair sex on account of his ordeal. *Der apfel fellt nicht gerne weit vom baume.*"

Le Veillard gave Ben a perplexed look.

"I apologize," Ben said. "It's an old German saying—'The apple usually doesn't fall far from the tree.'"

"I believe I understand it," Le Veillard said. "You could say that the fruit of my marriage acts much like the parent."

"At least like one of them," Ben replied.

The two finished their drinks. With the sun higher in the sky, the carriage ride home was much warmer. Ben napped.

Upon his return, he spent the remainder of the day composing his letter to Lord Shelburne. He focused on the potential for reconciliation between England and America. Ben would deliver the letter to Lord Cholmondely within a fortnight with the intent of planting a seed for peace.

Spring 1782

PARIS

"WHY AM I NOT allowed to go with you?" Marianne asked.

"Because it is for men only," Mesmer replied. He threw a black cape over his lavender robe.

"What exactly do you do at this 'Society of Universal Harmony'?" she asked suspiciously.

"Nothing."

"What do you mean 'nothing'? If you don't do anything, then why can't I come?"

"Because we discuss the scientific basis of *magnétisme animale*. You wouldn't understand."

Before Marianne could respond, Mesmer turned and left the apartment. He was halfway down the stairs before she could call after him.

"I could too understand." But her voice was so meek he undoubtedly could not hear it. She sounded defensive, even to herself.

Mesmer disappeared into the dusky *Place Vendôme*. Antoine the valet skirted Marianne as she stood fuming in the foyer. His arms were full of robes. He shrugged apologetically, but quickly he, too, disappeared. Marianne heard their carriage depart across the square. She stood for a moment in Mesmer's empty apartment.

"Secret society," she muttered. "They probably engage dancing girls or something."

Marianne wondered what she would do for the evening. After supper at their hotel, her mother had asked her to build up the fire so that she could keep warm, and Marianne had left her sleeping by the stove. Despite the balmy spring weather, Mother always complained of being cold. It worried Marianne.

She looked around the rapidly darkening apartment. If she were going to stay, she would have to light a lamp. She decided that she did not want to be there when Mesmer returned. She wondered why she tolerated him at all. He could have his dancing girls tonight—but he would not have her, she thought, a bit longingly, as she suddenly sensed her own desires. Marianne decided to walk.

The shops on the *Place Vendôme* were mostly closed. Few people walked the square at this gloomy hour. Marianne headed toward the Seine. She knew she would find people there.

Jaunty music greeted her as she approached the left bank on the *Pont Neuf*. Over the railing, Marianne could see five people surrounding a makeshift fire pit at the river's edge. A large houseboat was tied nearby. The flickering campfire revealed three male and two female figures. One of the men played a fiddle and stamped his foot for percussion, while another played a recorder. A man and a woman danced arm in arm. The final woman tended a roasting spit over the fire.

Marianne stood and watched for a moment from the bridge. She longed to join them. The man playing the fiddle appeared to notice her. He held a note. Involuntarily, she took a step back at being observed. He started playing again with renewed vigor, seeming to beckon her.

Marianne walked toward the Left Bank. On the street, artists were packing up their supplies, the daylight being almost completely gone. A vendor had one solitary baguette sticking out of his pushcart. Marianne reached into her pocket for a coin and gave it to the man in exchange. He pushed his empty cart away, whistling the same melody that floated up from the riverside.

Marianne found the nearest stairway down to the river. As she reached the lower path, she quickly spotted the group she sought. The musicians had finished their tune. Each man raised a flask to his lips. Marianne had a moment of doubt. However, just then, one of the women let out a delicious giggle. Marianne moved toward them. As she approached, she saw that they appeared to be about her age. Their clothes were shabby but clean. Marianne noticed no smell other than the delicious aroma of savory roasting meat mixed with rosemary. The fiddler stepped forward to greet her. The dancing couple seemed oblivious, wrapped up only in each other. The man with the recorder, Marianne realized, had just squeezed the woman tending the fire pit from behind—causing her to squeal. They now embraced as well.

"Will you join us for supper?" the fiddler asked. His voice was enticingly deep.

Marianne held out the loaf of bread. "Yes."

"What is your name?"

"Marianne."

"Ah, a lovely name."

"And yours?"

"Marko." His tone was strong, confident.

"Spanish?"

"Basque. You are not French, either?"

"Scottish originally."

"So beautiful."

Marianne was glad for the cover of darkness so that Marko could not see how deeply she blushed at his compliment.

"But forgive me, I have neglected to introduce you to my traveling companions," he said. He accepted the bread and put his arm around her shoulder to escort her toward the rest of the group.

Marianne could feel how muscular he was as he cradled her.

"This is Marianne," Marko announced. The others circled around to greet their visitor. "Marianne, this is Paulo and Alize, Yorge, and Lili."

Alize, the woman who had previously been tending the fire, spoke first. "We would be most honored if you would join us for supper. We are almost ready."

"I brought a loaf of bread."

"Good. We have everything else. Paulo, will you help me carve the roast? Yorge, Lili, will you set the table?"

Marianne looked around but didn't see a table in sight.

Marko must have caught her expression because he explained, "We'll eat on board our houseboat, come." He took her by the hand and walked her toward the river.

The houseboat was not big and hardly seemed seaworthy. "You traveled all that way in this boat?" she asked.

"Yes," Marko said. "For the second time. Last year we came with my wife Maria, in search of treatment for her condition. But she did not recover."

"I am so sorry," Marianne said.

"I'm starting to get used to it," Marko said. "It has been a year. Last spring, the six of us traveled to Paris—just like this." He pointed around. "From our home in Bilbao. We came to see the famous Doctor Mesmer. She suffered from a growth in the stomach. The doctors back home said there was nothing to be done. She constantly vomited blood. Even though she was weak, she made the journey.

"Doctor Mesmer tried his best, and his treatments seemed to be working—for a while. Her pain went away. She was calmer. Then one night, much like this one, she slipped away in my arms. We took her home to Bilbao and buried her on a hill. My friends and I decided to return here this spring to honor her."

"You should not let me interfere with your memorial," Marianne said, suddenly feeling embarrassed by her presence.

Marko looked hurt. "Oh no, please do not think that you are interfering. We are not here to mourn. That is done. We are here to celebrate. I want to keep Maria's memory alive the way that she would have wanted it—by living my life to the fullest."

"I am sure that is what she would want for you." Marianne gave him a friendly squeeze and was surprised to find how exciting she found touching him to be. He squeezed back. She felt her heart race.

The passion surely might have escalated had Lili not called from the deck of the houseboat.

The table had been set on the open part of the deck with six chairs around it. Overhead, the stars twinkled, and the slight rocking of the tethered boat was soothing. The rigging made soft clanking sounds with a distinct musical quality. Marianne contemplated the number of times the five friends must have sat around this table, missing Maria. She would not try to replace her. She felt honored to be there with them.

Marko, it turned out, was a Basque shipbuilder who had built the craft on which they dined tonight. Marianne watched his muscular forearms as he broke the bread, passing it around. He ate with gusto.

Marianne's plate was filled with small savory empanadas and carved meat. She took a bite of the rosemary-roasted meat.

"This is delicious," she said to Alize.

"Do you like it?"

"Yes, it tastes like chicken, only much more flavorful."

"We call it '*rata acuática*' when we find it near the Nervión River back home. I don't know what the French name for it is. There seem to be plenty of them around here."

"Did you say '*rata*'?" Marianne gulped hard. She recalled the huge river rat that had watched her one night from near this very spot.

"Yes, the Parisians are so fortunate to have such abundance."

Marianne put on the best smile she could muster. "That they are," she said and washed down the meat with a generous swig of Basque red wine.

Before too long, the dinner was finished. Marianne offered to assist the other women with cleanup inside. She was surprised at how well appointed the kitchen was—for a barge. The men disembarked to re-stoke the fire on shore. All three pulled out their pipes—tobacco smoke mixed with wood smoke to tickle Marianne's nose. Very quickly, the dinnerware was washed and put away.

The musicians resumed playing their instruments just as Marianne, Alize, and Lili emerged from inside. It turned out that Yorge was the percussionist, alternating between a tambourine and a small drum. They played what must have been a well-known Basque folk song, because both Alize and Lili started singing along almost as soon as the music started. They danced suggestively across the deck toward their men.

Marianne joined them, falling in step behind. While she didn't know the words to the song, she could follow the melody well enough. The other two women had decent singing voices, but Marianne's soon rose above them. As they stepped off the boat, the music stopped.

"What?" Marianne asked. Her mood of revelry was instantly broken.

Marko just stared at her.

"What?" she repeated, believing that she must have done something horribly wrong.

All five of them stared at her for what seemed an eternity before Marko said, "You sing like an angel."

Marianne felt her body, so tense only a moment before, go completely light.

Marko started to strum the fiddle again, and to sing. The others followed his lead. The barges down the way, laden with wood and coal, animal hides and country produce being delivered via the river to Paris, joined in as well, so that soon the whole river seemed to be singing along.

Later, they sat alone on the river's edge. "Are all these river vendors Basque?" Marianne asked.

Marko laughed. "No, of course not," he said. "They are French, German, Dutch, even English."

"Then how do they know your folk songs?"

"I don't know," he replied. "But we sing along with theirs too." He smiled with a smile that melted her heart. "Can you stay the night?"

Marianne thought of her mother sleeping by the fire. "No," she replied. "But I can stay for a while . . ." She smiled, and he did too.

Marko accompanied her on the short walk back to her hotel. The Paris streets were nearly deserted as the clock struck two. Marianne couldn't help thinking about how Ben used to walk her home in London. She realized that she had missed having a man want to protect her. Ben used to do it. Mesmer never did. Marko put his arm around her waist as they walked. Their cadence was synchronized so that they walked as one. He kissed her when she stopped in front of her hotel. The doorman slept on his stool.

"We return to Bilbao tomorrow," he whispered apologetically.

"Will you and your friends come back next year?"

"You can be sure of it."

"Why was she only attracted to men who would leave her?' she thought as she bundled her mother off to bed. The old woman seemed so frail that Marianne sat and listened to her labored breathing for quite some time before turning in herself.

Spring 1782

THE SOCIETY OF UNIVERSAL HARMONY, PARIS

WHEN TEMPLE OPENED the door to the Franklin lodgings, it was nearly midnight.

"Grandpa?" he whispered.

Ben was sitting by the fireplace. He put aside his book. A plaid blanket was draped over his legs. A half-empty bottle of Madeira sat on the table within easy reach. "How was the meeting?" he asked.

"Granddad, can we talk about it in the morning? I'm tired."

It was unlikely that Temple's head would hit the pillow before his grandfather was completely satisfied. Ben would hear nothing of going to bed without an explanation. He pressed on. "Who was there?"

"Mesmer, of course, D'Eslon too. John Paul Jones, your friend Le Roy, Monsieur de Gébelin, and perhaps a dozen others I didn't recognize," Temple said.

"And the presentation?"

Temple became more animated. "Granddad, they propose to initiate us in the healing ways of *magnétisme animale.*

"And what do they propose to charge you for this honor?"

"Well, they didn't put it exactly that way ... it is not a fee ... rather a donation to the Society of Universal Harmony."

"And what is this 'Society of Universal Harmony', might I ask?"

"A group of men, united by mutual interest, intent on curing the ills of the world." He spoke as if reciting a slogan he had heard many times that night.

"Hmmm, curing the ills of the world, eh?" Ben raised one eyebrow and peered at the lad through his bifocals.

"Yes, Granddad. It's an honor that I was invited," Temple said.

"To be sure," Ben replied sarcastically. "And what sort of donation to this 'Society of Universal Harmony' do they suggest?" He took a sip of Madeira.

"Two hundred louis, as a minimum," Temple answered matter-of-factly.

Ben almost spit out his drink. "Two hundred louis!" he exclaimed. "Where exactly were you planning on getting that kind of money? And what would you get in return?"

"Oh, Granddad," Temple said. "You should see what they can do. They cure people through their touch. Doctor D'Eslon showed us a woman who suffered terrible headaches. She would have been an attractive-looking young lady except that she appeared as if she had not slept in weeks. She had dark circles under her eyes. She rubbed her head constantly."

Ben had rarely seen Temple so excited. He radiated an evangelical fervor. "Go on," Ben said.

"Mesmer sat with her," Temple said. "He placed one hand on her chest and one on her thigh. He spoke to her softly. We couldn't hear what he was saying, but it must have been powerful. It looked like she fell asleep. Then, suddenly, she seemed to have a mild fit or convulsion. He held her. When the fit subsided, he commanded her to wake up. Once she recovered, she seemed not to recognize where she was.

"But she looked beautiful, Granddad ... peaceful. Her eyes were clear, as if she had just awakened from a full night's slumber. Mesmer asked her if her head hurt. She said it did not. In fact, the way she looked at him, it was as if her head had never bothered her. Yet she was so grateful for his attention that she kissed him in front of our whole group. I want to be able to help people like that."

"Do you want to help people ... or do you want to obtain kisses from pretty, appreciative young ladies?" Ben asked.

"You don't believe that Mesmer's technique works, do you?"

"Oh, I do believe that people feel better after his ministrations. What I don't believe is that he alone controls the fluid that he calls *magnétisme animale* ... if there is such a fluid. I am still waiting to see a measurement of it. And I don't believe that by paying him an outrageous sum of money, he will impart this secret technique on you."

"But Monsieur Le Roy says that, advanced as we are, there remain some fluids that we cannot measure."

"Yes, and he is right to a point, my lad. There are many aspects of the universe that we don't understand, many things we can't fathom yet. Trust me. I don't know all the factors that lead to healing. The body is a marvelous machine endowed by our Creator with a tremendous capacity to repair itself. I do not doubt that, in the future, doctors will find many more methods of augmenting healing than have already been discovered. Or better yet, stopping diseases from ever happening in the first place."

Ben pondered for a moment, then went on. "Consider inoculation—which has the potential to prevent many of the ravages of infectious illnesses. If the Church and others would accept it, I believe that it might offer the world freedom from plagues and poxes.

"No, my concern is that in Mesmer, you have a man who doesn't truly understand the force that he claims to be able to control. Not only that, but he proposes to sell others a portion of his incomplete knowledge so that they can go out and practice with unknown consequences."

Temple yawned. "Yes, Granddad. Goodnight." He headed upstairs to bed.

"Temple?" Ben called after him.

"Yes, Granddad?"

"I'll pay the two hundred louis if you will keep me informed of your training."

"Thank you, Granddad."

Ben leaned back in his chair by the fire. The spymaster of Passy sipped his fine Madeira.

Summer 1782

PARIS

A LIGHT MORNING BREEZE rustled the sheer curtains dressing the half-open windows of Room 11 at the *Cheval Sauvage*. Marianne's skin felt buttery smooth beneath Ben's hand. He stroked her gently, only intending to enjoy the sensation, not intending to wake her. She moaned softly. Her breathing quickened slightly. She opened her eyes.

"Ben, I must have dozed off," she said. "I was so relaxed."

"I love watching you sleep," Ben said.

She squeezed her warm body up against him, her soft breasts pressing against his chest. She wrapped her leg around his. She stroked his belly. Her hand headed further down.

"May we do it again?" she asked.

"Gladly," Ben responded, his own pulse now quickening. "But can I ask you something?"

"Of course, darling," she said dreamily.

"Must you leave Paris?"

She responded with a half-truth. "Mother is a hard taskmaster," she said.

"We have concerts planned all the way from Spa down to Florence ... where she wishes to spend the winter."

"Um," Ben said glumly.

Mesmer had arranged for the trip to Spa. He claimed that he needed time away from Paris once again. He had arranged with Mrs. Davies for a privately sponsored concert series, starring Marianne and Cecelia, of course. Marianne had been reluctant at first, but ultimately she agreed to accompany him.

She pouted. "Besides, I never get to see you anymore," she said. "You are constantly busy with your peace negotiations."

"Never too busy for you, my pet," Ben said. But in fact, he had deliberately become less available to Marianne over the past year. He wasn't entirely sure of his motivation himself. Had he secretly hoped that she would miss him, seek him out, and pursue him? Was that why he had withdrawn? Or was it that he was more frequently enjoying the company of the lovely and vivacious Madame Helvétius? Certainly, his carnal needs were nowadays being met on a regular basis in Auteuil. Notwithstanding all that, Ben knew that his interest in both women was about more than just lust.

Ben loved them both despite—and perhaps because of—their differences. Marianne was soft and round, voluptuous; Minette was sinewy and firm, lean, and muscular. Marianne was ripe peaches and *creme fraiche*, Minette was fine dark chocolate and cognac, aged to perfection. Each was equally satisfying, but in entirely different ways.

However, Marianne had also distanced herself from Ben since her long-awaited arrival in Paris. Their lovemaking had become more perfunctory, more mechanical, more about simple physical release than about passion and love—the kind of true love that they had known back in London. They had somehow lost the ability to lie together peacefully afterwards, looking into each other's eyes and speaking heart-to-heart.

Minette, on the other hand, threw herself into her relationship with Ben as she did everything in her life—with verve. There was never any question in his mind that Minette loved him, adored him, cared for his every need. Yet, she would never be entirely his. She belonged to the world;

she was a free spirit. No one man could ever know her fully. No man could own her. She was to have—not to hold. Ben wondered if this might be an aspect that the two women shared, only more subtle, more hidden in Marianne's case.

Ben realized that he was now the absent one in the room. His mind had wandered away for a moment. He turned his full attention back to Marianne, who, luckily, still seemed to be obliviously enraptured. He embraced her again with the comfortable love of many years, but somewhere deep in his heart, a sorrowful thought had taken root and started to grow. Ben couldn't help feeling that there would come a time when they would part.

Many workmen were already drinking and talking loudly at the bar when Ben walked Marianne down. They paid no attention to the lovers as they passed. Ben stood and watched Marianne from the vestibule, the bewitching motion of her long peach-colored skirt, until she vanished into the crowd. His eyes swept back across the street. A man watched her also from an open doorway. From that distance, Ben could not identify him. He didn't think much of it.

Ben turned back into the bar to locate Le Veillard. He found him sitting at his regular booth staring intently into the cleavage of a new barmaid. She was leaning seductively over his table. It appeared that perhaps a suitable replacement for Maggie had arrived.

"Ben, sit down and meet Gretchen," Le Veillard said. He smiled proudly.

"Hello, Gretchen. Or should I say *guten tag*?"

"*Guten tag*," she replied. "Do you also speak German, Herr Doctor?"

"Very little," Ben confessed. "Just enough to order a stein of beer and ask directions to the privy when visiting Frankfurt."

Gretchen laughed. "Well, that is about all you need there."

"Gretchen was just telling me about how Doctor Mesmer cured her," Le Veillard said.

"Really?" Ben replied. "You must tell me of your experience."

Gretchen looked at Le Veillard as if asking for his approval before continuing. However, there was suddenly a large commotion at the bar. The workmen began pounding their glasses on the large wooden counter demanding beer. It made a thunderous noise. The young barmaid behind the bar looked very nervous. Gretchen bounded away to aid her compatriot.

"I will return, don't leave," she yelled over her shoulder.

Ben watched as she artfully drew glasses and pitchers of beer for the boisterous laborers, her saucy countenance tantalizing and yet calming the throng. Ben reckoned that she would be engaged until the morning rush ended.

"She told me that she suffered from a digestive problem," Le Veillard said.

"Many do," Ben replied.

"Yes, but she said that Mesmer cured her."

"And how is he alleged to have accomplished this?"

"She went to his clinic in Vienna. She could not recall the entire process, but it ended with her having a strong compunction to avoid certain foods and take cream of tartar thrice daily."

"Cream of tartar is an established remedy for digestive problems."

"Yes, but she says that she felt better immediately upon undergoing the treatment. She has continued her treatments with him to this day. She left her family to follow him to Paris. Her symptoms never recurred."

"Interesting," Ben replied, "but certainly not proof."

"Yes, but Ben ... Don't you think?"

"Think what, Louis? Think that our good doctor somehow channeled a mysterious fluid that only he, and a select few who have paid their dues to him, can control to affect a cure on this lovely girl? Or that rather, through suggestion, expectation, and her own desire to be cured, she felt better until the cream of tartar and the change in her diet had time to work?"

Le Veillard looked like a deflated balloon. "I suppose that makes more sense," he said.

"Of course it does, Louis. But let me say this. I, for one, am not so interested in challenging these patients Mesmer has "cured." I have found them to be completely unable to articulate what happened to them, to glean any knowledge of the situation they were in. Arguing with them will come to no good."

When Gretchen finally returned to their table, the morning rush was subsiding.

Gretchen settled in and gave Ben her account of how Mesmer had cured her.

"I am truly glad that you are fully recovered," was all that Ben said when she was done. He smiled.

"*Danke*," she said with a demure smile.

"*Bitte schön*," Ben replied.

Le Veillard wore a bored look as the German was exchanged. But he snapped to attention when Gretchen asked Ben, "Was that Marianne Davies here with you this morning?" In response to the look of shock on Ben's face, she quickly added, "Not that I ever saw her here, of course."

"*Danke*," Ben said. He hoped he could count on her discretion. "How do you know her?"

"Oh, I don't really," she said. "I've only seen her at Doctor Mesmer's baquet. She is one of his most talented guides."

"You don't say." Ben was both surprised and a bit perplexed. "Tell me. What does one of Mesmer's guides do?"

"I am not sure that I can tell you entirely," she said. "They sit with you and guide you during your trance, I suppose. Mademoiselle Davies and Antoine seem to be the ones who Mesmer trusts most."

"Who is Antoine?"

"Mesmer's valet."

"Interesting." Ben placed his thumb on his chin. "Did Mademoiselle Davies guide your trance?"

"I don't fully recall. During the séance, I remember being seated with the doctor, *en rapport*. I felt very peaceful. I do vaguely recall hearing Doctor Mesmer speaking with a woman about my condition—but I think that woman was me, not Mademoiselle Davies. It was as if I was outside my own body, observing from afar. Yet I was able to peer inside my body. Doctor Mesmer asked me to observe certain things about my body, but I can't recall what I saw. Afterwards, I knew exactly what to do to solve my digestive problems. It certainly is a remarkable cure."

"It most certainly appears so."

Summer 1782

PASSY

AS THEY RODE HOME toward Passy, Le Veillard was exuberant. "So, do you like her?" he asked excitedly.

Ben was a thousand miles away, contemplating the morning with Marianne. "Who?" he asked.

"Gretchen, of course."

"She seems pleasant."

"I can hardly wait to bed her."

"You are incorrigible." Ben laughed. "What about Maggie?"

Le Veillard played dumb. "Who?" he replied.

"The pig farmer's wife."

Le Veillard touched his temple. "Forgotten," he responded.

"Forgotten?" Ben asked incredulously.

"Yes, quite forgotten."

"All right then ... long live Gretchen. May she fulfill all of your desires."

"Will you teach me to speak German?"

"As much as I know."

As they rode, Ben observed his friend with a sense of admiration. Here was a man who enjoyed the pleasures of life without any remorse or compunction. Not in an irresponsible or harmful way, but rather in an accepting, almost simple manner. Happy to receive the good fortunes that fate dealt him, and averse to dwelling on the bad ones. He simply went on living his life. He is living out his passions, Ben mused to himself.

The two rode on in silence for some time. The lovely summer day played out across the fields and meadows they passed. Farmers tended to their crops. A few looked up and waved. Intermittently, wagons lumbered down the road toward the market. On such a beautiful day, it was almost too soon that they arrived at the courtyard of the Hôtel de Valentinois.

As they handed their reins to the stable boy, Ben asked, "Would you join me for a cool drink in Madame Leray's garden?"

Le Veillard looked puzzled. "No ambassadorial business today?"

"Tomorrow I must meet all day with our delegation, including John Jay and John Adams in Paris. They have started to negotiate a treaty of peace with the British. But today, I am free."

"By all means, then. I will be most interested to hear the latest gossip from Marie-Thérèse."

"She does get all the best tittle-tattle," Ben said.

Upon entering the well-equipped kitchen, Ben could clearly see that dinner preparation was well underway. A host of savory aromas filled the air. Madame Leray was busy inspecting a tureen. Ben watched her as she lifted out a spoonful and tasted thoughtfully. She gave orders to one of the cooks standing nearby.

"It needs more salt ... and a little sage," she said. When she saw Ben and Le Veillard, she quickly bustled over.

"Did you boys get a good ride this morning?" she asked. Her *double entendre* was clear.

Ben and Louis looked at each other a bit sheepishly. Ben turned toward her.

"Yes, quite satisfying," he answered. His tone carried a precisely measured amount of inscrutability.

She seemed slightly miffed that Ben was able to dodge her innuendo so deftly. She changed the subject.

"That Mrs. Adams and the lovely Mrs. Jay are coming to dine with me today. You know how particular that Mrs. Adams can be. Everything must be perfect. And you know what a busybody she is. She will tell everyone in Paris if everything is not just so at the Hôtel de Valentinois."

Madame Leray had a simple code that Ben had quickly learned as a guest at her home in Passy. If she didn't like someone, she would refer to him or her as "*that* person"... as in "*that* Mrs. Adams." Conversely, having "*the* lovely" or "*the* dashing" appended before any name indicated she had a fondness for the person so referenced. Having neither appendage affixed would be considered neutral and usually meant that she hadn't developed strong feelings one way or the other. However, it struck Ben as odd that she would be calling Mrs. Adams, or anyone else, a busybody.

"What is the occasion?" Ben asked.

Madame Leray smacked the hand of Le Veillard as he was attempting to pilfer a small pastry from the tray behind her.

"Ouch," he protested.

She went on explaining to Ben. "It must have something to do with your peace negotiations. Both women are here with their husbands. I was told that they want to congratulate me for my role in supporting the war effort. It sounds like something that the lovely Mrs. Jay would do."

"I will come up and say hello to them if you send someone to my quarters to fetch me."

"Of course. They are not due for a few hours. You will have time to bathe and relax before then."

"Are you implying that I need a bath?" Ben asked.

She held her nose. "Oh no, please come just as you are. I would love to see what *that* Mrs. Adams has to say about you then."

"Marie-Thérèse, may we trouble you for a cool drink? Then we will leave your busy kitchen," Ben asked.

"By all means," she said. She snapped her fingers. A pretty

young girl dressed in a smock jumped immediately to her side. "Yes, ma'am?" the girl asked.

Le Veillard perked up instantly.

"Genevieve, please bring a pitcher of orange juice, two glasses, and a basket of muffins out to the garden for our guests."

"Yes, ma'am," the girl replied. She curtsied and quickly disappeared.

"Ben, if you will wait in the garden, Genevieve will bring your refreshments. I will join you as soon as I am able," Madame Leray said. She returned to her tasks with the precision of a woman who runs a tidy household.

Ben and Louis made their way to the garden off the back of the house. They settled at a table surrounded by several chairs. An arbor sheltered them from the sun, now approaching high noon. Thankfully, a light breeze provided welcome relief from the midday heat. It also brought in fresh country air fragrant with summer flowers. In the flowerbeds nearby, bees attended to their work, pollinating and carrying their rewards back to the hive. One of the Leray family dogs came over, wagging his tail, seeking attention ... or more likely food. Ben gave him a pet on his head, now happily resting on Ben's leg. The dog looked up plaintively.

"I want to live like that dog," Le Veillard said.

"What do you mean?"

"To be happy just to receive a little attention; a pet on the head; a morsel of food."

"Hmm, I believe that I see what you are saying. But a dog's life is not always as easy as this one, my friend."

"Oh, I know, Ben. But think about it. Even if this dog is inadvertently left out in the cold rain, once he is back in front of the fireplace, he is content. He doesn't let the pain of past events interfere with his enjoyment of the present. He lives his life from moment to moment."

"How do you know that?"

"Oh, of course, you want proof," Le Veillard said.

"Yes," Ben replied smugly.

"Well, I can't truly know his thoughts, but look at those eyes."

Ben looked down at the dog. His large brown eyes flicked back and forth between the two gentlemen ... as if trying to understand what they were saying. Ben chuckled.

"I have to admit—he seems to be intelligent. But how do you know that he does not let past events interfere with the present?"

"Ben, think of it this way: Suppose that neither of us feeds him a morsel of food here. Do you believe that he will mope around all the rest of the day, in a foul mood because of the slight? No, he will go off in search of a different morsel of food, chase a squirrel, or court a bitch. He will not take his misfortune as anything other than what it is ... a temporary setback, to be easily overcome by the pleasure of his next adventure."

"Granted that what you say is true about his behavior, but how do you know what he feels?"

"All right, Ben. Let me clarify my earlier statement. I admire the dog, for he doesn't give the outward appearance of any concern over past events." Le Veillard gave Ben an exasperated look. "How is that? Does that satisfy you?"

"That would be more scientifically correct, my friend."

Le Veillard laughed. "Yes, but also so much more boring," he said.

Genevieve arrived with a tray. She poured each man a large glass of fresh-squeezed orange juice and set a wicker basket of muffins on the table. Le Veillard looked her up and down.

She curtseyed to Ben and asked, "Will there be anything else that you gentlemen require?"

Ben looked at Le Veillard. It was clear that he wanted something off the menu.

"No, my dear," Ben replied kindly. "Thank you."

Genevieve disappeared.

"Ben, you could have at least sent her to fetch the butter," Le Veillard protested. He had already devoured half a muffin.

Ben laughed. "You will have to be content with satisfying only one of your many appetites, for now, my friend."

Le Veillard laughed too. He tossed a piece of muffin to the dog, who caught it in midair.

After a time, Madame Leray joined them. She brought another pitcher and a glass. After setting these down on the table, she flopped into a chair.

"I am exhausted," she said.

"Well, take a break with us. You must tell us about the latest news from Passy," Le Veillard said.

She instantly perked up, and over the next few minutes, in a rapid-fire discourse, she proceeded to divulge some very private information about nearly every one of their neighbors. As he listened, Ben couldn't help wondering what tidbits she offered about him when not in his presence. Le Veillard listened, also in rapt silence. When she had finished, she poured more orange juice into each glass and drank up.

"A remarkably thorough report, I must say," Ben said.

"Yes," Le Veillard chimed in. "It is unfortunate that Ben doesn't need any more spies."

Ben shut him up quickly with a glance, but added, "No, there are plenty of those around."

Madame Leray looked over at Le Veillard. "Your lovely wife will be here soon. She is dining with the ladies today."

"Then I had better get out of here," he said. "I'm headed back to the *Cheval Sauvage* anyway."

"Happy hunting," she called after him as he left the garden.

Once she heard the clip-clop of Diablo's hoofs in the courtyard, Madame Leray spoke again in a hushed tone, "Ben, we must talk."

"What is the matter?"

"You are aware, I believe, that John Paul is back?"

"Yes."

"Have you seen him?" she asked plaintively.

"No," Ben said. He hesitated, wondering if he should just leave it at that. "But Temple has. They have been attending meetings of the so-called 'Society of Universal Harmony' together.

"What society?"

"It is a group, organized by Mesmer, ostensibly promoting *magnétisme animale* as a cure for all of the world's ills—but I suspect it is more of a way for Herr Doctor to extract hefty subscriptions from young men interested in entrancing young women."

She looked puzzled. "And you let Temple join?" she asked.

"Yes. I believe that he can make his own decisions about the utility of the technique. Besides that, I needed a source of inside information about the Society."

"Ah, so Temple is acting as your spy." Madame Leray smiled knowingly.

"I wouldn't say that exactly. But he has been providing me with regular reports on the proceedings. So far, it all sounds fairly innocuous."

"And John Paul is a member also?" She paused. Then she sounded hurt as she moaned, "Ben, he won't see me."

"You will recall that I forbade him to do so."

"Yes, but certainly enough time has passed since then." Her voice was pleading. "You no longer require his services for your Navy. Why can't I have him once again as a lover?"

"That will be completely between you and Captain Jones."

"Ben, will you speak to him on my behalf?"

"I don't believe that it would be proper for me to ask him to be your lover."

No Ben ... and I would never ask you to do that. Just ask if he will meet with me. I will take care of the rest. Please?"

"Of course, if it is what you truly wish, I will ... at my earliest opportunity."

They stood up from their seats in the pleasant garden, the only sound the buzzing of the bees.

Madame Leray wore a look of genuine relief. "Thank you, Ben," she said. "But now I must return to my kitchen. God knows what the staff has been doing in my absence." Then she held her nose. "And you go take that bath, will you please?" She gave him a playful shove out of the garden toward his lodgings.

"All right, all right," Ben said. "I shall return a new man."

When Ben arrived, the four ladies were between courses of the luncheon. Servers busily entered and left the dining room carrying plates and bowls, drinks and utensils. Madame Le Veillard was describing the capture of her son by the British and his subsequent release. She sat to the right of her hostess. Across from Madame Leray, sat Mrs. John Jay. She was a tall woman by French standards, perhaps even taller than Marie Antoinette. She was strikingly beautiful. She sat with an aristocratic air that signified the best Colonial upbringing. The tailoring of her blue silk dress was perfect. She wore a simple matching blue hat atop well-groomed sandy brown tresses. She and her husband had recently arrived in Paris after his tenure as the American ambassador to Spain. John Jay would be a great help in the peace negotiations with the British, and Ben was glad to have his assistance. As he soaked up her gay laugh and her smiling countenance, Ben was glad to welcome Mrs. Jay as well.

Abigail Adams, wife of John Adams, sat with her back to the door. As much as Mrs. Jay was light and merry, Mrs. Adams was stern and prudish. There was nothing pleasant in the way she sat. A tight bun of black hair was tied with a gray ribbon, matching a plain gray dress. Though he could not see her face, Ben imagined that she wore a dour look despite the happy occasion. In Ben's mind, she represented the worst puritanical side of the American populace—strait-laced, intolerant, and fundamentalist in her religious beliefs. Ben doubted that she would ever be the "life of the party."

In fact, he recalled an occasion related to him by Madame Leray, when Mrs. Adams had visited the home of Madame Helvétius in Auteuil. Mrs. Adams had been "aghast" at the revealing dress worn by her hostess, and "shocked" by the loose manner with which Madame Helvétius ran her household.

Ben moved toward the table. "Probably it was wise of Madame Leray not to invite Minette to this luncheon," he thought.

Madame Leray noticed him enter. "Oh, Ben, there you are," she said.

"Hmmph," Mrs. Adams grunted. She became even more tense in her posture, if that were possible. She didn't turn her head at all. Ben walked over to stand by Madame Leray. Mrs. Jay gave him a warm smile across the table. Mrs. Le Veillard put down her fork. For the first time, Ben snuck a glance at Mrs. Adams's face. She looked livid, stone-faced, as she stared straight ahead.

"Ben, I am so glad that you could come say hello to my guests," Madame Leray said. She seemed unflustered by Mrs. Adams's rudeness. "You know Madame Le Veillard, of course."

"Of course," Ben said. He went over and planted a kiss on the back of her hand. She blushed. Mrs. Adams continued to stare straight ahead.

"And Mrs. Jay."

"Ah, the lovely Mrs. Jay," Ben said. He took her hand. "*Enchanté.* Welcome to Paris."

"Doctor Franklin, it is delightful to finally be here after our years in Spain. John is very excited about being a part of the peace negotiations."

"As I am pleased to have him as a member of the delegation. I am sure that he will prove invaluable. But you, my dear, are simply glowing." Ben said. He gave her hand a kiss.

"And you are an incorrigible flatterer," she said sweetly. She blushed, obviously enjoying his attention.

There was a strong "tsssk" sound from the direction of Mrs. Adams.

Ben looked up to catch her sour expression just as Madame Leray was saying, "And Mrs. Adams."

"Hello," Ben said formally. "So good of you to come." There would be no kissing of her hand, Ben was sure. Her icy stare left him cold.

The introductions ended, Ben begged his leave. But as he left, he could hear Mrs. Adams relaying to their hostess how improper the interruption of the ladies' luncheon had been. Madame Leray was apologizing, but she caught Ben's eye and gave him a wink.

Late Summer 1782

SPA, BELGIUM &
PASSY, FRANCE

MARIANNE FLOATED in a warm pool of mineral water. Her recent massage had left her skin tingling, and every muscle in her body relaxed. She had been at Spa for over two months now. These treatments with Mesmer had become nearly a daily routine. Even Mother seemed to question her comings and goings less this summer. Mesmer's funding of their concert series had the effect of keeping Mother from being overly inquisitive. Marianne appreciated being able to walk out the front door of the hotel, to avoid the pretense of having a headache, or having to use her window escape route. She wondered how much Mother knew about her and Mesmer, if she was aware of the bargain that had been struck. She was deep in contemplation when he brought her back.

"How did you learn your wonderful command of human anatomy?" Mesmer asked. The question was innocent enough.

"It was in London, many years ago," Marianne said wistfully. "William

Hewson, the anatomist, kept a laboratory in the basement of Ben's lodgings on Craven Street. It smelled terrible down there. Hewson's mother-in-law, Mrs. Stevenson, either never went down or had completely lost her sense of smell—otherwise, she would have made him clean it out. But I was fascinated by the idea of looking inside the human body. Ben introduced me to Hewson. The man was a genius. He died much too young. I once asked him to show me how the heart organ worked. He invited me down to the basement to view a body that he was dissecting. I was reluctant but curious. While he was showing me the heart organ, he launched into a ten-minute dissertation about the many variations in the coronary arteries that feed blood fluid back to the organ itself. I learned more than I could even take in that day."

"Impressive," Mesmer murmured. "And how did you come to meet Ben Franklin?"

Marianne began to wonder whether he was more interested in how she gained her knowledge of anatomy or about her time in London with Ben.

"That was also in London, and many years ago."

"Yes?"

"Well, there is not much to tell," she said.

"Go on."

She gave him a vexed look. "He attended one of my concerts and spoke to me kindly afterward." She hoped that might satisfy him. It didn't.

"He had his original glass armonica constructed for you, did he not?"

"Yes. You know that well enough. So what if he did?"

"Well, I was thinking that is an impressive present from a gentleman."

"All right, we were close friends in London. There, are you satisfied?"

"You don't have to explain your relationships to me, my dear," he said.

"Good."

"Have you seen him in Paris?"

"I thought that I didn't have to explain my relationships to you."

He couldn't completely cover his anxiety though he tried hard. "And?" he asked.

Despite his plaintive look, Marianne wasn't inclined to divulge the full extent of her relationship with Ben, either in London or Paris. She suspected that no good could come from Mesmer knowing.

Her response was at least half-true. "He is much too busy as American ambassador," she replied.

Mesmer seemed satisfied, for now. Either that, or he really didn't want to know, she thought. Marianne decided to change the subject.

"Tell me about the blind pianist," she asked. She tried to equal the veiled indifference of his prior questioning about Ben.

"Maria Paradis?"

"Um-hum," she said dreamily. She wondered if he would open up.

"Well, you know, my dear, I truly loved that girl."

Marianne felt her posture stiffen slightly. Mesmer had never expressed his love for anyone to her before, not his wife, not for her, not for anyone. She stifled her desire to confront him with that fact but said nothing.

"She was only seventeen when she came under my care, but what a temptress."

"Truly?" Marianne tried hard to feign only polite interest.

"You seem surprised but think of it this way: A young talented girl, blind from an early age, pushed relentlessly by her family to perform at the pianoforte, patronized by the Empress for her skills. She blossomed into womanhood with no one to appreciate it but me."

"No boyfriends?"

"Her parents wouldn't allow them, not that any came to call."

"Not even Wolfgang Mozart?"

"I am sure that they met on occasion, but you may recall that he did not live in Vienna until '81." Mesmer looked slightly misty-eyed. "She was so vulnerable, so incredibly talented, so sad. To hear her play the piano touched my very soul. She told me that she wished she could see."

"Um-hum."

"She asked me to cure her blindness."

"And you believed her to be curable?"

"Yes," Mesmer replied. He seemed slightly affronted at the question.

"But you know my technique. It involves a great deal of touching."

"I'll say ... but please go on." She did not want him to become distracted from his confession.

"Well, as you know, I had experienced considerable success using my technique with others by the time I was asked, by her parents mind you, to attend young Mademoiselle Paradis. I knew of her case, of course. Every doctor in Vienna did. She had already been treated by the most highly reputed physicians. These distinguished doctors had tried bleeding, purging, plasters applied to her head for so long that she developed welts. Doctor von Stoerk had tried everything he knew to renew her sight, and failed. It was reported that von Stoerk personally had applied over three thousand electrical shocks to her eyes without any result—except excruciating pain, of course. If only to stop this medical torture, I agreed to take her case."

"Three thousand shocks? That's barbaric."

"Yes, the first time I met with the girl, she withdrew from my touch— understandable given her experience with doctors."

"Of course."

"However, I assured her that I would not hurt her, and she relaxed somewhat. I asked her to play something for me on her piano. She gave me a puzzled look with those hauntingly vacant eyes, but obliged. As soon as she started to play, she relaxed. I sat down beside her. I could see that music was her treatment, her escape, her sanctum. She began with a sonata that I recognized as having been written by Wolfgang Mozart. Her fingers danced upon the keys with a lightness easily rivaling the young virtuoso.

"When she had finished, I asked her where she had learned this beautiful sonata. She told me that she had heard it performed three years earlier—in my own garden. She had memorized the entire sonata, playing it for me as if Mozart had written it for her. The emotion that she put into that piece—my God, Marianne—it nearly brought me to tears right then and there. When she had finished, I hugged her. She must have sensed my emotion as well because she started to weep too. We sat there together, on the piano bench, sobbing together. It was the beginning of our treatment."

"So, you cured her with sobbing therapy," Marianne said. She recognized that her sarcastic joke probably sounded overly mean.

Mesmer gave her a pained look. "No, of course not. That was how I gained her confidence—by letting her know that I was not going to treat her like all the other doctors that she had known."

"That seems certain," Marianne said.

He continued unperturbed. "So, I started my treatments. I channeled the *magnétisme animal* into her body by applying my hands to her hypochondrium and thigh. She was very sensitive to touch."

Marianne felt herself flush with jealousy but said nothing.

Mesmer didn't notice her reaction. He became even more serious in his tone. "Marianne," he whispered, "she started to be able to see."

"Truly?"

"I remain unsure how it worked exactly. It may have been very much like your own inner vision—she developed an ability to see without seeing. Whatever the mechanism, I could hold up any number of fingers, and she could tell me the correct number. She started to be able to distinguish dark from light. She laughed at the appearance of my nose. I brought in Doctor von Stoerk and showed him. He was impressed."

"So, what happened?"

"She liked my touch too much."

"Um-hum."

"Oh, it's not what you are thinking, my dear," Mesmer said. "I will admit that I wanted to please her. I wanted to help her find herself. She was like a butterfly emerging from a chrysalis. There may have been times when I allowed myself to go too far—to cross the line between a proper doctor-patient relationship and something else. Something that, looking back, she must have interpreted as more carnal."

"Why do you say that?"

"Because she started to pretend that she couldn't see."

"Pretend?"

"I don't know if 'pretend' is the correct word. To this day, I do not believe that she acted with any malice, and yet the results were the same. As you might anticipate, I needed to convince the medical community in Vienna of the effectiveness of my treatment. The second time that von Stoerk came to call, with a group of Viennese physicians, she failed their tests."

"She was blind again?"

"No, she told me later that she did not want to lose me."

"That doesn't seem to make sense. How might she 'lose you'?"

"She told me that if she proved to the other doctors that she was cured, there would be no reason for me to continue touching her. She failed the test in order to keep me."

"I believe I understand. What did you do?"

"I became angry. I told her that I would stop treating her anyway."

"Oh my."

"Then, *she* became angry. She insinuated to her parents that some inappropriate touching had occurred during the treatments."

"I can imagine their reaction."

"Yes, they forbade me to see her—practically kidnapped her from my clinic. They spread rumors among the Viennese, impugning my treatments. They suggested that I had taken liberties with their daughter. The gossip-mongering newspapers went wild with speculation. Soon the scandal was on everyone's lips in Vienna."

"I remember the uproar."

"Von Stoerk and the other physicians lobbied the Empress to have me investigated. Having only listened to my accusers, she commanded me to, in her words, 'Stop all this nonsense.' That is when I decided to leave Vienna."

"What happened to Mademoiselle Paradis?"

Mesmer shrugged. "The last I heard, she remains blind. She plays concerts to packed houses all over the continent. Quite the accomplished musician now, I'm told. Wolfgang visits her occasionally." His voice lacked emotion, but there was a profound sadness in his eyes.

Ben swam back toward Passy. He followed his usual channel in the Seine. He had hoped to encounter Minette, but she was not to be found in the river today. The late summer sun was warm, the water soothing to his skin. His mind wandered. Nearing home, he noticed a flock of small black birds flying above a grove of trees on shore. They split into two formations and then rejoined to form a single murmuration. The flock swooped out of sight for a moment, then reappeared. They seemed to be heading out over the water toward him.

Ben began to daydream. He found himself on the familiar *straße* in Vienna. It was raining. Everything was wet. Water cascaded off the awnings of the tidy shops, through rain gutters and onto the street. The street itself looked more like a small river. Rushing water lapped at Ben's ankles. Through the turbulent water, he could barely see the cobblestones. He looked up to see that the door to Mesmer's shop was slightly open, though it was dark inside. He could hear the faint eerie sounds of the glass armonica.

As Ben strained to listen, he became aware of another sound coming from up the street, the sound of wings fluttering. At first, he heard only a very low whoosh, but it became distinctly louder. He looked up to see a formation of small black birds performing their aerobatics. From this distance, he could not distinguish individual members, but with surprising speed, the throbbing rhythm of the flock was upon him. Despite the swiftness of their approach, Ben sensed no danger. The birds carefully avoided striking him as they swooped and dodged in an intricate pattern, in perfect control. Up close, Ben could see that each bird kept one eye on its neighbor, and one on the pathway in which it flew. The flock swirled around him.

The shops on the street disappeared as Ben had the sensation of being lifted up. His toes left the water. The flock engulfed him. He looked down to see the ground receding rapidly. The darkness inside the cocoon contrasted with the lush green landscape below. They ascended further, and Ben watched bright sunlight bathe the thick blanket of clouds. Soon, however,

Ben became aware that the light outside the flock had changed again. Where before there had been bright blue sky, now it was quickly transforming to an inky dark iridescent blue.

Then as swiftly as they had arrived, the flock dispersed, leaving Ben standing in an unknown place. He became aware that in his daydream, as in the river, he was naked. Yet he was not cold or even uncomfortable. He marveled at the twinkling of stars all around him.

Ben became aware that he was not alone. His gaze focused on the constellation Cassiopeia in the distance, at which point he began to move effortlessly toward the shimmering outline of a throne. As he drew closer, he saw two figures. One was the Queen seated on her radiant chair. She held a rod in one hand. Glittering rays issued from its tip. These seemed to be drawing him closer. Sitting at her side was Marianne. Ben came to a stop just before the two women. The Queen appeared to be in a trance and did not acknowledge his presence. But Marianne turned to him. She smiled the warm smile that had won his heart so many years ago.

"Hello, Ben," Marianne said serenely. She was dressed in a sheer flowing robe, and appeared peaceful, elegant.

"Marianne." Ben surprised himself at how calm he sounded as he spoke her name, considering his strange surroundings. "Where are we?"

"I don't know that this place has a name," she said. She held up her arms as if to show it off. "I know it only as the place that the flock brings me. I have been coming here for a long while now, but I'm not really sure that it truly exists. I suspect that it only exists in our minds. I wanted to show it to you."

"Thank you ... I think ... but how did we get here?"

"The flock has brought us here."

"So, where are our bodies?"

"Right where we left them."

"Do you mean to say that I am still swimming?"

"Yes, if that is where the flock found you."

"What if I should drown?" Ben thought that he might sound a bit anxious.

"I don't know. I suppose that you might stay here forever." She appreciated the look on his face and went on reassuringly. "But don't worry. The flock will always take you back to the same place where it found you."

"That's comforting," he said. He relaxed a bit. "What do you do here?"

"The Queen and I examine people."

"What do you mean *examine*?"

"We peer inside them."

"To what purpose?"

"To assist in their treatment and cure. When we go back, we are able to tell their doctors what we have seen."

"Do you mean Mesmer?" Ben asked. He tried to sound as unemotional as possible, given his suspicions about their relationship.

"And D'Eslon," she replied. "They take the information and use it to guide their treatment."

"What manner of things can you see?"

"Well, just have a look at yourself in this place, Ben."

She motioned for him to look down. For the first time, he realized that his body was no longer solid, but rather, it was translucent. He saw his heart organ rhythmically beating. He watched in amazement as the remnants of his breakfast traversed his upper intestine. As he looked farther down, he saw a small redness emanating from his great toe.

"My gout?" he asked expectantly.

"Yes, quiescent now ... but too much Madeira and red meat will bring it roaring back."

Ben looked resigned. "I know, I know," he said. "My physician, Madame Gout, has explained that her torture is aimed at improving my longevity by providing the consequence for my overindulgences."

"And right, she is."

Ben looked back toward his middle. He was shocked to see the size of the stone in his bladder.

"Is that my calculus?"

"Yes."

"I did not realize how large it had grown."

"Does it bother you?"

"From time to time ... and if it ever obstructs my outflow, I have a catheter of my own invention to relieve the obstruction."

Marianne gave him a puzzled look.

"It is a tube, known since Roman times, that is used to thread up the urinary channel and drain the urine from the bladder. My design is made of interlocking silver rings, polished smooth, just the right combination of stiffness and flexibility, and easy to keep clean," he explained.

"Ingenious, but you could have the stone removed by the surgeon."

"I would sooner die of it than submit to the butcher's knife."

She laughed. "As you wish," she said.

Having finished his internal self-examination, Ben returned to his inquiry about his whereabouts.

"How does this all work, Marianne?"

"I don't know, Ben. You just have to believe."

"You know that I need proof."

"Is not your being here sufficient proof for you? The proof of your own senses?"

"But can we always trust our senses?" Ben asked.

Marianne looked at him impatiently. "I only know what I can feel, and I believe that this place in which we find ourselves exists inside our minds. And not just your mind or my mind alone, but rather our minds working together, in harmony. Think of how the birds must communicate their movements in the flock. They don't say to each other, 'You go this way, I'll go that way.' They simply move together as one. They have developed a sense of intuition, a sense of the flock communicated by intricate minute gestures impossible to describe. This intuition tells them which way to go.

"I believe we humans have the same capability, but we don't use it as well as the birds. Perhaps we did when we were closer to nature. But we have lost the ability over generations of suppressing it. We now only get bits and pieces, scraps of such information that bubble up into our conscious mind from time to time. You might get the sense that you know what someone is thinking. You might have a premonition. You might perceive something meaningful in a dream. These are examples of the knowledge, the wisdom of the flock, of which I speak. Through Mesmer, I have learned to channel this ability. In this place, I have learned to understand the wisdom of the flock as it relates to others."

"And where is the doctor now?" Ben asked. He tried not to sound overly concerned.

"He is touching my corporal body."

Ben looked at Marianne's image more closely. He was surprised to see one disembodied hand pressed against her hypochondrium and another resting on her thigh. Ben bristled at the thought of Mesmer having such intimate contact with her. He quickly concentrated on her beautiful face in order to calm himself.

"So am I correct in assuming that you need him to get here?"

"I have never tried getting here without him. I wouldn't know how to start."

"Will he know that I am here?"

"Not unless I tell him."

Ben looked at her pleadingly. "Will you?"

"No, of course not. He doesn't need to know."

Ben wondered what other aspects of her life Marianne had kept from him. He decided not to ask.

"Thank you," he said.

The Queen awoke from her trance. She looked at Marianne, seeming to ignore Ben completely.

However, when she said softly to Marianne, "Now I understand why he pleases you so," Ben felt himself blush. Then she added, "But we must go."

Marianne simply nodded.

Before he could protest that he wished to stay longer, that he wished to further explore this strange land, the orb in the right hand of the Queen started to glow. The flock returned with a swooshing sound. A bright flash engulfed all of them in eerie green light.

Ben's head hit the dock of the Hôtel de Valentinois. "Ouch," he exclaimed.

The clear blue sky above the Seine was just where he had left it, a few wisps of cloud rolling by. The sun was warm, the water soothing. Everything was the same except for his head, now stinging from the collision.

"I must not have been paying the proper attention to my path," he thought. He looked back down the river to see the flock of birds flying away.

"How curious," he thought. He rubbed his head. He sat on the dock in his robe for some time, contemplating his experience.

PART
V

January 1783

PARIS

THE LODGE OF THE NINE SISTERS was quiet except for the raised voices of a small group of older freemasons who were smoking tobacco in the library. As he walked by the door, Ben overheard them talking, carrying on about what was wrong with the youth of today. He had no desire to join them. The smoke would torture his lungs, and besides that, he found nothing lacking in younger people other than that they had yet to gain the experience of their elders. Ben just smiled and walked on.

In the kitchen, he found the teakettle, stoked up the fire, and waited for it to boil. He prepared his tea. A clock chimed eight times in the hall. That sound and the crackling of the stove were all that he could hear in the kitchen. With a warm cup of tea, he strode to the parlor.

Ben lit a lamp. Its light did not nearly fill the large room but would provide enough illumination for his purpose. He sat down at the small desk and pulled from his pocket a folded drawing he had recently received. It represented an important pet project, nearing completion. The prior spring Ben had conceived a design of a medal he intended to produce to commemorate the end of the war in America. He had decided to name it the Libertas Americana medal. The drawing he now held was a first proof from the engraver.

On its face, a portrait of a young woman, appearing steadfast and defiant, was portrayed, representing Liberty. The back of the coin showed a scene depicting the struggle between America and the British, with France in her role as protector of the young republic. To portray America, Ben had specified an infant Hercules, for England, a lion, and for France, he chose the goddess Minerva. The proof he studied showed the three figures engaged in combat. Over the top was a quote from Horace, which read in Latin *"Non sine diis animosus infans"* meaning "The courageous child was aided by the gods." Below the scene were inscribed the dates of October 17, 1777, and October 19, 1781—the dates of the American victories in the battles at Saratoga and Yorktown.

Ben's smile turned to a frown as he focused on the tail of the lion. It was portrayed as being straight up in the air. Ben took up a pen, correcting the drawing so that the tail now went down between the legs of the beast—to better represent surrender. Being satisfied with that, he switched his attention to the obverse proof showing the young woman drawn by the artist Joseph Wright. Ben could almost feel her long hair, portrayed as flowing freely in the wind behind her. The expression on her face was solemn, resolute—just as it should be. Seen in profile, she looked straight ahead. Her nose was classic. Ben fancied that she looked slightly like Marianne in her youth—even though he knew that the artist had used his own niece as a model. The engraver had encircled the portrait, adding the words "Libertas Americana" above her head and the date 4 *Juil* 1776 below.

Somehow, the medal lacked something, Ben thought. Behind the woman, he added a pole topped with a pileus, the helmet on a staff being emblematic of freedom.

"Now that is complete," he said aloud to no one.

Ben addressed an envelope to Monsieur Dupré, the engraver, inserted the modified proofs along with a short letter of explanation authorizing the changes, and sealed it up with wax. He set the packet in the bin marked for the outgoing post.

Just as Ben had finished his work on the design of the medallion, there was a commotion in the entry hall. More masonic members were arriving. Ben could identify Temple, as well as John Paul Jones, speaking animatedly among the voices. Ben rose from his chair.

"The Society of Universal Harmony meeting must have let out," he thought. Ben ambled toward the entry hall, where members of the staff were gathering heavy coats and capes from the six members recently arrived. His grandson, John Paul Jones, and Pierre Cabanis were among this group of men.

These three were animatedly and repeatedly chanting, "*Allez, touchez, guérissez.*" Jean-Baptiste Le Roy, Antoine Court de Gébelin—the tarot card master, and a young nobleman Ben recognized as the Baron de Coberon, rounded out the group. All of the men were jovial, laughing. Temple and John Paul approached Ben first.

"Oh, Granddad," Temple enthused. "It was wonderful. Such a useful treatment."

Ben gave his grandson a look of some consternation but was silent. He looked over at John Paul.

"I am ready for a drink," Jones said. He moved toward the bar.

"Parched?" Ben asked. He headed out of the entry hall, arm in arm with Jones and Temple. Cabanis and Le Roy followed behind. De Gébelin and the Baron split off toward the kitchen.

"Yes. Mesmer does not allow any liquor, wine, beer, or coffee to be served at his meetings. I'm considering bringing a flask next time," Jones said.

"You will probably be a very popular member," Ben replied.

The bar was empty save for a couple of young initiates who jumped up at the entry of the distinguished party. With a glass of Madeira in hand, Ben restarted the conversation.

"Tell me how you intend to go forth, touch, and heal?" He posed the question to no one in particular.

Le Roy was the first to answer. "Ben, I know that you are not a believer in Mesmer's *magnétisme animale*, but I like a great deal of what he has to say."

"For example?"

"Well, so far, his teachings have been very general, but he advocates a healthy diet, moderation in indulgences of all types, and keeping the use of potions to a minimum."

"But what about his 'invisible fluid' that has neither form nor substance?"

"Well, of that I am skeptical, as I know you are. But are there not many things that modern science is only now starting to be able to explain? Consider this. In his twenty-seven propositions, Mesmer describes the influence of the heavenly bodies upon each other and upon us."

"I'll grant you that there are measurable effects of gravity and well-documented influences of the tides on people."

"Mesmer postulates that there is an ebb and flow of forces within animals and humans, which he found similar to magnetism."

"I would like to be able to measure such forces."

"So would I, but let us assume that we cannot, for the time being."

"As you wish."

Just then, the young medical student Cabanis yawned—no doubt sleep-deprived by his studies and the lateness of the hour. The yawn spread around the room, first to Temple, then John Paul, followed by one of the two servers and finally a cat sitting on the bar.

Le Roy smiled. "Did you observe that?" he asked Ben.

"What?"

"How that yawn went around the room."

"And so?" Ben looked perplexed.

"So, I believe that you have just seen a demonstration of the principle of which we were speaking."

"Jean-Baptiste, you have lost me completely."

"Ben, how would you explain that yawn being passed from one person to another around the room?"

"They are all completely bored with our dialogue?"

Le Roy laughed. "That could also be true," he said. "Pardon me, but I meant to ask how exactly you would explain that no one said anything to each other, no one touched anyone else, or applied any known force, yet most in the room yawned—including a nonhuman, the cat?"

"Sympathy," Ben replied.

Cabanis perked up. "Sympathy?" he remarked. "I am studying sympathy. From the Greek, literally meaning 'same feeling or same emotion.' The feeling of sympathy relates back to our own personal experiences of pain or pleasure. We must be able to sense and feel in order to know sympathy. Our nerves and brain provide the physical channels for that sensibility. Without sensibility, we would not become aware of the presence of external objects; we would not even have a means of perceiving our own existence—or rather, we would not exist. But from the moment at which we feel, we are. Taking it a step further, if we can each realize that we have sensibility and feelings, we can generalize that knowledge to others—assuming that they also have a similar experience. That may lead us to treat others the way we would like to be treated. Sympathy then becomes the foundation of our moral system."

Le Roy and Ben just looked at each other, both were impressed.

"You have been studying exceptionally well, my boy," Ben said with a smile. Cabanis looked slightly sheepish.

Le Roy summed up. "So whether it is through a yawn or a 'moral system,' I believe that you would agree that we are all connected through forces that we do not fully understand and cannot yet measure."

Ben recalled his recent daydream flying with the flock. "Yes," he said. "But I still want to see proof that these men can direct this force as they claim, using it to heal."

"And perhaps you will get that chance," Le Roy said.

Ben returned a questioning look. "How so?" he asked.

"There is talk in Versailles that the King may appoint a commission to investigate Mesmer's claims—but I've also heard that the Queen opposes the idea."

"She usually gets what she wants."

"Yes, but perhaps not this time. The Royal Society of Medicine and the whole medical community, aside from D'Eslon, are pushing hard for it."

"No doubt they have a pecuniary motive," Ben said.

"I am afraid that is the way it would be seen." Le Roy paused and turned more serious. He lowered his voice. "Ben, it would be helpful if I could let His Majesty know that you would be willing to lead such a commission. You would be viewed as impartial."

"Not by Mesmer … nor D'Eslon, methinks."

"I am not so sure, Ben. They both know your reputation as a man of science. I believe that, out of all the great men of science in France, Mesmer would like to prove his theory to you the most."

"You may be right," Ben said. He paused for a moment. "If the opportunity to assist with such a commission presented itself, I would be inclined to accept."

Le Roy looked as if a weight had been lifted from his shoulders. "Thank you, Ben," he said. "I will let the appropriate people know."

John Paul Jones started in on a dissertation aimed at Temple and Cabanis on the "proper" way to touch a woman in order to get the desired response. The two younger men were all ears, but Ben was disinclined to participate. He and Le Roy excused themselves to go visit the kitchen. Upon their entry, they encountered de Gébelin and the Baron de Coberon seated at the kitchen table, completely engrossed in their activity. Neither man noticed the intrusion. Only one small candle illuminated their space. In front of them was a spread of tarot cards in the form of a cross. De Gébelin was explaining emphatically in a whispered tone to the Baron, who was listening intently.

"The ninth card shows your hopes and fears in relation to the question," de Gébelin said. He waved his hand over the table before turning a card face up. "Ah, it is the Sun," he said with clear trepidation.

"But that should be good, is it not?" the Baron asked.

"Normally yes, but you will notice that it is reversed, which, in relation to your question, means a clouded future. I would interpret this as a sign that you fear the engagement might be canceled."

"Of course, a groom always has some concerns," de Coberon replied. "What about the last card?"

De Gébelin once again did a flourish with his hands, this time longer and even more mysterious, over the final card.

"The final card, the tenth, is the Culmination Card, which shows the end result of all of the previous nine cards," de Gébelin explained. He turned over The Star and gave a sigh that Ben interpreted as one of relief.

"What?" de Coberon asked. He seemed anxious to know de Gébelin's consul.

"I would interpret The Star as indicative of love, pleasure, faith, and balance in this situation. I believe that it is a very good sign for the upcoming nuptials."

De Coberon looked clearly relieved. "Thank you," he said.

Ben took the opportunity to clear his throat. "What was the question?" he said.

The two looked up, seeming to notice that they were not alone for the first time.

The Baron smiled sheepishly. "I asked Monsieur de Gébelin's prediction about my upcoming marriage."

"Ah," Ben replied. He smiled. "And so it appears that all is in order for a blissful union?"

"Yes, thankfully."

"Good. Then my friend Monsieur Le Roy and I may enter and locate a snack of cheese and bread?"

"Of course, please come in."

Ben lit another lamp. He proceeded to the cupboard, where he found a wedge of aged cheddar. He cut a large slice for himself and one for Le Roy. In the meantime, Jean-Baptiste had pulled a long baguette from the bread bin and was breaking it into chunks. The two men arrived at the table at the same time. They exchanged morsels.

"May I read your cards?" de Gébelin asked Ben.

"No, thank you. But I would gladly read yours," Ben replied.

De Gébelin was clearly taken aback. But he quickly replied, "As you wish. I didn't know that you were experienced in the reading of the Tarot."

"I am not, but I assume that you will help me if I go astray in my interpretation."

"Of course."

"Good, then let us begin." Ben collected the cards on the table. He shuffled them in with the remaining deck as though he knew what he was doing. He gave Le Roy a wink.

"Ten cards in a cross arrangement?" Ben asked as if only to confirm that his subject wished a traditional reading.

De Gébelin looked stunned. "Yes," he said.

"And your question?"

"I am concerned to know what the cards tell as to the course of my health."

Ben was surprised to be entrusted with such an important matter, especially given his inexperience with the Tarot. Nonetheless, as he believed the results would be meaningless, he answered simply, "As you wish."

Ben had a little trouble interpreting some of the minor cards. De Gébelin seemed to be unconcerned at this lack of knowledge and jumped in with his own interpretation several times. But Ben got an approving look from de Gébelin when he interpreted the upside-down Ace of Cups in the ninth position as representing a concern over confidence in his current physician. The reading seemed to be going very well until Ben got to the tenth card. Ben did an extended flourish with his hands before turning it over for effect.

There was a gasp around the table, including from Ben himself, as he turned over "*La Morte.*"

"I knew it," de Gébelin said. He exhaled and put his right hand to his chest.

"I am sorry," Ben said. He looked over at Le Roy, who appeared to be in a state of shock.

"It is all right, Ben. I get the same result every time I do it. I just wanted to confirm that it was not just me," de Gébelin replied.

"I doubt that it means anything," Ben said.

"I wish that I could believe that."

"It is getting late," de Coberon said. He looked as if he had seen a ghost. He got up haltingly from the table and quickly left. Ben and Le Roy sat in silence for a few more minutes before de Gébelin bid them a good night as well. They listened to his labored breathing as he slowly climbed the back staircase up to his room, half expecting to hear him collapse.

As they settled into the coach back to Passy, Jean-Baptiste sat across from Ben. Temple put his head on Ben's shoulder and was soon asleep.

"What do you think?" Le Roy asked.

"As I said—superstitious nonsense," Ben replied, but he wasn't quite so absolutely sure any longer.

March 1783

VERSAILLES

THE TRIP FROM PARIS to Versailles had been comfortable enough. Ben had enjoyed the all-too-infrequent opportunity to spend some time with his host in Passy, Jacques Leray. They were alone together for the entire five-hour coach ride. When they weren't talking about the business aspects of the peace negotiations between America and England, Ben delighted in observing the French countryside. It was still early spring, but the trees were starting to bud. Within a month, there would be cherry blossoms everywhere in Paris.

The road to Versailles remained rutted and muddy, and as the coach sped by, it splashed the passing peasants and their carts with a thick, brown slurry. Ben found himself increasingly troubled by the class disparities so obvious to him in France. He was troubled, as well, by his desire to avoid focusing on them. As he had been many times before, he became uncomfortably aware of the fact that, ever since his arrival, he had enjoyed the company and the largesse of the rich and powerful. In America, a revolution had freed the people from British overlords and their aristocratic dominance. Would that day come soon in France?

The dark earth was a backdrop for the vibrant green of the earliest spring vegetation. By the time they had arrived at the outer gates of Versailles, it was nearly sundown. Ben marveled at the precision with which they were checked at the gate, directed to the stable, and ushered into the palace for a light supper.

Ben was shown to a most comfortable room looking out over the garden, mostly brown still from winter, but glowing in the purple hues of evening. A fire already burned in his fireplace. Bed linens of a floral print adorned a comfortable-looking canopy bed. A bottle of Madeira sat on his bedside table along with a tray containing an assortment of cheeses and crusty breads. He wondered, briefly, if the peasants he had passed on the road had even reached their destination or had a decent meal to eat.

Ben unpacked his bag and hung his outfit in the armoire. He removed a small wooden presentation box and placed it carefully on the writing desk. He donned a pair of soft linen *pājāma* trousers he had acquired many years before in England. Though Ben slept in the nude at home, he had adopted an old English practice of wearing this loose-fitting garment to bed when traveling. That way, there would be no need to worry that he might offend anyone if he wandered to the privy at night.

He walked over and cracked open the window to let in some fresh air, then turned down the duvet and pulled it over him. The softness of the bed and the crackling of the fire carried him off to sleep almost immediately.

Morning came slowly at the royal palace. Ben recognized that there must be activity on the part of the staff, but they went about their work so quietly that he was unaware of any of it. He awoke with the first morning light. As comfortable as the mattress and duvet had been, he quit them, never one to let the day waste away lying in bed. He donned a thick robe hung nearby for his use. Ben stoked up the fire to warm the room. Sitting at the writing desk, he penned a note to Minette.

Ben wrote that he would miss her presence today but that he understood her distaste for such formal royal events. He sealed the letter and placed it in a small basket labeled "*Poste.*"

Then he turned his attention to the presentation box. He opened the polished mahogany lid to reveal two gold Libertas Americana medals secured side by side on red felt, each showing a different side, and glimmering in the early morning light. Ben smiled as he thought that these would be the first of many commemorative medals he would give away. He also thought it fitting that the only two medals he had struck in gold would be presented to the King and Queen of France for their role in assisting with the American cause. The silver and copper versions were not even pressed yet. To date, the mint had only been able to produce these two. He closed the box, tying it with a red ribbon.

Ben walked back over toward the bed. There he pulled the cord to summon the butler. Within a minute, there was a soft knock at his door. Ben opened it.

The impeccably dressed butler entered. "*Oui, Docteur?*" he inquired. He carried a newspaper and a small vase with a flower.

"May I have some hot water to bathe?" Ben asked.

"But of course." The butler set the newspaper and the vase on the desk. He spotted the letter. "For the morning post?" he asked.

"Yes."

The butler inspected Ben's letter. "It will be delivered to Auteuil this afternoon, Monsieur," he said.

The butler tended the fire, then picked up the leftover cheese and bread tray. "You are finished with this tray, I trust?" he asked.

"Yes, thank you." Ben marveled at the efficiency of his actions.

"I will be returning in a few minutes with your water for bathing. Is there anything else that I can bring you?"

"Tea ... with milk, *s'il vous plaît.*"

"Of course, doctor. I believe there are fresh scones as well. May I have a tray brought to you?"

"The King eats scones?" Ben asked.

"No, the Queen perhaps…" the butler replied. He looked slightly impish. "I believe His Majesty would probably bounce them off my head if I tried to serve them to him. They have origins in Scotland, do they not? The King eats only French food. No sir, these scones were prepared especially for you."

"Remarkable," Ben replied. He was now even more astonished at the level of preparation that must have preceded his visit. "But I truly enjoy French food too," he said. He patted his slightly protuberant stomach.

"We will have plenty of that today as well, sir," the butler said. He disappeared.

Ben had barely gotten back to his chair when there was another soft knock at the door. This time a pretty maid appeared with a tray of scones and a silver tea service. Her dark brown hair was cut shorter than Ben had seen on any of the French ladies. The combination of her fiery dark brown eyes, the pert cut of her hair, and a few freckles dappled on her cheekbones gave Ben the distinct impression that she would have no difficulty attracting men well above her station in life.

"Is there anything else that I can do for you, Doctor?" she asked. "No, thank you," he heard himself say. All the while, thinking that Le Veillard would probably cringe had he been witness to such a waste of a good opportunity in the company of this captivating young woman.

She breezed out as airily as she had arrived, but her essence lingered for a long time.

To his dismay, three husky men rather than the pretty maid delivered it. But after bathing with hot soapy water, Ben felt revived. He decided to get dressed and explore the palace.

Ben donned a pair of white stockings and a ruffled silk shirt from his bag. From the armoire, Ben pulled out his black velvet suit and pulled on the knee breeches. He buttoned the vest over his shirt and put the long jacket over the top. Finally, he slipped on a pair of comfortable, but not particularly stylish, leather shoes with pewter rectangular buckles on top. He strode to the full-length mirror and checked for anything out of place. Reassured that he looked his finest, he tucked his bifocals in one breast pocket and the presentation box in the other. Then he attached his pocket watch to his belt, checked it for accuracy against the mantle clock, and clicked the jewel-like timepiece shut. As he left his room, the butler jumped up from where he was stationed in the hall.

"You did not need any assistance dressing?" he asked.

Ben laughed. "No," he said. "I didn't attain the age of seventy-seven years and never learn to dress myself."

"Of course not, sir … but begging your pardon, sir … no wig?" He motioned at Ben's wavy silver shoulder-length hair flowing down from his mostly baldpate.

"I can't stand the things. Terribly hot and itchy. Torture devices, I'd say."

The butler shrugged. "The gentleman's prerogative," he said. "Dispensing with it will certainly make dressing easier."

"I was hoping to stretch my legs a bit this morning. Is there anywhere that I should not walk in the palace?"

"Doctor Franklin, you have no restrictions. However, the royal court will be in session this morning. I would suggest that, if you wish to observe, you do so discreetly from the gallery. I believe that your presence on the floor might be a distraction. Other than that, and the royal apartments, you are free to roam wherever you please except where there are guards posted outside the doors. Would you like me to find someone familiar with the palace to guide you?"

"Perhaps that delightful maid who brought my scones this morning," Ben said, only half in jest.

"Brigit?" the butler replied, his eyebrow raised. "I regret she has other responsibilities this morning."

"No doubt," said Ben, plainly disappointed.

Ben was instead introduced to a stern woman who provided guidance as they walked. She talked rapidly, and without stopping—a steady didactic stream of information about the rooms, furniture, paintings, art, and other objects that they passed. While her monotone voice grated on him, Ben had to admit that she knew her way around the palace.

The place was enormous. More than once, he would have been completely lost had she not been with him. Ben listened to the proceedings of the court from the gallery for some time. The pettiness of most of the concerns voiced by the stream of attorneys and courtiers amazed him. It seemed to Ben that the few genuine issues that needed the attention of the King were far outweighed by the minor griping and complaining he witnessed that morning. By the time that he and his guide were returning from the morning tour, Ben's feet were getting tired from all the walking, and they hadn't even stepped outside the palace to the gardens.

Ben checked his watch. It was nearing time for the festivities to begin. As he and his escort approached the hall, Ben heard a male voice speaking just inside the entrance. His voice was familiar, but Ben couldn't place it. Then he heard a woman laugh. It was unmistakably, the lovely Sarah Jay.

Ben entered the large hall to find her standing, along with her husband John, Henry Laurens, and a woman he didn't recognize. The unknown woman stood with her back toward the door. She was athletic, aristocratic, striking. Ben thought that she looked vaguely familiar from the rear.

When she turned around, he was astounded to find that it was Minette. Her silver hair was done up and powdered with beads and flowers braided into it. It was no wonder that he hadn't recognized her. Ben could not remember a time when he had ever seen her so made up.

John Jay was the first to speak. "Ben," he exclaimed as if greeting a long-lost friend. "We rushed all the way from Paris to be here for your coronation."

Ben barely heard him. His eyes were fixed on Minette and found himself embracing her almost instantly without realizing he had crossed the floor.

"I thought that you weren't coming," he whispered, pulling her close to him. He was unexpectedly overcome with emotion.

"How could I miss this?" she responded. She pulled him close to her as well.

"And look at you." He let her go and took a step back.

She twirled around. "What do you think?" she asked. "Ready for court?"

"Perfectly," Ben said. "You may cause a scene."

"Flatterer ... but don't get to like it too much. I'm washing it out as soon as we are done here."

"Of course, I like it much better *au natural.* It is just so different."

Ben finally turned his attention to the others in the room.

"John ... Sarah ... Henry," he said apologetically. He shook each man's hand. He planted a kiss on the back of the hand Mrs. Jay presented and accompanied the kiss with a deep bow, but he kept Minette's hand locked in his own even as he did so. He didn't want to let her go.

John Jay started up the conversation once again. "Ben, as I was saying, we headed out early this morning, picking up Madame Helvétius on the way."

"Who convinced her to come?" Ben asked the group.

"I guess that would be me," Sarah Jay replied, raising her hand. "Madame Leray helped too, of course ... but I do not believe that your Minette needed much convincing."

"Marie-Thérèse did not make the journey with you?" Ben asked.

"No, she sends her regrets but was unavoidably detained with business at the Hôtel de Valentinois," John Jay said.

More guests were now entering the hall. Ben recognized John Adams and *that* Mrs. Adams enter together, each wearing a sour expression despite the joyous occasion. Madame Brillon was strikingly beautiful in contrast to her frumpy husband. Ben watched as Jean-Baptiste Le Roy entered with a group of other scientists, including Condorcet, Lavoisier, and Bailly.

Ben found it interesting to observe that the scientists did not mingle with the courtiers, the physicians did not mingle with the politicians, the city folk did not mingle with the country ones, et cetera. Only he and Minette seemed able to move freely among these groups. Perhaps, he mused, this was because they had interests in all of these areas and could converse, at least a little bit, in each. Perhaps it also helped that he was the guest of honor today. The room was close to being full when Ben spotted Temple with a group of young men, including Pierre Cabanis. Notably missing was John-Paul Jones.

A trumpet fanfare brought the conversations in the room to a stop, and a hush fell over the crowd. Charles Gravier Compte de Vergennes, the French Foreign Minister under King Louis XVI, entered the hall with an honor guard. He carried, on his outstretched arms, a square red plush pillow with gold tassels dangling from each corner. Atop the pillow lay a green laurel wreath. The crowd parted to let him pass. He approached Ben, now positioned near the middle of the rectangular hall. Minette attempted to pull away, but Ben held her firm. Vergennes and the guard came to a stop directly in front of them. The crowd redistributed itself around the central figures as a large hall fell completely silent.

Ben was just beginning to wonder how the Queen would make her entrance when it happened. The hush of the crowd instantly changed to a palpable buzz. A few people turned, but Vergennes kept looking straight forward at Ben as if he had done this a thousand times before. Ben reckoned that he himself was getting used to the way the Queen made her entrances. He could feel her presence but was only slightly tempted to watch her approach. She must have entered through a side door, for she deftly cut through the crowd, arriving next to Ben in much less time than if she had entered through the main doorway. Vergennes and the guard turned precisely to allow her to become the third side of the triangular grouping.

A trumpet fanfare sounded again, lower and sweeter this time, then died away.

Her Majesty greeted Ben softly with a warm smile. She looked at him approvingly, which evoked a squeeze of his hand from Minette, who apparently noticed the attention.

"Your Majesty," Ben said. He bowed deeply and kissed her hand. "Are you ready, Ben?" the Queen prompted.

Ben gave a solemn nod. "Yes," he replied.

"Hello, cousin," Marie Antoinette said to Minette. Her greeting was considerably more on the cool side. "I love what you have done with your hair."

"Thank you." Minette stayed calm. Ben squeezed her hand now. She squeezed back.

"Ladies and gentlemen," Vergennes bellowed, filling the cavernous reception hall with his rich baritone voice for the first time. "Our Queen will address you now."

Marie Antoinette stood at the center of the large throng of people. Her voice was strong but not excessively loud. There was no pressure to her speech. Yet everyone was able to hear her because it was so quiet in the large hall and she enunciated so perfectly.

"*Mesdames et Messieurs,*" she said. "We have come together today to honor our good friend and American Ambassador, Doctor Benjamin Franklin. Ben came to our country seven years ago with one goal. That goal was for America to become a sovereign nation. His strategy was to secure an alliance with France in the courageous fight against England.

"France rose to the occasion. Our Comte de Rochambeau and the Marquis de La Fayette are two well-recognized heroes who have fought side by side with the Americans in their cause. Today, with the help of many of you in this room, we are on the precipice of a historic event. Peace talks are now being conducted in Paris with the goal of crafting an agreement recognizing America as a new country. Many of you know well the risks that we have all taken in the pursuit of this goal. Today, we honor Benjamin Franklin in his role as the representative for the American people ... and their victory over the British in their war for independence."

She took a breath and turned toward Vergennes. "The laurel wreath is a symbol bestowed on victors since ancient Greek times. This wreath represents the American victories at Yorktown, and more recently at Saratoga, resulting in British capitulation and surrender."

She picked up the laurel wreath from the pillow. With her right hand, she held it above Ben's head.

"Ben, wear this wreath as evidence of your successful battle against British occupation and tyranny." She lowered the wreath softly on his baldpate. It was slightly prickly.

Emotion was welling up in Ben's throat as he addressed Marie Antoinette. "None of this would have been possible without the dedication and support of the French people. America owes you an eternal debt of gratitude for our freedom. As a token of our appreciation, I would like to present you and His Majesty with a small memento," he said. He pulled the box from his pocket and presented it to Marie Antoinette.

Marie Antoinette opened the box. For a woman who was surely accustomed to receiving the most lavish gifts, the look on her face showed genuine appreciation.

"Ben, the King and I will cherish these medallions as long as we live," she said.

There was thunderous applause as the room erupted in celebration. Ben wore the prickly crown for a few minutes, but then found it too irritating to his skin and removed it. The Queen disappeared as quickly and discreetly as she had arrived.

In one corner of the hall, a band struck up. They played a tune Ben recognized as *Marche des insurgents* composed by Madame Brillon. He looked around to find her flirting animatedly with three finely dressed courtiers, her husband nowhere in sight. Servers descended with large trays of carved meats, cellar vegetables, tureens, and desserts. The wine flowed. As the afternoon progressed, a few of the revelers departed to get an early start on the long ride back to Paris. Mr. and Mrs. John Adams were the first to depart. The Brillon's left soon after—although Madame Brillon did not look at all happy about it.

Most of the guests continued to enjoy themselves, however. Ben and Minette circulated among them, at times together, at times separately, but they always found each other again at intervals, joining hands and greeting well-wishers as a couple. As the event wound down, Ben pulled Minette aside.

"Stay tonight," he pleaded. "I have a lovely room, and there is a seat in Jacques Leray's coach for you to travel home with us tomorrow."

Her objection was weak. "I have to wash my hair," she said.

"I am sure that we can find you a bathtub somewhere in this palace."

"But I have nothing else to wear."

Ben thought for a moment, then a mischievous look spread over his face. "My dear Minette, how much do you need?"

The following morning, Jacques Leray decided to remain in Versailles, ostensibly for business, giving Ben and Minette the coach to themselves for the ride back to Paris. They talked the whole way except for a short time when Minette took a nap, her head resting on Ben's shoulder. She slept like an angel. Ben didn't want to let her go when the coach pulled up in front of her house in Auteuil. He made her promise to invite him for dinner by the weekend.

Ben traveled on alone for the short trip to Passy. He found himself contemplating the mysteries of love. He wondered if love could be ever measured in some way. Clearly, his love for Minette was growing, and his love for Marianne changing, perhaps even dissipating. Yet, how could one calculate or put a value on such a thing? One woman was not better or more important than the other in his life. Love was so difficult to quantify—such a personal, subjective emotion; an objective outside observer, a scientist, would never be able to calibrate or attune it. No one could connect a meter or instrument to measure it. He recalled a passage written by Descartes over a hundred years before:

Love is an emotion of the soul caused by a movement of the spirits, which impels the soul to join itself willingly to objects that appear to be agreeable to it.

Even if it were true that human emotions engendered by particles traveling through the nerves (the spirits) as Descartes suggested, Ben wasn't sure that love could, or even should be measured that way.

He arrived at the gate of the Hôtel de Valentinois, hungry and tired from the adventures of his travel, glad to be home.

Marie-Thérèse met him at the *porte-cochère*, before he could even step down from the coach. She seemed hurried, and a bit concerned. Yet her skin possessed a glow that he had not seen in some time. It was an interesting mixture of emotions. She peered into the coach past Ben.

"Jacques did not return with you?" she asked.

"No, he stayed at the palace on business."

"Good."

"Good?"

"Yes, good. I must speak with you." Then, always the perfect hostess, she asked, "Are you hungry?"

"Famished."

"All right then, come to my kitchen."

Ben followed along through the well-kept house. It didn't seem to him that anything had visibly changed since he had left a few days before, but something was different.

Sitting in the warm kitchen, Ben listened as Madame Leray instructed the cook to go to the root cellar on an errand designed to keep her out of earshot for a while. He took a bite of cheese while his hostess poured a healthy measure of red wine for each of them. She sat down next to him at the large wooden table.

Ben decided to open the conversation. "John Paul was here," he said matter-of-factly.

She let out a small gasp. "Is it so obvious?"

"Only to me, my dear," he said reassuringly. "I doubt that anyone else would have noticed your mutual absence at my coronation."

"I am so sorry that I missed it, Ben," she said. "But I needed the time to get some things sorted out."

"I understand. How did it go?"

"I believe that I am finally over him."

"I doubt that."

She started sobbing softly. Ben put his arm around her.

"You are right, of course," she managed. "I'll never stop loving him, but I have to try to forget him. He doesn't love me."

"There, there," Ben said consolingly. "Tell me about it."

"Oh Ben, he is so big, so strong, so powerful. Making love to him is the most pleasurable thing I have ever done."

Ben's expression turned to a mock frown. "I don't need to know all the details," he said.

"Yes, of course." She laughed slightly, her mood lifting.

Ben reached over and wiped a tear from her eye with his handkerchief. "So, how did it end?"

"Well, I asked him to be with me one more time ... and he obliged."

"Very accommodating of him," Ben said.

Madame Leray gave him a vulnerable look.

"Go on," Ben said.

"We talked. He told me that there was no future for us. I already knew that, but to hear him say those words. Ben ..." She started to sob again. "But in the end, I told him that he was free. I love him too much to try to make him into someone he is not. I can't make him love me."

"No, you can't."

"I told him that I would not pursue him ... and that I would appreciate it if he would not pursue me."

"It sounds done then."

"Yes, all but this gaping hole in my heart. It hurts so much, Ben."

"I know, I know." He tried to be as consoling as possible. "But your heart is strong. It will heal with time."

"I hope you are right." She brightened up. "Now, you must tell me all about the coronation. Who was there, what they wore, everything."

Ben eagerly described the whole scene for his hostess. He thanked her profusely for her role in helping to convince Minette to attend. By the time the cook returned to the kitchen from her errand, Madame Leray was animatedly regaling Ben with the latest gossip from Passy.

May 1783

FLORENCE, ITALY

MARIANNE WAS RESTLESS. The coach trip from Florence to Paris would be arduous, Marianne expected, but she was glad to set out. Not that there was anything wrong with Florence, it remained one of the jewels of the Habsburg-Lorraine empire. Though Marianne felt that the city had not received quite as much care and attention since the passing of the Empress Maria Theresa three years earlier. The streets were not as clean as they once were. Nonetheless, the city remained vibrant with art—and music—which at least had allowed the Davies sisters to make a living there. Cecelia had become a genuine star. She was one of the very few non-Italians regularly singing on the operatic stage in Florence.

Perhaps because of Cecelia's solo success, the city had become a lonely place for Marianne. Her engagements were few and far between. She missed Ben—at least the way things had been with him. She wondered if they could rekindle their passion. She missed Marie Antoinette. She missed the feeling of community around Mesmer's baquet in Paris. She missed helping heal people. She yearned to sit on the houseboat in the

Seine with Marko and his friends. She even missed Mesmer.

To make matters worse, Mrs. Davies had succumbed to pneumonia the past autumn, not long after their arrival. Marianne's relationship with her mother had been strained many times over the years, but now that she was gone, Marianne encountered a deep loneliness that she hadn't encountered ever before. Over the winter, she'd tumbled again and again into the abyss of melancholia. Now that she had finally crawled back out, she felt that she needed to get out of Florence to preserve her sanity.

"At least I won't have to slink out of my bedroom window ever again," she thought. Marianne stared out the window of the stagecoach into the bright morning haze.

Before leaving Florence, the coach came to a halt in front of a hotel frequented by businessmen. Marianne wondered if other passengers would join her on the long trip to Paris. She wished that Cecelia had been able to accompany her—if for no other reason than that she would not be forced to talk to strangers.

Marianne had written a sorrowful letter to Ben the month before. In it, she described her profound discontent. After her mother's passing, Marianne and Cecelia had entrusted much of their money to a man who promised to invest it wisely, but he had speculated with the funds instead, and now their mother's small estate was mostly gone.

While Cecelia's career in the opera was proceeding well, and they were able to get by, there was little extra money. Marianne lamented in her letter to Ben that many other musicians were now playing the glass armonica. This made it harder for her to get any jobs. She requested that Ben somehow protect her right to play it exclusively. But he hadn't responded. Perhaps the letter had gone missing or never got to him. Perhaps he was no longer inclined to help her as he had done in London. Perhaps he no longer loved her.

Thus, when Mesmer had offered to pay for her trip to Paris, Marianne surprised herself by how quickly she had accepted—despite the prospect of two weeks aboard this bumpy stagecoach and the nagging sense that Mesmer might want her in Paris for reasons other than her assistance at his séances.

Marianne had dressed for travel. She wore a comfortable dress of soft linen and, over that, a cape that covered her from head to toe. She kept her thick strawberry-blonde hair pulled back severely and tied with a ribbon behind her head.

Yet despite her precautions, it was impossible to hide the fact that she was a woman traveling alone. The two Italian businessmen who boarded the coach at the hotel gave her an interested glance but quickly returned to their conversation when she did not reciprocate. She was delighted to overhear that they would travel only as far as Bologna—especially when they started smoking their pipes. Tomorrow they would be gone.

Marianne spent her first restless night away from home in a roadside hotel fit only for transients. Finding no lock on her door, she wedged a chair against the door latch instead. The following morning, Marianne breathed a sigh of relief as two priests and a nun traveling from Rome joined her in the coach. After they settled in, they seemed primarily interested in studying their Bibles and quoting passages to each other in Latin. However, the nun struck up a conversation with Marianne.

"Oh, to where might you be traveling, my dear?" she asked with a spritely singsong voice as the coach stopped momentarily to let a herd of sheep cross the road.

"Paris," Marianne replied.

"My, that is a long way." The nun sounded impressed. "By yourself?"

"Yes."

"Bless you, my child," she intoned.

"Thank you, Sister. And what brings you on the long road to Geneva?"

"Oh, it is a mission, my dear," the nun said. "And we must travel even farther than Geneva. We will go on to Vienna to try to save the Mariazell Abbey from closing."

"I see," Marianne said.

"I hope you do," the nun said kindly, but with a tone that made Marianne feel reprimanded. "That monastery has flourished since the twelfth century. But Emperor Joseph has just disbanded it ... after all these years." She looked sad. "Without the monks, who will care for the shrine?"

"I am truly sorry to hear of that situation," Marianne replied with considerably more compassion. "I hope to soon see the Emperor's sister in Paris. Perhaps I can put in a good word?"

"Queen Marie Antoinette?"

"Yes, I taught her to play the harpsichord when she was a young girl. The Empress Maria Theresa was my patron a long time ago in Vienna."

"Oh my dear, would you be able to say something on behalf of the monks at Mariazell?"

"I cannot promise it will do any good, but I will be more than happy to speak for them."

"Thank you, my child," the nun said, taking her by the hand. Her touch felt warm and reassuring.

Marianne soon lapsed back to daydreaming as the clerical party returned to quoting chapter and verse, and in no time, she found herself deep in contemplation.

After her mother had died, Marianne spent many weeks—in fact, nearly the entire winter—languishing in bed. She had no appetite and refused to eat, even when Cecelia tried to force her. Nothing gave her pleasure, not even the thought of her music. She felt wooden, dead. She slept most of the day and night. During her short times awake, she could only rock, groan, and sob. Cecelia tried everything she knew to comfort her sister. She brought fresh flowers to her room almost every day. The flowers always looked gray to Marianne, though she knew that they ought to be brightly colored.

When not rehearsing or singing at the opera, Cecelia would sit in Marianne's room. Sometimes she would read aloud from a book of Shakespeare's comedies. Marianne took no pleasure in even the most hilarious passages. Several times over the winter, Marianne wondered if she had permanently lost the ability to laugh. When Cecelia's stage manager dropped off a box of Marianne's favorite chocolates, they sat untouched for so long that the cocoa became covered with the fine white film of oxidation, and Cecelia eventually threw them away. It seemed like the depth of Marianne's melancholia knew no bounds.

But finally, gradually, the dark cloud began to lift. One morning in spring, Marianne awoke to the sound of birds singing outside her window. To her surprise, she actually enjoyed listening to them. She recalled the date exactly. It had been Saturday, April 26th.

Marianne quit her bed. She went to the writing desk and penned the letter to Ben. She bathed, dressed, and decided to go for a walk. She posted her letter. She stopped by the market. Everyone seemed to be moving in fast motion around her. There was a tumult of activity in the crowded straw market under the loggia. Yet somehow, the commotion seemed comforting to her. She wandered around the market until she came upon the bronze statue of a boar known locally as *Il Porcellino*. Marianne rubbed his shiny snout for good luck. She smiled. It felt strange to do so, but surprisingly good. She found that her legs felt tired, a sensation she enjoyed.

She recalled buying a *pandoro* topped with sugary icing that reminded her of the snow-capped Alps now laid out in front of her in the distance. She had consumed the small cake right there in front of the slightly bemused vendor. It was the first food that had tasted good to her in a very long time, and it fortified her for the walk home.

Back at their apartment, Marianne realized that Cecelia must have been worried about her when she found her sister anxiously quizzing the neighbor lady as to her whereabouts. As soon as Cecelia recognized Marianne—out of bed, dressed, and walking—she cried with joy. They had hugged in the sun-dappled courtyard in front of their apartment. At that moment, Marianne had known what she had to do. She had to get back to Paris.

Several days further along the road, the coach began its climb into the Alps. Marianne knew from experience that this would be the most difficult part of their journey. Even this late in May, it was still early in the summer season, and the pass known as Saint Bernard's could be impassable due to heavy snow. At the very top, a building called the hospice sat ready to assist travelers in need.

Marianne remembered her father telling stories of having to disassemble their wagon and trek over the summit on foot. Marianne hoped that she would never have to do that ... especially not today. Modern coaches were much better equipped, yet the trip could be harrowing. She smiled as she looked at the robust Tyrolean boots she wore just in case. This was not the day for wearing dainty French shoes—she would persuade Mesmer to buy her a pair when she reached Paris.

As the coach took the steep grade past the foothills, the temperature became perceptibly colder. When they crossed above the tree line, Marianne shivered. Cold white sunlight drenched the small yellow and purple alpine flowers dotting the pale green tundra. Soon, she noticed dark clouds hovering over the mountain in front of them. When the sun ducked behind the clouds, Marianne cinched up her cape.

The cabin of the coach became alternately dark and light as the travelers navigated the twisting switchbacks on the mountain's flank. About three-quarters of the way up, it started to snow. At first, it was just a light flurry, but the snow became increasingly heavy the higher they climbed. The road became a white ribbon carved into the side of the rugged mountain. Their progress slowed as the wagon wheels slipped, and the brace of horses strained against the weight, trying to gain a footing on the icy road. The falling sheets of white blinkered Marianne's view out the window, and the ground seemed to shift beneath the coach.

The nun reached over and took Marianne's hand, as if she could sense Marianne's anxiety. Or perhaps she just wanted to hold someone's hand as well. Either way, Marianne didn't mind. An increasingly fierce wind buffeted the coach, which began to creak in a way that frightened Marianne. Outside her window, the road had now disappeared. Just as she was about to turn and make a comment to the nun still holding her hand, there was an awful crack. The coach sharply lurched to the side, and the door flew open.

The last thing Marianne remembered, she was flying through the whiteness. Individual snowflakes danced in front of her, beautiful, each one different. Enlarged as they were, she could see their stunning patterns. Beautiful snowflakes everywhere, surrounding her, dancing, shifting, darting mostly downward at first. Then suddenly, all at once, they stopped, hovering directly in front of her face. In slow motion, one landed on her lip and melted. It tasted sweeter than any water she had ever known.

The world sped up again, the coordinated ballet of snowflakes now rushing past her face—or was it that she was falling? Marianne heard herself cry out. The bright whiteness surrounding her dimmed perceptibly. Did she hear a fluttering of wings? Marianne knew that sound. Could it be? Then a sharp pain as her head struck a rock, and everything went black.

Marianne slowly became aware of hot, musty breath close to her face, but everything was a blur, a fuzzy yellow glow. It was toasty, and she could smell the comforting smokiness of a fire in a fireplace nearby. It felt as if she still held the nun's dainty hand in hers. Marianne tried to move, but there was a soft, warm weight on her chest. Shortly, her eyes began to focus. She perceived two big brown eyes staring at her. The musty breath came from the huge dog resting his head on her left shoulder and chest. His soulful eyes flicked back and forth as he watched her with warm concern. She brought her right arm up to her face where there was a bandage on her forehead. Her head throbbed.

Marianne moaned.

The nun yawned, awakening from her own nap with a slight start. "Oh, hello, dear," she said sweetly.

"What happened? Where are we?"

"My child, the wagon wheel broke," the nun explained. "You fell out of the carriage. Hit your head. Luckily we were only a short way from the hospice. This big fellow came bounding down the mountain. Jumped right into the snowbank and pulled you out, he did. Carried you on his back up to the building where the staff bandaged you."

Marianne took her hand from her aching head and placed it on the dog.

He was massive. She could not even reach around his midsection. His long fur was soft and smooth. She gave him a pat.

She looked straight into his big brown eyes. "Good boy," she said. The dog gave her a lick on her cheek with his warm wet tongue. It felt good despite the pain.

"The monks of Saint Bernard have insisted that we stay here tonight for our safety and your health," the nun said. "One of our priests has medical training. He said that your head wound is not so deep. No broken bones either, he believes. I say it is a miracle. Imagine, dear, if that ledge hadn't been there to catch you! It is a long way down this mountain." She shuddered. "God saved you, my child."

"Thank you, Sister," Marianne said. "God and this dog."

"God sent the dog, my dear."

Once again, Marianne felt reprimanded. She was about to ask if God had also sent the snow and then the flock but thought better of it. "Yes, of course," was all she said. "I do not believe that I could travel tonight if I had to," Marianne went on. "What is his name?"

"Who?"

"My savior," she said meaningfully.

"Max."

"Good night, Max," Marianne said. She gave the huge dog another hug and quickly fell asleep.

The remainder of Marianne's trip to Paris was much less eventful, but by no means boring. The clergy disembarked as expected at Geneva. No travelers replaced them. With the coach all to herself, Marianne spent a few days marveling at the sights of southern France out her window. Farmers busily plowed their fields for sowing. The trees became a dazzling green. Patches of wildflowers abounded. The road bustled with springtime activity in both directions as wagons brought supplies to the farms. Marianne wondered if Marko might be sailing up the Atlantic coast from Bilbao even now.

A day south of Dijon, Marianne bedded down in a comfortable roadside hotel run by a delightful older Italian husband and wife. They were happy to hear the latest news from Florence as they doted over their only guest for the evening. Marianne curled up under the covers after a delicious bouillabaisse accompanied by a measure more of crisp Loire Valley wine than she usually imbibed. At some point during the night, Marianne thought that she heard a commotion. Only partially aroused from her deep sleep, she awoke in the morning wondering if she had only dreamt it. However, after dressing and carefully repacking, she went downstairs. She was surprised to find a man sitting in the dining room sipping coffee. Marianne sized him up as a fellow traveler. Apparently, he had arrived after she had gone to bed, resulting in the commotion she recalled.

He was a gray-haired gentleman, distinguished in his appearance and dress, but clearly a well-worn traveler. He was tanned. He studied a book intently. However, as soon as Marianne entered the room, he looked up. He acknowledged her with a warm smile. She was about to sit at a separate table when he spoke.

"Won't you join me here?" he asked politely, standing up from his table. "It appears that we will be traveling together in the coach today." His voice was deep and warm. Clearly Italian, possibly Venetian in accent.

"All right," Marianne responded. He seemed pleasant enough. She sat down at his table. His face showed deep lines etched by an interesting life. It was pockmarked by the scars characteristic of one who has survived smallpox at a young age. His hooked nose and angular jaw provided further definition to the face that Marianne thought must have once been quite classically handsome. His lips were full. They looked as though many women would yearn to kiss them. But his eyes were his most striking feature. Marianne found herself staring into his huge hazel eyes, swirling with emotion. She was just beginning to get lost in them when the Italian innkeeper's wife appeared with a pot of coffee.

"*Buon, Mama, gentilmente verserete il mio ospite un certo caffè?*" he asked the woman in fluent Italian.

The innkeeper turned to Marianne as if to confirm that she indeed wanted coffee.

"*Sì, caffè, grazie,*" she said in her rudimentary Italian with a smile.

"Ah, you speak Italian?" he asked.

"*Poco.*"

He laughed. "One doesn't find many Scots with even the slightest knowledge of our language."

"You are right in that I originally hail from Scotland, but I have lived in Florence long enough to pick up a little bit," she explained. She was not sure she wanted to reveal too much information to a stranger.

"You speak very well. You must have a wonderful singing voice as well."

Marianne felt herself blush. It had been too long since she had experienced the thrill of a man complimenting her. His words warmed her like a ray of sunshine. She gave up any thought of hiding information from him.

"Thank you, but my sister is the singer, not I," she said.

"Might I know of your sister?"

"She goes by the stage name of Le Inglesina."

A look of revelation washed over his face. "Of course, that explains it," he said. "So, if your sister is Cecelia, then you must be the famous Marianne Davies."

"I was not aware that the Davies sisters were so well known in Venice," Marianne said. If he had surmised that she was Scottish, then she could venture her own guess.

He laughed. "Yes, I am originally from Venice, but as you may also gather, I have traveled extensively. If one added up the years, I have lived away from my home city more than I have lived there. In fact, I have recently been banished from there once again." He looked a bit forlorn but brightened up quickly. "Please forgive me for not introducing myself. I am Giacomo Casanova de Seingalt."

Marianne stifled a small gasp as he delivered the name synonymous for more than thirty years with love, passion, and infidelity.

"Monsieur Casanova, so charming to meet you," she said with as much confidence as she could muster. She presented her hand with more than a bit of trepidation. He planted a kiss on the back of it with his full, moist, warm lips. Marianne felt the sensation travel directly to her groin. She didn't try to pull her hand away at all.

The coach pulled up outside the roadhouse just at that moment. As Casanova helped the innkeeper and his wife load the bags and the mail pouches onto the coach, they spoke animatedly in Italian.

Marianne got the distinct impression that this was not the first time Casanova had stayed at this place. When the coach was loaded and the two travelers seated aboard, she said, "It seems that you are quite acquainted with the innkeeper and his wife."

"Giuseppe and Maria? They are like family to me. Probably closer than my own family, in reality. You see, I am one of six children born to my actress mother. I suspect that my real father was not my mother's husband. I was mostly raised by my grandmother until I was nine years of age—at which time I was packed off to a boarding school. You could say that I had no real family. Yet, I have developed many close relationships over the years."

"I have read of some of your exploits," Marianne remarked.

A slightly pained look came over Casanova's face. "Mostly rumor and innuendo...the product of small minds, I can assure you. I intend one day to write an accurate account of my life to counteract the misinformation that abounds."

"I will look forward to reading it."

"But let me ask something about yourself, if I may."

"Of course," Marianne said politely. She could feel herself withdraw slightly in apprehension; she was once again not entirely sure that she wanted to share her secrets with her traveling companion.

"You have recently had a near-death experience, have you not?"

Marianne was not expecting his question in the least. Her jaw dropped. "How ... how did you know?"

Casanova explained. "The cut on your forehead is healing, but I suspect it is slightly less than a week old. If I calculate correctly, the coach coming from Bologna would have been navigating the Alps about that time. Having traversed those mountains many times in my travels, I suspect that is where the damage was done. Also, I detect a few long dog hairs clinging to your wool cape. The colors of these hairs are black, brown, and white—exactly the colors of the large dogs who are trained by the brothers of Saint Bernard to come to the aid of injured and lost travelers."

"What incredible powers of deduction you possess, Monsieur," Marianne said.

"I know more than that about you," he said.

Marianne felt a flutter in her stomach. Here she was, alone in a coach with the most famous, or infamous, lover of her age.

"All right," she said. "What do you know?"

"I know that you can fly with the flock. I know that you can travel to a place that is not of this world, a special place inside the mind. I know that you can see inside people's bodies, help determine what is wrong with them, and aid their physicians in their diagnosis and treatment. I know that you sometimes see things that will happen in the future. I know that you are clairvoyant."

Marianne was incredulous. She was not aware that anyone other than those in Mesmer's circle knew of her 'powers,' and she had never thought of herself as clairvoyant.

"How do you know these things?"

"Marianne," he said softly. He paused for a moment as if to collect his thoughts. Out the coach window, the greens and blues of spring flew by. They were cocooned inside the warm coach. There seemed not to be a bump on the road. He wore a gentle, warm expression that was completely non-threatening.

Casanova spoke again. "I have been trained as an abbé, a physician, a writer, and a librarian. In my life, I have been a charlatan, a thief, a gambler, a lover, and an alchemist. I have read the Cabal, followed Rosenkreuz, studied Freemasonry and Mithraism. In all that I studied and experienced, I have searched for the threads that tied these philosophies together. I have attempted to discover the common aspects in these human pursuits that were otherwise unique."

"And what have you learned from being a gambler and a thief?"

Casanova looked slightly piqued. "I have had no scruples about deceiving nitwits, scoundrels, and fools when I found it necessary. We avenge intelligence when we deceive a fool, and ... deceiving a fool is an exploit worthy of an intelligent person."

"So what, may I ask, do you believe ties all these diverse ideologies together?"

"First, let me say that I am not a student of Mesmer. I have found in my life that I could attract all the women that I wanted without resorting to putting them into a trance."

"I am sure that you could," Marianne replied. "But I have to believe there is more to Mesmer's discovery than mere seduction."

"Yes, of course. You are very perceptive, my dear. I believe that if you study the pinnacle of *any* method for achieving the level of transcendence that you have attained—the seventh degree of Mithraism, the thirty-third Masonic level, the enlightenment of the Buddhists, or the rapture of the Christians, to name only a few—you will find more similarities than differences."

"I never thought about it in that way."

"Marianne, you have reached a very special plane. Few humans have attained the vision that you have. You are able to see across our human boundaries. To my way of thinking, you have mastered a method—*magnétisme animale* in your case—that transcends the day-to-day conscious world. Others have used different methods to achieve the same end. I hope that I will be remembered as having mastered the art of love."

"Love?"

"Yes, love. Consider this—why do you think that we refer to the climactic moment of love-making as '*le petite morte*'?"

"I'm not sure that I have ever considered it before," Marianne said.

"We humans are never truly aware of our vitality except in comparison to death. I have noted that at that final climax of our coupling, we peer momentarily through the window into the full meaning of life. At that moment of 'the little death,' we sense why we are here on earth—to reproduce ... why we couple with one another—to enjoy closeness, intimacy ... why we live—to ultimately die, but not to be gone, simply forgotten ... rather to ultimately live on through our deeds and our progeny.

"We see that we are not alone. That we can fly with the flock. That we are not isolated, but rather connected in so many ways to the rest of humanity. If we open our hearts to it, we discover that we are not living as a solitary being, but rather as an integral part of the family of mankind. That is why I chose—as my method of transcendence—love."

Marianne's expression showed a twinge of sadness. "I do not have any progeny, nor will I ever," Marianne said. She put her hand on her belly.

"I am truly sorry to hear that. But consider this—you have loved, have you not?"

"Of course."

"And you are married?"

"No," she replied. She was not entirely sure where he was leading.

"So would I be correct in assuming that you do not feel that it is exclusively through the institution of marriage alone that people find love?"

"I suppose. I never thought of it."

"Marriage is an invention of the Church and State to maintain control over the populace," he said. "Monogamy is an artificial construct." His tone led Marianne to believe he had given this diatribe before. It was practiced.

Marianne smiled. "It is no wonder that the Doge wanted to be rid of you."

"The Venetian government enjoys my sleuthing and spying when it serves their purposes, but they are intolerant of even the slightest criticism." He gave Marianne a wink. "But the Church and State are temporary institutions. They will fade away. Yet the love that you experience will live forever. It is immortal." Casanova smiled a knowing smile that made Marianne feel quite content.

"I hope so," she replied. She was quiet for a moment, reflecting on how her love for Ben—once so strong, so vibrant—had changed. It made her uncomfortable, and she decided to change the subject. "What happened to me when I was so near death on the pass?"

"I don't know entirely. I have been close to death many times. A pistol duel in Warsaw nearly twenty years ago left me with this." He held up his left hand to reveal an ugly scar. "The doctors advised me to amputate my hand because of the severity of the infection."

"A pistol duel over a woman, I suspect," Marianne said.

"What else would be worth fighting over?" Casanova said in all sincerity. "But I also recall another near-death experience escaping from the Doge's palace in Venice. There I was ... standing on the roof ... the fog swirling around me." He waved his hands dramatically around his head. "I could hear the sound of water lapping in the lagoon far below."

Marianne could almost see the scene, impossibly romantic—Casanova, standing on slippery terra cotta tiles, wearing a black cloak, enveloped in thick fog, his dark eyes blazing.

"I simply sat down, at last unfettered after having been imprisoned for so long and so unjustly and contemplated my own death."

"What happened?" Marianne asked. It was beginning to dawn on her that this old traveler likely had more than a few good stories to tell.

"I was cold, and I was frightened, but I was *outside*—free—after spending nearly two years under the bleakest conditions, underfed, unkempt, and considerably underdressed." He smiled. "And I felt wonderful. Instead of being despondent, ready to expire, I felt as if I were back from the dead. I was alive. Marianne, the experience enriched me."

"Being in prison enriched you?" Marianne said. She sounded skeptical.

"Not exactly," he went on. "The experience of facing death and surviving enriched me. I emerged more fully aware of how much I loved life. I threw myself back into life with more verve than ever. Your experience on the mountain has hopefully pointed out to you the preciousness of your life. I believe that is how you will remember your experience."

"I believe that I already do," Marianne said.

The next day Casanova caught the coach from Dijon heading toward Spa in Belgium. Marianne was sad to see him leave. She could have listened to many more of his stories to make the hours pass by. At Fontainebleau, she enjoyed a lovely room provided by the Queen, who was not currently in residence. Marianne luxuriated in her bath. She spent a blissful hour playing a grand pianoforte ... the product of Monsieur Érard, she noted. The long journey was nearly done—for tomorrow, she would reach Paris.

Upon her arrival in Paris, Marianne sent word to Mesmer. He showed up at her hotel with a bouquet of fresh spring flowers—daffodils and Spanish bluebells, hyacinth, and tulips. Later, she eagerly walked to the *Pont Neuf* only to find that there was no Basque houseboat docked below. She bought a baguette from the vendor there. She descended the stairs to where Marko's boat should have been moored and ate the bread alone by the side of the river. Marianne was disappointed that Marko was missing, but it felt good to be back in Paris. Given Mesmer's recent enthusiasm, and the likelihood that Marko would soon return, she decided to postpone letting Ben know that she was back. He was probably too busy to see her anyway.

Summer 1783

PARIS

PARIS WAS ABUZZ with excitement all summer. On June 5th, the Montgolfier brothers had sent up a heated air balloon near Lyon. It had reportedly traveled aloft for over a mile. Parisians were aghast that their country cousins had been the first to witness such a historic event. They clamored for a repeat performance in Paris. The brothers tried to respond with another launch but were beaten to it by a physicist by the name of Jacques Charles.

Ben read the announcement aloud at the dinner table in Passy.

"On Wednesday, August 27th, departing from the Champ de Mars, Monsieur Charles and his colleagues shall launch a balloon of monumental significance, the first to be launched in Paris. All are welcome to attend."

"Balloons, ridiculous folly," Jacques Leray said. He took a bite of mutton.

"It sounds so dangerous, these things flying up in the sky ... someone will surely get hurt," Marie-Thérèse lamented.

"Granddad, might we go?" Temple asked.

"Of course, my boy. I wouldn't miss it," Ben said.

Wednesday was rainy in Passy, as it was in Paris. Warm summer rains had moved in during the week, providing much-needed water for the farmer's fields, but not portending well for a balloon launch. Nonetheless, Ben decided to brave the trip to the *Champ de Mars*. He and Temple boarded the coach and, on the way, collected Le Roy at the side door of the *Château de la Muette* where he was standing under the portico, wearing a heavy oilcloth cape. He climbed in, folded up his rain gear, and placed it on a seat occupied only by four collapsed umbrellas. The wet oilcloth smelled pungent in the humid air of the coach.

"I couldn't find my umbrella," Le Roy explained.

"I brought extras, just in case," Ben replied. "An ounce of prevention is worth a pound of cure, I always say. You won't want to be wearing that heavy garment very long in this weather."

"No, indeed," Le Roy said.

"What have you heard about the balloon launch?" Ben asked.

"As you know," Le Roy said. He looked at Ben's grandson, who probably didn't know, and went on. "Monsieur Charles is a well-respected member of the Academy of Science. He has been experimenting with what we previously knew as 'inflammatory air,' but now call 'hydrogen'—a name coined by our friend Professor Lavoisier from the Greek meaning 'water-former.'"

"Why did he rename the air 'water former'?" Temple asked.

Ben pitched in. "Because when this gas burns, water is the result. Lavoisier was the first to recognize that water is composed of hydrogen and a substance we now know as oxygen," he said.

"Granddad, I'm confused. If this hydrogen turns into water when burned, how does it make a balloon fly?"

"Good question, my boy," Ben said. "In its pure form, unburned hydrogen has been shown to be much lighter than regular air. If a sufficient quantity is kept contained by a vessel, that vessel will lift up into the surrounding air."

"It sounds like magic. How does anyone keep this stuff in his laboratory? Wouldn't it fly away?"

"Yes, if released, the hydrogen would dissipate back into the atmosphere. But kept in a heavy glass container, it is trapped. One method to prove that it is lighter than regular air is to weigh two containers, one with plain air and the other filled with hydrogen. What do you think the result of such an experiment would be?"

Temple thought for a moment. He responded tentatively, "The one filled with hydrogen will weigh less?"

"Excellent, my boy. Yes, a glass container filled with hydrogen would weigh less, but only slightly. Imagine then that you proceeded to contain a quantity of hydrogen in successively lighter and lighter vessels. Then what do you think would happen?"

"At some point, the vessel would weigh nothing?"

"*Magnifique*," Le Roy chimed in. "Your grandson has the makings of a good scientist."

Ben went on, "And once a sufficiently light vessel 'weighs' nothing in this series of experiments, it will lift off the scale—and off the ground. It is not magic, it is science."

"Oh, now I understand," Temple said. He smiled mischievously. "So why don't we all just strap hydrogen-filled vessels to our bodies and fly where we want to go?"

Ben's expression instantly changed from pride to consternation. He sighed.

"I'll take this one," Le Roy said. "It is not quite so simple, my dear lad. Someday man may be able to fly with the aid of hydrogen. But consider this. For the demonstration of balloon flight that we are hoping to witness today, I understand that Monsieur Charles used one thousand pounds of iron filings and five hundred pounds of sulfuric acid to produce the hydrogen. It took him four days to prepare the quantity required to lift a balloon made of silk coated with gum and with a diameter of thirteen feet."

"So how much hydrogen would it take to lift me?" Temple asked earnestly.

"I don't know," Le Roy replied. But I would anticipate considerably more than that."

Ben jumped back into the discussion. "In addition to the problem of creating a large quantity of hydrogen, we don't really even know that a man could survive such a flight."

"Why not?" Temple asked. "Birds fly up there all the time."

"Yes, but perhaps they are built differently than we."

"What about climbing a mountain? Wouldn't that be similar, Granddad?"

"I suppose so..." Ben thought for a moment. "But your feet would remain attached to the ground as you ascend a mountain. Freely flying in a balloon might be more dangerous in some way that we are not able to anticipate. For example, the quality of the air, the temperature, the effect of the wind, the chance of falling back to earth too abruptly... I'm not sure what all we might encounter. However, I am anxious to see further experimentation in this interesting area."

By the time their coach reached the *Pont Royal* to cross the Seine, traffic was already heavy. Despite the rain, thousands of people were making their way to the large grassy field of the *Champs de Mars*. Those on foot carried folding chairs, picnic baskets, and umbrellas. Yet, in spite of the dismal weather, there was a festive feel to the event. The Leray coach could proceed only slowly along the muddy road. At the entrance to the *Champ de Mars,* a guard on horseback directed them toward a large open tent. As they approached, Ben could see that many aristocrats were alighting from their coaches directly under the shelter of the expansive canopy. In front of the tent, the brightly colored balloon was tethered. The rain gave it a shiny, ornamental appearance – reminiscent of a decorative German glass bowl Ben had seen. Only it was floating in the gray sky.

Ben made his way through the throng of important people gathered under the tent. He was aiming for the balloon but was unable to proceed more than a few feet without someone wishing to stop and talk with him. Le Roy and Temple seemed to be making a bit better headway.

A finely dressed lady was blocking Ben's path. "Excuse me," he said with more than a little irritation. She sported a large hairdo done up to look like a large balloon. Ben just shook his head in disbelief at the sight of it.

When he finally got to the far edge of the tent, Le Roy was already there. He had opened up an umbrella. He motioned for Ben to step out toward the balloon. Recognizing Ben, the guard opened the rope barrier meant to keep onlookers inside the tent. The two scientists and Temple walked across a short strip of soggy grass to where Monsieur Charles and his team were making final preparations. They appeared to be carefully weighing bags of material before placing them in a basket attached to the base of the balloon.

As Ben approached, he cleared his throat. Monsieur Charles looked up.

"Ah, Doctor Franklin, I am so glad that you could attend," he said.

"And I am happy to be here. You know Professor Le Roy... and this is my grandson, Temple Franklin. But please call me Ben."

"All right, Ben," Charles replied. He then turned to Le Roy. "It is my distinct pleasure to make my demonstration in the presence of the director of the King's Scientific Laboratory."

"The pleasure is mine," Le Roy responded politely.

Turning to Temple, Charles said, "Welcome, young man. If you turn out to be one-tenth the scientist that your grandfather is, the world will be a better place for it."

"Will you be able to launch in this weather?" Ben asked.

"Yes, there is very little wind despite the rain ... so I believe it will be safe. We are weighing the ballast again now. These sandbags have soaked up quite a bit of water. I must know the exact weight of the cargo if I am to judge the success of the flight."

"Of course. Please do not let us keep you from your work," Ben said. He stepped back slightly.

"No, Ben. We are almost ready. I would be honored if you would release the final rope."

"You want me to launch her?"

"Yes. I would be deeply honored."

"Then, I will do it when you instruct me."

The rain let up ever so slightly. Monsieur Charles got up from where he was working to reveal that his trousers were soaked. He had mud all over his hands. Yet, he had a broad smile on his face.

"We are ready," Monsieur Charles announced loudly. A hush fell over the crowd in a wave.

Ben looked behind him to see the tent packed with people, all pushed up expectantly against the rope barriers. Outside the tent, a sea of faces stood in near silence. Ben looked across and up the hill to see that the multitude of rain-soaked onlookers must have numbered well into the thousands. He turned his attention back to the balloon. Charles had one rope in his hand. Three members of his team were stationed by the other ropes tethering the balloon. Charles motioned to Ben to step forward. He handed over his rope. The balloon seemed to sense imminent freedom. It undulated sensually just above Ben's head.

Charles took a step back as if appreciating his work. "On the count of three," he bellowed. "One, two...three!"

The other men let go of their ropes immediately, but Ben only eased his grip. The rope started sliding slowly through his hand. It became warm, then hot. Ben was aware of a tremendous roar from the crowd all around him. He dropped the rope and looked up. The glistening globe was ascending slowly, above the *Champ de Mars*. He stood there in the light rain, entranced by the shiny balloon lightly dancing in the sky, seemingly glad to be free. The small prevailing wind pushed the balloon toward the north. The crowd followed as far as they could. Even many of the aristocrats watching from under the tent left their shelter to pursue the balloon, their fancy boots being quickly ruined by the muddy ground. No one seemed to care about his or her footwear. The throng headed toward the river, leaving the *Champ de Mars* nearly vacant. Charles was collecting his equipment. His men loaded boxes onto a wagon.

Le Roy was the first to speak. "Well, I would call that experiment an unqualified success," he said. He had a look of pride as if he had built the balloon himself.

"There was over one hundred pounds of ballast on board that balloon," Charles said to no one in particular.

"A slightly larger one would carry a man," Ben observed.

"Yes," Charles said thoughtfully.

Madame Leray delivered Ben's newspaper in the morning. She unfolded it as he prepared them a pot of tea.

"It says here that the small town of Gonesse, some fifteen miles to the northeast of Paris, was terrorized yesterday afternoon by Monsieur Charles's balloon." She started chuckling and read on. "Thinking that some form of demon was descending upon them, the townspeople attacked the strange globe with pitchforks." She broke out in full guffaws, barely able to continue. "After they had subdued it, they tied it to a horse and dragged it through the town until it was surely dead." She threw the newspaper down on the table so as to be able to hold her sides. "I told you that machine was dangerous."

Ben picked up the newspaper. Next to the article about the misguided townsfolk was an official announcement from the government. He read it out loud:

Anyone who shall see in the sky such a globe, which resembles the moon in eclipse, should be aware that, far from being an alarming phenomenon, it is only a machine that cannot possibly cause any harm, and which will someday prove useful to the wants of society.

"I'm not sure that proclamation will be very reassuring to illiterate peasants," Ben said. "A mob's a monster; heads enough but no brains," he went on, quoting an old saying from his Poor Richard's almanac. "I hope that the first men to ascend in a balloon are able to talk themselves out of the fate suffered by Monsieur Charles's first unmanned globe."

"Perhaps they should send up lawyers," Marie-Thérèse proposed. She put a finger on her cheek.

"Heavens no," Ben said. He laughed. "*They* surely would be killed."

She poured the tea into their cups. "Oh, how sad," she said.

September 3rd, 1783

CHEVAL SAUVAGE, OUTSKIRTS OF PARIS

BEN WATCHED MARIANNE dress. It was getting light outside. The addition of early morning sunlight would enhance most rooms, but Room 11 appeared shabbier to Ben the more it became illuminated.

"When was the last time we were here?" he asked. Ben could truly not remember how long it had been since they had partaken in the enjoyment of one another.

"Last summer," she replied. "Why?"

"We used to do this once or twice a week."

"Ben, I was traveling ... Spa, Vienna, and over the winter in Florence ... Mother passed away ... ."

"I know," Ben said. "I am sorry about your mother." His voice was filled with sincerity despite the fact that he was not sorry in the least that she was gone—other than for Marianne's loss, of course.

"Thank you, Ben," Marianne said. "But, I know that you never liked her."

"I never got a chance to know her. I didn't like that she kept us apart."

"No, neither did I."

"How did Cecelia take it?"

"Better than I, I'm afraid. She was the one who had to hold us together. I went into a fit of melancholia so deep I couldn't see the light of day. Didn't you get my letter?"

"Yes, I got it."

"And?"

"Marianne, you know that I cannot respond when you are in that condition."

"Why not?" The sun ducked behind a cloud, darkening the room.

Ben was not sure that he could explain his own feelings on the matter. In her melancholia, Marianne was a different person—a person so radically foreign to him that he could not even relate to her. A person he didn't know—didn't love. It occurred to him that this might be a failing on his part. During her melancholic episodes, she was so dependent, so vulnerable. She had always needed him at those times especially, and he had always run away, abandoning her for those who would attend to his needs—not the other way around.

"I just can't," he said. "I'm sorry."

The sun came back out. Ben tried to change the subject, lighten things up, tell a joke. Marianne would want that, wouldn't she?

"Which is the favorite word among women?" he asked.

Marianne appeared sullen. "I don't know," she replied.

"The last one."

No laugh, no response. Marianne gazed at him for a moment, as if deciding something, then turned away. "It has always been this way with us, Ben. The scales in this affair are tipped heavily to you. That balance will never change." Without another look, she slipped her shoes on, left the room, and closed the door.

Ben leaned back on the bed and sighed. He was sad that the click of the latch surely meant the end of their long relationship. Then he closed his eyes, trying to erase the prick of guilt he felt that his relief to be free of her expectations outweighed his sadness at her departure.

He was asleep before he could even admit it to himself.

September 3rd, 1783

PARIS

"BEN ... BEN, WAKE UP." The slightly muffled voice was that of Le Veillard. His words were accompanied by insistent knocking on the door of Room 11. Marianne was gone. Noise from the morning street traffic came in the open window. Ben wondered how long he had been asleep.

"Don't go back to sleep. Today is the signing."

Ben practically leapt out of bed upon realizing that he was expected at the *Hôtel d'York* at noon. "What time is it?" he asked through the door. He fumbled for his bifocals on the bedside table.

"Nearly eleven o'clock. We should leave soon."

"I could use some tea."

"I'll have Gretchen prepare some for you ... if you promise to get dressed."

"I promise," Ben replied. "Now, go away."

The clomping of Le Veillard's heavy riding boots receded down the hall toward the stairs. Ben doused his face with water from the washbasin. Marianne's fragrance remained in the air. He combed his hair, found his clothes, and dressed quickly.

Downstairs in the noisy bar, Ben found Le Veillard sitting at his usual table. A cup of steaming tea sat next to him. Gretchen was tending bar. Ben poured a small amount of cream into the tea. He was about to sit down at the table when Le Veillard stood up.

"Ben, we should go," he said.

"Louis, I believe that you are more nervous about today than I," Ben said. He took a sip of the fragrant, hot liquid. "Besides which, it won't take us more than twenty minutes to ride to the *Hôtel d'York*."

"Yes, but you will need to change. You can't sign the treaty in those riding clothes. There is the sitting for the portrait ... and what about the signing?" Le Veillard fretted. He sounded more like a doting secretary than his usual unflappable self.

"All right, all right." Ben laughed at seeing his friend in this frenzied state. He took another gulp of tea. "Let us be off." He put the cup down on the table, along with some change from his pocket.

Le Veillard practically bolted for the door. Gretchen gave him a longing look from behind the bar as he flew past her without so much as a goodbye.

The two rode into Paris to the *Rue Jacob* with hardly a word. Upon their arrival at the *Hôtel d'York*, Ben noted the Leray coach was just pulling up in front.

Temple stepped out of the coach. Ben almost didn't recognize him. He sported a brand-new forest green suit on his lanky twenty-three-year-old frame. But what really made him appear unusual was the powdered wig on his still boyish head. He carried a bundle under his arm. Ben guessed it contained his formal suit for the ceremony. He handed his reins to Le Veillard and dismounted.

"Hello, my boy," Ben said. He put his arm around his grandson with a smile.

Despite his dapper appearance, Temple clearly seemed uncomfortable.

"What's wrong?" Ben asked.

"Nothing."

"Come on, out with it."

Temple's hand shot up above his left ear. He started scratching. "This thing is miserable," he whined. He tried to stick a finger underneath his wig.

"Why do you think I never wear them?"

"I wish I had never let Madame Leray talk me into it."

"Come on." Ben started into the hotel arm in arm with his grandson. "You can take it off as soon as the ceremony is over."

As they entered the lobby, Ben immediately spotted John Jay. Tall and lean, the man towered over the other hotel patrons milling around. Next to Jay stood John Adams sporting his usual scowl. Unfortunately, it appeared both had chosen the same suit for the occasion. While the jacket worn by Jay had a collar and Adams's did not, the warm brown color of the material was identical. The two stood out like two brown cows in a field of black ones. He laughed out loud but stifled it before he got close to the men. He did not wish to make Adams any more cross than he seemed already.

"Good day, John. And John," Ben said.

John Jay returned Ben's greeting with a strong handshake. "It's a historic day," he said.

John Adams simply mumbled and shook his head grimly.

The Comte de Vergennes strode across the lobby to greet the Americans, resplendent in a dark suit with gold piping. The royal coat of arms was embroidered over his left chest. A gray satin sash topped his ensemble, cutting from his right shoulder to his left hip.

"How is the American delegation this fine day?" he asked. He looked slightly askance at the two brown cows, but diplomatically ignored the fashion *faux pas*.

"Quite well, thank you," Ben said. He answered for all—even though John Adams appeared as though he suffered from intestinal gas.

"The signing of the treaty will proceed thusly." Vergennes began giving instructions like a man used to the intricacies and formalities of international diplomacy. Clearly, he had worked out every detail of the plan well in advance. "The artist, Monsieur West, is in the drawing room. He will be having each of you sit for your portrait to commemorate this event. Monsieur Laurens, as he arrived earlier, went in first. He is sitting for the artist now. Ben, might I suggest that you go in next? I have not seen the British representative, Monsieur Hartley, although I am aware that he is staying at this hotel."

"David will be at the signing," Ben said. "He is not in the most comfortable position – being the sole representative of the British crown to this agreement. Nonetheless, he is a good man, and he carries the authority of Lord Shelburne's parliament with him. King George will honor the agreement that he signs today."

Temple bent forward to whisper in Ben's ear. "Granddad, may I sit next for the portrait?"

"Why, my boy?"

"I must get this wig off as soon as possible."

Ben laughed. "Of course," he said. Then to Vergennes he directed, "Temple will sit next for the portrait. I must dress now."

The Americans dispersed, and Ben was led to a changing area. There a butler offered to press his suit as he donned his undergarments and stockings. Ben combed his hair in the mirror. He splashed water everywhere he thought needed cleaning. A bottle of cologne sat on the dressing table. Ben applied it conservatively. The butler returned and assisted Ben with his trousers and jacket, both of which were made of black velvet. Ben marveled at how there was not a speck of lint on them. The butler looked around for a wig box with a puzzled look on his face.

"No wig," Ben said.

"As you wish, sir."

Ben looked himself over in the full-length mirror as the butler straightened his coat from the back. He thanked the butler with a coin from his purse and headed off to have his portrait done.

Ben finished quickly with Mr. West. He found Vergennes waiting just outside the room.

"Everyone is assembled," the Foreign Minister said.

He led Ben down the hall to a room Ben recognized as the one where they had signed the preliminary treaty the previous November. It was a comfortable library with a table surrounded by six chairs. The last time he'd been here, a fire blazed in the fireplace; it now stood dormant, unneeded in this mild September weather. In fact, the windows were wide open, letting in a gentle breeze and sounds from the *Rue Jacob* outside.

Temple sat at the table, no wig in sight, doodling on a pad of paper. John Jay and John Adams sat too, intently studying the documents in front of them. Henry Laurens stood wearing a red jacket. Ben cringed to think that it might be his way of affronting the British. But since Laurens had the distinction of being the only American ever held captive in the Tower of London as a prisoner of war during the Revolution, Ben reckoned he deserved to be allowed the demonstration—if that were his goal. He looked gaunt, preoccupied with smoking near the window. The first to recognize Ben's entry into the room was David Hartley, who strode briskly across the room.

He shook Ben's hand with genuine affection. "Do you recall when we first discussed the possibility of peace between the United States and Britain?" he asked.

"Yes. It has been too many years in coming, David. I am glad to see this day."

"Lord Shelburne sends his regards."

"Please convey my warmest regards to him upon your return to London," Ben replied. "Shall we begin?"

The Articles of Peace were passed around to all in attendance except Temple. He took notes on his pad in case any minor corrections were identified.

Ben looked at the document. It consisted of ten articles. A thrill passed through him as his eye landed on the first article of the treaty. It read:

Article 1:

His Brittanic Majesty acknowledges the said United States, viz., New Hampshire, Massachusetts Bay, Rhode Island, and Providence Plantations, Connecticut, New York, New Jersey, Pennsylvania, Delaware, Maryland, Virginia, North Carolina, South Carolina, and Georgia, to be free sovereign and independent states, that he treats with them as such, and for himself, his heirs, and successors, relinquishes all claims to the government, propriety, and territorial rights of the same and every part thereof.

Ben looked at it again just to be sure. 'To be free sovereign and independent states' had been his goal for such a long time that he could recall many days when he might have been easily convinced that this one would never arrive. But here it was.

The other American ambassadors scrutinized the documents, pointing out an error here, a possible alternate interpretation there. In the end, they all signed and sealed the documents. Hartley signed for King George. They rolled up copies to go back to London. They rolled up copies to be sent back to the Continental Congress. Ben rolled up a copy for himself. He handed one to Temple.

"Lock this in the iron chest when you get back to Passy," he instructed.

"All right, Granddad. But will you not be riding home with me in the coach?"

"No, I will ride with Le Veillard. I need the exercise."

Ben changed back into his riding clothes. The changing room happened to be directly next door to the room being used by Benjamin West to paint portraits of the diplomats. Ben looked in to observe the painter sitting glumly in front of his canvas. The large canvas showed five men sitting at the table. Ben recognized himself, Adams, Jay, Laurens, and his grandson. The portraits were well done, but Temple looked particularly uncomfortable under his white wig, Ben thought. The right side of the canvas was conspicuously blank, void of any portrait of David Hartley. Vergennes was standing nearby, wearing a look of consternation.

Ben entered the room. "Why so despondent?" he asked.

Vergennes spoke first. "Monsieur Hartley has departed," he said.

"Do you mean that he won't sit for his portrait?" Ben asked.

The artist appeared to be in a state of shock. He was collecting his paints and packing them into a wooden box. He remained silent.

"I do not believe that he refused to sit," Vergennes continued. "He simply left."

Ben instantly realized the implications of the defection. "How unfortunate," he said. The painting would remain unfinished.

"What should I do with this?" the artist asked. He motioned to the canvas.

"Crate it up and ship it to the Continental Congress," Ben instructed. "I will send a letter explaining the circumstances. Your fee will be paid, I assure you."

Ben walked out into the warm afternoon sunlight bathing the *Rue Jacob*. The street was alive with activity as businessmen and shoppers milled past on the sidewalk. One woman, in particular, caught Ben's eye. She wore a fashionable dress of green satin trimmed with fine white lace. Her skirt hoops were so wide that people had difficulty passing her without stepping into the street. Luckily, there had been no recent rain. Yet Ben wondered if the dressmaker had specifically measured the width of the sidewalk in determining the proportions of the dress, as if it were calculated to make people get out of her way. But even more remarkable was her hair. She sported a towering creation piled high with feathers, and brightly colored flowers. However, the most astounding feature of her headdress was the half dozen miniature balloons floating like a crown above her head. The small balloons were tethered by satin strings of contrasting colors. Ben wondered how she kept her balance. Luckily there was no wind, or her creation would have quickly become a tangled mess. She walked on, seemingly oblivious to the scene she was causing, as traffic literally stopped to gaze at her. In a moment, she was gone.

Le Veillard sat across the street in an outdoor café, the horses tied nearby. His riding clothes gave him the appearance of a country gentleman at leisure among the mundane businessmen hustling by. The sunlight bathed him in a golden glow that made his skin shimmer. He seemed not to have noticed the woman with balloons in her hair, as he was deep in flirtation with a serving girl. The café had few customers at this time of day. Had there been others, they would have found the service lacking, Ben thought with a smile. He made his way across the street between the passing coaches.

Ben cleared his throat loudly as he approached.

His friend looked up from his dalliance swiftly. "Hello, Ben. All of your business concluded satisfactorily?"

"Yes." Ben patted his pocket containing his rolled-up copy of the treaty.

"Good. Then we will be off." Louis cast his gaze back to where the serving girl had been, but she had already disappeared. Rising up, he tossed a coin on the table.

"Are you sure?" Ben asked jokingly. "I wouldn't want to interrupt anything important."

"Oh no," Le Veillard replied with equal humor. "Not to worry, my friend, she will still be here the next time."

"All right then. Let us ride before the sun goes any lower."

Ben mounted his horse as Louis untied the reins. Once aloft, Ben scanned the street for an opening in the traffic. The opportunity soon presented itself, and the two riders headed in the direction of Passy.

As the traffic thinned and the bustle of the city receded, they talked about the events of the afternoon. Ben described the treaty signing in detail. Le Veillard laughed at Ben's recounting of Temple's itchy wig. Soon though, the story of the signing of the Treaty of Paris had been told, and they rode on in silence for some time, enjoying each other's company without saying a word.

"And what of this morning?" Le Veillard asked after a while, breaking the quiet.

Ben paused for a moment, not immediately replying.

"Only if you want to talk about it," Le Veillard added.

"Louis, I've lost her," Ben finally said with profound sadness.

"What causes you to say that?"

"She no longer laughs at my jokes."

"Ah, my friend . . ." Le Veillard replied as consolingly as possible. "In my experience, when a woman ceases to laugh at your jokes, the relationship will soon be over."

The sun was setting behind the buildings flanking the Seine. Long shadows fell onto the boats docked along its banks. Their rigging clanked merrily in the balmy breeze. Brightly colored paper lanterns twinkled. The smell of roasting meats filled the air. On a certain Basque houseboat, wine flowed at the dinner party. Marko was relaying a humorous story about a corrupt ship inspector back home and how he had been skillfully outwitted. If the other guests had heard the tale before, it didn't matter, they all laughed appropriately. But Marianne laughed heartily, and most of all.

September 4th, 1783

PARIS

"I MUST RETURN TO FLORENCE soon, my Queen," Marianne announced with sadness. "Cecelia needs me." She sat at the foot of the iridescent throne in Cassiopeia. The flock receded into the blue-black sky shimmering with stars. "But we will be returning in the spring," she added. "And you should have a new baby by then."

"I do not have a good feeling about this baby," the Queen said wistfully. She patted her belly, still very small for her six months gestation.

Marianne was about to ask if she should take a look when the Queen interjected. "No, you must go attend to the needs of your sister. Nature will take its course here."

"I do not want to wait much longer to make the passing over the Alps."

"Of course not." The Queen gave a sly smile. "Perhaps you will meet up with Monsieur Casanova again."

Marianne scrunched up her nose. "He didn't even attempt to bed me," she said. Her tone was laced with disappointment.

"He is not known as a rapist. I was only five years old the last time he was in Paris, but I have heard from some of the older courtesans that your Casanova was a master at determining what a woman wants, what she needs—and giving it to her."

"He is not 'my Casanova', as you say."

"All right, my dear. I'm just suggesting that if you had knocked on his door that night near Dijon ... two travelers, lonely, on the road together ..." Her voice trailed off. She flashed a coquettish smile that quickly turned to a frown. "But it is probably for the best that you didn't. Who knows what form of venereal disease you might have caught from that man."

"Yes, I suppose that you are right. What I needed at that time was his companionship, his insights ... and that is exactly what I got." Marianne changed the subject. "What is our business here tonight, my lady?"

"I would like you to examine someone for me."

"Of course, my Queen. Who?"

The Queen directed her scepter at the dazzling star Spica in the constellation Virgo. As the luminous orb approached, Marianne started to appreciate the image of a young man, an officer, inside it. As it came closer up, she could see his uniform was not French, English, or American. He cut a dashing figure nonetheless. His features were fine, chiseled. He had sandy brown hair, cropped close. Expressive brown eyes presaged wisdom beyond his years. He wore a white kerchief around his neck. He did not appear to be any stranger to manual work by his toned physique, yet he had the refined posture of royalty.

"He's gorgeous," Marianne said. "My Queen, where have you been hiding him?"

"I have not been hiding him at all," the Queen protested. "He has been fighting alongside Rochambeau in America for over three years. He just recently returned to France."

"Who is he?"

"Count Axel von Fersen, of Sweden." The Queen brought his shimmering image to rest in front of them. As they looked into his sphere, Marianne noted that he seemed to be crying.

"What is the matter?" she asked.

"Today, he learned that he must accompany King Gustave of Sweden on his Grand Tour of Italy and France for a year."

"A year is not so long."

"Yes, I know ... but just when I got him back from America."

"You got him back?" Marianne asked. "Is he yours?"

"He could be. We met in '74 when we were both merely eighteen years of age. I am sure that he was as smitten with me as I was with him—but at the time, I was desperately trying to conceive a son for Louis, as you will recall. I couldn't follow my heart to him then—even though I wanted to."

"I understand."

"We have kept in touch all these years. Today is his twenty-eighth birthday. Marianne, I believe that if I have ever loved any man in my life, that man is Axel."

"My Queen, I never knew."

"No one does—except now you, of course."

"Your secret is safe with me."

"Thank you, Marianne. What can you see about him?"

"He is a fine male specimen," Marianne said. She sighed as she appreciated his muscles rippling over an aristocratic frame. "He seems to have suffered a bit of frostbite to one little toe on the campaign fighting alongside the American insurgents, but otherwise I don't see anything wrong with him. The fact that he weeps over the prospect of leaving Paris, and you, leads me to believe that he is a sensitive man, not intimidated by his feelings."

"Marianne, you know that I don't want you to tell me the events of the future, correct?"

"Yes," Marianne answered hesitantly. It sounded to her as if the Queen was now requesting just the opposite.

"But can you tell me..." Her voice cracked with emotion. "Will he ever be mine?"

"My Queen," Marianne said. "My abilities to foresee the future are rudimentary at best. I am not even sure that what I see will come true. But

I do see that if you want him to be yours, he can be yours. I also sense that there may come a time when this Axel Fersen shows himself to be your one true friend. Do you really want to know any more?"

"No," the Queen replied. She started to sob softly.

"Your Majesty, I did not intend to upset you."

The Queen composed herself quickly. "Marianne, you have been most obliging and helpful," she said. "Let us go home now."

The glowing image of the Adonis-like Axel von Fersen receded back into the blue-black cosmos as the sound of fluttering wings surrounded the two women, obliterating everything.

November 21st, 1783

KINGSWOOD

THE *Château de la Muette* was overrun with onlookers. Ben had taken the trail through Kingswood on horseback, lest he become delayed by the coach traffic on the road. Arriving at Monsieur Le Roy's side door, he was amazed at the assortment of coaches parked in every corner of the yard. They stretched as far up the road as Ben could see. More were arriving by the moment. Ben entered the house to find Madame Le Roy in the kitchen. He gave her a squeeze from behind. She squealed, first with surprise and then delight when she realized who had accosted her.

"You had better watch out, Doctor Franklin," she said amiably. "My husband is just out front."

"I'm sure he wouldn't mind sharing," Ben said. Despite their repartee, Ben didn't seriously consider Madame Le Roy a love interest. He wasn't quite sure that she felt the same way, however. More than once, she had put herself in situations where something might have happened. She had invited Ben to dinner when Le Roy was in Versailles, for example. She'd written him flirty and provocative letters. She referred to herself in writing as his 'pocket wife'.

Nonetheless, Ben considered her only a friend. He enjoyed flirting with her but carefully limited the extent to which he let anything progress. Besides, she was a wonderful cook. Ben was never one to discourage anyone who wished to cook for him.

"What he doesn't know can't hurt him," she said.

"You are not interested in the balloon launch?" Ben asked, changing the subject.

"I find them to be foul-smelling and frightening," she replied. She pinched her nose.

"I have to agree on the smell," Ben said. "It seems that the Montgolfier brothers believe that the smokier and more fetid the heated air, the better the lift for their creations."

"I will keep to my kitchen, if you please."

"It smells much better in here," Ben observed.

"Then you must stay for supper after the balloon launch."

"Of course, your wish is my command."

"My every wish?"

"Well, almost," Ben replied. He hesitated briefly. "Now, I must go find your husband."

She gave him a playful shove out toward the laboratory.

Ben made his way through the tidy apartment. The noise of the crowd in the front courtyard became louder as he approached the Royal Scientific Laboratory side of the building. Walking through the lab, Ben noted that there were no technicians attending to their experiments today. All of the equipment stood dormant. No lamps burned. No apparati whirred. In fact, the laboratory looked as though it had been thoroughly scrubbed in anticipation of today's event. The brass was shiny, the glass glimmering in the dim light. Even the floors, normally covered in debris produced by the various machines, were squeaky clean beneath his shoes.

Ben found a terrace overlooking the main courtyard. He gasped at the extraordinary scene in front of him.

A bulging fabric bladder about fifty feet in diameter hovered above the courtyard. The Montgolfier brothers fanned the flames of a smoky fire and directed the exhaust as best they could into the opening at the base of the balloon. A wooden ringed walkway sat on the ground next to the balloon, which was attached by ropes to its underside. As he stood there, amazed by the sheer size and wonder of the behemoth, Ben became aware of a voice next to him.

"Ben, I'm so glad that you could come." It was Le Roy.

"Jean-Baptiste, how could I possibly miss the first manned balloon flight?"

"The first untethered manned balloon flight," his friend corrected.

"All right, the first untethered manned balloon flight. Nonetheless, it seems like a historic occasion."

"I must agree ... especially if all goes well. We have already had one mishap. The balloon had to be repaired when a gust of wind caused the ropes to gash her." Le Roy seemed anxious. Trepidation was a side of his personality that Ben rarely, if ever, saw.

"Jean-Baptiste, whatever happens, today is a triumph for you. You fought hard to move this flight from Versailles. Now we must only observe. We must enjoy the grand experiment taking place in front of us."

"Of course you are right ... as always, Ben."

Le Roy seemed to relax somewhat. Then, almost immediately, he became excited again.

"Ben, I want to introduce you to Doctor Rozier." Le Roy pulled Ben toward a grandstand on the terrace. Ben realized that he had previously been completely unaware of the existence of anyone else on the terrace on account of his rapture with the balloon. As he looked up at the grandstand, Ben recognized Marie Antoinette and King Louis XVI. The Comte Vergennes and several other cabinet members were in attendance.

"No wonder the laboratory is so clean today," Ben thought. He said nothing to Le Roy.

Jean-Baptiste directed Ben toward a baby-faced man with a sharp nose who appeared completely preoccupied. He sat alone at the front of the grandstand, busily biting the nail on his right thumb. It appeared to Ben as if he were sucking his thumb.

"François, I want you to meet Ben Franklin," Le Roy said.

The young physician immediately dropped his hand into his lap. He looked up almost with a sigh of relief as if hoping that the presence of the esteemed natural philosopher might assure his success today.

"I understand that you have already flown once?" Ben said.

"Yes, last month at Versailles. After the sheep, the duck, and the rooster flew in September, I am the first of God's creatures to have ascended into the sky attached to a balloon," Rozier replied.

"I understand that you had to convince the King to send you up instead of a convict?"

"The King had been inclined to risk only a man already condemned to death. I convinced him to send me instead."

"You are a brave man."

"No, sir. I only believe that humanity shall be better served if a man of science is able to record the event."

"How did you find the tethered flight?" Ben asked.

"Spectacular, sir." The young physician's face became more animated. "Even though I flew to a height of only eighty-four feet—the length of the rope tethering me to Earth—I came to understand the sensation of free flight. I am ready to experience that feeling again, and more, today."

Ben looked into Doctor Rozier's eyes. There he found the resolute gaze of a man who has seen the future—and knows that he will be part of it.

"And so you shall," Ben said. He put his arm around the man's shoulder. Ben felt him trembling. He let the aeronaut go with a pat on the back. Ben found his seat on the terrace between a newspaper reporter and an older courtier he didn't recognize.

The Montgolfier brothers, at last, seemed satisfied that everything was in order for the flight. They rushed up to the terrace, looking for their passengers. Doctor Rozier and the Marquis d'Arlandes jumped up. The two young men filed down toward the balloon to thunderous applause from the onlookers in attendance. Once standing on the ringed walkway underneath the globe, they waved. The band played a triumphant tune. Ben could now see the balloon fully inflated in front of him. It was made of a royal blue silk, its glossy body emblazoned with golden emblems and zodiac signs, spectacular in contrast to the sunlit brown and evergreen foliage of late autumn. Like the first balloon that Ben had witnessed on the *Champ de Mars*, this one too seemed to want only to be let free. It swayed in the air in front of where Ben sat on the terrace, seemingly pleading to be let loose from its shackles. The Montgolfier brothers hefted additional bales of straw and wool onto the walkway. They threw a few large chunks of cow dung and an old pair of shoes on the fire for good measure. Lastly, they placed a bucket of water and a sponge on board, just in case the fire in the pit escaped.

The balloon riders looked apprehensive to Ben, but tenacious. He silently wished them well. Fully a dozen men manned the ropes securing the balloon to the courtyard. At the end of the countdown, led by the Montgolfier brothers with help from the attendees, all of the men holding the balloon let go.

The marvelous machine lifted off slowly. Ben watched in awe as the balloon riders ascended from below his gaze, to eye level, to above him. At about two hundred and fifty feet, the aeronauts lowered their hats to salute the crowd.

Mercifully, the moderate wind in the courtyard had been blowing from the northwest, away from the terrace, during the balloon's preparation. However, as the balloon lifted, the wind turned ever so slightly in the opposite direction, and black smoke washed over the grandstand—acrid, oily smoke with a disgusting odor. There was a groan from the crowd sitting on the terrace. Many started coughing or pulling out their handkerchiefs to cover their faces. The older man sitting next to Ben spoke for the first time.

"What possible good can come from that contrivance?" he choked out with disdain. He wiped the tears from his burning eyes.

Ben thought for a moment, and then responded with what had leapt to mind. "Of what good is a newborn babe?" he asked.

The reporter scribbled in his notebook. The crowd started to disperse. Ben got up to search out Le Roy in order to offer his congratulations and procure a dram of his cheap brandy.

The following morning, Madame Leray showed up at Ben's door. Whenever she personally delivered his morning newspaper, Ben knew that something was up.

She popped into his lodgings, carrying a tray. "You're in the newspaper," she sang gaily.

"I am? Whatever for?"

She unfolded the newspaper and started reading. "It says here that upon viewing the first-ever manned balloon flight, you were asked 'What good might come from such a contrivance?' to which you answered . . ."

Ben cut her off. "Of what good is a newborn babe?"

"Yes, Ben, that was a brilliant *bon mot*. You know that I think those balloons are dangerous ... and that dashing young Doctor Rozier will likely end up dead one day if he keeps flying them ... but I must admit that mankind's ability to fly opens up a new world of possibilities. Much like a newborn babe."

"Marie-Thérèse, I believe that you are right, as usual. Hopefully, mankind will find peaceful uses for this new machine, not bellicose ones. Does the newspaper report the outcome of yesterday's flight?"

"Oh yes, it is front-page news," she said. She started reading again. "It says here that Doctor Rozier and the Marquis d'Arlandes flew more than six miles across Paris yesterday, finally landing on the *Butte aux Cailles*. Their flight lasted twenty-five minutes. Both men landed in good health. They are to report their findings to the King next week."

"Le Roy will be very proud that this historic flight started at his Royal Scientific Laboratory."

"It seems fitting to me. Do you care for a scone?" she asked. She revealed a basket of freshly baked breads on her tray.

November 23rd, 1783

PARIS

THE STONE STEPS of the old Louvre were covered in a slimy mixture of late autumn rain and pigeon droppings. Ben slipped hurrying up them and nearly fell but caught the arm of Le Roy just in time. He carefully wiped his shoes on a mat by the door. The marble hallways inside would be even more slippery. The two found their way to the meeting of the Academy of Science already underway. A report was being presented regarding the Montgolfier balloon flight. Ben was uncertain that he would learn anything new, having attended the original event. But regardless, he went to support Le Roy. As they entered, Condorcet was asking if there might be any way to steer the craft—seeing as it had only followed the path of the wind on its flight. Ben found his seat at the end of the front row near a set of glass doors. He glanced outside. The rain had let up, leaving cold gray clouds streaking low over the courtyard below. Wind sent a few leaves whirling in the small balcony just outside the doors. A large oak leaf stuck to the iron railing for a moment then was blown away. Several members stood up in succession and offered proposed methods of balloon maneuvering. Ben dozed off.

He awoke with a start. The meeting was taking a break. Several members got up to stretch. Ben watched a man open the glass doors and walk out to the balcony. His appearance was striking; not that of your usual scientist by any means. A distinguished older gentleman, he wore the clothes more of a courtier, or a dandy. His dark green velvet topcoat was fitted tightly at the torso but then flared out below his waist. Underneath the topcoat, he wore a silk suit jacket of a lighter green hue, a ruffled white silk shirt, and a shade of green leggings to match his suit down to the knee, with white stockings below. Atop his head, he sported a gray wig, short with many curls.

Ben pointed the man out to Le Roy. "Quite a lot of trouble to go to for an Academy meeting," he said.

Le Roy laughed. "That is Monsieur Casanova, for you. It is unlikely that he will find any women to seduce here today, yet he always dresses for the occasion."

As the two watched, Casanova turned to face back toward the glass door and struck a pose. He turned his head to the right, closed his eyes, crossed the right arm over the left with both hands palm up, crossed his right foot in front of his left, and stood as if frozen like a statue.

"How odd," Ben said.

"Yes, most likely, the venereal disease has addled his brain," Le Roy replied. It appeared that he might say more but was quickly distracted by well-wishers wanting to congratulate him on the successful balloon launch.

Ben watched as Casanova stood silently in his pose for a moment longer. Then he gracefully unwrapped his arms, then his legs, and slowly turned his head back toward Ben. His eyes opened. They met Ben's with a jolt. Ben wasn't sure what to do next. He didn't feel that he could look away. Casanova smiled. Ben felt himself smile back. Casanova shook his arms and legs out. He walked over to the glass doors and re-entered the room. He walked directly over to Ben and stuck out his hand. Ben shook it.

"I am Giacomo Casanova de Seingalt."

"Benjamin Franklin ... but please call me Ben."

"It is an honor to meet you, Ben."

"And you."

"Would you walk with me in the garden?"

Ben recalled how he had been dozing only a few moments before. "I could well stretch my legs," he replied.

The two left the room full of scientists, still milling around at the break. Ben looked over his shoulder to see Le Roy with Condorcet and one of the Montgolfier brothers engaged in a heated discussion.

Ben and Casanova walked the empty halls of the Louvre, their footsteps echoing as they strode. Since the royal family had moved to Versailles over a century before, the building was used primarily for office space. Ben noted that most of the artwork had been removed from the walls, but here and there, a minor piece had been left behind.

"What form of contortion was that you performed on the balcony?" Ben asked, intending to start up a conversation.

"It's a pose, taught to me by an Indian yogi many years ago. I don't know that it has a name."

"Interesting. To what purpose is it?"

"It is a form of meditation. I find that even if I assume the pose for only a moment, I can clear my thoughts, return more focused to the matter at hand. Do you meditate?"

"I have not been trained."

"That is not what I asked," Casanova said.

They entered the garden. A few evergreen plants seemed the only foliage remaining. The still air was cool and moist around them.

Ben stopped. He felt very comfortable with this man, even though they had just met. Everything about his demeanor was soothing. He spoke with soft, lush tones. The meter of his voice was not too rushed or too slow. His eyes beckoned one to spill all. Ben could instantly understand why so many women succumbed to him.

"I believe that I do meditate in my own way," Ben said. "When I am swimming in the Seine, I reach a state of peacefulness, a place of calm tranquility that I find remarkably soothing. I can think there, open my mind up to many things."

"Do you commune with God in that way?"

"Yes, I suppose so. I am not religious in the sense of feeling a need to attend church regularly. I find inconsistencies and hypocrisy with the Church."

"Myself as well. And you are also a Freemason, I believe?"

"Yes. You seem to know a lot about me."

"A blessing and a curse. I have trained in many forms of transcendence. Through those ways, I have developed an inner vision. I often feel that I know things about people, people I have just met, such as you, or even people that I may see on the street. I like to check to see if my intuition is correct."

"And what does your intuition tell you about me?"

"I believe that you are a man conflicted."

Ben was about to object, but Casanova put his index finger up to his mouth. Ben listened instead of speaking. Casanova went on. "You want proof, is that not so?"

"Yes."

"But what of the things in this world that we cannot prove?"

"Perhaps someday, through the scientific method, we will."

"But what if we shouldn't try to prove or disprove certain things?"

"Such as?"

Casanova paused for a moment. "Let me ask you this," he said. "These scientific marvels ... the balloon we discuss today, your precious electrical fluid, the discovery of new chemicals and compounds ... should these wonders be used for the good of humanity, or rather for evil?"

"Good, I should hope."

"I hope so too ... but what makes you say that? How would you go about proving it?"

"*Prima facie,*" Ben replied, "It's obvious on the face of it."

"So you will agree with me that there are certain things that need no proof? How about love, for example?"

"Are you speaking of the love of one specific person for another, or in general?"

"They are the same in my mind. Either—or both."

Ben looked lost. "Please explain," he said.

"You are able to recognize that you are an individual, correct?"

"Yes, most definitely," Ben said proudly.

"And yet you live in society. You are not a hermit. You choose to live with others, also correct?"

"Yes."

"Why do you believe this is?"

"I enjoy the company of other people."

"Yes, but why? When I was imprisoned in the Doge's palace, mostly in solitary confinement for nearly two years, I thought a great deal about why we humans need others."

"What is your explanation?"

"I have come to believe that it is because of love that we choose to live together. It is because of love that we pursue scientific discoveries to benefit humanity. It is because of love that we have developed our society, our moral systems. I believe that love is the fluid that binds all people together. I believe that this invisible force connects us all."

A sardonic look swept over Ben's face. "An invisible force emanating from the stars?" he said mockingly. "Surely, you can't be another follower of Mesmer."

"No, I am not a follower of any one theory of transcendence. I believe that all methods of enlightenment have the capability of delivering one to a higher plane. Faithfully studied and practiced, each has the potential to free us from our day-to-day conscious ministrations, allow us to connect with one another through the power of love, and help us to reach our full potential as human beings."

"Christianity?"

Casanova nodded. He went on, "And Buddhism, Mithraism, your own Freemasonry, even *magnétisme animale*—if you will permit me—are only a means to an end. Some techniques work for some, others for others."

"And what of the claims that one man controls this power?"

"Hogwash ... but ponder this Ben ... the Pope maintains the keys to Heaven, does he not?"

Ben thought for a moment. The rain started again. A soft mist fell over the garden. The two men stepped back inside. They headed in the direction of the meeting room.

"Yes, I suppose so," Ben said. "But one need not necessarily tithe to the Church in order to receive their blessings."

Casanova laughed. "The Holy See may be able to afford to be magnanimous now, but I doubt that it was always so."

"Probably true, also."

"But Ben, don't you see that by carefully attending to any one of these methods, by practicing any form of transcendence, we connect with our fellow humans, we tap into the collective wisdom of generations back to Adam and Eve."

"And you practice love as your method?"

"What more pure form of transcendence is there? Consider this, Ben ... what do you believe to be the true meaning of life?"

"Please enlighten me."

"I believe that, ultimately, the true meaning of life is to procreate."

"That is a very scientific answer."

"Yes, but more than that, if all people did was procreate and die, would the world ever become a better place?"

"I think not."

"And given that in the day-to-day conscious world, it is very difficult to do anything other than simply procreate and die, shouldn't we yearn to have life mean something more?"

"I should think so."

"Then my argument rests on the fact that by learning to practice a method of transcendence, whichever one you choose, love in my case, people may contribute to the collective wisdom of humankind—the wisdom of the flock, if you will. Through doing so, we find meaning in life. Through doing so, we become immortal."

"I believe that I understand your theory, but it would not be at all easy to prove."

"We all know instinctively that this other plane exists. As I said before, there are some things that require no proof."

"I must have proof."

"Then I sincerely hope that you find your proof someday but doubt that you ever will. Ben, I said that you are a man conflicted because I see in you a man with a substantial inner vision, a great natural capacity to peer into the other plane of existence that I have just described, and yet you choose to insist on denying it."

"I don't deny it; I simply don't have proof of its existence."

"Ben, it is all around you." Casanova closed his eyes. He spread his arms open wide over his head and brought them back together, palms up, at the level of his navel. He stood there for a moment as if in a trance. His eyes opened.

"I must leave now," he said abruptly.

With that, Casanova whisked away down the dreary hall of the Louvre. Ben stood for a moment and watched him disappear. He made his way back to the meeting room, still packed with scientists discussing aeronautics. Ben reclaimed his seat but did not hear any of the remaining speaker's presentations. He thought instead about his encounter with Casanova. He thought about Marianne flying with the flock, and the place where the flock brought her.

As the meeting disbanded, Le Roy turned to Ben and said, "That Casanova is an interesting fellow, is he not? A capable librarian, but what a libertine."

"Yes, but his mind has most likely deteriorated through the venereal disease or the toxic medicines he has consumed attempting to treat it. He is quite convinced of the power of love."

"And you ... not so?"

"I'm not sure."

Christmas 1783

AUTEUIL

IT HAD ALREADY BEEN a particularly snowy and cold month, but somehow the wintry weather was comforting to Ben. He could sit and watch the snow falling lightly to the ground from the window of his lodgings. The pristine white made the whole world seem quiet and at peace. It reminded Ben of being home in Philadelphia. Thankfully his gout had remained quiescent despite the harsh weather. Since Saint Nicholas's Day on the 6th, Ben had been reveling in the holiday spirit. He enjoyed giving out small presents to the young children of his friends and neighbors in France. The youngest of the Leray children was already a teenager – past the age to be visited by *Père Noël*—but the Hôtel de Valentinois nonetheless was quite festive for the holidays. Ben enjoyed simply walking through the house to see what new ornaments and decorations Madame Leray had put up. He received many invitations to Christmas Eve dinner but accepted only the one that came from the *Notre-Dame d'Auteuil.*

Ben dressed in a dark red velvet suit. He donned black boots and a belt. His pocket watch read half-past five, but as was his custom when visiting

Minette, he would leave it on the dresser tonight. As he checked his appearance in the mirror, he patted his protuberant belly and fancied that if he could only grow a decent beard, he might resemble Saint Nicholas. This thought made him chuckle out loud. In the drawer of his writing desk, he found a long unused pipe, and tucked it into his breast pocket. Then he donned a heavy wool overcoat and beaver hat and pulled the flaps down over his ears. He extinguished the lamps before heading up the hill toward the main house.

"We will miss you tonight, Ben," Madame Leray said. She wore a look of genuine sadness as she took his arm, walking him through the foyer.

"You have your family."

"Yes, but you have become part of the family."

"Thank you, Marie-Thérèse. Next year, I promise I will stay home."

"By next Christmas, you may be back in Philadelphia."

"Then, I will have to sail across the ocean in order to keep my promise."

"Oh, go on and have a good time," she said. "We won't wait up."

"Thank you ... and merry Christmas," Ben called out over his shoulder. He boarded the coach waiting outside.

The ride to Auteuil was nothing less than magical. Snow-covered fields sparkled in the moonlight on both sides of the quiet road. Countless stars winked overhead in the clear black sky. Ben might have been warmer if he had drawn the curtains over the windows of the coach, but he found that he couldn't look away from the wondrous scene outside. The golden sliver of moon seemed to hover just above the horizon. It darted in and out from behind the clusters of bare trees, seemingly chasing him across the countryside. The only sound Ben could hear was the muted ringing of the bells worn by the draught horses as they pranced through the winter air. When the coach arrived at the home of Madame Helvétius, Ben was slightly disappointed that the show was over ... but not so much that he was tempted to ride on. He yearned to see Minette.

The house was brightly lit in all rooms visible from the walk. That warmth and the smell of oak burning in the fireplaces invited him in. Ben was not a bit surprised that the courtier cats did not come out in the snow to escort him from the gate to the house. He was greeted at the door by the sound of carols being sung from inside. Ben hung his hat and coat in the foyer.

The courtier cats gathered to form his entourage as he proceeded toward the library and the sound of singing. Ben was beginning to know the cats by name. He recognized Giacomo, one of the larger cats, also known as The Chevalier, by his sleek orange coat and muscular build. Also, part of the welcoming committee was a smaller friendly cat named Claude. As Claude was the name of Minette's dead husband, Ben wondered if the names of the other cats held any significance. The other six or seven cats in attendance must have names as well, Ben thought. He determined that he would endeavor to learn them all.

Upon entering the library, Ben recognized the two abbés and student doctor Cabanis locked arm in arm singing "*Adeste Fideles*" at the top of their lungs. The smell of spiced wine filled the air, leading Ben to believe that the festivities had begun without him. He did not see Minette, however. The three singers abruptly stopped when Ben approached.

Abbé Morellet was the first to speak. "Merry Christmas, Ben," he said. He brandished a bigger smile than Ben could ever recall adorning the normally reserved clergyman.

"André, and the best of the season to you as well."

"Ben, we desperately need your baritone to make us into a decent quartet. What say you?" the Abbé de la Roche pleaded.

"Find me a large mug of your spiced wine, and I'll consider it," Ben said.

"I'll fetch it," Cabanis said. He bolted toward the kitchen.

"Where is Minette?" Ben asked, despite the fact that he thought that he already knew the answer.

"Dressing," the two abbés answered simultaneously. They laughed so hard they had to support each other.

"All right then," Ben said. He joined in their laughter.

Ben believed that he had never seen these two men of the cloth in such high spirits. Cabanis returned with a pewter mug the size of a pitcher. He handed it to Ben, who downed a good swig. The wine was warm, slightly sweet, with aromatic clove and other delicate spices. He wiped his mouth ceremonially on his sleeve.

"Anyone for a game of chess?" Ben asked.

By the time Minette made her appearance, the abbés had both nodded off by the fire. Ben was on his third game of chess with Cabanis. The more-than-slightly drunk medical student was playing poorly and yawning frequently. Ben first perceived Minette's approach when the courtier cats became alert. The Chevalier jumped up and trotted toward the foyer, followed closely by the rest of the cat entourage. Cabanis dropped off to sleep, his head supported by his right arm in the soft chair. Ben rose and followed the cats out of the library. They were gathered in the foyer in a semicircle, each looking upstairs. Ben also looked up to see Minette emerge at the top. She wore a white silk dress, with red satin accents and a bow. Her long silver-gray hair was tied back with a scarlet ribbon. Her lush red lips met his as soon as she reached the foyer. Her aroma was heavenly. Ben felt his body heat rise. They stood together under the flickering glow of the chandelier, encircled by the courtier cats.

"Where are the boys?" she asked after a kiss that left Ben breathless.

"Asleep by the fire," Ben whispered.

"Good. I want to take you out."

Ben had been hoping to increase his body temperature rather than decrease it by going outside in the cold, but he acquiesced.

Minette took his hand and led him toward the door. He assisted Minette with her wrap and then donned his.

"Wait," she said. She ran toward the kitchen. In a moment she returned with a handful of fleecy wool and some string.

"You'll be needing your beard, *Père Noël*," she said. They bounded for the coach waiting outside, laughing like schoolchildren.

In the course of the short coach ride into the town of Auteuil, Minette managed to fashion a respectable-looking beard out of the wool. She attached it to Ben's face with string and fashioned a hole in front before giving him another passionate kiss on the eager lips that she had exposed.

"Umm, I like you with a beard," she cooed. Then she scrunched up her nose. "It tickles."

"Well, don't get too used to it. I can't grow a decent one to save my life."

"That's all right. It is still fun to pretend. I don't think I ever kissed Father Christmas before." She pushed herself away from Ben's chest slightly. "Do you suppose it is a sin?" she asked with mock concern.

"Not one that won't be quickly expunged," Ben replied. He drew her close to him. He pressed his lips to hers again, forcefully.

The coach pulled up at the beginning of a row of small shops and houses that constituted the town of Auteuil. Most people lived in the surrounding countryside and came into town for business or to go to the small local church. The few people who lived in town were the shopkeepers. Auteuil had none of the hustle and bustle of Paris, which is exactly what gave the quaint town its charm. Ben stepped down from the coach onto the wooden sidewalk, holding his hand out for Minette to alight. The air was cold but calm. He took the pipe from his pocket, placing it between his teeth through his beard.

Many of the shops were closed, but candles lit the windows, imparting a warm glow to both sides of the street. The townspeople were settled in their homes, preparing for the traditional feast with family and friends to follow midnight mass. A small group of carolers passed, singing robustly. Ben and Minette joined in behind them and sang along. At each building, they would pause to sing a carol or two before proceeding up the boardwalk. At the end of the street sat the small wooden church. The carolers crossed the street to work their way back down the opposite side, but Minette held Ben back.

Ben looked at the church. It was tidy but by no means ornate. Fully lit from the inside, the colorful windows flickered with scenes of many saints. The carved front door was closed. It was not yet time for midnight mass.

Minette tugged Ben's hand. "Let's go in," she said.

The door creaked as they entered the small space. Ben noted only four rows of pews on each side of the single center aisle. The church might hold thirty people, Ben thought. There were one or two worshipers scattered throughout the pews. They appeared to be immersed in prayer. The priest stood near a small altar at the front engrossed in his preparations for mass. When the door creaked, he turned to see who had entered.

"Hello, Minette," he said almost instantly. "It has been a long time since you have been here."

"Yes, Father ... I know," she replied softly. Her voice was tinged with a slight hint of sorrow. "I send my tithe," she added.

"We appreciate your money. It keeps this place running." He motioned with his arms at his surroundings, decorated for the High Holiday. Then he added, "But I would rather have you."

"Yes, I know."

"May I bless you ... and your friend?" For the first time, Ben felt the priest recognize him.

"Of course."

The priest walked slowly down the aisle, holding an aspergillum in his hand. He shook a sprinkling of holy water toward them as he approached. Both Minette and Ben bent down on one knee. The priest put a hand on her head. He whispered a short prayer, then said, "Bless you... and may the Lord keep you, my child."

He turned his attention to Ben. "I don't believe that I have ever blessed *Père Noël* before," he muttered bemusedly.

"Everyone can use a blessing, Father."

"Then, may God bless you."

"Thank you, Father," Ben and Minette said simultaneously.

"Will the remainder of your household be joining us for midnight Mass tonight?"

"Yes, Father, if they awaken in time."

The priest looked slightly perplexed. He responded only by saying, "Minette, I hope that one day you will join them once again."

"I understand," Minette said. Her voice was kind but devoid of any hint of a commitment.

Back outside the church, Ben and Minette walked hand in hand along the quiet street back toward the coach.

"I didn't realize that you were estranged from the Church," Ben said.

"I'm not *estranged*," she protested. "And what about you? I do not believe that you regularly attend services."

"I am more spiritual than religious."

"What does that mean?"

"That means that I have found that I can commune with God more easily swimming in the Seine, or riding my horse through the flowery fields of Passy, or quietly contemplating life on my own, than I can while sitting in a stuffy church being lectured to by a parish priest."

"I agree with you, Ben." She squeezed his hand. "I have no need for the Church or its canon."

"Then why do you support them financially?"

"Because I understand the importance that the Church can have in peoples' lives. Take my dear abbés as an example. They both live out their spiritual lives through the Church. Neither one could conceive a life not connected with it. For many others in this town and elsewhere, religion represents the foundation of the social order. Births, weddings, funerals ... people measure their lives through the ministrations of the Church. It is important to the well-being of society."

"But you don't feel a need to attend?"

"No, Ben. You must understand. I believe I have told you of my upbringing in the monastery. The sisters were mostly quite sweet to me, but they all lived such sheltered lives. As a young woman, I yearned to know more ... to develop a broader understanding of the world ... to live fully."

"And you can't do that within the Church?"

"Ben, the Church, to me, represents confinement. It represents a box that asks people to be satisfied with what they have."

Ben looked puzzled but said nothing.

"I don't mean just material things," she went on. "I mean that the Church asks us to accept a framework, their rules, their limitations on what we can do as humans ... limitations that I eventually found overly restrictive."

"Limitations such as having intimate relations only within the confines of marriage?"

She gave him a stern look. "Don't even get started down that path," she warned. Then she gave him a sly smile. "You do want your Christmas present, don't you?"

Ben shut up quickly, remembering how he yearned to release her red satin ribbon as soon as they got back to her bedroom. Tonight he wasn't inclined to start an argument about her unwillingness to marry him.

They climbed up into the still-warm coach. "Besides," she said. "How many 'good married Catholics' do you know who take the 'love thy neighbor' doctrine much more literally than the Church would approve?"

Ben pulled off his bearded disguise. He rubbed his face. He thought for a moment. He observed his beautiful companion bathed in soft moonlight.

"I will certainly agree with you there. The hypocrisy of many of the Puritans and the 'holier than thou' set has always rankled me," he said. "Some use their affiliation with the Church as a way to suppress or control others."

"My way of resolving the issue for myself has been to set limits on my participation with the Church. I grew up with the Church, I know its cant intimately, I support them financially ... but I keep my soul, my spirituality as you call it, between me and God Himself."

"Or Herself," Ben said. He gave her hand a squeeze.

"Or Herself," she replied.

Just then, the coach pulled back up in front of her house. "Come on inside," Minette said. "I believe that God has provided us with a unique opportunity. The boys will soon leave for midnight Mass. Let us be grateful and not squander it." She flashed him a wonderfully mischievous smile. "I have the oysters and Champagne already chilled."

Two hours later, by the time the two abbés and Cabanis returned from midnight Mass, Ben was formulating an idea. Minette was upstairs, relaxing in a hot bath. Ben stood in the library, examining a book when the church-going party arrived home. He tucked a piece of paper into his pocket.

The table was lavishly set for the Christmas feast. Minette sat next to Ben. As was traditional, no one sat at the head of the table in deference to Monsieur Helvétius. The two abbés sat across from Ben and Minette, with Cabanis anchoring the foot of the table. Tureen after tureen of confit, cassoulet, hearty stews, and root vegetables arrived. In good time, the Christmas goose made an elegant presentation to a round of applause from the dining party.

After the dinner plates had been cleared, but before dessert arrived, Ben took the paper from his pocket. Minette looked puzzled.

"I would like to read you this poem," he announced.

"Ben, I didn't know that you were also a poet," she exclaimed.

"I am not," Ben admitted. "This is a poem by Edmund Halley."

"The discoverer of the comet?"

"One and the same. Also, the publisher of the first edition of Newton's *Principia Mathematica,* which I found in your library."

"Let's hear it!" cried the abbés in unison.

Ben adjusted his bifocals. He took a long sip of mulled red wine and began to read out loud.

Edmund Halley: Poem for Isaac Newton's Principia Mathematica.

Behold! You grasp the Science of the Pole,
Earth's wondrous Mass, how pois 'd the mighty Whole,
Jove's Reckoning, the Laws, when first he made

All Things' Beginnings, by his Will obey'd,
Those the Creator as the World's Foundations laid.
The secret Chambers of the conquer'd Skies
Open to View. Hidden no longer lies
What Binds the World's Frame, and the constant Force
Which rolls the farthest Planet in his Course....

Ben finished the poem. He put the paper down and peered at the assembled company over his bifocals. There was silence around the table. All of the occupants of the Helvétius household sat immobilized, as if under a spell.

"Would you like me to tell you why I wanted to read you that poem?" he asked the group.

"Yes ... please ... enlighten us," came the responses from around the table.

"All right," Ben said. He slowly looked over at Cabanis. "It occurred to me, as I was first reading this poem, that one ingenious characteristic of Sir Isaac Newton's work was that he applied experimentation to confirm or disprove his astute observations of Nature and God's creation."

"Ben, Newton was certainly not the first or last to do so. Think of Copernicus, Descartes, even your own experimentation with electricity," the Abbé Morellet said.

"Yes, but it struck me that perhaps there might be a role for experimentation in the medical arts, particularly as it relates to the influence of the planets."

Cabanis instantly perked up, hearing that the conversation had moved from the metaphysical realm to something closer to his own interests.

"What do you mean, Ben?" he asked.

The coffee service arrived. Ben was about to request tea when a server placed a small porcelain pot in front of him. He glanced over at Minette to let her know he appreciated the small things she did to take care of him. She gave him a wink in return.

"My boy," Ben went on, looking back toward Cabanis. "Professor Le Roy and Professor Lavoisier are of late asking me to head a commission.

A commission empowered by the King and charged with investigating *magnétisme animale* as practiced at Paris. But I had no real inkling of how I might proceed with this inquiry until I discovered this poem tonight."

Cabanis bore a confused look on his face. "What was it about the poem that enlightened you?"

"As I read Halley's poem, it occurred to me what Newton had done. He had observed a natural force—gravity in this case—and used experimental methods to document it. He made predictions about how the force would behave, and then he designed tests to determine if gravity followed the rules that he had proposed for it. A force previously shrouded in mystery was instead found to be understandable, predictable, and capable of aiding mankind rather than vexing us."

"I believe I am beginning to understand," Cabanis said. "If such experimental methods could be applied to medical treatments, then we could find out if they are effective or not."

"Yes, yes, my lad," Ben said excitedly.

Ben noticed a troubled look on Minette's face. "But Ben," she said slowly. "People are not apples."

"I am not sure that I'm following you," Ben replied. Seeing her expression, his excitement deflated like a balloon.

"Apples are not self-aware," she went on. "They fall from trees under the effects of gravity, whether they want to or not. They are not active participants in the process. You have said yourself that the same treatment, given to two different people, can have very differing effects – to the point of one outcome being considered curative and the other not. The difference may just be that one person *wants* to be cured."

"Hmm." Ben pondered her reasoning as he cradled his chin in his hand. "You have a brilliant mind, my dear. The treatment of human disease is made considerably more complicated by the presence of consciousness and will."

"Ben," the Abbé Morellet interjected. "you must find a way to direct the commission and address the issue. Your leadership will convey a credence few others could bring to the subject."

Ben thought for a moment. "I believe I have a solution," he exclaimed. "Accepting that the human mind interplays considerably with sickness and health."

"Yes?" Minette asked.

"I believe that the best way to proceed will be to attempt to prove or disprove the presence of *magnétisme animale* as a physical force or fluid— rather than its purported effects."

"And how might you go about doing that?" Cabanis asked.

"I am not entirely sure as of yet," Ben said. "But I am sure that it will involve experimentation."

PART
VI

THE ROYAL SCIENTIFIC LABORATORY

LE ROY RAPPED HIS FIST three times with authority. "I call this meeting to order," he announced. The small group of scientists sat around a sturdy worktable in a corner of Le Roy's laboratory in the *Château de la Muette*. It was early evening. The staff was gone for the day. Dusk fell over the silent scientific equipment, which sparkled in the flickering lamplight.

Ben had been engaged in conversation with Professor Lavoisier about new processes to more efficiently generate hydrogen gas. He stopped talking and gazed over at Le Roy. Professor Bailly and Doctor Guillotin continued, however. They were engrossed in a discussion regarding the need for a humane method of executing condemned prisoners. Ben listened with cordial interest for a moment. He had heard the doctor present his favorite cause many times before. He hated to see even condemned prisoners suffer during their execution. This time, though, he was describing a device of his own design to Bailly. The device Guillotin described would quickly and effectively decapitate a prisoner without any prolonged suffering or the risk of failure that plagued current execution methods. Guillotin envisioned a weighted blade, released along a track from a height. He was expounding about how he had calculated the necessary weight and height precisely. It seemed like an oddly macabre conversation to Ben, so he was glad when Le Roy interrupted again.

"Gentlemen," Le Roy said. He cleared his throat loudly in an attempt to halt all conversation, which finally stopped.

"Ben," Le Roy said. "Would you be so kind as to introduce the topic of our meeting?"

"Certainly," Ben said. He stood up. "Tomorrow, I expect to receive word that the King has listened to the advice of our friend Professor Le Roy here, the Royal Academy of Sciences, and the Faculty of Medicine. It is my understanding that the King intends to designate me as the head of a commission to investigate the practice of *magnétisme animale*. You gentlemen have agreed to join me in this endeavor. I thank you for your willingness to do so. I have chosen each of you because of your unique talents, ones that I hope to apply to our task."

Ben turned and indicated each member seated at the table in turn. "Professor Bailly, for your expansive knowledge of astronomy; Doctor Guillotin, for your thorough understanding of the medical arts; Professor Lavoisier for your pioneering work with chemistry; and last, but certainly not least, Professor Le Roy, because of your keen scientific mind . . ." Ben raised his glass. "As well as your seemingly inexhaustible supply of cheap brandy."

There was a good laugh around the table. Ben went on.

"Doctor Mesmer has proposed that he has discovered an invisible fluid emanating from the stars—a fluid to which he has given the name *magnétisme animale*. A fluid with the power to heal. A fluid only he and his trained disciples can control. The King will ask us to investigate these claims scientifically and will expect a report by this summer."

The group of scientists may have been stunned by the short time frame Ben revealed for their work, but none reacted negatively.

"Ben, how do you propose to accomplish this task?" Le Roy asked.

"I believe that I need not remind this esteemed group of the first law of natural philosophy ... 'To admit no new causes without an absolute necessity.' I propose that we approach the problem scientifically."

"All very well and good," Doctor Guillotin interrupted. "But how will we prove whether the Mesmeric treatment works or not?"

A smile came over Ben's face. "I am glad to be asked that question, Doctor," he replied. "*Magnétisme animale* may indeed exist without being useful, but it cannot be useful if it does not exist."

Guillotin looked lost. "Ben, what do you suggest?" he asked.

"Here is my proposal. First, I believe that we should attempt to measure the force of *magnétisme animale* with any and all of today's most advanced instruments." He pointed around the room for effect. "I suspect that we will find it unmeasurable."

"No surprise there," Professor Bailly said. "We cannot measure light either, but yet we know it exists."

"Ah, I agree, Professor," Ben replied. "But we can perceive light with our own eyes. Therefore, I propose that we should next determine if we can detect the *magnétisme animale* with any of our five senses."

"I doubt that if we are unsuccessful in measuring *magnétisme animale,* we will convince many believers of its nonexistence," Lavoisier said.

"Yes, I doubt this as well," Ben went on. "So, as further evidence, I propose that we test for the effects of *magnétisme animale.*"

"Do you mean that we attempt to judge whether patients are cured of their diseases or not?" Guillotin asked.

"No, Doctor," Ben said. "I do not believe I need to tell you that Nature cures diseases. Human diseases go through a natural progression, and most often, a cure is reached. Even modern Medicine must admit that the part played by the physician is usually limited. Didn't Moliere write, 'The role of the physician is to entertain the patient while the disease runs its course.'"

"I sincerely hope that someday it will not be so true," Guillotin said. Heads nodded around the table.

"Yes," Ben said. "I propose that we test for any measurable physical effects of *magnétisme animale*."

"For example?" Guillotine asked.

"An increase in the rapidity of heartbeats, a rise in body temperature or sweating, an increased respiration—any measurable physical effect that you care to detect. I can examine the effect of my own physical activities, such as swimming or climbing the stairs, on my body by these measures."

"Certainly, the effects of which you speak will happen when a man places his hand on the bare hypochondrium of a receptive woman," Guillotin said jokingly.

"Ah, an astute observation, my dear doctor. There you have hit upon another aspect that I would like to explore. Mesmer claims that physical contact or touching is not a requirement for the *magnétisme animale* to flow. Would it not be interesting to test whether the same physical effects occur when the subject is blindfolded?" Ben said.

"Yes, yes." There was general agreement around the table.

The discussion of ways to test for the presence or absence of a force called *magnétisme animale* carried on deep into the evening, taxing Le Roy's supply of cheap brandy to its limit.

March 11th, 1784

PARIS

MARIANNE CARRIED THE CRUMPLED piece of newspaper in her pocket as she moved briskly through the lamplit streets of Paris. She was fuming. Only recently returned with Cecelia from Florence, in her huff, she barely noticed the street musicians and artists. As she crossed the *Pont Neuf*, she checked to see if Marko's houseboat was docked there. It was not. She walked on.

It was a cool spring evening. Marianne was glad to keep her hood over her head. At the *Place Vendôme*, Antoine opened the door to Mesmer's apartment.

"Good evening, Mademoiselle. You are back early this year..." Antoine said cordially enough. Yet, his tone indicated that she was not expected.

Marianne breezed past him without as much as a 'Hello.' She found Mesmer sitting in the study, reading a book. She took the paper from her pocket, recrumpled it, and threw it at him. It struck him in the head.

"Marianne," Mesmer exclaimed. "What was that for?"

Marianne picked up the paper and smoothed it out as best she could.

"Do you know about this?" she asked angrily.

"Whatever is it?" Mesmer asked.

"'The *Concert Spirituel* proudly announces the arrival of renowned Austrian pianist Maria Paradis for a series of concerts in April,'" she read. "'These concerts will be conducted at the *Salle des Cent Suisses* in the *Tuileries* Palace. Tickets are now available. All are welcome to attend.'"

"So now, with Mother dead, you read the newspaper?" Mesmer taunted.

Marianne crossed her arms, seething. "So, what do you know about this?"

"Nothing." He kept his gaze focused on his book.

"Liar," she hissed. "Have you seen her?"

"No." He stood, paying her his full attention. "Marianne, I don't believe that I have ever seen you jealous before ... and so soon upon your return. Come, come here, My Dear." He held out his arms, but Marianne ignored him.

"Jealous, I'm not jealous!" she wailed. "Why in the world should I be jealous of a blind twenty-year-old pianist?"

"She is nearly twenty-five."

Marianne dove at him with her fist, striking him on his chest. Mesmer grabbed her arms to avoid her taking a second shot.

"I can't stand her," she sobbed.

Mesmer finally seemed to realize how truly upset she had become. "Marianne, she means nothing to me," he said soothingly. He continued to hold her. "I swear to you. What we shared ended a long time ago."

"Will you be attending her performance?"

"I was not planning on it."

"Good."

"And you won't see her anymore?"

"No."

"All right."

She seemed to calm down a bit with each of his reassurances.

"I believe that you could well do with a glass of cognac," Mesmer said, letting go of her only in order to fix her a drink from the bar.

"Thank you," she replied as he handed her a snifter. She downed a generous gulp.

"Will you stay for supper?"

"Cecelia . . ." she said. Marianne was planning to resist, but then succumbed to his beseeching brown eyes. "I can only stay for a while." She collected herself, savoring another sip from the snifter. She knew, as he did, that Cecelia wouldn't be looking for her anymore tonight.

Mesmer rang the bell to summon Antoine. When the valet appeared, Mesmer instructed him to set another place for supper.

"*Bon soir*, Antoine," Marianne said sheepishly. She recalled her brusque entry only a few moments earlier.

"Welcome, Mademoiselle," he responded. "Supper will be served in ten minutes."

A pan-fried beefsteak, accompanied by hearty mushroom soup and a buttered baguette soothed her considerably. She reluctantly refused dessert. Antoine brought her fresh coffee instead. Mesmer consumed a piece of cake large enough for both of them.

Just after the hall clock finished chiming nine, the doorbell rang. Marianne recognized the voice of Doctor D'Eslon speaking to Antoine in the foyer. He entered the dining room, looking upset.

"What is the matter, Charles?" Mesmer asked.

D'Eslon looked at Marianne as if trying to decide if he should speak or not. Mesmer caught the look. He said, "You may speak freely."

"The King has charged a commission to investigate *magnétisme animale*," D'Eslon said.

Mesmer seemed unconcerned. "It will not be the first, nor the last, time that someone has tried to investigate my discovery. I shall simply refuse to cooperate."

"Benjamin Franklin will lead the commission."

Marianne let out a small gasp at the mention of Ben's name, unexpectedly

430

coming as it did from D'Eslon. She was fairly sure that Mesmer had noticed her response, but he said nothing to her.

Mesmer stiffened, and his eyes narrowed. "It won't make any difference who they have lead it," Mesmer snapped. "I know this effort is being subsidized by the Faculty of Medicine. They all want to stop my practice—and yours too, my friend. They have all seen the remarkable cures that we have produced. From their way of thinking, we are stealing their patients left and right. They claim that my discovery does not work; yet their patients leave their practices in droves to seek out healing through *magnétisme animale*. They would like nothing more than to find a way to stop us from practicing."

"But should we not prove them wrong?" D'Eslon asked beseechingly.

"These quacks could not possibly understand my methods," Mesmer said. "If they truly wanted to learn, they would all join the Society of Universal Harmony. No, they seek only to criticize and obstruct."

D'Eslon seemed to have heard this tirade many times before. He changed tack. "Have you spoken with the Queen? What does she say? Might she be of help?"

Marianne gazed at Mesmer to judge his reaction. Since his 'open letters' to Marie Antoinette demanding an Institute for *magnétisme animale*, a large pension, and other remuneration had been published in the newspapers, Marianne doubted the Queen could provide much support, whatever her personal beliefs about his treatments. Mesmer had burned his bridges.

"You could ask her more easily than I," Mesmer said.

"I believe that my ability to ask her to intercede has passed," D'Eslon replied. "We must now assist the commission in its work."

"No!" Mesmer shouted, banging his fist on the table. "I refuse to cooperate with these naysayers, these imbeciles."

"But how will we convince them if we don't cooperate?"

"Charles, I am warning you," Mesmer said, his voice cold. "If you, or any member of the Society of Universal Harmony, cooperates with this commission, it will be in clear violation of the oath of secrecy you each signed. I will prosecute my rights in this matter vigorously."

"That oath calls for a member to be liable if they divulge your materials."

Mesmer looked as if his head might explode. "No," he said, as if speaking to a tedious child. "It applies not only to my printed materials—but also my methods, my teachings, my entire secret formula. My discovery had better not be given away by anyone."

D'Eslon wore an expression Marianne interpreted as representing his unaltered convictions in the matter that cooperation was the better path. However, he seemed to recognize the futility of arguing with Mesmer when he was in this state. Turning on his heels, D'Eslon left without so much as a goodbye.

"I never liked that man," Marianne said after he was gone, attempting to break the steely silence.

Mesmer, deep in thought, said nothing.

"Perhaps I should go now, too," she suggested.

"No," he replied with a pleading tone that she knew well.

The bed was warm. If Mesmer had been distracted by the earlier altercation with D'Eslon, it hadn't shown in his sexual attention to her. His hands had done their usual excellent work. Marianne only wished that she could make other parts of his body respond so well. The rejuvenation of their 'normal' relations that she had once enjoyed at Spa had long since faded. Yet, he seemed to be satisfied with satisfying her ... and if that was the case, then so be it.

"Did you enjoy that?" he asked.

"Oh yes," Marianne said in a rush of emotion.

"Good. I like pleasing you."

"I am glad that you do."

"May I ask you something?"

"Of course."

"Can Franklin make you reach *le petit morte* like that?"

His words shocked her, and Marianne felt herself tense up immediately.

Her mind raced. She thought back to her reaction to Ben's name earlier that evening. Perhaps Mesmer was just fishing. He had done it before. She remained silent.

"I know about the *Cheval Sauvage*," he said.

Her heart sank.

"How?" she asked.

"It was not so easy, but I followed you."

"You followed me?"

"Yes. I watched you go into the *Cheval Sauvage*. I saw you come out some time later. I waited a while longer and saw the good doctor leave. If your paramour had been some average workman, I admit that I would have been stumped. But when I recognized Franklin, I knew."

"What will you do?" Marianne asked with some trepidation. She had known that her affair with Ben might someday be exposed, but she had never dreamed that it would be like this.

"Oh nothing ... for now," Mesmer said triumphantly. Then it appeared that he had had an idea. "But you know ... this commission?"

She guessed what he was thinking. "No," she said. "You can't ask me to interfere."

"And why can't I?"

"Because it would have no effect. Ben is a man of principle. He wouldn't change his opinion or his report because of anything that I might say or do."

"I suppose that you will just have to try, my dear. Imagine the outcry if it were to become known that you have been carrying on an affair with a married man for all this time."

"Mother is dead, and Cecelia wouldn't care. Besides that, you are the married man, Ben is widowed."

"Oh yes, but that wasn't always the case. Anyway, I don't expect to have to use my information. You will find a way to help me stop this commission."

"It seems that I have no choice in the matter."

"You don't."

Marianne slunk through the streets of Paris, berating herself for being so careless as to let Mesmer track her to the *Cheval Sauvage*. She had gone to him today to castigate him for his relationship with the blind pianist, and he had turned the tables on her completely. She wondered how she would ever be able to face Ben again, let alone attempt the subterfuge that Mesmer required of her. Not that she bore any great devotion to Franklin any longer. Hadn't he deserted her when she was in the depths of her melancholia? He couldn't even explain why he'd reacted that way. Hadn't he refused to help her in her time of need? Refused to help her protect her right to play the instrument that he had made for her? What kind of a friend was that? He only wanted her when it was convenient for him.

With Mesmer, at least, she held some measure of control. Mesmer jumped when she called. He tried to please her. If he wasn't so damned pig-headed about his 'discovery' of *magnétisme animale*, perhaps she could even be more of an aid to him. Marianne suspected, however, that much of his secrecy about *magnétisme animale* was due to his lack of understanding. It occurred to Marianne that he might not truly comprehend its power or its source any more than she did, and perhaps less. He might be able to use big words to describe his theories, yet it was she who flew with the flock, she who had come to know its wisdom. She smiled.

Late March 1784

PARIS

"LOUIS JOSEPH HAS A FEVER," Marie Antoinette confided. She and Marianne sat among the blue-black clouds in the place where the flock brought them. Her translucent throne gleamed.

"He has never been the heartiest of children," Marianne said cautiously, with as much sensitivity as she could.

"I know that Marianne, but he is the Dauphin. What will happen to the kingdom if he should not survive?"

Marianne looked to the north to observe the elegant camelopard bend its graceful neck down to drink from the big dipper. She gazed back to appreciate the worried look on the Queen's face, the anxiety, and stress of normal motherhood, further burdened by the weight of the crown.

"Fevers come and go," Marianne said. "How old is he, four years now? In a few days, he will be right as an adamant."

"He won't be four until October. I do hope that you are correct. The boy is small and sickly, but I love him so."

"I don't doubt it, considering what you went through to conceive him, let alone the difficult labor," Marianne said. The Queen's face seemed to relax a bit, and she settled more comfortably into her throne.

"Would you examine him for me, Marianne?"

"Are you certain that is what you would have me do?"

"Yes."

"Then, of course, I will."

The Queen aimed her scepter at a small constellation with two bright stars and two smaller, dimmer ones nearby. Marianne couldn't help noticing that there were two gaseous nebulae close by as well.

"Oh, my Queen," Marianne exclaimed. She quickly recognized what she was observing. "You still have two more children to come."

The Queen said nothing but flicked a ball of light from her scepter at one of the small stars in the royal family constellation. It returned with a shimmering image of the Dauphin. He was playing with a wooden toy under the watchful eye of a nursemaid, who coughed frequently. The boy coughed, too.

As he approached her position, Marianne peered into the shimmering body of the gaunt lad. She focused her attention on his lungs, which looked like Emmentaler cheese—full of holes.

"Oh," Marianne said.

The Queen's worst fears seemed to have been realized. She put her hand to her reddening throat. "What is it?"

"I am so sorry."

"Marianne, please tell me."

"I believe that your son has the Consumption. The nursemaid too."

Phthisis had been known to be fatal since the time of Hippocrates. The fevers, bloody cough, and wasting were characteristic signs.

"Then there is nothing that can be done?"

"You could send him to the country. The fresh air might help for a while."

The Queen stopped asking further questions. Nothing more remained to be said. Both women knew the outcome. The boy would likely not live to become a man. Marianne became acutely aware of how painful the loss of the child would be. Yet, she knew that the Queen was stoic. She would never let her feelings show in public, and little in private. Marianne watched the boy float back into the constellation, playing happily as he receded.

After a moment of silence, Marianne spoke. "My Queen ... may I now ask your advice?"

"Of course." The Queen's voice remained tinged with grief, but she seemed eager to change to subject.

"What can you tell me about the commission to which Ben has been appointed by the King?"

"The commission investigating *magnétisme animale*?"

"Yes."

"You are aware that my husband has been hounded by the Faculty of Medicine to do something about Mesmer. As always, it is about money and power. I must admit that Mesmer has worn me down with his incessant demands. For the longest time, I interceded with His Majesty in order to block this investigation. But I can do so no more. What must be, will be."

"But the commission will likely be skeptical and may discredit what we do."

"Marianne, both you and I know that *magnétisme animale* works. Our sitting here together now is proof of that. But *how* does it work? Did you ever ponder that? Is it truly an invisible fluid that streams to earth from the stars? Even up here, where we seem to have eyes that can see as none have seen before, its sources remain invisible. Is that not strange to you?"

The peaceful celestial scene swirled around them, the translucent images of the constellations shifting ever so slowly. Leo, the lion, roared faintly in the distance. The two fish of Pisces dangled on their string. Pegasus stamped his hoof.

"I admit to not fully understanding it," Marianne said.

"Perhaps Mesmer's true genius is in the naming of the thing. *Magnétisme animale*—the force that binds us all together, that connects us, that makes us One. I have come to believe that what we do when we are here together, you and I, is something we have found within ourselves. Something we might well have found even had there been no Mesmer."

"You are right, of course. But he did direct us here."

"It is true that Mesmer and D'Eslon guided us on this journey—but where are they now? Back in the 'real' world with their hands placed on our thighs and chests." She gave a sly smile. "Enjoying themselves, I trust.

"However, you and I have reaped the true benefits of *magnétisme animale* and freely given our help to others through our own natural abilities and some hard work. We have discovered many wondrous things about ourselves in the process. You took advantage of it to cure your own melancholia. Mesmer didn't do that."

Marianne thought back to her sad winter in Florence. "Yes, but as we know, the cure can be transient," she said. "After Mother died, I was quite powerless to affect my own temperament. Yet, I suppose you are correct, my Queen. Mesmer didn't cure me—or anyone else. We have all cured ourselves," Marianne said.

"So then, let me ask you this. Do you think that the world is ready for Mesmer's 'discovery'?"

"What do you mean?"

"Marianne, knowing what you know about the world, do you think that the average person of today is capable of understanding that they could be much happier and healthier if they only allowed themselves to be? If they used any form of introspection, any method of transcendence at all, to become more in touch with their real feelings? If they listened to their true wants and needs? I am not talking about material wants and needs here, but human emotional ones."

"I never thought about it in quite that way."

"Mesmer didn't invent this," the Queen continued. She motioned around her at the cosmos, moving slowly in synchronized precision. "He showed us a path to explore it—yes, but this visionary realm, this realm of our common understanding has always existed within our minds. Not our everyday conscious minds, but rather a special place we can only locate if we try. Most people keep this place locked away. They don't seem able to find it. They can't embrace it, submit to it, release it, and channel it as the birds do."

As Marianne sat there, the universe shimmered. She realized what she heard was a precious rare thing—a wisdom born of insight, a cosmic poetry directed through the voice of this young, sometimes vain, impetuous, and high-born woman. Yet, true wisdom, nonetheless. She listened in awe.

"For some," the Queen went on, "this realm may even be filled with demons. They fear it. Others simply do not know that it exists, or when confronted with it, they balk at opening up this aspect of their mind. They resist it. They would stab it with their pitchforks and try to kill it, much like the backwards townspeople who attacked that balloon descending from the sky. They would try to lock it away. Mostly, they would deny it even exists. That is why I do not believe that the world is ready to embrace it.

"But we can see its benefit. You, in particular, have been able to use the wisdom of the flock to help many people. Marianne, you have a rare talent, a true intuition. By opening yourself up to *magnétisme animale*, you have not only improved your own understanding of yourself but are also making the world a better place."

"And the commission?"

"Ah, the commission," the Queen said. She smiled. "Ben is the perfect man to head the commission. He is rational, pragmatic, and scientific. He must have proof. Nothing else will satisfy him. And Marianne, this place where we currently sit, is neither provable nor tangible. This realm, so beautiful, that we have come to know so well, is outside the purview of the conscious mind. It is a human possibility, like love. I defy you to prove that love exists."

"I wouldn't even want to begin," Marianne mused. "Trying to prove the existence of love would besmirch it. Believing in love makes it special."

"But trying to prove the existence of *magnétisme animale* will not besmirch it. I believe that these learned gentlemen, led by your own Ben Franklin, *will* successfully show that modern science cannot prove the existence of *magnétisme animale*. Nor will they be able to disprove it through their examination. They may or may not enlighten the world about the true meaning of this marvelous human quality—I doubt that they will—but it is certainly my hope that they will discredit Mesmer as the sole owner, inventor, and proprietor of the force that we know exists.

"Someday mankind may come to appreciate the full capacity of the unconscious mind in sickness and in health, the ways in which we are all connected, the wisdom of the flock. Unfortunately, I do not believe that time is now." The Queen regarded Marianne for a moment. "Have you seen Ben since your return to Paris?"

"No."

"And why not?"

Marianne blushed. "I can't face Ben knowing that Mesmer wants me to spy for him."

"I see."

"My Queen," Marianne went on solemnly. "I am not sure that you understand fully—for I am not sure that even I understand what has happened between Ben and me. He has become more distant in the past few years. He doesn't answer my letters. He doesn't try to comfort me when I am sad. I have not seen him since my return because he is not the Ben I knew in London."

"People do change. Love sometimes comes to an end."

"Yes."

The two women sat quietly for a long time.

Marianne broke the silence. "And what of you and me?" she asked plaintively.

"Marianne, you have a wonderful gift, the ability to see what is wrong with people through the power of *magnétisme animale*. I hope that you will continue to aid mankind through it. I trust by now, I need not tell you that you can do all that you do already—and more—without the hand of Herr Doctor Mesmer." She paused. "As for me . . ."

The Queen sat, serenely peaceful, upon her throne and looked out in the direction of Libra. The scales tipped slowly to one side.

"What of you, my Queen?" Marianne asked.

"Marianne, I have seen many marvelous things in our travels here. But just now, I am concerned to see the storm clouds of civil unrest gathering over our kingdom. After the revolutionary experience in America—an effort His Majesty and I fully supported—there is some danger for any monarchy. In my dreams, I have seen a terrible machine, an instrument of death, a sharp steel blade, and it frightens me to my bones. I fear that I may have peered too deeply into Pandora's jar already."

The Queen shuddered. "Marianne—this will be my last flight with you. I must stay in the 'real' world now. I want to care for my children and my husband. I want to care for my kingdom as best I can. You must travel alone from now on."

Marianne started to sob at the thought of losing her friend. The flock soon gathered around them.

The walk home from the *Place Vendôme* was lonely for Marianne despite the festive atmosphere of the Paris streets in spring. She glanced over the *Pont Neuf*, hoping to hear Basque folk singing. There was none. She wondered what it would take to make her happy once again.

April 4th, 1784

PARIS

JACQUES LERAY SUBSCRIBED to a box at the *Concert Spirituel* every year, although he rarely, if ever, attended. Ben enjoyed the public concerts for their variety. Started in 1725 to fill a gap in the theatrical and operatic calendar over the high holidays, they had become a welcome addition to the spring social scene in Paris. Where the opera had become rigid and overly regimented, obsessed with literal interpretations of the classical works, the *Concert Spirituel* series, was, in contrast, lively and unpredictable. Joseph Legros, the famous operatic star, had ably directed it for the past seven seasons. He did not shy away from staging concerts with music written by some less acknowledged, but still living, composers such as Wolfgang Mozart and Joseph Haydn. Their works provided an energy and freshness not likely to be found at the more established venues.

Ben was particularly looking forward to tonight's concert by Maria Theresa Paradis. After the stories Madame Leray had told him about her, Ben would not have missed this concert for anything. He wondered if Mesmer would be there.

The coach buzzed with excited banter as Ben, Madame Leray, and Benny rode from Passy toward the *Tuileries* Palace. On their way into Paris, they would pick up Minette and Mrs. Jay at their respective homes in Auteuil. Benny, now fifteen, seemed unable to stop talking. He was interested in everything, from printing to kite flying. The coach approached Paris just as the sun was beginning to set. The light streamed across the cherry trees standing ready to explode with flowers. The air was fresh with spring. The warm glow of early twilight hovered over the city as they breezed past the *Tuileries Jardin* toward the Palace.

"Ah, there is no place on earth that compares with Paris in April," Sarah Jay said. Everyone agreed.

The coach pulled up at the door of the Palace. An impressive façade greeted the concertgoers as they gaily piled out onto the street. The two guards flanking the door were dressed for the occasion. Ceremonial pikes in hand, they stood silently by as the Leray party was admitted by the man checking names. Once inside, the ladies went to freshen up their powder.

Ben and Benny made their way through the lobby of the *Salle des Machines*. As they proceeded up the stairs, Ben was perturbed to find his foot had begun bothering him. After they found their way to the Leray box, Ben took a seat and removed his shoe. The theater floor below was filling up. Benny went to the railing overlooking the grand space.

"Granddad," he said, "this place is huge!"

"Yes, it is the largest theater on the Continent," Ben replied. He rubbed his great toe. "Perhaps the world."

"What is that?" Benny asked. He pointed to a large machine at the back of the stage.

Ben looked up. "That is one of the machines from which this theater gets its name."

The device had a gondola attached to a crane by thick ropes. A series of pulleys and gears was partially exposed as stagehands worked to move props around the set.

Benny watched the men work on the machinery. "It looks complicated," he said.

"Perhaps a bit, but it is simply an application of modern physical principles, my boy. I've heard that they sometimes fly actors, and even the royal family, around in it."

"That sounds like fun. May we ride in it?" Benny asked.

Ben chuckled. "Not tonight, my lad," Ben said.

The ladies entered the box from the hallway. Minette noticed Ben rubbing his foot.

She sat in the seat next to him. "Are you all right?" she asked.

"Yes, it is just Madame Gout tormenting me."

"Well, no more red wine and rich food for you."

"Harrumph," Ben said.

"Oh my!" Madame Leray exclaimed. She sat up abruptly in her seat.

Ben and Minette looked up to see what the matter was.

"What is it?" Ben asked.

"Isn't that ... Herr Mesmer?" she asked in a hushed tone.

"Where?"

Madame Leray turned her head toward Ben and Minette. "In the box across from us ... Don't all look now," she said. But it was too late. All of the occupants of their box stared across the cavernous space to the opposite side.

There sat Mesmer, smirking. The box was empty save for him. Ben was relieved to see that Marianne was not beside him. Mesmer wore his lavender robe embroidered with swirling mystical symbols. The thread used to make these designs must have been silver or gold, for they glinted in the late afternoon sunlight streaming in through the theater's clerestory windows. Had Mesmer worn a plain dark suit, he might have gone unnoticed. But his vanity had unmasked him. Through the choice of his costume, he had asked to be noticed, to stand out, to be seen as exceptional.

The theater, now nearly full of concertgoers, turned to recognize the wizard in their midst as if a wave had swept across the floor below them. The sound of hushed and random conversations turned to gasps, followed by more active jeers, followed by organized booing. A man threw a large tomato up from the floor of the theater toward where Mesmer was seated. Ben looked up in time to see the tomato splatter on the back wall of the empty box seat. Mesmer was gone; he had vanished, disappeared.

"I suppose many people must know the story of Maria Paradis and Mesmer—even in Paris," Madame Leray mused. The audience resumed its cheerful random banter.

"Yes, I suppose," Ben said. "But I wouldn't have expected that people coming to hear this young pianist would be armed."

"I always carry a tomato," Minette said blithely. "Just in case."

"In case of what?" Ben asked.

"In case of a really bad performance." She reached into her bag, produced a juicy red fruit, and pretended to hurl it.

"You wouldn't," Madame Leray said. She wore a shocked look on her face. "Not from my box!"

"No, of course not," Minette said. She laughed mischievously. She took a big bite from the tomato, then offered it to Ben.

"And you shan't assault Miss Paradis with it if the fruit has been devoured," he said. He took a bite. Juice dribbled down his chin.

"Tomato is undoubtedly good for the gout as well," Minette said. She daintily wiped the juice from his face.

Ben took his handkerchief out and dabbed the corners of her mouth lovingly.

"You two love birds make me ill," Madame Leray said with mock disgust.

A fanfare from the orchestra pit brought a hush over the crowd. As the curtain went up, Mademoiselle Paradis was revealed sitting motionless at the pianoforte center stage. If she had been affected in any way by the earlier presence of Mesmer, she didn't show it. Monsieur Legros introduced her, to generous applause. She turned her head toward the audience, acknowledging its attention, but said nothing. There was no sheet music in front of her. She appeared uncommonly thin to Ben, a wisp of a girl with long dark hair tied in a blue bow. Her formal dress appeared to be made of flowing black satin. It ended just above her feet, clad in dainty black shoes, which rested on a small wooden box designed to keep her legs from dangling. Her sinewy arms, bare from just below her shoulders, terminated in fine hands with unusually long fingers that Ben could appreciate even from this distance.

As she began to play, the huge *Salle* became completely silent. She played with such soaring emotion that Ben felt it well up in his throat several times. He looked over at the ladies. They all had tears in their eyes. Benny was the only one who seemed unaffected by the music. He had his head propped on his hand, apparently bored or sleeping. Mademoiselle Paradis played several pieces of her own composition, as well as some that Ben recognized by Wolfgang Mozart. She played a portion of one concerto in B flat major that Ben found out later had been written especially for her, but not yet finished by the young master. She ended with a Haydn concerto in D Major that brought the house down with thunderous applause – finally arousing Benny from his lethargy.

The party was much more subdued on the way home. Talk of the power of music found everyone in agreement that it was a universal language.

"Music is a moral law. It gives soul to the universe, wings to the mind, flight to the imagination, and charm and gaiety to life and to everything," Ben said.

"You quote Plato," Minette affirmed. "If music be the food of love, play on," she went on dreamily.

"Shakespeare's Twelfth Night," Ben replied. He squeezed her hand.

It was dark outside as they whisked away from the city. After they dropped off Mrs. Jay at her home in Auteuil, Minette tugged on Ben's sleeve. She gave him a wink. Nothing more needed to be communicated. Ben asked Madame Leray if she would assure that Benny got straight to bed. She said that she would, with a knowing smile.

April 26th, 1784

PASSY

BEN SCRIBBLED A FEW NOTES in his pocket journal. He had just finished his morning tea when Madame Leray knocked on the door of his lodgings. His foot was propped up. The throbbing of his great toe felt only slightly better now, covered as it was by a cool, wet towel.

"Come in," Ben bellowed. He did not wish to get up.

"*Bonjour*," Madame Leray said gaily. She entered with a tray of scones.

"Good morning," he grumbled. He rubbed his great toe. He tucked the journal into his pants pocket.

"So, grumpy! I am sorry to see that you are not well," she said. "Have you been disregarding the advice of Madame Gout?" She put the tray within his reach on the table but removed the butter.

"No, I have been quite austere in my libations."

"Then, I shall be forced to inform your lady friends that you need more exercise."

"Thank you, Marie-Thérèse, but I can take care of that. I think that I shall go for a swim."

The cool waters of the Seine once again worked their magical healing powers on Ben's gouty foot. His mind wandered.

Ben glided through the smooth water and studied the forms of the clouds rolling by overhead. Unfortunately, one looked like a man wearing a wizard's robe. The cloud seemed to be pursuing him. It blocked the sun. Ben tried to ignore it.

Ben spied a kite flying over the river. He followed it. The red diamond-shaped paper rose and dipped jauntily in the bright blue sky. Ben tried to trace its string back to the earth and was surprised to see that it appeared to originate in the middle of the river. Ben triangulated his position and the effect of the river current to intercept the origination of the string, then he stepped up his stroke to reach that spot. As Ben approached the position, he recognized that another swimmer was anchoring the string.

"Benny," Ben yelled. "Whatever are you doing?" Ben took a closer look at the lad, who had a harness fashioned around his chest to which the kite string was attached. He appeared to be in tow behind the large kite, which was acting as a sail.

"I am flying a kite while swimming."

"I can see that. To what end?"

"I wanted to see if the kite would power my swim."

"How is your experiment going?"

"Well, I have traveled farther than ever before," the boy said proudly.

"And how are you planning to get back?"

"I hadn't thought of that," Benny said. He looked worried.

"Well, I reckon that you had better cut that thing loose before it pulls you too close to the city side. I can tell you that the river water is not nearly so pleasant nearer the opposite bank."

"All right, Granddad." Benny sounded disappointed but flipped onto his back and released the kite string from his harness. The wind swiftly carried it out of sight toward the far shore. The wizard-shaped cloud had also vanished.

As the two swimmers arrived at the dock of the Hôtel de Valentinois, Ben was tired, but Benny appeared exhausted. The lad dragged himself out of the river onto the sun-warmed boards and simply lay there panting for a few moments. Ben donned his robe. He threw a towel at the prostrate boy.

"Part of any successful experiment is to plan for contingencies," Ben said, beginning to lecture.

Benny lay with his eyes closed but said nothing.

Ben realized he was being a pedant and that he didn't need to rub it in. "All right, I hope you've gained some knowledge from this experience."

Benny sat up. He toweled off his mop of dark brown hair. Ben went over and tousled it. They both laughed.

"Granddad?" Benny asked. "Will you help me set some type today?"

Ben recalled his schedule. Other than nursing his gouty foot, it was clear. "Yes, as long as I do not have to stand."

"Of course, Granddad," Benny said. "I will do all the press work."

Several blissful hours passed that day in the press shop at the Hôtel de Valentinois. Madame Leray brought down sliced meats, cheeses, and bread around one o'clock in the afternoon. The day proved warm enough to keep all the doors and windows of the shop wide open. It was after three, and Benny was pulling a final proof off the press, when Ben heard a horse arriving. He looked up from rearranging his typeset box to find Jean-Baptiste Le Roy dismounting. He tied up his horse and knocked on the open door of the shop.

The wiry scientist entered, a newspaper tucked under his arm.

"Ben," Le Roy exclaimed. He unfolded the morning newspaper, patting it for effect. "Your letter to the editor describing the cost savings of resetting the clocks to more reflect the hours of daylight is *magnifique*. You have outdone yourself once again."

"Thank you, my friend. But hopefully, you did not travel across Kingswood only to congratulate me."

"No, of course not," Le Roy said. "Am I the 'learned natural philosopher' you referred to in the letter?"

"Jean-Baptiste, the letter was a product of my whimsy. I was not specifically envisioning any real person as the 'learned natural philosopher.' You and I have discussed many topics over the course of our friendship including, light, darkness, and keeping the windows open. So, of course, in many ways, your wise counsel has shaped my thinking over these years."

"Then let me say this," Le Roy replied. He became more animated. "The logic that you used in this printed letter is impeccable. Another reason for my visit today, aside from enjoying your warm company, Ben, is to ask that you contemplate how we might apply some of the same logical principles to the upcoming commission investigation."

"You must have been reading my mind," Ben said. "I have already been thinking of methods to set up just such experiments." He pulled the small journal from his pocket. By the time Madame Leray brought supper to them, the two scientists had mapped out a plan.

April 27th, 1784

PARIS

MARIANNE WAS INCREDULOUS. "You did what?" She dropped her fork.

Marko sounded proud. "We busted them up," he said.

He, Paulo, and Yorge lifted their goblets full of red wine in a toast. All three looked as if they had imbibed too much already. Alize rolled her eyes. Lili covered hers with a thumb on one temple and her index finger on the other. The two women were only too accustomed to the antics of the three young men, Marianne surmised.

"Please don't tell me that you have committed a crime," Marianne beseeched.

"I don't think so," Marko said, but with enough hesitancy that it quickly deflated his boasting. The others were silent.

"All right, then recount for me what happened from the beginning."

"It all began when the wizard showed up here yesterday morning."

"Mesmer?"

"Yes."

"The day you arrived in Paris? He must have been waiting for you. I didn't even discover that you were here until today."

"And I am so glad that you came to dine with us tonight," Marko said. He gave an inebriated tip of his hat.

"Go on," Marianne prodded. "What happened with Mesmer?"

"Well, as you say, the wizard shows up just as soon as we arrive. He is not wearing his robe ... just a regular suit of clothes ... a fine suit mind you ..."

"Go on."

"He says he has a job for me and my men, as he calls them." Marko pointed to Paulo and Yorge, who had returned to eating.

"What kind of job?"

"He says that someone stole some machines from him," Marko said, "but he doesn't want them back ... he just wants them broken. Says that he is willing to pay a good sum of money.

Well, I had paid Mesmer handsomely, hoping for a cure for my Maria. So, he offers half of what I paid him. Give me the whole amount, I say. We settle on three fourths. He tells me that his machines are way out in Kingswood, in the Royal Scientific Laboratory."

Marianne was stunned by the news. Mesmer had never done anything like this before, at least to her knowledge.

"Didn't that seem odd to you, that he would send you way out there to destroy some machines?"

Marko looked a bit sheepish. "Not at the time ... no," he said.

"Go on."

"So, he gives me a description of the machines he wants broken. Tells me that only the director's wife will be home in the evening."

"How did he know that?"

"I have no idea."

"Go on."

"So, we rent horses, and the boys and I ride out there last night. It is not the easiest place to find in the dark, mind you, but getting in was easy. The place was empty. No one about at all. We each take up a big plank and start smashing things. Did the job real good if you ask me."

"I am sure that you did. What about Mesmer?"

"He came around this morning, did he, with a fat purse and tossed it from the bridge. You don't think we did anything illegal, do you?" He looked sheepish again.

Marianne glanced at him to ascertain whether or not he was kidding. Surely the laws of Spain and France could not be so different. "Let's see ... breaking and entering, destroying public property, conspiracy ... no, nothing illegal."

"But he said the stuff was his."

"And you believed him?"

"Yes, I guess so."

"Have you gone mad? How could you be so foolish? I wouldn't go boasting about your escapades last night to anyone else." Marianne gave him an angry shove. "But you may want to think about heading back to Bilbao early this year. And no more 'jobs' for Herr Mesmer, all right?"

"Yes. But we just got here. Do you really think that we should head home early?"

"Possibly ... if there are repercussions to your actions ... but not tonight, though." She smiled.

"No, definitely not tonight." He smiled back at her.

April 29th, 1784

PASSY

JEAN-BAPTISTE LE ROY burst into Ben's lodgings at the Hôtel Valentinois. "Ben, they are all smashed!" he exclaimed.

"Jean-Baptiste, whatever *are* you on about?" Ben asked. He looked up from his morning newspaper.

"While I was out at the Society of Universal Harmony meeting two nights ago, someone broke into the Laboratory and smashed the electrical instruments."

"Who would do such a thing? Have you alerted the gendarmerie?"

"Yes, but they have no suspects. The grounds were deserted except for my wife … and she says she heard nothing. She went to bed early. No one was seen. The gendarmes will have little to go on except for some hoof prints."

"Can the instruments be replaced?"

"Happily, I have a completely new set locked up in storage."

"You do?"

"Ben, His Majesty is very generous with funding for the laboratory equipment. I would have had the new instruments out sooner, but you know how I don't like to waste anything. I was waiting until the old ones were completely worn out."

Ben laughed. "That is just like you, my friend. Well, I suppose that you will now have to install the new ones."

"Yes." Then Le Roy looked pensive. "Would you consider that someone was attempting to stop the commission by this attack?"

"I wonder . . ."

"Mesmer was at the meeting I attended that night."

"Yes, but he knew that you would be there also."

"Do you mean that he could have sent someone to do it?"

"I don't know. Just the same, I believe that we should keep this as quiet as we can. It would be in our best interests if our adversary, whoever that is, does not know that you have all new equipment."

"Agreed. And I have requested that a guard be posted at the laboratory around the clock until we are done with the commission work."

"Good."

April 30th, 1784

PARIS

BEN WAS INTENT ON ENJOYING the opera tonight. He would share the Leray box with his hostess and Mrs. Jay. Even better, Minette had invited him over for a nightcap afterward. It promised to be a perfect evening.

The opera house was resplendent. *Les Danaïdes* had opened on the 26th to good reviews but also some controversy. Originally billed as having been written by Glück, it was now becoming clear that Antonio Salieri was the true composer. The newspapers were having a field day with the revelation. Ben had no love for the work of Glück, the composer was well past his prime. He was glad that the young Salieri was getting the credit he deserved.

Ben waved at Madame Brillon across the way as he found his seat in the Leray box. Her posture was exquisite. She looked like a porcelain doll, beautiful but cold.

Ben knew the tragic story of this opera well. The first act began with Danaus betrothing his fifty daughters to wed the fifty sons of his dead brother, and enemy, Egyptus. The wedding was intended to reconcile the family, but the goddess of vengeance, Nemesis, would not be placated. The characters of Lyncée and Hypermnestre, eldest son and daughter of Egyptus and Danaus respectively, were beautifully portrayed. They sang of their love for one another even while Ben, and most of the audience, knew of the tragedy that awaited them; Danaus planned to have all of his daughters kill their husbands on their wedding night.

As the opera came to its climatic fifth act, with the palace of Danaus going up in flames, Ben began to feel queasy. He put his hand on his stomach, but it was not upset. He felt his pulse. It was quicker than normal, unusual. His gaze kept returning to the mock flames on stage with a feeling of vague discomfort.

The curtain came down, and the house lights were lit. "You don't look well," Madame Leray said to Ben.

"I don't feel well, either," Ben said.

"I am sorry. I hope that my supper did not upset your stomach."

"No, I don't believe that is the problem ... but I am not sure exactly what is."

"Perhaps some fresh air will do you good."

"I hope so," Ben said. He made his way down the stairs of the theater with one lady on each arm.

Well-wishers practically mobbed him in the foyer, but Ben barely heard them.

As soon as the trio made it out to the street, Ben recognized one of the Leray stable boys on horseback alongside their coach. It was then he knew something must be wrong. The boy jumped down. He ran over toward their group, fighting his way through the crowd. On the other side of the street, a familiar menacing figure in a lavender satin robe stood alone under a streetlamp.

"Mr. Ben, Mr. Ben," the boy was yelling as he rushed through the crowd. "There has been a fire!"

Several of the nearby operagoers turned toward the boy with alarmed expressions. Ben pulled him close. He glanced across the street, but the robed figure had vanished.

"Tell me what happened, my boy," he said.

"Mr. Ben, there has been a fire at your lodgings ... the printing press building," he said breathlessly. "The butler sent me to fetch you, but they said I could not go in until the show was over."

"That is understandable. Is everything all right at the Hôtel de Valentinois?"

"Yes, at least I believe it to be so. They were still working on putting out the fire when I ran to fetch you. But it was discovered early and contained to the one building as far as I know."

"Thank you, my boy," Ben said. He gave the lad an affectionate pat on the back of his head. "Would you do something else for me?"

"Yes, sir."

"Would you ride now to the home of Madame Helvétius in Auteuil? And when you get there, tell her what happened tonight and that I will not be able to visit her just now."

The boy ran to his horse and leapt on with a youthful exuberance at which Ben could only marvel. Ben and the ladies boarded the coach. Madame Leray instructed the driver to make for home with the utmost haste. There was little talk of the *Les Danaïdes*. Everyone sat in tense silence.

Despite the late hour, the coach was met at the Hôtel de Valentinois by what appeared to be the entire house staff.

Ben stepped down after Madame Leray. He was quickly escorted down the hill by the butler and a few of the stable hands. He was told that the blaze had been put out but that some damage had been done. No one knew the cause of the conflagration but given that it had occurred away from the kitchen, it seemed suspicious. One of the maids had reported that she had seen a man leaving the grounds on horseback just as the alarm was sounded. No one had recognized him.

Benny stood in the building that had housed the printing press, staring down at a tray of what used to be rows of lead typeface, now a molten blob.

"Benny, are you alright?" Ben asked with concern as soon as he entered the building.

"Yes, Granddad, but look at this mess."

"Don't worry, my boy," Ben said consolingly. "We can get more type. What happened?"

"I was sleeping when I smelled smoke," Benny said. "I looked outside and saw the press building on fire. I ran up the hill and yelled, and everyone came running with buckets of water from the main house. We started a bucket brigade from the river to here. The fire burned up the back of the building but never got in. The heat through the wall melted these lines of type." He pointed to the leaden mess.

"Yes, I can see that. I am just glad that you are safe." He gave his grandson a hug.

Ben went around to the back of the building with a lantern. The air smelled thickly of oily smoke, but it was too dark to see very much. Deciding that he would investigate further in the morning, he went back and told Benny to go to bed. The house staff finished up cleaning as best they could and headed back up the hill.

Ben took off his clothes and climbed into his own bed, feeling uneasy. It seemed that someone was targeting him. Trying to scare him off. And who else but Mesmer? After all, the wizard had been brazen enough to appear outside the opera. Or had he been a figment of his imagination? Ben knew it must have to do with the commission. He was still sitting up in his bed when he heard a gentle knock. Thinking that it was Benny unable to sleep, he wrapped a blanket around himself and went to the door. He opened it only to find Minette standing there.

"Would you like some company?" she asked.

"Yes, of course," Ben said.

"Good, then open up that blanket and let me in next to you. I'm frozen."

"By all means."

"Where have you been? You smell of smoke." Marianne asked Antoine as he entered Mesmer's apartment. She had just been preparing to head back to her hotel when she'd heard the front door open. Mesmer snored down the hall.

"Never mind. Where is the Doctor?"

"Sleeping."

Marianne took a closer look at Mesmer's valet. He looked upset. "Come on, out with it," she said. "You look shaken. How about a drink?"

Antoine softened slightly. "All right."

They walked into the kitchen. Marianne cut two large wedges of cheese and poured out two good draughts of wine. Antoine, usually the cook as well as the valet, found a baguette and brought it over to the table with two pewter plates.

"He ordered me to do it," Antoine muttered.

"To do what?"

"To set fire to Franklin's lodgings."

"What?" Marianne exclaimed so loudly that she stopped to listen for the snoring down the hall. It continued unabated. "What exactly did you do?"

"He told me that Franklin needed to be stopped from proceeding with his commission."

"So, he proposed arson as the method?"

"I didn't want to hurt anyone. I simply went to Passy to do as I was ordered. I set a small fire to the back of one of the buildings at the Hôtel de Valentinois. Then I ran. They were already putting it out when I left."

"Antoine, you should know better than this. Someone could have gotten hurt … or killed."

"Yes. I rode back home feeling terrible. I don't care if he dismisses me. I won't do anything like that for him again."

"Good."

As Marianne walked alone through the deserted streets, she thought about what Mesmer was doing. First, the destruction of the equipment at the Royal Scientific Laboratory and now the attempt to intimidate Ben through arson. She decided that she needed to confront him.

Gretchen, Le Veillard's barmaid, sat *en rapport* with Mesmer when Marianne arrived at the storefront clinic the next day. She waited until they were done, then followed his lavender robe into the small back office. He sat down in his chair.

"You are a bastard."

"I love you too," he said dismissively. "What is this about, Marianne?"

"It is about setting fire to Ben's printing press building."

"I didn't do it," Mesmer objected.

"But you caused it to be done—it is the same thing."

"Perhaps," he replied. "I should have done it myself. That incompetent valet of mine doesn't know a printing press building from an apartment."

"Do you mean to say that you intended to burn down his lodgings?" Marianne asked incredulously.

"He was at the opera."

"But his grandson was sleeping, according to the newspaper report. What if the boy had been killed?"

Mesmer shook his head briefly, as if to dismiss her question and rose to his feet. He gestured at her with agitation. "That man must be stopped," he said.

"And why is that?"

"Because he is jeopardizing all this." Mesmer motioned around him.

"He is only doing what the King has asked."

"Oh, Marianne," Mesmer said. "Do you truly believe that? By attempting to discredit or disprove *magnétisme animale*, your Ben Franklin is acting out of motives even he does not understand. He is jealous of me—of my fame and importance, but also of the fact that I have you in my bed. He wants to punish me. And he also wants to stop me for the same reason as all those other quacks and imposters. They want to steal my discovery. They want to make the profit that is rightfully mine. Yet none of them can even begin to understand what I have discovered—so instead, they condemn it."

He was on a rant, recounting the all-too-familiar litany of doctors and scientists who dismissed his work, the injustice that he was not recognized for his genius, his determination to ruin his enemies. Marianne knew that to argue with him now would only prolong it. She slumped in a chair, buffeted for a full ten minutes by his manic anger.

"Now, are you finally ready to help me?" Mesmer asked.

"What do you want from me?" she said, her weary tone covering her trepidation.

"I want you to ask Franklin to stop the commission."

"And you believe he would do that for me?"

"Yes, I do," Mesmer said flatly.

"You're wrong," Marianne said. "And besides, I won't do it."

"Oh, yes, you will." He sounded more threatening than Marianne had ever heard him before.

"What if I don't?"

"I will take away your power. I will cut you off from *magnétisme animale*. I will ban you from the flock. I will send you to depths of melancholia so foul that you will never return."

Marianne fell silent for a moment, stunned by the vituperation of his threat. She realized that some of what he claimed he would do was mere bluster, but she wasn't entirely sure how extensive his powers were.

In the end, she agreed to talk with Ben. She made no promises about the outcome.

May 6th, 1784

CHEVAL SAUVAGE,
OUTSKIRTS OF PARIS

The early morning ride with Le Veillard was pleasant, yet Ben was filled with an apprehension that would not abate. Something about Marianne's invitation .... It was written in the same inscrutably small script that he had struggled with for so many years. It smelled the same. It arrived tied up with the same pink ribbon. Yet something was different about this one. Perhaps it was that the message was so terse. It simply read:

> *Ben, are you able to meet me at Room 11 on Thursday, May 6th? Early.*

> M

There was no expression of love in it. There were no frills, no playfulness, no flirtation. Perhaps that was it. Or perhaps it was the memory of the way that they had ended their last meeting there in September, eight months ago now. It had appeared that everything might be over between them then.

Room 11 looked particularly dingy as Ben opened the creaky door. A few dust particles danced in the weak beams of sunlight streaming from between the lacy curtains. Initially, he didn't notice Marianne sitting, arms folded, in a wing chair, obscured as she was by shadows. Only when she moved to take down the hood of her cape did she appear.

"Oh, you *are* here," Ben said.

"Yes." Her tone was impossible to read.

Marianne moved to get up and walked over toward Ben. She wore a plain dress under her cape and appeared to have been crying. It was quite a different mood than their first encounter here.

"Ben, I am worried about you," she said, tentatively.

"Why?" He took the cape from her shoulders. She didn't resist ... but she didn't assist either.

"Because you could have been hurt. The fire at your lodgings."

"I was at the opera when it happened. What do you know about the fire?" Ben asked. He put his hands on her hips. Once again, she didn't resist his advance but didn't reciprocate. She kept her hands at her sides.

"Only what I read in the newspaper," she said.

Ben put his hands on her shoulders and unfastened her dress. She allowed her dress to drop to the floor.

"It was an amateurish attempt at arson," Ben said. He buried his face in her hair. Her aroma was the same, yet there was something wrong. She stood there, limply.

"It might have had a much worse outcome," Marianne said.

"Yes, I suppose."

"Ben, do you believe that it was on account of the commission?"

"What makes you say that?" Ben removed his hands from her bare shoulders. He took a step back, his amorous concentration broken.

"I don't know. It just seems that someone might be trying to warn you."

"I am not easily scared off," Ben said proudly. "Do you recall the time in London when I was being harassed after presenting the American case at Parliament? It seemed I might be thrown in the Tower on charges of being a spy—or worse."

"Yes, I remember," she said. But she said it in such a weak voice that Ben wondered if she truly did.

"So, this is nothing. A demented wizard who wants only to maintain his pecuniary advantage."

"He is not demented."

Ben looked at her askance. "Oh?"

Her tone softened. "He is many things," she said. "But he is not demented."

"Marianne, let's not fight. What are we here to do?" Ben slid his hands down to her hips.

Marianne's expression changed. While up until now she had been calm, even passive, she quickly became angry. She pushed him away.

"I am asking something of you, and all you can think about is my body," she said coldly. "Nothing ever affects you. You go through life as if nothing you do has any consequences for those around you."

"That is not true," Ben replied weakly.

"So won't you stop this foolishness with the commission?"

"It is not 'foolishness'. And no, I won't stop."

Marianne put on her dress and left in a huff. Ben briefly thought about chasing after her, but he didn't.

Marianne stormed down the stairs of the *Cheval Sauvage*. Ben had acted not at all as she had hoped. She had hoped that possibly he would soften; perhaps he would even acquiesce. But even before she got all the way down the stairs, she realized that he was just being Ben. It was she who was asking the impossible this time. She wondered if she should run back upstairs and throw her arms around him. A part of her wanted to go back and make love to him. Yet, she didn't turn around. She kept walking away.

As she crossed the door leading into the bar, Marianne saw Gretchen preparing something that looked like tea. There was no one else in the bar yet. It seemed odd.

"Gretchen, what are you doing?"

With a start, the young barmaid dropped a ring she was holding on the wooden bar. "What?" she said, clearly startled. She looked directly at Marianne. It seemed as if she had just awakened from a trance.

"I asked what you were doing," Marianne said.

She could see that the ring was heavy and ornate, with a flat embossed surface. The top was hinged, and had sprung open, revealing a secret compartment.

Marianne recognized the ring. She had seen it on Mesmer many times. Its chalky gray contents had spilled across the polished wood of the bar.

"Fixing Doctor Franklin's tea," Gretchen said. She moved to sweep up the substance with her hands.

"No!" Marianne cried out. She rushed for the bar. She was able to grab Gretchen's hands just before they touched the powder.

"A delicious and refreshing tea," Gretchen said dreamily.

"Wake up, Gretchen." Marianne shook her gently. The barmaid seemed to come around more now.

"Oh my," she exclaimed as she saw the mess on the bar.

"What is that powder, Gretchen?"

"I don't know," Gretchen said. She looked frightened.

"Don't touch it. I fear it may be poison." Marianne grabbed a wet rag from a nearby pail and wiped the bar clean. "Where did you get that ring?" She picked up the now empty jewelry, closed its secret compartment, and tucked it in her pocket.

"I don't know," Gretchen repeated. She now seemed more befuddled.

"Have you been working with Doctor Mesmer recently?"

"Yes, why only a few days ago . . ." Her voice trailed off.

"Will you be so kind as to thoroughly wash everything that you have touched this morning and then fix Ben a strong cup of fresh tea?"

"Yes, of course."

"Good."

"Marianne, I won't be in trouble, will I?"

"Not now, you won't ... but I would stay away from Doctor Mesmer for a while if I were you." Marianne put on the most reassuring smile that she could under the circumstances.

"Yes, if you say so."

Marianne pulled her cape back over her head. She swept out of the *Cheval Sauvage* onto the brightening avenue still empty at this early hour.

Ben watched her disappear up the street for the last time. He closed Room 11, intending to have a good hot cup of tea downstairs before heading home.

Marianne walked briskly into the city, heading toward Mesmer's clinic. Along the way, she crossed the *Pont Neuf*. She peered down to see two uniformed officers speaking with Marko. They seemed to be having a heated discussion. Marianne put her head down and walked on.

At the clinic, she confronted Mesmer directly, not waiting for him to retreat to the privacy of his office. She walked toward him as he was in the middle of conducting a séance. She took the ring from her pocket and hurled it at him.

He howled as the missile hit its mark. A trickle of blood ran down his forehead.

"You monster," Marianne yelled.

Mesmer recovered his bearing quickly and picked up the ring from the floor. "Let us discuss your grievance in the privacy of my office," he said calmly as if the rest of his followers might take her to be a disgruntled patient. Then he grabbed her firmly by the arm and led her away.

Marianne stood in his office. "You tried to poison him," she fumed.

He walked over to a chair and sat. "I did not," he said. "How can you accuse me of such a thing?" He dabbed his forehead gingerly with a piece of gauze.

"What was in that ring of yours?"

"What ring?"

"The ring I threw at you. The one you now hold in your hand. The one I found this morning at the *Cheval Sauvage.*"

"A sleeping draught."

"You're lying," Marianne said.

"I keep it handy in case I need it. Or one of my patients does. It went missing a few days ago. I assumed that barmaid stole it."

"Why would Gretchen do such a thing?"

"I have no clue. It is pretty." He looked at the ring as he slipped it back on his finger. "Perhaps it might be worth something." He popped open the now empty reservoir. "But what has happened to the powder?" He spoke as if he had rehearsed these lines in case the poison ring were ever traced to him in a police inquiry.

"She was going to put it in his tea. I stopped her. She had no idea what she was doing."

"Poor girl," Mesmer said. "I don't know what is wrong with her."

"Are you going to sit there and tell me that you did not try to poison Ben?"

He looked at her intently. "I did not try to poison your Dr. Franklin," he said. "Now, may I ask you something?"

"What?"

"Did he agree to put a stop to the commission when you petitioned him?"

"No. I told you he would not."

"So you failed also ... ."

"Your words give you away, Monsieur." She turned to walk out.

As she left, Marianne heard Mesmer mutter in a low voice, "I must stop that man." She wondered what he might do next.

Walking back over the *Pont Neuf,* Marianne noted that Marko and his friends were all busily at work on the deck of the houseboat. As she drew closer, she saw that they were tying up ropes, packing boxes, putting away tables, and chairs. She realized that they were taking her advice and preparing to leave. Marianne ran the rest of the way across the bridge and down the steps to the river.

Marko spotted her running toward him. "Marianne," he yelled.

She nearly knocked him over as she fell into his arms. "What is happening?" she asked breathlessly.

"I am so glad that you arrived. We must leave."

"The *gendarmes*?"

"Yes, they discovered that we rented horses from the livery that night. I explained that we went out hunting for pheasant, but I do not expect that the officers believed me. They will be back with more questions."

"What will you do?"

"Return home to Bilbao."

Marianne started to sob. "Will you come back?"

"Not anytime soon. May I write to you?"

"Yes, but in Florence, not here in Paris."

Marko looked surprised. "You will leave also?"

"Yes, Marko, there is little left for me here now." Marianne's voice broke. "Be careful crossing the Alps."

"And you be careful sailing the Atlantic."

"I will miss you, Marianne."

"And I you, Marko."

Marianne felt sorry for herself all the way home. She went directly to bed. She mostly blamed Mesmer for her loss of both Ben and Marko, although the loss of Ben had been approaching for at least the last few years. She and Ben had grown apart, she realized, on many planes. His persistent clamoring for proof—even for things that could not, or should not, to her way of thinking, be proven—had caused a chasm between them that could no longer be bridged. The development of her inner vision, her ability to understand the wisdom of the flock, her desire and need to help people heal—Ben would scoff, and never understand. His part-time commitment— he loved her when she was gay but left her desolate and unconsoled when she was melancholy—she could never fathom. Why wouldn't he want to love her all the time? She would fall asleep thinking of his powerful hands touching her. When it came down to wanting a man's hands on her, they would always be Ben's. Yet, she couldn't help feeling that she might only have the memory of them left now.

At sunrise, Marianne donned a long dress with a flower print. Sitting next to each other in her closet were a pair of fashionable high-heeled pumps she had made Mesmer buy and her now well-worn Tyrolean hiking boots. She chose the boots. Marianne donned her cape and was about to leave through the window—force of habit—when she grabbed the pair of dainty shoes and tucked them under her arm. She strode out the door.

The street merchants, artists, and shopkeepers were all preparing for a routine day as Marianne walked toward the *Place Vendôme*. No one paid any attention to her. She started to hike over the *Pont Neuf* with mild apprehension. As she gazed over the side, she saw a vacancy where Marko's boat had been. Marianne pulled out the dainty shoes and tossed them into the river. They barely made a splash—but a nearby river rat dove for cover at the intrusion. Marianne laughed. It felt good.

"I had better go keep my eye on that bastard Mesmer," she thought. She hiked on.

PART
VII

May 9th, 1784

PARIS

THE COMMISSIONERS had arranged to meet at the home of Doctor Charles D'Eslon in Paris. True to his word, Mesmer had steadfastly refused to open up his clinic or practice. However, D'Eslon, having been convinced by Doctor Guillotin, had said that he would be willing to demonstrate the effects of *magnétisme animale* to the members of the commission.

The street in front of D'Eslon's stately home was lined with coaches. Ben arrived in the Leray coach. He had picked up Professor Le Roy on his way into Paris. The two stepped down to find the street in a carnival atmosphere. A technician from the Royal Scientific Laboratory was unloading a wagonful of sparkling new instruments in front of them. The *gendarmes* had created a corridor from the street to the entrance of the house, attempting to keep back the curious public and the newspaper reporters crowding around. Ben and Jean-Baptiste made their way inside. A doorman guided them to the library.

Ben greeted the other distinguished members of the commission already gathered. In addition to Bailly, Lavoisier, and Guillotin, Ben recognized Majault, D'Arcet, Sallin, and DeBory. Nine commissioners stood around nine chairs, arranged three across by three deep. They all sat down just as Doctor D'Eslon entered the room, looking dour. He wore a dark red flowing robe with mystical symbols embroidered on it, similar to the garment Ben associated with Mesmer. The commissioners fell silent.

"Gentlemen," D'Eslon began, with a deadly serious demeanor. "There is but one nature, one distemper, and one remedy ... and that remedy is *magnétisme animale.*"

There were a few coughs, but after a brief pause, D'Eslon pressed ahead with an icy stare at anyone who might dare to interrupt.

"Those are the words of Doctor Franz Anton Mesmer. Today, I intend to present to you the theory and practice of *magnétisme animale.*"

Ben had to admire his courage. Ostracized by the Faculty of Medicine for his beliefs, hounded by the reporters, and speaking to the commissioners today in what Ben assumed must be a clear violation of his signed oath of confidentiality, yet he appeared confident, clearheaded, and organized. How much easier it would have been for D'Eslon simply to refuse to cooperate as well, continue his lucrative practice, and laugh up his sleeve at his detractors. For him to even be here today took pluck, as well as clear faith and belief in what he was attempting to prove. As much as he might have disliked the man personally, Ben resolved that he would endeavor to assure that D'Eslon did not become a victim of the commission process.

"There is a healing fluid that emanates from the stars ... Planetary influences on the human body ... Tides and cycles affect sickness and health . . ." D'Eslon droned on with the Mesmeric dogma Ben had heard since soon after his arrival in Paris. His mind drifted. Ben became more interested as the doctor began to describe the technique of *en rapport.*

D'Eslon unveiled a large anatomical drawing of the female body—quite lifelike in Ben's estimation—that prompted a few hushed comments from the distinguished scientists, but no one asked for her to be covered up. D'Eslon theorized the nervous connections between the hypochondrium and thigh with certain parts of the brain. A question was raised as to the anatomical legitimacy of these connections—a question to which D'Eslon did not have a cogent answer. After an hour of didactic theory, the lecture ended, and D'Eslon asked the commissioners to step into the large treatment room next door.

There they found that a baquet had been set up in the center of the darkened room. Soothing armonica music played. Around the periphery of the tub, patients sat in various states of rapport with staff. D'Eslon stood in front of the baquet as he described the design. It was filled with 'magnetized' water, he explained, and the rods that rose from the baquet communicated the magnetic fluid to the injured or suffering body part. He showed the commissioners the method of attaching a rope around the patients at the baquet to encircle and contain the *magnétisme animale*.

A technician had set up an electrometer in the room. Under the commissioners' instructions, the leads were attached to various rods and to other metal surfaces of the baquet, in several configurations. No electricity registered with any configuration. Ben made a note of it. Next, a needle of iron not touched with a lodestone—a device capable of detecting very small effects of mineral magnetism—was brought into proximity with the various metal parts of the baquet. Once again, no effect was noted. Ben scribbled on his pad that there was no detectable electrical fluid or magnetical substance associated with the baquet or rods.

The commissioners carefully observed the group of patients undergoing treatment. There were three distinct reactions, Ben noted. One type of patient remained calm, often sitting with eyes closed as if in a very restful state throughout the entire process. A second one would cough, or expectorate. This type of patient might show other physical symptoms—beads of sweat on the brow, an uncomfortable expression on the face, or report a burning sensation where the rod from the baquet touched the body.

The third type of patient was the one who developed a 'convulsion' upon contact with the baquet or rod. Ben watched as a woman grabbed hold of the rod and thrust it inside her dress. She placed it under her left breast. Almost immediately, she developed a wild look in her eyes. She began to vocalize, alternating between shrill shrieks and immoderate laughter. Her limbs began to twitch. Suddenly she fell to the floor in what looked to Ben very much like an epileptic fit. Doctor Guillotin rushed to her side. He supported her head, but then he looked perplexed.

Ben knelt down next to the doctor and the stricken woman. "What is it?" he asked.

"I do not believe that this is an epileptic seizure," Guillotin replied.

"Why do you say that?"

"Ben, look at her face. Her body is undergoing these rigors, these contorted movements, yet they do not affect her face. Observe how she continues to maintain this iron rod clutched to her breast. See how she flails, yet she manages not to strike anything. She does no damage to her limbs with the motions. She has lost no urinary or bowel continence as far as I can tell."

Ben examined the woman's face. Her eyes were looking straight ahead, not rolled back in her head. Her mouth was slightly open. There was no clenching of her jaw, no biting of her tongue. Her breathing was not unusually rapid.

"I must agree with you that this state is like no epileptic fit I have ever seen," Ben said.

"It is no epileptic fit at all," Guillotin replied.

Just at that moment, the music changed. The effect was almost instantaneous. Around the treatment room, several other patients started to shriek and moan. Ben observed that several of them dropped slowly to the floor with their arms and legs flailing. After a short time, the music changed once again. Calmness swept over the eerie scene. Ben shifted his attention from the convulsing patients to see D'Eslon sitting *en rapport* with the pretty German barmaid from the *Cheval Sauvage*, friend of Louis LeVeillard. She stared straight ahead.

As Ben approached, D'Eslon acknowledged him. "Doctor Franklin, I would like you to meet Gretchen."

"Hello, Gretchen," Ben said as if they had never met. She said nothing.

"Gretchen, say hello to Doctor Franklin," D'Eslon instructed.

"Hello, Doctor Franklin," she said. Her eyes stayed fixed straight ahead.

"Gretchen, may I have you demonstrate some of the effects of *magnétisme animale* for Doctor Franklin?"

"Yes."

"Gretchen, it is becoming very warm in the room. It is as if someone has put a few too many logs on the fire, or you are sitting too close. Unfortunately, you cannot move."

Ben turned his attention to Gretchen, who started to sweat profusely. Her skin had become more pink and mottled. Her breathing accelerated. She fanned herself with her hand.

"Good," D'Eslon said as he observed her reaction. "Now you have left the fire and gone outside. It is a cold, snowy day. Not a beautiful warm day like today. You have forgotten to take your coat. It is bitterly cold."

Ben looked back at Gretchen to see her shivering. She wrapped her arms around her chest. Her teeth started chattering.

"Good," D'Eslon said again. "Now, let's go back inside the warm house."

She relaxed. She rubbed her hands together as if in front of a fire.

"Now Gretchen," D'Eslon went on. "I am going to give you an instruction. Do you understand?"

"Yes."

"It is a very important instruction, and I don't want you to forget it."

"I won't."

D'Eslon looked pensive for a moment, and then he spoke. "When the commissioners are leaving today. I want you to give Doctor Franklin a kiss goodbye."

"But I hardly know him."

"It need not be a romantic kiss, just a peck on the cheek as he is leaving. Will you do that for me?"

"Yes."

"Now, when I clap my hands, I want you to wake up. You will not remember anything of your experience today. You will feel rested, refreshed—as if you had a short nap. You will feel perfectly well. All right?"

"All right."

D'Eslon clapped his hands. Gretchen snapped out of her trance with a slight jolt.

"Oh, my," she exclaimed. She looked around at the commissioners who had all gathered around for the demonstration.

"How do you feel?" Bailly asked.

"Wonderful," she replied, stretching luxuriantly.

The commissioners returned to the library, where D'Eslon resumed the didactic approach.

"This rod," he said, holding up a polished foot-long metal object resembling a semi-erect phallus, "is the conductor of *magnétisme animale*, which is concentrated at its point. Sound also transmits the fluid, and vice versa, so that when there is music in the treatment room, it potentiates the effect—as you saw demonstrated today. The rope, which is passed around the bodies of the patients, augments the effects as well. Lastly, the baquet is specially constructed to concentrate the *magnétisme animale* and is a grand reservoir from which the fluid is distributed through the iron rods."

The commissioners asked many questions of D'Eslon, and he patiently answered for quite some time.

"Was there any special preparation of the water in the baquet?"

"No, it was merely magnetized."

"How was it magnetized?"

D'Eslon pointed his finger at a glass of water. "Thusly."

"Is that water now magnetized?"

"Yes."

"So, if I were to drink it, would I feel better?"

"Yes."

"If another patient did not see you magnetize the water, would it still have the same effect?"

"Yes."

"Can you magnetize other objects besides water?"

"Yes."

"What, for example?"

"Just about anything can be magnetized, but trees and ceramic bowls or basins are often done so."

"Why trees and bowls?"

"Trees are naturally magnetic. To augment their natural healing powers is one of the easiest feats of the follower of Mesmeric theory. Bowls are simply a handy vessel for *magnétisme animale.*"

"If you magnetize these objects, do they carry the same effect as you magnetizing a patient?"

"Yes. They can be used as a surrogate. Mesmer has been known to magnetize a particular tree—which has then continued to heal for a long time after he is gone."

"Have you magnetized trees?"

"Yes."

At the end of the marathon afternoon, Ben thanked Doctor D'Eslon profusely for his cooperation. Ben could tell by the comments he overheard among his colleagues that none was any more convinced of the veracity of *magnétisme animale* than they had been upon their arrival so many hours ago. Nonetheless, Ben felt that they had made some significant progress. The null measurements of electricity and mineral magnetism were the first step that he had outlined in his plan with Le Roy. Those had come out as expected. Next, they would test to see if any of the commissioners could sense *magnétisme animale* themselves. Also, Ben had been heartened to hear D'Eslon corroborate that other objects could be magnetized and would hold the magnetic charge long after the magnetizer had left. He planned to test that property as well.

Ben and Le Roy walked across the foyer toward the front door, discussing their next steps in the investigation. Ben had completely forgotten about Gretchen. Out of the corner of his eye, he perceived someone rushing at him from the direction of the treatment room. He braced himself. Le Roy hoisted his cane as if to ward off an attacker. Gretchen thrust herself at Ben, landing a delightful kiss on his cheek as she held his head tenderly.

"Goodbye, Doctor Franklin," she said out loud. But then she whispered in his ear, "And please be careful."

May 10th, 1784

KINGSWOOD

BEN WAS TIRED after a long day. His foot throbbed. The fireplace at the Hôtel de Valentinois crackled with warmth, and at supper, Madame Leray urged him strongly to stay home. As an incentive, she produced a bottle of vintage Madeira after the meal. It sat on the table, pleading with him not to leave.

Ben could easily have reneged on Le Roy's invitation based on the weather alone. While yesterday had been a pleasant late spring day, this morning had brought blustery cold weather back down from the north. Rainsqualls swept over Kingswood, which separated Passy from the Royal Scientific Laboratory. It appeared pitch black out the window of the parlor after supper. But Jean-Baptiste's urgency and his secrecy had piqued Ben's curiosity enough to make the trip inevitable.

Le Roy had been uncharacteristically cryptic in his invitation. He wanted to show Ben something... 'a new discovery', 'a new proof.' Ben could get nothing more out of him. Why he had chosen this particular night, Ben couldn't fathom.

Ben waited for the wind to settle down from a howl to a hushed roar, then ordered his horse. The lull wouldn't last long on a raw night, such as this one. He would have much preferred to travel in the dry interior of the Leray coach, but the narrow path through the woods wouldn't allow it. Besides, he would feel guilty making a driver go out in this weather, especially not knowing the amount of time it would take Le Roy to reveal his 'secret.' Ben cinched up the hood of his heaviest cape around his face so that only his eyes were exposed. He mounted his horse in front of the stable boy who appeared incredulous that any sane person would ride out in such conditions.

"*Taïaut*," Ben bellowed. He smacked the rump of the steed with his crop. The horse bolted out of the courtyard into the night. In the darkness, the branches of the trees swayed wildly, making a ghostly creaking as they were buffeted by the winds. Ben guided his horse toward the path that led through the forest. The steed snorted but then dove into the wood. At least there would be no other travelers to contend with on a night such as this. Ben ducked, barely avoiding a low hanging branch pushed down by the swirling winds.

"Damn you, Le Roy. I will be lucky to survive this night," he said, as he rode on.

The canopy of trees overhead sheltered him, at least partly from the pelting rain. At last, the lights of the Royal Scientific Laboratory appeared in front of him, signaling the end of his harrowing ride. An unfamiliar coach was parked near the front door. Ben rode up to the side door of the Le Roy residence, expecting a stable boy to greet him. An oil lamp flickered under the portico, but no one appeared to assist with his horse.

"This is odd," Ben thought. After a moment, he dismounted. He recalled Gretchen's warning from the prior day and resolved to take extra care. Ben shook out his cape and hung it near where he'd tied up his horse. With no one about to tend to the animal, Ben hauled a water bucket over within easy reach. The horse drank heartily. Ben looked around. Rain continued to pelt the path outside the shelter of the portico. The door to Le Roy's residence was closed, but lamplight shone through the adjacent window.

Had he made a mistake? Perhaps Le Roy had assumed that Ben would not be coming out in this weather. That would explain the absence of the stable attendant and the lack of any sort of a welcome. Perhaps Le Roy and his wife had already gone to bed. Then he recalled that Le Roy had said that his wife was visiting her sister and *le jeune* in Bordeaux for a fortnight. Ben decided that he would at least roust his friend to let him know he had traversed the treacherous gloom at his request.

Ben knocked on the door. No one responded. He knocked again, harder. Still nothing. Ben looked through the window. A lamp burned in the foyer, but no one seemed about. He tried the door. To his surprise, it opened easily. He hesitated for a moment, then entered. He knew the layout of the house well, having been a guest here almost weekly since his arrival in France eight years ago. He proceeded to the study where he fully expected to find Le Roy nodded off in front of the fire, a spent glass of cheap brandy nearby. Instead, he found that the fire had burned down to a few embers, unattended. Ben threw a log on the grate and continued his search.

"Jean-Baptiste," he called out. No response. "He must be in the laboratory," Ben mumbled to himself after he had verified that no one was in the apartment. As Ben returned to the study, he recalled the secret passage that Le Roy had used on the occasion when he had first shown Ben his electric eel. Rather than walk outside to the front entrance of the laboratory in the rain, Ben decided to try to use the passage. He approached the bookcase, wondering if he could find the hidden button to activate the mechanism.

Ben felt along each shelf until his finger found a small indentation. He pushed. The bookcase silently swung inwards with the precision of a finely tuned machine. "Son of a watchmaker," he mumbled appreciatively. Ben commandeered an oil lamp from a nearby table and entered the dark passageway. The cool air smelled damp and musty. His lamp threw strange dancing shadows onto the sweaty limestone blocks as he inched his way along the ancient corridor. Ahead of him, he began to hear noises coming through the darkness. He paused.

Perhaps his mind was playing tricks on him. "I will be glad to find that son-of-a-bitch Le Roy and give him a scolding for his treatment of me this night," he grumbled. He began to move forward again. As he finally approached the door to the secret laboratory, Ben was sure he heard voices coming from the other side, but he could not discern what was being said. It sounded like two different men—and possibly a woman. Ben listened for a moment but still could not pick out individual words. He peered through the darkness off to his right to see the escape passage that Le Roy had told him led to a cabin in Kingswood. His lamp illuminated only the first few feet of the tunnel.

He turned back toward the door. The voices were clearly becoming more animated. It sounded to Ben as if the discussion, whatever it was about, was becoming heated. One of the voices could be Le Roy's, Ben thought. He wished that he had brought a pistol—or even a sword from above the fireplace in the study—in case he was about to enter the scene of a robbery. But he doubted that Le Roy would be arguing with robbers. "Only one way to find out," he thought as he reached for the door handle.

"He will be here soon," Le Roy was saying as Ben entered, his back to the door. In front of Le Roy stood Franz Mesmer and Antoine Court de Gébelin with scowls on their faces, their arms folded across their chests. Ben was relieved to see no weapons drawn, although he was disconcerted to see that Mesmer wore a pistol on his hip. He had a nasty fresh gash on his forehead. Ben saw no woman in his quick scan of the room. The electric eel undulated in her glass enclosure, air bubbles dancing up the sides of the tank. Other scientific equipment filled the room, just as Ben had seen before. However, he also noted an empty wooden baquet now stood beside the aquarium.

"What is this about?" Ben said.

Le Roy wheeled around. "Ah, Ben," he exclaimed. "You have come at last." He looked genuinely relieved to have some support, but also frightened. "These men asked me to invite you here tonight, claiming to be able to offer you proof of Mesmer's fluid, but I have just now found out that they intend instead to silence our report."

"There is no proof of Mesmer's fluid," Ben said. "You should know that,

Jean-Baptiste." He walked over and put his arm around his friend, trying to exude confidence in a clearly dangerous situation.

"*Magnétisme animale* is real," Mesmer hissed.

"Yes, it is real. I believe in it," de Gébelin chimed in. He seemed self-righteous and smug.

"Brother de Gébelin, you believe in the ability of your Tarot cards to predict the future. Your beliefs cannot be taken seriously," Ben said. "I need real proof, reproducible scientific proof."

De Gébelin shut up.

"But I have proven again and again the effectiveness of my fluid. You have witnessed my successes," Mesmer said angrily. "No one can doubt my cures."

"I don't believe you have proven anything," Ben said. "The results could just as well be due to the overwhelming desire of your patients to be cured—so much so that they imagine any positive sign as evidence."

"I have subjected my treatments to rigorous study."

"Then you should have no quarrel with the commission's method—as we shall do the same."

"But you used only the patients and methods of my student, Doctor D'Eslon, far inferior to my own."

"Because you made yours unavailable."

"I have nothing to prove to you," Mesmer said. "Yet, I doubt that the King will publish your precious commission results with its leader dead."

Mesmer pulled his pistol, aiming it directly at Ben's chest.

Ben instinctively jumped backwards, thinking of nothing but escape. From the corner of his eye, he caught a glimpse of strawberry-blonde hair. A figure lunged from behind the baquet. Ben's eye followed Marianne as she struck Mesmer's arm just as he pulled the trigger.

The misdirected shot shattered the glass aquarium. There was a scream. Ben watched as Marianne fell in slow motion away from him. He felt a spray of water followed immediately by the unmistakable crackle of electricity in the air. Water rushed over his boots. Shards of glass struck his side. Ben turned his face away. He heard a thud. The room became eerily quiet.

As the haze cleared, Ben turned to see the newly freed eel entangled with a limp, scarlet-faced de Gébelin. The pair had somehow landed in the baquet. Le Roy had the dazed Mesmer pinned to the floor in a headlock. Ben attended to Marianne lying face down on the floor. She moaned as he turned her over. Ben saw glass shards in her wet hair, but she did not seem to be bleeding.

She revived quickly in his arms and looked at him with sad, terrified eyes.

"Thank you for saving my life," he said softly.

"I'm so sorry, Ben," she said.

Ben tried to smile, but his expression could not hide his disappointment. She must have known of Mesmer's plot to kill him, yet she had failed to warn him. He started to ask Marianne why she had come in the first place but thought better of it. He knew the answer. He knew that she had been with Mesmer for a long time, longer even than he cared to admit to himself. His mind raced. He knew that even earlier this very week, when they had been together for their final time at the *Cheval Sauvage*, she had tried her best to convince him to stop the commission. Her action tonight, in saving his life, must have been done out of her love for him—but he also knew that she belonged to Mesmer. Ben knew that he could never see her again. It would hurt too much.

"I am sorry, too," he said.

"I have an idea of what to do with him," Le Roy said. He kept Mesmer pinned on the floor. The wizard squirmed and groaned and called out weakly to Marianne for help.

Ben got up and dusted himself off. Marianne found a chair. She sat, looking down at the floor, broken.

"What do you suggest?" Ben asked.

Le Roy had a devilish expression on his face. "I was just pondering how we could reload his pistol and shoot the already dead Monsieur de Gébelin with it. Then we could alert the police that a murder had been committed. I am sure that a murder trial would not be good for Herr Doctor's business."

"Or perhaps," Ben said, "the good Doctor would like to test his animal magnetism against another animal's electricity."

Mesmer said nothing. He looked dazed.

"No, Ben, you couldn't…" Marianne whimpered softly. She started to sob.

"I appreciate your idea, Jean-Baptiste, but in all honesty, I think it will be sufficiently damaging to his reputation if we simply let it be known that de Gébelin died in an electrical experiment at Mesmer's hand," Ben said calmly. His own heart rate was only now starting to return to its normal pace.

Le Roy ordered Mesmer and Marianne out, and they offered no resistance. He and Ben escorted the pair to the front door of the Royal Scientific Laboratory, and Ben watched as they drove off into the pouring rain. He found that his chest ached, not only from his anger and dismay over Marianne's betrayal, but at his sudden grief upon realizing that the end of their relationship had come in this manner.

Ben and Le Roy donned heavy rubber gloves to shield themselves from electrical shock and carefully disentangled the lifeless body of de Gébelin from the electric eel. For the time being, they left her confined in the baquet half-full of water. So as to avoid even the possibility of being observed, they carried the body out through the secret passage to the hunting cabin in the woods.

Ben waited nervously as Le Roy went back through the secret passage. He shivered in the dark as flashes of lightning intermittently revealed the sparse furnishings of the room. He thought about the remarkable events of the evening and could not help but wish that things had turned out differently. He hated the fact that this meeting with Marianne would be his last. Though he wasn't sure how he had wished their relationship to end, he knew that a pistol shot, shattered aquarium glass, and de Gébelin's electrocution had not played a part in his wish.

Le Roy returned after what seemed like an eternity. He drove up to the front door of the cabin on a farm wagon drawn by two stout horses. The rain had let up just enough to see that he had also retrieved Ben's horse. Le Roy entered the cabin enshrouded in a dripping oilcloth cape. He tossed over a bundle. Ben was pleased to find that it contained his own warm cape, as well as a large burlap sheet and a length of rope. The two wrapped de Gébelin up. They worked silently together to place their parcel into the wagon. As Ben took his seat on the hard wooden bench, Le Roy produced a flask from underneath his cloak.

"Here," he said. He handed the flask to Ben as he snapped the reins.

Ben felt the sharp bite of Le Roy's cheap brandy hit his palate. The stinging sensation seemed immensely appropriate to the situation. He handed the flask back to his friend, who downed a good slug as well.

"Perhaps he was right about one thing," Le Roy mused as they reached the back alley entrance to the Lodge of the Nine Sisters.

"Who?"

"De Gébelin."

"What?"

"The Tarot predicted his death."

"Everyone eventually dies, my friend. I will die someday. Because I can predict that, does it make me clairvoyant?"

"No, I suppose not."

They placed de Gébelin's body in his own bathtub at the lodge. The newspapers reported that he had died while undergoing an electrical experiment directed by Doctor Mesmer aimed at curing his heart condition. The aquarium tank was rebuilt, but Le Roy transferred the electric eel to another laboratory for further study.

As Ben later relived that night, usually in his dreams, Mesmer and the eel combined to form a horrible creature, half-human, slippery, and hissing. The apparition wielded terrible power. Marianne was substituted for de Gébelin. She would end up, cold and lifeless, entangled with the eel in the baquet. Ben always awoke in a cold sweat from that dream.

May 20th, 1784

PARIS

AT LEAST A HALF A DOZEN reporters swarmed around Mesmer as he entered the coach station. Marianne watched from a bench where she sat with Cecelia. The sisters were unnoticed by the scandal sheet writers badgering Mesmer—that is until he strode directly over toward them. Marianne flipped the hood of her cape up. Not that she would be unrecognizable even so, and not that she cared, as she did not intend to return to Paris anytime soon.

"What say you to rumors that de Gébelin died at your hand?" Marianne heard a particularly loud reporter ask.

"I deny it," Mesmer shouted.

"What of Franklin's commission?"

"A sham."

The stationmaster was attempting to announce that the coach to Spa was boarding but was having some difficulty being heard over the din created by Mesmer and the reporters. But Mesmer must have heard him because he ushered the sisters out toward the waiting coach. Luckily none of the reporters had a ticket to ride. The coachman stopped them at the door.

They were still shouting out impertinent questions as Mesmer, Marianne and Cecelia embarked.

Once outside of the city gates, it became much quieter. Cecelia laid her head down on Marianne's shoulder and fell asleep. Mesmer remained agitated, however. He fidgeted with his pocket watch, opening and closing it with an annoying clicking noise.

"Will you be so kind as to put that away?" Marianne asked.

Mesmer did so but remained jumpy, on edge. Marianne thought that perhaps he fretted over the death of de Gébelin.

"Do you expect an inquiry into the death?" she asked.

"If the police had wanted to detain me, I am sure that they would not have let me board this coach. No, as a physician, I would not expect that there would be an inquiry into why a frail man, weak from a disease of the heart, died."

Marianne raised an eyebrow. "Even if he died from an electrical experiment you performed as reported by the newspapers—let alone the true circumstances of his demise?"

"A trifle ... of no consequence," he said.

"What is it that has you so agitated, then?"

Mesmer was quiet for a moment. He glanced over at Cecelia as if to be sure that she was asleep. "I will not be staying at Spa. I will be traveling on to Vienna."

The announcement caught Marianne completely by surprise. "On to Vienna? But I thought that we would perform at your house in Spa for the summer. Franz, you promised to engage us for the summer concerts." She could feel the heat rise at the back of her neck.

"I am afraid that will no longer be possible," he replied coolly. "You may stay at my house in Spa for the summer if you wish," he offered.

The meaning of his abandonment sunk in. "But we have no other engagements. We have no income—or savings. How will we live?"

"I don't know. It is not my concern."

Marianne started to sob. "Franz, what happened to cause your change of heart?"

"Anna Maria wants me back in Vienna."

"Your wife?" Marianne exclaimed. She sat up, nearly awakening Cecelia in the process.

"She wrote and asked if I would return to our home in Vienna," Mesmer continued almost apologetically.

"And since when do you do whatever she says?" Even as the words came out, Marianne recalled the incident in the *Christkindlmarkt* and how henpecked he had appeared that day.

"She needs me."

"For what ... to carry her Christmas packages?" Marianne muttered.

Mesmer appeared not to catch her meaning. He shot her a blank stare but didn't respond.

Marianne wasn't going to push it. If he wished to go back to her, then so be it. "And what of our work with *magnétisme animale*?" she said. She sounded pleading, even to herself.

"Your Doctor Franklin claims it does not work."

"He must have proof," Marianne replied. "And I believe that *magnétisme animale* is not provable ... at least not with the methods of the science of today. Perhaps, it shouldn't be proven. Perhaps, like the power of love ... or our faith in God ... we besmirch it by requiring proof that it exists. But Franz, do you comprehend the true power of *magnétisme animale* yourself?"

"Of course," he said, sounding peeved. "I channel the *magnétisme animale* from the stars to heal."

"No, that is not it at all. The power is within each of us, Franz. You have a wonderful ability to open us up to it ... to allow us to discover the healing powers of *magnétisme animale*, but you do not own it. It is not the province of one man. *Magnétisme animale* belongs to all mankind."

"It *is* mine. I own it," he protested. "I will not give it away."

Marianne realized that she would not convince him of the true nature of *magnétisme animale* or the advantage of sharing it openly with the world. Perhaps, as the Queen had said, the world wasn't even ready for it. She gave up trying and fell silent.

At Spa, Mesmer boarded the coach headed east toward Vienna. He left without so much as a kiss goodbye. Marianne found that she was not sad to see him go—except for his broken promise of an engagement for the summer. She and Cecelia decided to head south. They had at least enough money to make it to Florence—and some hope for work there.

A day south of Dijon, the sisters stayed at the roadside inn owned by Giuseppe and Maria. They ate the best meal of their entire journey that evening—on the house. Marianne was delighted, and only slightly surprised, to find that Casanova was staying at the inn. He offered to travel to Florence with them. Marianne gladly accepted. The sisters were regaled by stories of his many adventures all the way over the Alps and beyond.

June 1784

PASSY

THE COMMISSIONERS HAD quite a busy few weeks following the death of de Gébelin. They met in Paris almost daily.

Ben, meanwhile, recuperated in Passy. The night he'd spent hauling the body of de Gébelin around had badly aggravated his gouty foot. To make matters worse, his bladder stone now seemed to be flaring up as well. Horseback riding proved to be pure torture. Even the normally comfortable Leray coach produced a lancinating pain in either his foot or his lower abdomen with every bump in the road. In addition, he'd fallen into a funk as the finality of his affair with Marianne sunk in. He was confined to Passy.

Le Veillard was always of some small consolation with his jokes and his *laissez-faire* attitude toward life. Madame Leray provided a sympathetic shoulder to cry on. But Minette was gone to visit her daughters in the country, and Ben wished it were she who was there to comfort him the way that only she could. Swimming was his sole solace.

Le Roy kept Ben informed of the commissioners' progress. None of them, even those with known illnesses, had felt any noticeable effect when D'Eslon's *magnétisme animale* fluid was directed at them, except for one who perceived a slight pain from the pressure of the iron rod placed upon his abdomen. D'Eslon had ultimately conceded to the commissioners that the fluid had no qualities detectable by vision, hearing, smell, or taste—although all of these had at one time or another been reported by patients.

Also, the commissioners had compared the effects on participants paid for their time versus those who had volunteered—finding that those who were paid participants, usually from a lower socioeconomic class and less well educated, tended to respond with more reports of feeling 'something' when magnetized than did the unpaid volunteers. They concluded that paying the participants might have influenced them towards feeling that they needed to report something.

The commissioners had also begun to experiment with blindfolded participants. They found that susceptible patients, in whom a crisis was readily evidenced when able to see the magnetizer, became immune to the same effect when blindfolded and left untouched.

One of the commissioners, M. Sigault, having no prior training in the application of *magnétisme animale* at all other than having briefly observed D'Eslon, tried magnetizing a woman patient. She promptly started to shake and vomited up her lunch. Afterwards she claimed she felt better.

Ben prevailed upon the commissioners to reconvene in Passy—so as to limit his travel but allow him to continue to participate in the experiments.

Today, the commissioners would be conducting experiments with trees in the apricot orchard adjacent to the Hôtel de Valentinois. They continued to benefit from the cooperation of D'Eslon, although a few of the more suspicious members of the commission were concerned that the doctor might be passing signals in some manner to his patients, thereby making it appear that he had some power over them. They would gladly have left him at home had he not insisted that he would be unable to guarantee the success of magnetizing a tree without being physically present to point a cane or finger at it.

As he waited for the other commissioners to arrive, Ben went for a leisurely swim. As he floated past Auteuil, he daydreamed about Minette. He imagined her lithe body, shiny and sun-kissed. Her warm smile, her hearty laugh. Her fancily dressed courtier cats named, it just now occurred to him, for her former husband and lovers. Her household full of scholars, the abbés and young Cabanis, all revolving around her like the planets around the Sun.

He returned to the dock of the Hôtel de Valentinois with thoughts of natural forces, both planetary and human emotional, swirling in his head.

Le Roy was waiting there for him. Holding up a towel, he turned his head and let out an embarrassed cough as Ben hauled his naked frame up onto the dock.

"Jean-Baptiste. Is it time for the experiments to begin?" Ben asked.

"Everyone is assembled in the orchard awaiting the esteemed Doctor Franklin. Madame Leray directed me here to fetch you."

"I must apologize then. Time got away from me," Ben said. He toweled off. "Swimming in this river is the only thing that does my foot any good."

They stopped by Ben's lodgings, where he quickly dressed. Even walking up the hill to the apricot orchard taxed his tolerance for pain. When they reached the orchard, Ben saw that Madame Leray had made provisions for him to sit in the shade. Several of the commissioners milled around.

Ben quickly spotted D'Eslon, who was engaged in a discussion with Doctor Guillotin. Ben greeted the other commissioners and D'Eslon briefly. He sat. Madame Leray had thoughtfully positioned an ottoman so that he might elevate his foot. A chairside table held a tall glass filled with *eau de Passy*, chips of ice, and a wedge of lemon. Ben sat and took a cool drink.

Le Roy made some brief introductions about the nature of the experiment that had been prepared for today. He described the subject, a boy of twelve years of age, of D'Eslon's own choosing, and very susceptible to *magnétisme animale*. He was currently ensconced inside so as not to be influenced by the set up of the experiment or to discover which tree was to be magnetized. Le Roy then turned the podium over to D'Eslon.

D'Eslon began. He seemed more comfortable now in his role as consultant to the commission than he had the last time Ben had seen him in Paris, perhaps because Mesmer was gone.

"All trees are magnetic to some extent," D'Eslon said. "However, when a tree has been touched according to the principles and method of *magnétisme animale,* every person who stops under it will experience, to a greater or lesser degree, the effects of this magnetizing. There have even been some in this situation who have swooned or experienced convulsions."

"The set up of the experiment is this," Le Roy interjected. "We will ask Doctor D'Eslon to magnetize one particular tree in this orchard. Doctor Franklin, will you please point out the tree for us?"

Ben pointed to a singular apricot tree, set apart slightly from the others but still well within line of sight from where the commissioners observed. "That one," Ben said.

"Very good," Le Roy affirmed. "Doctor D'Eslon, will you please be so kind as to magnetize that tree?"

D'Eslon marched across the orchard to the base of the apricot tree Ben had identified. He stood in front of it for a moment, his back to the commissioners. Then he raised his right hand. He made several passes with the hands back and forth, up and down. Finally, he took his cane and pointed it at the trunk of the tree. Walking backwards, he kept the point of the cane directed at the tree until he reached the area where the commissioners gathered.

"It is done," he said with a flourish.

"Must you continue to point at it with your cane?" one of the commissioners asked. "The subject may identify the tree by your pointing to it."

"It is not absolutely necessary," D'Eslon said. "However, I believe that the transfer of the fluid will be more effective in this manner."

"Must you be seen by the subject for this experiment to work?"

"No, of course not," D'Eslon replied testily.

Le Roy stepped up. "I have an idea," he said. "What if we have a few of the commissioners form a sort of human shield—so that the boy will have no visual contact with the Doctor?"

"Here, here," the commissioners affirmed. They surrounded D'Eslon in a semicircle. D'Eslon was taller than most of the men, but the tree to which his cane pointed was no longer visible after the maneuver.

"Will that be satisfactory?" Le Roy inquired.

"I suppose so," D'Eslon responded with dry resignation.

Upon a hand signal from Le Roy, the slender boy was led out of the house wearing a blindfold. Madame Leray guided him by his right arm. The late morning sun was bright, but there was a haze in the upper atmosphere, resulting in an unusual iridescent quality to the light when combined with the late spring exuberance of the foliage surging across the orchard. Adding to the eeriness, the strains of lilting flute music began to emanate from the open windows of the house. The commissioners all watched in attentive silence as the scene played out in front of them.

Le Roy intercepted Madame Leray, joining her about halfway across the lush green lawn. He took the boy's other arm and said something that Ben could not hear at that distance. However, Madame Leray retreated toward the house. Ben surmised that Le Roy must have released her.

Le Roy removed the blindfold and directed the boy toward the closest non-magnetized tree. Once he was there, Le Roy instructed the boy to embrace the trunk, which he did, enthusiastically. After less than a minute, the boy coughed, then spit on the ground, his reaction evident even at the distance from which Ben observed. Le Roy moved the boy to a second non-magnetized tree a bit farther away from the one D'Eslon had prepared. After a short time, the boy put his hand up to his head. He appeared to swoon slightly. Le Roy moved the boy to a third non-magnetized tree even farther away. The boy appeared to be nearing a crisis ... staggering, his hand held up to his head. At the fourth non-magnetized tree, the boy fell into a full-blown fit. He collapsed to the ground, his arms and legs shaking tremendously. The commissioners and D'Eslon bolted across the lawn to attend him. Ben also got up from his seat and hobbled over, though his gouty foot tortured him. At this point, the boy was nowhere near the magnetized tree.

The commissioners parted as Ben approached. As a group, they stood over the stricken boy. D'Eslon knelt at his side, along with Doctor Guillotin. D'Eslon stroked the boy's hand. Miraculously, it was the only one of his limbs not shaking.

Doctor Guillotin gave Ben a disgusted look. "Not a bonafide fit," Ben heard him mutter. D'Eslon continued to minister to the boy, who came around slowly. He moaned less and less agitatedly. The shaking of his limbs transformed slowly into more choreiform movements. His eyes were open but looked blankly forward as he jerked about. Slowly the shaking stopped altogether, and he lay limp on the ground breathing heavily. D'Eslon caressed his willowy limbs a bit too sensually for Ben's taste. Someone asked if he wanted to sit up. The boy nodded but did not speak. They sat him up, at which point he seemed to come around more fully. He glanced about with a dazed expression and asked for a drink of water. Madame Leray appeared with a wet washcloth for his forehead, and then promptly headed back to the house to fetch a glass.

By the time she returned, the experiment was over. Once he was more fully revived, Madame Leray led the boy back to the house for some rest, out of the sun. He appeared only slightly wobbly. D'Eslon watched him go with the first look of true compassion that Ben had ever seen on the man's face. After all the excitement had died down, the commissioners gathered around Ben.

"What do you make of this experiment, Dr. Franklin?" Le Roy asked.

"It appears that the result of this experiment is entirely contrary to the theory of *magnétisme animale*," Ben said.

"As I stated at the outset, all trees are somewhat magnetic," D'Eslon objected, appearing to have composed himself in the interim. "It is more likely, in my opinion, that the natural magnetism of all of your apricot trees has been enhanced by my presence here today."

"If this is a demonstration of the magnetic properties occasioned by any and all trees, I would surely wonder how this poor lad, or any other person susceptible to *magnétisme animale*, should ever be able to walk in a forest," Ben said drolly.

June 1784

PARIS

THE COMMISSIONERS CONDUCTED yet further experiments using objects magnetized by D'Eslon, this time at the home of Professor Lavoisier in Paris, also known as The Arsenal. Lavoisier, master chemist to the King, was in charge of both the manufacture and safekeeping of the kingdom's supply of black powder. For some experiments, the commissioners chose as their subject a certain Dame P., a woman reputed to be especially sensitive to *magnétisme animale*. She gave the commission her consent to be the subject of an experiment sanctioned by Doctor D'Eslon.

Le Roy met her coach outside The Arsenal. She was an aristocratic woman in her late fifties, impeccably, if conservatively, dressed. As she took Le Roy's offer of a hand to descend from the carriage, she appeared ideally cast as the matriarch of one of the finest families of the *ancien regime*. Le Roy was well acquainted with her type. She said nothing and maintained her haughty bearing as she paraded through the house. As they entered the antechamber, she started to swoon simply from the expectation that she was about to see D'Eslon. When she had adequately recovered, she was led into the room to be used for the experiment. There she was directed to a comfortable wing chair with the commissioners seated at a table directly across from her. On the table sat five ceramic basins filled with water. The basins were undecorated, identical in color and size. They were shallow but wide at the top, like those intended for washing face and hands.

She settled into her chair. "Your Ladyship," Lavoisier said. "Thank you for coming today and agreeing to be a part of our experiments."

"You are welcome," she responded pleasantly enough, if coolly.

"Doctor D'Eslon has magnetized one of these five bowls, especially for you," Lavoisier explained. He pointed to the row of basins laid out before him. "He has informed us that the effect of bringing the one magnetized bowl close to you will have the same effect as if he were in contact with you himself."

"Oh?" she replied. She seemed to realize for the first time that D'Eslon was not actually going to be present.

"Yes." Lavoisier went on setting up the experiment. "Doctor D'Eslon has provided us with this one specially magnetized basin so that we can observe your reaction to it. Is that all right?"

"I suppose."

"Good. Then we shall proceed. For the first part of our experiment, we would like to apply a blindfold to your eyes. Would that be all right?"

"A blindfold?"

"Yes, you know, a bandage." Lavoisier motioned toward commissioner Majault, who held up a folded strip of cloth.

"I suppose," she replied with a tone of suspicion.

"Thank you."

Lavoisier instructed Majault to affix the blindfold. Once it was in place, Majault signaled to Le Roy. Majault continued to carry on a polite distracting conversation with her about the weather. Le Roy took the magnetized basin and quietly walked behind her. He held the magnetized bowl directly behind her head—as close as he could get it without actually touching her. Nothing happened. He put it next to her ear. Nothing. Le Roy shrugged his shoulders at Lavoisier. He held the bowl in various positions around her head as the trivial conversation continued between the lady and Majault. Once that was concluded, he stealthily returned the bowl to the table.

"Your Ladyship?" Lavoisier asked.

"Yes?"

"We are ready to proceed. My colleague Monsieur Le Roy will present each bowl to you in sequence. We are interested in your experience with each one. Do you understand?"

"Yes."

"Monsieur Le Roy, will you present the first basin to Madame?"

"Of course," Le Roy said. He moved around as noisily as possible to pick up an unmagnetized bowl and carry it toward the subject. "I am in position," he announced. He held the first bowl next to her head.

"Do you feel anything?" Lavoisier asked.

"Nothing, sir," she responded.

"We will now try another bowl," Lavoisier said.

Le Roy once again walked loudly over to the table and collected another unmagnetized vessel. He brought it into position and announced, "I am now placing the second bowl near the subject."

Dame P. started to breathe faster. A few beads of sweat broke out on her brow.

"Are you feeling something now?" Lavoisier asked.

"Yes, oh yes," she said breathily.

"Can you describe what you are feeling?"

"Warm, not hot, just very warm. This may be the bowl, but I'm not entirely sure."

"We will try a third then," Lavoisier said. He motioned to Le Roy to take another basin.

Once in position, Le Roy said loudly, "I now have the third bowl in proximity to her head."

"Oh, my ... Oh, my," she said, swooning.

"Do you believe this one to be the magnetized basin, my Lady?" Lavoisier asked.

"It might be, it could be," she responded with increased agitation. Her breathing was becoming more labored. She rocked back and forth slowly.

"Let us try the fourth," Lavoisier said.

By the time Le Roy could get back with the fourth bowl, Dame P. appeared to be in a state of complete crisis. She flung her head back and started to moan. Her arms and legs trembled while she slumped on her chair. She was panting and sweating profusely.

The commissioners looked upon this autoerotic display with amazement, and some had to stifle a laugh at this snooty, aristocratic woman creating a scene more apropos of a drunken wench. She gyrated her hips and heaved her breasts with abandon. She shrieked, she groaned, she appeared to be alternately in some form of pain or ecstasy. Her crisis finally reached a crescendo, *à la le petite morte*, and then slowly waned in front of the amused commissioners.

Only slowly did Dame P. resume a more ladylike pose in her chair. "May I have a drink of water?" she asked.

Lavoisier asked that her blindfold be removed. Majault obliged.

Le Roy poured some water into the fifth bowl, the only one that had been magnetized by D'Eslon, and presented it to her. She took it to her lips and drank from the vessel without so much as a twitch or a moan. The commissioners noted her reaction.

"How do you feel?" Lavoisier asked.

"Very well," she responded as if nothing had happened.

"What do you believe to have occurred just now?"

"You performed a transfer of the *magnétisme animale* fluid into me using these bowls."

"But we did nothing to you. The basin magnetized by Doctor D'Eslon had no effect on you."

"If you did nothing to me, I would not now be in my current condition."

"Nonetheless, such is the case Madame," Lavoisier said. "Your expectation that you would experience the effects of *magnétisme animale* today is what produced the condition."

"Harrumph," she replied. She adjusted her clothing and stormed out of the house without another word to anyone.

Le Roy related the events of the day in great detail to Ben, stuck as he was nursing his gouty foot in Passy. "You should have seen it," Jean-Baptiste exclaimed. "The snooty woman made a complete ass of herself, thinking that she was being magnetized by D'Eslon."

"Who hath deceived thee as often as thyself," Ben said with a wink.

June 1784

PARIS

THE HOME OF DOCTOR MAJAULT was the site of another interesting experiment during early June. A certain Doctor Jumelin presented
himself to the commission. Ben was able to attend the session on account
of a reprieve by Madame Gout and listened thoughtfully as the serious
young man explained how he had completely independently discovered his
magnetizing technique. He claimed to be a disciple of neither Mesmer nor
D'Eslon. He postulated that the fluid Mesmer called *magnétisme animale*
was actually a force intrinsic to the human body – not hailing from the stars
at all. Jumelin professed that, like all known fluids, the *magnétisme animale*
tended toward equilibrium. Therefore, *magnétisme animale* would flow
from an area of greater quantity to one of lesser quantity. He proposed that
this flow could occur from one person to another through the application of
touch—or even within an individual if they were experienced at guiding it.

Jumelin brought with him as a subject a woman of about twenty years
of age. He had discovered that he could cause her to become mute through
his application of *magnétisme animale.* He proceeded to demonstrate the

effect for the commissioners. Seated *en rapport*, Jumelin placed a hand on the hypochondrium of the young lady. She appeared to quickly slip into a trance. He spoke to her softly. He asked her to repeat several sentences. She did so with perfect clarity. Then he suggested that, upon awakening, she would be unable to speak until he snapped his fingers. He gently woke her. The commissioners verified that she was completely mute upon awakening from the trance. They tried everything to make her speak. Nothing worked. Once the commissioners were convinced that she could not, or would not speak, they requested that Jumelin release the proscription. He snapped his fingers, and she started to talk almost immediately.

The commissioners endeavored to ascertain the answer to several questions in her case. First, they wished to know if the same effect could be produced without the operation as performed by Jumelin. Also, they were interested in whether sight or touch was required for this effect to occur.

They started by blindfolding the young woman. She was tall, with wide-set eyes, but not without considerable charms. Her shoulder-length, chestnut brown hair had a healthy sheen. She sported high cheekbones, a long graceful neck, and full wet lips. She sat stiffly with an erect posture; willowy arms folded in her lap. Doctor Jumelin sat across from her. Once she was blindfolded, Lavoisier gave a hand signal to Ben, who silently switched places with Jumelin, who swiftly circled behind Ben, leaning forward so as to place his head just above Ben's right shoulder.

"Shall we begin?" Lavoisier asked.

"Yes," Jumelin said. Ben remained silent.

"We shall attempt to replicate your finding with your subject blindfolded," Lavoisier continued. There was no hint in his voice that there had been a substitution of the magnetizer.

The young lady shifted her shoulders. The front of her dress opened slightly, enticingly. Ben looked over at Jumelin, who nodded affirmatively and pointed his finger at her chest. Ben inserted his right hand through the opening in her dress. His open palm came to rest on the smooth skin of her bare hypochondrium. She reacted almost imperceptibly. Presumably, she believed it to be the hand of Jumelin—which had obviously been there many times before. The physical contact produced a most pleasant sensation for Ben. It took some effort on his part to stifle a contented sigh at the feeling of her smooth skin. He placed his other hand on her forehead as he had seen Jumelin do previously ... only now just above the blindfold covering her eyes. Jumelin began to induce a trance in the subject. He spoke the same soothing words that had been effective earlier. However, after a few minutes, it was clear that something was different. She was not responding in the same manner as before. Even after he instructed her to be mute, she continued to be able to speak when asked.

"Perhaps we should remove the blindfold now?" suggested Jumelin.

The commissioners deliberated momentarily. Then Lavoisier replied. "Yes, of course." Majault untied the cloth bandage from her head.

When the young woman realized that it was, in fact, Ben's hand that was pressed to her chest, she exclaimed, "Oh, my."

"What do you think we did wrong?" Ben asked.

"Your hand now applied to my forehead should descend past the level of my nose," the woman replied serenely.

They started again. Ben waited a moment for Jumelin to confirm that she remained in the appropriate trance state. Then, on Jumelin's signal, he started to move his hand down from her forehead slowly toward her nose, mouth, and throat. As soon as he got to her chin, she made a guttural noise. He stopped.

"Can you speak?" one of the commissioners asked.

Ben could appreciate that her larynx moved up and down, but no sound was produced. Her tongue and lips attempted to mouth words, but no voice came forth. Despite the abnormality, she did not appear in the least distressed by her mute condition. She appeared calm and relaxed. Her breathing was unlabored. Her pulse was slow and strong. Ben had a wonderful monitor on her physiological functioning as his right palm measured every respiration and heartbeat.

Ben looked into her face. Her gaze seemed far away, and Ben began to wonder what she visualized. She resembled, Ben thought, a young antelope. Ben envisioned that she saw herself on an African savanna, testing her strong legs against the pursuit of a hungry lioness. He entered her trance. He saw her deer-like body—sleek, taut, and sinewy. Every muscle and tissue had a purpose. He observed her bounding, leaping, escaping to freedom through the brush; reveling in the thrill of being chased but also appreciating being able to live to run another day. He watched her stop to savor a cool drink of water by the river. Ben observed her as she taunted the male antelopes, playing hard to get before she picked a suitable mate. She wanted a mate that was as intelligent, strong, and quick as she. Much too soon for Ben's liking, the moment came for Jumelin to release her. Ben's vision dissipated. He returned to reality. Ben reluctantly removed his hand from her chest. She blushed ever so slightly as he did so. She spoke again with the clearest voice Ben had heard in a long time, perhaps ever.

"Please forgive me, Doctor Franklin," she said.

"No need to apologize, my dear," he replied, a bit breathless himself after the experience.

"I do hope that I was a good subject for your commission today."

"Yes, of course, you were marvelous," Ben heard himself say. He was recollecting more the intimacy that they seemed to have shared than anything he might have learned about *magnétisme animale.* "What is your name?"

"Gazelle," she replied.

"It fits," Ben said.

Doctor Jumelin and Gazelle departed, and the commissioners regrouped to discuss the outcomes of the day.

"I believe that this most recent experiment shows the power of the sense of sight over the imagination," Ben proposed to the group.

"What do you mean, Ben?" Le Roy asked.

"Even as D'Eslon says, 'The eyes possess, in an eminent degree, the power of magnetizing.' This lovely young woman had to be able to see her magnetizer in order for the effect to be present."

"Yes, but that magnetizer was you, Ben," Lavoisier said. "Did you know that you had such power?"

"Professor, I truly believe that the power resides completely in the subject. It is their imagination that fuels the effects of the *magnétisme animale*," Ben said.

"Ben, I don't understand," Le Roy said. "How would you explain the response of the blind pianist Maria Paradis?"

Ben thought for a moment. Then he said, "As you know Jean-Baptiste, the eyes convey the most energetic expressions of passion. All that the human character has in terms of the commanding or the attractive is developed within them. It is natural, therefore, that the eyes should be the source of very high power. But this power exists only in the aptitude the eyes possess of moving the imagination. For those who have lost the sense of sight, other senses take over to the extent that they are able. A person going through life without the sense of sight might experience her passion more through sound—as in music—or touch, taste, or even smell. It is the imagination, fueled by passion, that produces the effects of *magnétisme animale*." He stopped short of relating his experience with Gazelle on the savanna. He had no proof of its existence.

"From these experiments," Lavoisier summarized, "I believe that we may conclude that the imagination is the true cause of the effects attributed to *magnétisme animale*."

"More than that," Ben went on, "the truth thus stated not only explains the effects of the *magnétisme animale*, but also the physical effects of the imagination. For the affectations of the soul make their first corporal impression on the nervous center,"—he pointed to his own hypochondri-um—"which commonly leads a subject to describe the feeling of a weight upon their stomach or a sensation of suffocation."

"Yes, yes," Guillotin chimed in excitedly. "The diaphragm enters into this business, from whence originate the sighs, the tears, and the expressions of mirth. The viscera of the lower belly then experience a reaction ... surprise occasions the colic, terror causes a diarrhea, melancholy is the origin of hysterical distempers. The history of medicine presents to us an infinity of examples of the power of the imagination on the body."

"The terror occasioned by a house fire, a violent degree of desire, a strong and undoubting hope," Ben continued, "have restored the use of his limbs to one who has been crippled with the gout or to a paralytic person."

"A strong and unanticipated degree of joy has dissipated a *quartan ague* of two months' standing," Doctor Guillotin added enthusiastically.

"I beg your pardon?" Ben asked.

"Oh, I apologize for the medical term ... a fever that recurs every fourth day."

"Of course," Ben replied.

Guillotin resumed his discourse. "Close attention is a remedy for the hiccough, and persons, who by some accident have been deprived of the faculty of speech, have recovered it as a consequence of some vehement emotion of the soul."

"Your last example," Lavoisier said, "appears indeed to be what we witnessed with Doctor Jumelin's subject here today."

"Yes," Guillotin concluded. "The action and reaction of the physical upon the mental, and the mental upon the physical systems have been acknowledged ever since the phenomena of medical science have been remarked upon—that is, ever since the origin of natural philosophy. Tears, laughter, coughs, hiccoughs, and in general all the effects which have been observed in the crises of *magnétisme animale* do thereby originate either by the interruption of the functions of the diaphragm by a touch or pressure, or by the power with which the imagination is endowed of acting upon this organ and interrupting its functions."

"Hear, hear," the commissioners all resoundingly agreed.

As the backslapping and congratulations died down, Ben glanced around with a concerned expression. "Did anyone get all this down on paper?" he asked anxiously.

From the corner, Le Roy raised his head from where he had been furiously scribbling in his journal. "I believe I did," he said.

"Good man!" Ben cried with relief. "We will need your notes to prepare our report."

June 19th, 1784

PASSY

THE COMMISSION INVITED D'Eslon to a meeting at the Hôtel
de Valentinois. The doctor arrived, holding his head high, yet appearing
apprehensive. Ben thought that perhaps he expected an inquisition. But
there would be no further probing today. The commission had concluded
its work. However, Ben wanted to discuss their findings with D'Eslon before
they went to press with the report. He felt he owed the man that much.

Madame Leray had prepared her library for the occasion. It was a warm,
breezy day in Passy, and she had opened all the windows to let in the country
air. Sheer curtains waved in the gentle wind. Roses adorned vases throughout the house. Ten chairs were positioned in a circular arrangement in the
library. It was to be a less formal format today. The commissioners milled
around the room, but as soon as D'Eslon entered, they ceased their side
conversations and moved toward their seats. Madame Leray and her staff
appeared with refreshments.

After taking a cool drink of water, Ben stood and spoke.

"I would like to welcome all of you once again to the Hôtel de Valentinois, my home in Passy." He nodded to each member of the commission as he spoke their name. "Doctor Majault, Professor Le Roy, Professor Sallin, Professor Bailly, Professor D'Arcet, Doctor De Bory, Doctor Guillotin, and of course, Professor Lavoisier." He took another drink. "We are especially honored today to be joined by Doctor D'Eslon, without whom the work of this commission would have been much more difficult—if not impossible."

D'Eslon sat rigidly in his seat. A sardonic smile briefly moved across his otherwise impassive face. As Ben sat, Lavoisier rose to speak.

"Compression, imagination, and imitation are the true causes of the effects attributed to *magnétisme animale*," he began. Ben observed that D'Eslon remained expressionless.

Lavoisier continued. "Such is the result of the experiments of the commission and the observations we made upon the means employed and the effects produced. This agent, this fluid, has no independent existence."

D'Eslon started to rise from his seat as if he might bolt from the proceedings.

"No, please remain seated, Doctor," Ben requested. D'Eslon acquiesced.

Ben stood up. "It cannot be denied that we are all surrounded by a fluid which particularly belongs to us. The insensible perspiration forms around us an atmosphere of insensible vapors ... but I maintain that we have found this fluid has no usefulness except as is common to other atmospheres. We have not found it to be able to be communicated by the touch—it is not capable of being directed by conductors, nor by the eyes, nor the will. It is neither propagated by sound nor reflected by mirrors. Notwithstanding all that I have said, the imagination of sick persons has unquestionably a very frequent and considerable share in the cure of their diseases," he said.

D'Eslon looked only slightly more comfortable. He spoke for the first time. "I have long considered that the imagination might have the greatest share of the effects of *magnétisme animale*. In fact, this new agent might be no other than what we call imagination itself, whose power is as extensive as it is little known. I have always maintained, when speaking to the faculty of medicine, my concern in this matter."

"Yes, it is true," Doctor Guillotin spoke up, vouching for him.

"Thank you, Doctor," D'Eslon said. He seemed to relax even a bit. "In my experience with *magnétisme animale*, many people have been either entirely cured or infinitely amended in their state of health by this technique."

"And what if the cure is only imaginary?" Lavoisier asked.

"What of it?" D'Eslon replied. "If the imagination might be thus directed to the relief of the suffering of humanity, would not that be a most valuable means in the hands of the medical profession? *Magnétisme animale* gives people hope."

There was a rumbling around the room as the commissioners mulled the implications of D'Eslon's words.

"I invite you ... nay, I implore you to investigate this power of the imagination afforded by my practice, to study its procedure and its effects on people. I, for one, shall await—and embrace when it arrives—a scientific explanation for *magnétisme animale*."

With that, he arose from his seat. Ben studied his stern face. Without D'Eslon saying anything more, Ben felt that he knew the man's mind. D'Eslon understood that the commission could not measure *magnétisme animale*, and though they had observed the healing effects of it, their report would testify to the lack of evidence of any measurable fluid. D'Eslon, as well, understood that his plea for further study into how patients heal under the decidedly subconscious influence of *magnétisme animale* might well fall on deaf ears in a group that was so invested in experimental physical science and traditional medical practice.

D'Eslon walked out the front door of the Hôtel de Valentinois, back to his lucrative practice, back to his patients and their suffering. He carried with him Ben's respect.

"I want you all to ponder something," Ben said as the group returned to their seats. "It is a known adage that, in physic as well as religion, men are saved by faith. This faith is the product of imagination. In these cases, the imagination is working by gentle means. It is transfusing tranquility over the senses. It is restoring the harmony of the functions. It is recalling into play every principle under the genial influence of hope."

He paused as he gazed into the rapt attention of the eight commissioners sitting in a circle before him.

"Gentlemen, hope is essential to human life. The man who provides us the first contributes to restore to us the other. You heard D'Eslon say it—*magnétisme animale* gives people hope. Without hope, many would suffer more. I firmly believe that Nature cures diseases. But I believe just as fervently that the human suffering associated with those same diseases might be reduced by the encouragement of hope. The doctor who recognizes that, and by his actions, whatever they are, is able to restore and maintain hope within his patients, is indeed a wise man—and will be more successful in his practice for it."

Ben floated on his back in the Seine. The commission's work had officially ended. Le Roy promised a draft manuscript for Ben to see within a week. For now, there was nothing to do but contemplate life. Soon his preparations to return to America would begin. Ben hoped that he would be able to return to Philadelphia by the next summer. He wished to bring Minette with him, although he doubted if she would ever agree.

Thomas Jefferson was preparing to leave America to join Ben in France. Ben anticipated that Jefferson would then be sent to negotiate a treaty between the United States and Prussia. At the conclusion of that negotiation, Jefferson would return to Paris and relieve him in his post as the American ambassador to France. That would free Franklin entirely.

Ben suddenly yearned to be back in Philadelphia. He yearned to see his daughter Sally, his son-in-law Richard, and the grandchildren they had produced while Ben was away. He yearned to return Benny to his parents and a life in America. He even wondered if reconciliation might be possible with his son William, now forced to live in England as a result of his loyalist actions while Governor of New Jersey. Yet it seemed doubtful that father and son would ever again see eye to eye after the events of the war.

Ben observed a flock of small black birds circle out over the river and then fly back toward the city. He wondered if the human quality of imagination existed in other creatures as well. Could it be that the birds of the flock share a single imagination that allowed them to know which way to turn? Could it be that a fluid of thought, feelings, emotions—perhaps even love as Casanova suggested—was the commonality shared by the flock? Ben wondered if even these small creatures might share a common vision. A common vision of a better future ... Is that not a definition of hope?

When he had first arrived in Paris, when he had first heard of *magnétisme animale*, he had been skeptical, even dismissive. He, along with his learned colleagues, had found the theory propounded by Mesmer to be dubious. Mesmer's boastful claims would not stand the rigorous experimentation of science, they found. There was no demonstrable force, but what if *magnétisme animale* existed in the murkier and more mysterious places of the human subconscious mind and soul? What if *magnétisme animale* truly was a manifestation of human imagination?

Ben realized that he had been changed by his time in France—by his unexpected love for Minette, by the waning of his relationship with Marianne—by the birthing of a new nation, which represented a new hope for the future of all people—and by his experiences leading the commission. He had found a loving home in France. He had made new friends for whom he felt much gratitude and love, and although they had different customs and a different heritage, were they not his brothers and sisters, were they not his flock? Of course, he remained guided by logic and reason, but he had been shown a side of himself that revealed he had been too rigid in his thinking before. The flock had its own instinctive wisdom; the imagination was capable of anything. He had perched among the stars with the Queen and Marianne. He had romped on the savanna with Gazelle. He had faced Mesmer in his dreams and in reality—and he had won. He appreciated Casanova's concept of the transcendence of love—even if he did not fully understand it and couldn't prove any of it. And he respected the insights of Dr. D'Eslon about the healing power of hope. Ben's original out-of-hand disregard for *magnétisme animale* had given way to a kind of wonder. He wondered if mankind could ever fully understand or be able to harness the utility of the unprovable, yet undoubtedly powerful, force called *magnétisme animale*.

July 5th, 1785

PASSY & AUTEUIL

OVER THE PAST WINTER and spring, Ben had once again been the toast of Paris. Congratulations on the culmination of the war in America and Ben's artful resolution of the commission poured in. While Ben appreciated the attention, it was sobering to realize that he might never see these friends and acquaintances again. Some, such as Madame Brillon and Louis LeVeillard, had distanced themselves... pulling away slowly but inexorably. Might this be a way for them to defend against the pain of separation—or were they simply getting on with their lives?

The movers had been packing up his belongings at the Hôtel de Valentinois with mercurial efficiency. Ben felt a compulsion to escape his lodgings. He didn't want to be in their way, but more than that, he couldn't stand to watch them. It saddened him to see his worldly goods packed up—even if he knew that he would reunite with them in Philadelphia. Ben decided to sit in the small garden outside Madame Leray's kitchen instead. He hiked up the hill to the main house for nearly the last time.

When Ben arrived, the garden outside the kitchen was empty except for one of the family dogs. He was sitting with his back toward the low garden fence as Ben approached and was intently watching something in the corner. A large poodle mix, he appeared to be wet from a recent swim in the river. The curly locks on his back gleamed in the late morning sun. Ben thought it odd that he was not waiting by the kitchen door for a morsel discarded by the cook.

As Ben entered the garden, the dog remained motionless. His back muscles twitched. Then, at that instant, the dog lunged at the corner. Ben's eye jumped to the dark recess, expecting to see a rat or some other river vermin about to become a well-deserved snack. Instead, he saw nothing. But he heard a yelp as the dog jumped back, his paw applied to his snout. Ben peered into the dark recess again. This time he spied a small gray ball of fluff, no bigger than his fist, standing with its back arched, tail high, claws uncovered.

The dog was only momentarily stunned. He reared up. At least a hundred times the size of the kitten, he must have realized that there was no match, despite the early aggression. He was about to close in for the kill when Ben yelled, "No!"

The dog stopped. He shot Ben a pained look but heeded. Ben rushed forward and scooped up the kitten. It weighed next to nothing. The dog stared at them for a moment, then flashed Ben a look of disdain for spoiling his fun and ran down the hill toward the river. Ben held the kitten close to him. He could feel its ribs. It was breathing hard, and trembling.

"You're very brave ... taking on that big dog," Ben said comfortingly.

Madame Leray came running out the kitchen door, apparently having heard the fuss.

"Ben, what is the matter?" she exclaimed.

Ben looked at her. He held up the kitten.

"This little fellow just about met his maker."

"Oh, isn't he the cutest thing," she said.

"And brave too! Took on one of your dogs, he did."

"Impressive," she said. She put her finger to her cheek. "Keep him there with you for just a minute." She ran back inside.

Ben stood in the garden, the small newfound life in his hands, on nearly the eve of his departure from France. An idea began to form in his mind.

Madame Leray reappeared with a saucer of milk. "Here we are," she said. She set it down on the table.

Ben put the kitten on the table in front of the saucer, where he started to lap up the milk immediately.

"He's a hungry little fellow," she said.

Ben and Marie-Thérèse watched, enthralled, as the famished kitten licked the entire saucer dry. When finished, his stomach appeared swollen. Ben picked him up again. He was considerably heavier.

"What shall we do with him?" Madame Leray asked. "He can't stay here. One of the dogs will kill him next time to be sure."

"I have an idea," Ben said. An impish look came over his face. "Do you have any satin ribbon?"

The kitten started to purr in his arms. Ben hadn't felt a kitten purr in quite some time, and he found it comforting.

A half hour later, while the kitten slept peacefully, a ruffled collar and vest of red satin had been fashioned from measurements Madame Leray had taken. She giggled through the entire sewing experience, assisting Ben with the critical parts.

Ben slipped the garments on the sleeping kitten. He woke up and immediately started to claw at his new collar in an attempt to remove it. Ben held his paw.

"Now, now, young prince," he said. "These garments are your ticket to a good life. Do not remove them."

As if he understood the words Ben said, the kitten immediately stopped fussing with his *accoutrements*.

"All right, we must now depart for your new home."

Madame Leray watched, amused, as Ben, the embellished kitten tucked under one arm, rousted the coachman with instructions to take him to

Auteuil. He headed out with no invitation to dinner, no time to send an announcement that he would be coming, not even knowing if Minette would be found at home. Yet, Ben felt the uncontrollable urge to go to her. There was not very much time left.

The gray kitten dressed in courtier garb slept the entire way to Auteuil. Upon arriving, Ben was gratified to note no unidentified carriages in front of the Helvétius house.

It was just after noon when Ben alighted from the Leray coach carrying his purring surprise. The usual courtier cats met him at the gate. They did not seem to notice the interloper he secretly transported into their midst. The Chevalier led the entourage as they escorted Ben to the front door.

Ben knocked. There was no immediate answer. He opened the door, not entirely sure what awaited him inside.

"Hello!" Ben shouted as he entered.

Medical student Cabanis was the first to acknowledge his presence.

"Ben," the anxious appearing young man exclaimed. "What are you doing here? Were you expected?"

"No, I present myself unannounced," Ben said proudly. "Is her ladyship at home?"

"Yes ... at least I think so," Cabanis said.

"I will see her then," Ben replied.

Cabanis dashed away quickly, but only brought back the Abbé de la Roche.

"Ben, we weren't expecting you," Martin said. His bushy eyebrows writhed.

"Martin, is Minette at home? I would only take a moment if she is."

"Ben, I assure you that she is. But may I also tell you she is not in the best state?"

"Why is that, Martin?"

"You're leaving, Ben. She has taken it very hard."

"I have offered to bring her with me to America so many times that I cannot recall them all."

"Yes, but that creates a dilemma for her—don't you see? I have never seen Madame so torn. You know that she loves her freedom."

"Yes."

"But she loves you too. Ben, this is tearing her apart."

"I don't want her to be unhappy."

"No ... of course not."

"Martin, I only want to speak with her for a moment."

"I will ask."

The Abbé walked slowly up the stairs. He seemed to be composing his speech as he went. Ben waited patiently, but as he stood there, the kitten seemed to have found new energy in his hiding place under Ben's arm. Ben pulled him out and tried to settle him down.

Ben looked the kitten in the eye. "Hush now. Stop struggling," he said.

For the first time, Ben got a good look at the young cat's fierce and determined eyes. Fully revived from his encounter with the poodle, he looked squarely at Ben as if to say 'I will do what I want.' Except that he actually did stop struggling and lay still once again in Ben's arms.

Minette appeared at the top of the stairs in a shorter time than Ben could ever recall. Even from that distance, Ben could tell she had been crying. Her eyes were red and swollen. She wore a plain white linen dress that looked as if she had slept in it for a few nights. Her hair was a mess. She attempted to flatten it out as she descended.

"Oh, Ben," she moaned. "You shouldn't see me like this."

"You look beautiful to me."

She burst into tears as she ran to his arms. Ben held her as she sobbed.

"Ben, I can't bear you going away."

"Come with me then."

"You know that I cannot."

"Why is that?"

"Ben, I don't speak the language. I don't know the customs. I would not know anyone in America."

"All weak excuses ... and I've heard them all before," Ben replied as sensitively as he could. "You would make new friends, we could be married, I have a lovely home in Philadelphia—at least it was lovely the last time I saw it ... before the War."

Minette looked as if she might burst into tears again. "Ben," she said, "you could stay here in France. We wouldn't have to get married. I would be able to love you and care for you. In America, could I live the free life that I have here? No, I think not. What would your puritanical neighbors in Philadelphia think of this French country lady, her free-roaming cats, her swimming in the nude? It would never do.

"No, you have created a new country in America that now needs you. You must go. France has aided you in your quest in battling the inequities of British rule. Yet, I have a feeling that my own country may soon need my voice, my ideas, if we are ever to move away from the inequities of the *ancien regime*. I must stay."

"Minette, you are right, as always. It does not make any sense. Why two people who love each other so much should have to part."

"I know, I know, and that is precisely why I weep. Ben, we have been so happy together these last few years. To lose you makes me very sad."

"Do not be sad for things we cannot change, my darling," Ben said, lightening up a bit. "I have brought you a present to remember me by."

Ben pulled out the gray kitten from beneath his jacket. The kitten yawned as if just awakening from a nap. He batted at the courtier collar around his neck. Ben held his paw and warned him with a shake of his finger.

He presented the squirming cat to Minette. "I want you to call him Ben," he said.

She accepted him into her arms with a warm smile. She laughed. For a moment, she was the old carefree Minette, and her laugh warmed Ben to his toes.

"Ah, a little *chat gris*," she chided. "Are you trying to tell me something? Did not you once famously say 'as in the dark all cats are gray'?"

A pained look came over Ben's face. "Minette," he said. "You know that you are irreplaceable."

"Yes, as are you, my dear." She held the kitten up to have a better look at him. "He is so adorable. I will cherish him," she said.

"Yes, but feisty too," Ben warned. The kitten started to squirm. "He took on one of Madame Leray's dogs—and lived to tell of it."

Minette looked the kitten in the eye. "So you are both gorgeous and brave ... just like your namesake," she said. The kitten started to purr loudly. "I do not believe that I will have any trouble handling you," she said.

"Just like his namesake," Ben said.

Minette turned her attention back to Ben. "Can you stay for dinner?" she asked.

"Marie-Thérèse will be expecting me."

"Might I not have you just one more night?" she pleaded.

"Of course. I would have it no other way."

The following morning Ben stumbled sleepily into the kitchen to find Cabanis and the Abbé de la Roche already up. They were teaching the new kitten tricks at the table.

"Ben, this cat has already learned more tricks than any other—and it is just his first day!" Martin exclaimed.

"He is a talented one, to be sure," Ben said like a proud parent. "High-spirited too. I have only one aspiration for him, though."

"What is that?" the Abbé asked.

Ben looked the kitten in the eye. "I want you to rule the roost, young Ben. I want you to show *that* Giacomo who is the real boss of this house. I want you to put Claude, Jacques, Pierre, and every other one of those courtier cats in their place when the time comes. I want you to grow up to be the man of the Helvétius household. I will not be here. You must do so in my place. I expect you to lead the entourage." The kitten looked at Ben as if he understood.

July 12th, 1785

FLORENCE

MARIANNE HELD MARKO'S HAND as they strolled through the Boboli Gardens. It promised to be another hot day. The morning mist had been cool earlier but was now burning off. They stood on the terrace of the building known as the "kaffeehaus" which offered a commanding view of the city.

"You can see the turret of the *Torre della Sardigna* from here," Marianne said.

"My boat is moored just beyond," Marko relied. "But I can't quite see it."

Marko had sailed across the Mediterranean and up the Arno river to be with her. He had no need or want to travel to Paris anymore. She had welcomed his companionship this summer but warned him that he would need to travel home before the Fall rains arrived.

A flock of birds circled overhead. "What of *magnétisme animale?*" Marko asked.

"I now know that Mesmer does not control it, as I have been able to continue to avoid the the darkness by channeling my own inner vision without him."

"Good, you are better off without him." Marianne thought that he sounded slightly jealous—but also relieved that Mesmer was out of her life.

"I must be careful with my power now, though. I have not used it to examine others as in Paris. There is a Society of Harmony in Strasbourg, run by the Marquis de Puységur, that cautions that some ailments of the healed may be transferred to the magnetizer."

Marko appeared shocked. "Do you believe that to be true?" he said.

"Not necessarily. And I have never suffered such an experience. However, I do not wish to find out the hard way. I'll practice privately from now on."

"That is good. And what of Doctor Franklin?"

"On his way back to America, I presume." I have not heard from him, nor do I wish to."

"Also good," Marko said, but there was a tinge of sadness in his voice. "Won't you accompany me when I return to Bilbao?" he pleaded.

"Marko, I don't know a bit of Spanish."

"Yes, but you know Italian, it's close. And I would teach you. You know the best way to learn a foreign language, don't you?"

"No."

"Between the sheets."

Marianne laughed heartily, but then became more serious. "You could stay here," she said.

"What would I do—sell sand from the *Pescaia di Santa Rosa*?"

"Why not? Many do."

"Yes, but I need to get back to building boats. I can't do that here."

"I know. But I must stay. Cecelia needs me." Marko knew that she couldn't leave Florence, didn't he? "Let us speak of this no more. Let us simply enjoy each other while we can," she said.

As they walked slowly back down toward the Porta Roma through the lush gardens, past the ancient statuary and fountains, Marianne secretly wished that she could run away with Marko back to Bilbao. Had she finally found the gold coin under the shell—only to lose it once again by her own choosing?

July 12th, 1785

PASSY

THE QUEEN'S PERSONAL CARRIAGE arrived in the courtyard of the Hôtel de Valentinois to transport Ben, Benny, and Temple to Le Havre. The exquisitely inlaid wooden carriage gleamed in the late morning sun. The spokes on the four enormous wheels were painted in bright contrasting colors of red, white, and blue—the colors of the French flag, recently adopted by the Americans. The royal crest was emblazoned on each door. The door was so high off the ground that a stepladder of four good-sized steps was required to enter the seating compartment. The cabin itself perched on a system of robust springs, seemingly guaranteed to minimize bumps in the road that might inflame Ben's bladder stone. The entire staff of the Hôtel de Valentinois poured out to gawk at the marvelous machine—but also to bid a fond farewell to their famous lodger, Doctor Benjamin Franklin.

Ben felt strange, taking one last lingering walk around the lodgings he had called home for more than eight years. All of his belongings had already been packed and were gone, even now heading down the river by barge. The entire accumulation would soon be loaded on his ship in Le Havre, bound first for

England and then home to Philadelphia. During the days since the barge had departed, Ben had been drinking Jacques Leray's best Bordeaux as Ben's own collection of several thousand bottles was now bound for America.

Not that Monsieur Leray knew of the raiding of his cellar. More than ever, Ben's host had been absent from the Hôtel de Valentinois. Madame Leray chose the wine to go with dinner every day, and she seemed to be intentionally picking the finest ones.

Marie-Thérèse knocked at the door just as that revelation struck Ben. He sat at the same table where so many times she had brought his morning newspaper and a tray of scones. Today she arrived empty-handed.

"The Queen's carriage is waiting," she said softly. Her voice cracked with emotion.

"You have been uncorking Jacques' best Grand Cru all week, haven't you?"

"He won't miss it," she said. She flashed an expression of contempt, but then smiled warmly at Ben.

"Walk with me down to the river," she pleaded.

"Right you are. It is time to leave here," Ben said.

She took Ben by the arm. They walked away from the house down the sloping lawn toward the dock on the river Seine. As they stepped onto the creaky wooden structure, two startled ducks flew away quacking loudly.

"The waterfowl will have no one to disturb them tomorrow," Ben said.

"Oh, Ben, we will all miss you so terribly." She looked as though she was about to cry again.

"And I you, Marie-Thérèse. Tell me, what are your plans?"

"You know that there will not be much for me here without you, Benny, and Temple. My children are all gone now. They have their own families to tend to. Jacques stays for the most part in Versailles—which is fine with me. I have asked him for the château at Chaumont."

"You will live there?"

"Yes. He has not given me the château outright, mind you. But Jacques has agreed that he will no longer consider it his home. He will consider it to be *my* home. He will provide me with an allowance. I will be free to live out my life there as I choose."

"Marie-Thérèse," Ben said with a look of concern. "Is this what you truly want?"

"Yes, Ben," she said. "It is exactly what I want."

"I hope that you will find the happiness there that you deserve." Ben gave his hostess a warm squeeze around her shoulder.

"And what of your new life in Philadelphia?"

"My fledgling country needs me now at home. I hope to be able to provide some valuable service."

"I have no doubt that you underestimate your value ... as usual." She smiled. "You will write, won't you?"

"Of course." Ben felt a lump in his throat. He could say no more.

The boys were already aboard the coach when Ben climbed in. He waved out the window as they pulled away. Ben watched a murmuration of birds circle over the river behind the house and then disappear. He was glad to be starting the journey home.

The End, or rather—Au Revoir

EPILOGUE

BEN FRANKLIN left Passy for America on July 12th, 1785. As expected, Minette did not accompany him. After a brief side trip to London, which included a failed attempt at reconciliation with his son, he sailed for The United States of America on July 27th, 1785. He arrived in Philadelphia on September 14th to a hero's welcome. Ben reunited with his daughter Sally and her husband Richard Bache. He continued to stay active in the new United States but declined to be nominated for public office. He did not return to France. Ben died on April 17th, 1790, in Philadelphia. He is buried in the Christ Church burial ground with his wife Deborah.

FRANZ ANTON MESMER returned to his wife and medical practice in Vienna. He later practiced medicine in Switzerland and southern Germany, where he died in 1815. He never achieved the fame or fortune he believed that he deserved for his "discovery." However, there is no historical evidence that he intentionally tried to harm Franklin physically—that is pure fiction. The Marquis de Puységur followed Mesmer and expanded on his work in France, but the theory of *magnétisme animale* was largely forgotten in his Mesmer's time. Ultimately it became what we know today as hypnotism—as the result of experiments in the 1800s by British physician James Braid. We now think of being "mesmerized" in a negative connotation as having been put into a trance or controlled by another person, idea, or object. The true power of the human imagination and the subconscious mind remains to be elucidated.

MARIANNE DAVIES and her sister Cecilia continued to perform around the European continent but avoided Vienna. While historians have occasionally wondered about Marianne's relationship with Ben Franklin, particularly as to why he might have invented the glass armonica for her, there is little historical record to go on. Her relationships with Franz Mesmer and Marko, the Basque ship builder, are fictitious. The Davies sisters eventually returned to Britain and taught private music lessons in England and Scotland. Marianne died around 1818. It is not known where she is buried. Cecelia lived until 1836 and passed away at the age of eighty years. Little more is known about the later years of their lives. However, there is no historical record of any further communication between Marianne and Ben after he left Paris.

MADAME HELVETIUS (Minette) continued to hold regular salons at her home in Auteuil. She encouraged freedom of thought in science, philosophy, and the arts. She did not remarry or see Ben again after he left France, although they communicated via letters until his death in 1790. She survived the French revolution, perhaps due to the protection of friends like Jean-Paul Marat. She died in Auteuil on August 12th, 1800. One can only hope that she is reunited with Ben on the Elysian Fields.

THE FRENCH REVOLUTION began in 1789, with the storming of the Bastille on July 14th of that year seen as a pivotal event. Both King Louis XVI and Marie Antionette were executed by Dr. Guillotin's invention in 1793.

AXEL VON FERSEN conspired in an escape attempt of the Royal Family in June 1791. When his role was discovered, an arrest warrant was issued, and he fled France. He tried to convince Marie Antoinette's brother

Leopold (at that time the Holy Roman Emperor in Vienna) to declare war on France, but it was not to be. His affair with Marie Antoinette has long been suspected by many historians, but never proven.

PROFESSORS LAVOISIER, Condorcet, and Bailly (along with many others of the French intellectual elite) perished in the French revolution. However, Jean-Baptiste Le Roy, and Dr's. Cabanis and Guillotin survived. Contrary to popular belief, Dr. Guillotin was not killed by his own invention.

LOUIS LEVEILLARD was elected mayor of Passy soon after Ben left for America. He died by the guillotine in 1794 during the French revolution.

MADAME LERAY moved to the Chaumont estate in the Loire Valley. She and her husband led separate lives after Ben left Passy. Jacques Leray was bankrupted by, but survived, the French revolution. He died in 1803. Marie-Thérèse lived until 1819.

JOHN PAUL JONES finished his service with the US Navy and subsequently accepted a position in the Russian navy where he fought against the Ottoman Empire. Never one to avoid controversy, he was arrested and accused of rape in 1789 by the Russian naval commander. While he was acquitted of the crime, he left Russia embittered and returned to Paris. He was found dead in his Paris apartment on July 18th, 1792, at the age of forty-five. The official cause of death was interstitial nephritis (kidney disease). He was initially buried in Paris, but his body was later exhumed and now resides at the US Naval Academy in Annapolis, Maryland.

ANNE LOUISE BRILLON, continued to play and compose for the harpsichord and the piano until her death in 1824. Her glass armonica now resides at the Bakken Museum in Minneapolis, Minnesota.

GIACOMO CASANOVA quit Paris for good in 1785, taking up the position of librarian to a Count in Dux, Bohemia—in the current day Czech Republic. He wrote his memoirs during his remaining years there, which were published after his death in 1798. He never returned to his birthplace in Venice, even after the fall of the Doge and the Venetian empire. Over time, his name has become synonymous with a promiscuous or unscrupulous lover—perhaps because of the escapades he described in his memoirs. Unfortunately, his qualities of brilliant intelligence, spiritualism, and sharp wit have not been as well remembered.

PIERRE BEAUMARCHAIS continued his irreverence toward the aristocracy (as demonstrated in his plays)—which probably saved him during the French revolution. However, he was subsequently exiled in absentia while traveling out of the country when his enemies falsely declared him to be a loyalist of the old regime. He was able to return to Paris in 1796, where he passed away in 1799. He is buried in Paris.

WOLFGANG AMADEUS MOZART left Paris prior to the French revolution. He went on to pen the music to the opera *The Marriage of Figaro*, which opened in Vienna in 1786. He died of a fever at his home there in 1791. In his short but illustrious lifetime, he composed more than 600 musical works.

THE REVEREND WILLIAM SMITH was not welcome in Pennsylvania during the American Revolution as he was suspected of being a loyalist to England. He was forced to move from Philadelphia to Maryland, where he headed Washington College during the war. His role in this book as a spy is fictitious—but plausible. However, after the American Revolution ended, he returned to Philadelphia and became head of the newly formed University of Pennsylvania. He lived until 1803.

PIERRE SAMUEL DU PONT DE NEMOURS left France with his second wife (his first wife, Nicole, portrayed in this book, died of typhoid in 1784) and son after a failed attempt rescue King Louis XVI and Marie Antoinette in 1792. His son Éleuthère Irénée (E.I.) du Pont had studied under Lavoisier and learned how to make explosives (black powder). The family moved to America where E.I. established the du Pont de Nemours company in 1801—the company we know as DuPont today. He passed away in 1817.

EDWARD BANCROFT continued his role as a stock market investor/manipulator and entrepreneur after the American Revolution in England and France. His role as a British spy was confirmed by diplomatic papers released after his death in 1821. However, it has long been suspected by historians that he was truly a "double agent" during the American Revolution, working for both the Americans and the British.

BENJAMIN "BENNY" FRANKLIN BACHE returned to America from France with his grandfather in 1785. He became a journalist and publisher in Philadelphia. He died in the yellow fever epidemic of 1798 at the age of twenty-nine.

WILLIAM "TEMPLE" FRANKLIN also returned with his grandfather to America in 1785, but after Ben's death in 1790, he returned for a short time to England and then Paris. He had a somewhat tumultuous career as a land speculator there, but ultimately edited and published Ben's autobiography and letters between 1816 and 1819. He died in Paris in 1823.

TEMPLE'S FATHER AND BEN'S SON, William Franklin, remained in England after the American revolution and never reconciled with his father. He died in 1813 and is buried in London.

JOHN ADAMS AND THOMAS JEFFERSON went on to become the second and third presidents of the United States respectively. When Adams died on July 4th, 1826, his last words reportedly included an acknowledgment of his longtime friend and rival: "Thomas Jefferson survives." Adams was unaware that Jefferson had died several hours prior.

Bibliography

Amacher, Richard E. *Franklin's Wit and Folly: The Bagatelles*. New Brunswick, New Jersey: Rutgers University Press, 1953.

Alvarado, Carlos S. "Human Radiations: Concepts of Force in Mesmerism, Spiritualism and Psychical Research." *J. Soc. Psychical Research*. 70, no. 3 (July 2006): 138-162.

Beaumarchais, Pierre Augustin Caron de and David Coward. *The Figaro Trilogy*. Oxford World's Classics. New York: Oxford University Press, 2003.

Best, Mark A., Duncan Neuhauser, and Lee Slavin. *Benjamin Franklin: Verification and Validation of the Scientific Process in Healthcare, as Demonstrated by the Report of the Royal Commission on Animal Magnetism and Mesmerism*. Victoria, British Columbia: Trafford Publishing, 2003.

Bigelow, John. "Franklin's Home and Host in France." *The Century Magazine* 35, no. 5 (March 1888): 741-754

Boros, Gábor. "Love as a Guiding Principle of Descartes's Late Philosophy." *History of Philosophy Quarterly* 20, no. 2 (April 2003): 149-163.

Buranelli, Vincent. *The Wizard from Vienna*. New York: Coward, McCann & Geoghegan, Inc, 1975.

Cabanis, Pierre J. G. *On the Relations between the Physical and Moral Aspects of Man*. Baltimore: Johns Hopkins University Press, 1981.

Casanova, Giacomo. *The Memoirs of Jacques Casanova*. New York: The Modern Library, 1929.

Clark, Ronald W. *Benjamin Franklin*. London: Phoenix Press, 1983.

Conner, Clifford D. *Jean-Paul Marat*. Amherst, New York: Humanities Press, 1998.

Darnton, Robert. *Mesmerism and the End of the Enlightenment in France*. Cambridge: Harvard University Press, 1968.

Donaldson, I. M. L. "Mesmer's 1780 Proposal for a Controlled Trial to Test His Method of Treatment using 'Animal Magnetism.'" *Journal of the Royal Society of Medicine* 98, no. 12 (Dec 2005): 572-575. doi:10.1177/014107680509801226.

Fersen, Hans Axel von. *Diary and Correspondence of Count Axel Fersen: Grand-Marshal of Sweden Relating to the Court of France*. Elibron Classics. Elibron Classics, 2005.

Finger, Stanley. *Doctor Franklin's Medicine*. Philadelphia: University of Pennsylvania Press, 2006.

Fischer, David Hackett. *Liberty and Freedom: A Visual History of America's Founding Ideas*. New York: Oxford University Press, 2005.

Franklin, Benjamin, et al., *"Report of Dr. Benjamin Franklin, and Other Commissioners, Charged by the King of France, with the Examination of the Animal Magnetism, as Now Practised at Paris."* Translated from the French with an Historical Introduction 1785. London: J. Johnson.

McPharlin, P. *Benjamin Franklin Satires and Bagatelles*. Detroit: Fine Book Circle, 1937.

Franklin, James L. "Mozart, Mesmer and Medicine." Paper given at the Chicago Literary Club February 16, 2004. Reprinted in Hektoen Institute Journal of Medical Humanities 2017 Accessed 7/6/2020 https://hekint.org/2017/01/30/mozart-mesmer-and-medicine/

Fruchtman, Jack. *Atlantic Cousins*. New York: Thunder's Mouth Press, 2005.

Gallo, David A. and Stanley Finger. "The Power of a Musical Instrument: Franklin, the Mozarts, Mesmer, and the Glass Armonica." *History of Psychology* 3, no. 4 (2000): 326-343. doi:10.1037//1093-4510.3.4.326.

Gauld, Alan. *A History of Hypnotism*. Cambridge: Cambridge University Press, 1992.

Gay, Peter. *The Enlightenment*. New York: W. W. Norton & Company, Inc, 1969.

Goldsmith, Margaret. *Franz Anton Mesmer*. Garden City, New York: Doran & Company, Inc (Doubleday), 1934.

Hadlock, Heather. *Mad Loves: Women and Music in Offenbach's Les Contes D'Hoffmann*. Princeton: Princeton University Press, 2000.

Hale, Edward E., and Hale, Edward E. Jr. 1887 *Franklin in France*. Boston: Roberts Brothers

Heilbron, J.L. "Plus and Minus: Franklin's Zero-Sum Way of Thinking." *Proc. Amer. Philosophical Soc.* 150, no. 4(2006): 607-617.

Hepworth, Kate. *Eighteenth Century Women and the Business of Making Glass Music*. Thesis/Dissertation. Hist. 461 (June 2017). Accessed 7/6/2020 http://digitalcommons.calpoly.edu/histsp/38

Higgins, Maria Mihalik. *Benjamin Franklin: Revolutionary Inventor*. Sterling Biographies. New York: Sterling, 2007.

Hort, G. M., Richard Basil Ince, and William P. Swainson. *Three Famous Occultists*. London: Rider & Co, 1939.

Isaacson, Walter. *Benjamin Franklin*. New York: Simon & Schuster Paperbacks, 2004.

Japin, Arthur. *In Lucia's Eyes*. New York: Alfred A. Knopf, 2005.

Kelly, Ian. *Casanova*. New York: Jeremy P. Tarcher/Penguin, 2008.

Lopez, Claude-Anne. "Franklin and Mesmer: An Encounter." *Yale Journal of Biology and Medicine* 66, no. 4 (July 1993): 325-331.

Lopez, Claude-Anne. *Mon Cher Papa: Franklin and the Ladies of Paris.* New Haven: Yale University Press, 1967.

Lopez, Claude-Anne. *My Life with Benjamin Franklin.* New Haven: Yale University Press, 2000.

Lopez, Claude-Anne. *Le Sceptre Et La Foudre.* Paris: Mercure de France, 1966.

Lopez, Claude-Anne and Eugenia W. Herbert. *The Private Franklin: The Man and His Family.* New York: W. W. Norton & Company, Inc., 1975.

Marks, Robert W. *The Story of Hypnotism.* 1st ed. New York: Prentice-Hall, Inc., 1947.

Matthews, Betty. "The Davies Sisters, J. C. Bach and the Glass Harmonica." *Music & Letters* 56, no. 2 (April 1975): 150-169. doi:10.1093/ml/56.2.150.

McConkey, Kevin M. and Campbell Perry. "Benjamin Franklin and Mesmerism." *International Journal of Clinical and Experimental Hypnosis* 33, no. 2 (1985): 122-130. doi:10.1080/00207140208410108.

Mead, Corey. *Angelic Music.* New York: Simon & Schuster, 2016.

Mesmer, Franz Anton. *Mesmerism.* London: Macdonald & Co, 1948.

Mesmer, Franz Anton. *Mesmerism: The Discovery of Animal Magnetism.* Sequim, Washington: Holmes Publishing Group, 2006.

Middlekauff, Robert. *Benjamin Franklin and His Enemies.* Berkeley: University of California Press, 1996.

Mottelay, Paul F. *Bibliographical History of Electricity and Magnetism.* London: Charles Griffin & Company Limited, 1922.

Nash, Michael R. "The International Journal of Clinical and Experimental Hypnosis: 50th Anniversary Special Issue: Mesmer, Franklin, and the Royal Commission." 50, no. 4 (October 2002).

Newton, Isaac and Stephen Hawking. *Principia.* Philadelphia: Running Press, 2002.

O'Doherty, Brian. *The Strange Case of Mademoiselle P.* London: Arcadia Books, 2001.

Pattie, Frank A. *Mesmer and Animal Magnetism.* Hamilton, New York: Edmonston Publishing, Inc., 1994.

Rhoden, Nancy L. and Ian K. Steele. *The Human Tradition in the American Revolution.* The Human Tradition in America. Wilmington, Delaware: Scholarly Resources Inc., 2000.

Schaeper, Thomas J. *Edward Bancroft.* New Haven: Yale University Press, 2011.

Schaeper, Thomas J. *France and America in the Revolutionary Era.* Providence: Berghahn Books, 1995.

Schiff, Stacy. *A Great Improvisation.* New York: Henry Holt and Company, 2005.

Schwartz, Stephan A. 2005 "The Blind Protocol and Its Place in Consciousness Research." *Explore* 1 (4) (July): 284-289. doi. org/10.1016/j.explore.2005.04.013

Staum, Martin S. *Cabanis*. Princeton: Princeton University Press, 1980.

Szasz, Thomas. *The Myth of Psychotherapy*. Garden City, New York: Anchor Press (Doubleday), 1978.

Turner, Christopher. "Mesmeromania, or, the Tale of the Tub." *Cabinet*, (2006) 1-11.

Ullrich, Hermann. "Maria Theresia Paradis and Mozart." *Music and Letters* 27 no. 4 (October 1946): 224-233.

Zeitler, William. *The Glass Armonica*. San Bernardino, California: Musica Arcana, 2013.

ABOUT THE AUTHOR

STEVE GNATZ IS A WRITER, physician, bicyclist, photographer, traveler, and aspiring ukulele player. The son of a history professor and a nurse, it seems that both medicine and history are in his blood. Writing historical fiction came naturally. An undergraduate degree in biology was complemented by a minor in classics. After completing medical school, he embarked on an academic medical career specializing in Physical Medicine and Rehabilitation. There was little time for writing during those years, other than research papers and a technical primer on electromyography. Now retired from the practice of medicine, he devotes himself to the craft of fiction. The history of science is of particular interest, but also the dynamics of human relationships. People want to be good scientists, but sometimes human nature gets in the way. That makes for interesting stories. When not writing or traveling, he enjoys restoring vintage Italian racing bicycles at home in Chicago with his wife and daughters.

If you enjoyed
The Wisdom of the Flock,
please take a moment to leave a review
on Amazon or Goodreads.

For more interesting fun facts and
illustrations about Franklin and his
time in France, please visit my blog at
stevegnatz.com/blog
or the website at
thewisdomoftheflock.com

Made in the USA
Monee, IL
11 January 2021